LONDON
UNDERGROUND

LONDON
UNDERGROUND

A THRILLER

CHRIS ANGUS

YUCCA

Yucca Publishing books may be purchased in bulk at special discounts for sales promotion, corporate gifts, fund-raising, or educational purposes. Special editions can also be created to specifications. For details, contact the Special Sales Department, Yucca Publishing, 307 West 36th Street, 11th Floor, New York, NY 10018 or yucca@ skyhorsepublishing.com.

Yucca Publishing® is an imprint of Skyhorse Publishing, Inc.®, a Delaware corporation.

Visit our website at www.yuccapub.com.

10 9 8 7 6 5 4 3 2 1

Library of Congress Cataloging-in-Publication Data is available on file.

Cover design by Yucca Publishing

Print ISBN: 978-1-63158-050-5
Ebook ISBN: 978-1-63158-060-4

Printed in the United States of America

LONDON
UNDERGROUND

1

London — May 1528
The Reign of King Henry VIII

The French Ambassador to the English court, Du Bellai, contemplated his young aide. The lad was barely seventeen, but he would grow older before this day was out . . . if any of them lived so long.

"Tell me again," Du Bellai demanded. "And stop babbling. Speak clearly."

The boy took a deep breath, then looked around with frightened eyes, as if that simple act might condemn him.

"One of the filles de chambre of Mlle Boleyn was taken ill. She was laid low very quickly. Mlle Boleyn called for her physician, who examined the girl and then spoke quickly to my lady. They both immediately left the chamber. I overheard the physician say he feared it was the Sweat."

Du Bellai felt a cold hand squeeze his heart. It had been a dozen years since the last outbreak of the dreaded disease. Some called it the "Affliction of the Henrys," for it first appeared at the start of the reign of Henry VII in 1485. It had caused great mortality and become known by its special symptom as the "sweating sickness." Distinct from the plague, it was noted for its even more rapid and fatal course.

He had read the treatise, written in Latin, by Thomas Forestier concerning the 1485 epidemic, which included the description: " . . . the exterior is calm in this fever, the interior excited . . . the heat in the pestilent fever many times does not appear excessive to the doctor, nor the heat of the sweat itself particularly high . . . But it is on account of the ill-natured, fetid, corrupt, putrid, and loathsome vapors close to the region of the heart and of the lungs whereby the panting of the breath magnifies and increases and restricts itself . . . "

The young aide shook with fear, desperate to get away from this awful place. "The king and Mlle Boleyn have fled the city. All of my lady's attendants have disappeared as well. The afflicted woman is dead. There is no one to remove her body."

"You and I will remove the body," said the ambassador.

The boy was horrified. "It will be a death sentence. I cannot."

"Listen to me. You have already been exposed. Either you will get the sickness or you will not. But the body must be removed and burned at once."

He grabbed the boy by the arm and dragged him back into Mlle Boleyn's deserted apartments, pausing long enough to prepare face masks and to place garlic around both of their necks. When they reached the bedroom, the body of the young lady in waiting lay contorted on drenched bedding. Her face was white, characteristic of the terrible illness, and there were no outbreaks on her fair skin.

"Tear down those drapes," he ordered the aide, who moved forward as if in a dream.

Together, they wrapped the body in the drapes, trying not to touch any bare skin that showed. They carried it and the remaining bedding out into the nearest courtyard, where they dumped it unceremoniously. They piled what wood they could find on top of it, saturated everything with lamp oil and set it ablaze.

As Du Bellai stood back, so as not to breathe in the vapors and smoke, his young aide scampered away, leaving him alone. It no longer mattered, and the ambassador could hardly blame him. He wanted to run as well, but believed it would do no good.

He had read the history of the first outbreaks. It was thought that the Sweat might have been brought to England at the end of the Wars of the Roses by the French mercenaries Henry VII used to gain the English throne. Those mercenaries had seemed immune to the disease. He wondered if, by some miracle, his nationality might also save him.

As the woman's body was consumed, he considered whether he ought to set fire to the entire palace . . .

2

London was in chaos. Tens of thousands lay dead from the outbreak of the Sweat. Anyone in the city who could afford to do so fled to the outlying towns, spreading the scourge even farther in the process. The first to flee—like rats leaving a sinking ship—were the royal family and its retainers. The common people were well aware that they had been abandoned to their fates. There was nothing new about this and they were resigned to it.

Those who had homes remained inside, appearing as necessary at their doors to thrust their dead into the streets, where they were picked up in carts by the lowliest workers in the city. Those who lived in the streets—and there were thousands of them—got drunk and roamed the cobbled byways in search of carnal pleasures to help wile away their final hours. Despair was absolute. There was no treatment, no safe haven, no one to turn to for succor. The bodies piled ever higher.

A dozen miles outside the city, King Henry VIII sat in his tent in a farmer's field next to a peaceful stream. Servants bustled about the clearing, raising more tents, building an enclosure for animals and posting guards to keep any of the sick or just plain curious, away. Henry's wife Catherine had been out of the city when the great affliction broke out. Though he was king, his lot was cast with those who cared for him. He could not exist without the retainers he was so used to having around him. If any of them were already infected, then he would be too.

This included Anne Boleyn. It was a risk to be with her, for it was her chambermaid who had become ill. But Henry was infatuated by Anne. Nothing could keep them apart.

With uncommon foresight for one so young, Anne kept that fervor alive by refusing to submit to Henry until he divorced Catherine and agreed to marry her.

Now she sat beside him, stroking his forehead. "Do not fear, my Lord. The Sweat would not dare infect the King of England."

"We know you are right, Anne. Still, we will stay here in the country until we hear that the danger is past." He put his arms around her. "There is something else we have ordered."

"My Lord?"

"It is a secret we wish to tell you—to show our love. Before the scourge fell upon us, we ordered a part of our treasures to be hidden. We have long believed this to be a worthy idea in the event of some terrible catastrophe as has recently visited our people. The city will soon be in riot, and there is no one to protect the king's treasury."

"Surely the people will be too sick to take advantage of such a situation—and they will fear your retribution."

"That they should!" Henry's fist pounded the arm of his chair. "But the safety of the royal fortune has long worried us. There are those in the court, foreigners and Frenchmen who would not hesitate to steal from us."

She sighed. "I fear it may be true. But what can be done?"

He looked at her slyly. "We are not king for nothing, my lovely Anne. Only in recent weeks did our navy take possession of one of the richest Spanish galleons ever captured at sea. We have had this treasure hidden, along with other valuables from our personal collection. If the treasury is looted, there will be enough left to replenish our fortune."

"What of the men who undertook this task for the king? In the chaos of the sickness, will they not seek to enrich themselves?"

"The men involved have been dealt with. And there is this to tell you, Anne. We intend to leave this treasure well and truly buried even after the pestilence passes, as a security for the realm."

He pulled her close and whispered the location of the treasure. Her eyes gleamed at the confidence. She was privy to the most important secret of the realm. Placing her hands on Henry's florid cheeks, she stared into his eyes. "You are a great king, Henry, and one day I will be your wife and have fine sons for you. Your people are fortunate to have a leader who looks to their future welfare." She kissed him. "Pray, tell me, what does the future hold for me?"

"You have a beautiful head on your shoulders, Anne. It will have a roll all its own in the future of our country."

3

London — Present Day

Knees cramped against the dashboard, Inspector Sherwood Peets massaged his aching calves and eyed his driver's relaxed slouch. He was supposed to have his new patrol car by now, but as usual there had been a delay. One of the perks of his recent promotion to inspector would be the added leg space of a larger vehicle.

He stared bleakly out the window as they passed the Coram's Fields football grounds, the game otherwise known as soccer in the United States. He'd virtually grown up on the grounds and for a while thought he might make a stab at being a professional player. He had been that good. But then he kept growing, all the way through college. His long, lanky body had simply outgrown his athletic ability. He still felt the disappointment keenly.

They passed down Guilford Street and circled Russell Square. A late September frost lay like confetti on the grass. The benches were white and stark. A couple of teenagers with backpacks sprawled out, looking huddled and miserable. Then the British Museum loomed, wrought iron gates glistening with moisture. It had been an unusually damp and gloomy month.

Down Great Russell Street to Tottenham Court Road, Charing Cross and then Shaftsbury Avenue. Past the Palace Theater, the Gielgud and the Apollo.

"Stop the car!"

Sherwood uncoiled his long body from the cramped seat and watched as Harry Forsyth, his stocky young sergeant, scrambled out and came round to stand beside him.

"What are we doing?" he sniffed, annoyed at the prospect of walking. "We're still two blocks from the subway entrance."

"I need to stretch my legs," said Sherwood. "They were getting twitchy. Plus it'll give us a chance to go over what we know."

Harry looked put out. It took two of his own strides to match one of his boss's. He hated walking anywhere with Sherwood. He hated walking period. "We don't know dick," he said. "Some workers down in the Piccadilly Line found a couple of stiffs."

"Not bodies," Sherwood corrected. "Body *parts*. Skulls, skeletonized remains. Had to have been dead for years. Maybe decades, for all we know."

"So? Coupl'a derelicts, sleeping it off on the tracks, get clipped by a train. It's happened before."

"From what I understand, they weren't near the trains at all, they were in some sort of maintenance tunnel well above the tracks."

Harry grunted. "Could be someone left over from the war. Plenty of blokes went missing, were burned or buried alive during the Blitz. Lot of the damaged places were just plowed under. They didn't have the time or resources to do extensive searches." He searched his own thinning, brown hair with one hand, located the itch that was annoying him and proceeded to scratch at length, even as he danced a stutter step to keep up.

Sherwood said nothing, ducking under a low street sign. He always kept a watchful eye when walking the street. He'd banged his head more times than he could count. His ex-wife claimed it had addled his brain.

He thought briefly about Adria. Their marriage had been a train wreck, due mostly to her clinical depression. For a long time, he had managed to help her, talk her down, so to speak, when she got really bad. But she refused to take her medicine, and inevitably things grew worse. Finally, he felt her neediness sucking him into his own dark place and knew it was time to leave. Surprisingly, she seemed to be doing better on her own.

They neared the Piccadilly entrance. He glanced down Glasshouse Street to the low budget Regent Palace Hotel. Harry had lived there for a while in a tiny room, subsidized by the department. Then he got married, and the closest place to central London he and his wife could afford was a forty-five minute commute from New Scotland Yard. The sergeant spent a lot of time on the tube. He deeply resented the daily hour and a half it took away from time with his family.

Sherwood started to turn in but Harry grabbed his arm and steered him away. "Next block," he said. "Service entrance used for maintenance."

A uniformed constable stood by the tube entrance, head down against the early morning cold. Sherwood nodded to him.

"Disposal crews already down there, sir," said the man, saluting casually. He pulled up an overhead door and pointed the way to a set of gritty steps.

"Sheesh! Don't we get to ride the lift?" asked Harry.

"It's a 150 feet down to the tracks," the man said. "But the remains were in a maintenance tunnel not more than twenty feet below ground."

Sherwood eyed the large lift as they descended the steps. He wasn't unhappy to avoid it. Riding London's tube lifts always felt like a thirty-second fall from grace. The ancient machines issued forth a continuous series of ominous sounds, inevitably coming to a halt with a loud clank, as though Lucifer himself were rattling his chains in anticipation of their arrival.

They stepped into a dingy corridor at the bottom of the stairs, lit by a row of forty-watt lightbulbs. The gloom was heavy and ominous.

"Jeez," Harry said. "You'd think they'd need more light to work down in this pit."

They proceeded along the hall toward a distant light and the grinding sound of a portable generator. Heavy cords snaked into the opening, and they could see an area a hundred yards farther bathed in bright work lights. A clutch of dark figures appeared to be working on something.

A pock-marked face looked up as they approached. "Bloody time you showed up. They're ready to take this lot out." It was the medical examiner. His job was to make an initial examination, secure the location and oversee the removal of bodies to the morgue.

Sherwood shook his limp hand, looking around. "Where are they?" he asked.

The examiner pointed to a crumbling opening in the side of the tunnel.

Harry peered into the hole. "How in bloody hell did someone stumble across them down there?"

The man shrugged. "Apparently one of the archaeologists working at the Coram's Fields site was poking around and found them."

Sherwood stepped over the crumbling bricks and picked his way down into what appeared to be a sub-tunnel. He could see lights and two men preparing to bag up the bones. Harry joined him, grumbling, and they stood staring at the pitiful remains.

"Not much left of these poor blokes," said one of the men.

There were two gray skulls, glistening with dampness, and an assortment of other bones, hardly enough to make up two bodies.

"That's all there is?" Sherwood asked.

"Yes, sir, that's it. Only way we knew for sure there was two is 'cause of the skulls."

"Well where's the bloody rest of them?" asked Harry.

"They've been chewed on some, prob'ly by rats," the man said. "Soon as we get this lot bagged, we'll search some more. But the critters coulda spread 'em around pretty good."

Sherwood eased his long legs into the tight space and squatted. "Any clothing?" he asked.

"Nah. It's damp down here. What was there prob'ly disintegrated."

"Bag lady stuff," Harry sniffed. "Mostly it disintegrates while they're still wearing it."

Sherwood couldn't imagine how any sort of derelict, much less a bag lady, could get down here. It was more like someone had deliberately tried to hide the bodies. He stared at the opening.

"Any other way into this place?"

One of the men shook his head. "See how those bricks crumbled away? I bet no one even knew this sub-tunnel was here. Once they're bricked over like that and a hundred years go by, people forget about 'em."

Sherwood started to get up when something shiny caught his eye. He took a pen out of his pocket and gently rolled one of the skulls over. What he had seen shining through the eye socket appeared to be an earring. He picked it up. It was filthy and very crude.

"Anyone see this?"

The men shook their heads.

"All right, I'll keep it." He slipped it into a plastic bag. "You can finish up the rest. Harry, let's look around."

Sherwood produced a torch and they began to walk down the sub-tunnel. The ground was uneven and wet. They could have been two thousand feet underground in a coal mine.

"I just remembered why I like being a copper," said Harry. "The superior work conditions." He swore as he stepped into a puddle and went down into six inches of slime.

Sherwood spun the torch as he heard something. There was a lightning-fast scurry of movement, just detectable, but nothing clearly visible.

"What was that?" asked Harry.

"Rats." But Sherwood looked curiously at a small drain that emptied at chest height. He pointed the light into it. It was about a foot in diameter and stretched back until it angled off at the edge of the light's range.

"I hate rats," Harry said, helpfully. "Like to plug every one of the nasties."

"Shhh . . . listen."

They could hear something coming from the pipe, the sound of something moving. There was a strange sucking sound.

"What the hell . . . ?" Harry backed away from the drain.

Sherwood pulled the light back as well. "That doesn't sound like rats to me," he said. It was hard to pin down the location of the noise. They listened as it grew fainter and then stopped altogether.

Sherwood poked the light back into the drain and peered inside. Then he stuck his long arm in as far as he could reach.

"Jesus! I wouldn't put my hand in there for all the tea in China," said Harry.

"I think I can reach it," Sherwood said.

Harry moved in closer. "Reach what?"

"I can almost touch it," Then, suddenly, Sherwood's arm jolted into the hole up to his shoulder. "It's got me, Harry!" he cried.

"Holy Christ!" Harry grabbed Sherwood around the waist. "I got you. I got you, boss! What is it?"

Then Sherwood collapsed into laughter and drew his arm out, still holding the light. "Let go, Harry, before the boys decide we've got a thing for each other."

Harry stared at him with wide eyes, then let go of him like he was a hot poker.

"Asshole!" he said, turning away. "No wonder they made you an inspector."

Still smiling, Sherwood said, "Let's follow this tunnel a ways." He headed off, not waiting for Harry, who he knew would sulk for at least thirty seconds.

The tunnel began to slope more steeply, a trickle of water running down the middle. The top of the space was barely high enough for Sherwood to walk without stooping and he could touch both walls if he stretched out his arms.

"Pretty strange maintenance tunnel," said Harry. "Too small to get any serious equipment in here. And what the hell would they be maintaining anyway?"

Sherwood nodded, then realized Harry couldn't see him behind the torch. "I have to agree with you, Officer Forsyth. There's no evidence anyone's been in here for a long time. No tools left behind, not even any footprints I can see."

He stopped and examined the walls of the tunnel. They were crudely constructed. Most of London rested on dense clay. There was very little rock, which had made construction of the tube system an engineering tour de force.

"You know, this doesn't look like modern construction at all. See the way the wall has these sorts of scallop-shaped cuts in it, like they were made by someone swinging a pickaxe or some kind of hand tool. They haven't cut tunnels by hand down here at least since the early 20th century."

Again they heard the sound of something heavy moving, almost dragging or scrabbling over the ground. This time, a sort of singsong murmuring sound accompanied it. Sherwood looked at Harry, whose eyes were round as saucers.

"It's coming from farther down the tunnel," Sherwood said. "Come on." He led the way into the gloom, splashing now through wetness and mud.

"It's just rats," Harry said. "What are we going to do? Interview them? Who the hell cares?"

"When was the last time you heard a rat sing?"

There was definitely a detectable humming sound coming from the tunnel. They proceeded another thirty feet when Sherwood stopped abruptly and they both stared at something that came shuffling toward them out of the dark.

"What the bloody hell!" said Harry, taking a step back.

"Wait," said Sherwood.

The apparition slowly approached until they could see that it was human—more or less. It appeared larger than a normal person. Then they saw that it was a woman, dressed in multiple layers of clothing. She had a blue stocking cap on her head and a worn pair of army boots on her feet. Long, stringy blonde hair hung down over her shoulders. As she came up to them, they could hear her humming and alternately talking to herself. Sherwood stared, incredulous, at a young woman, probably not more than twenty years old. He eased the light out of her face, pointing it at her feet.

"Uh . . . hello miss. Could you tell us what you're doing down here?"

Her face was almost cherubic with smudged red cheeks and a pug nose. She might have been pretty, if she weren't so filthy. Her smell was indescribable. She stared at the two men, then looked away and began to talk—babble really.

"She's not right in the head," said Harry. "You won't get anything out of her."

Sherwood eased closer to the woman, put out a hand and gently touched her shoulder. She stopped talking, then leaned her cheek down into his hand, almost purring. The humming began again. Then she stopped abruptly and said, "Don't go down there. Lila says. They're down there. Waiting."

She grabbed Sherwood's hand with both of her own and stroked it like a favorite pet.

"What's down there?" Sherwood asked softly.

"A secret place," she said. "Where they hide secret things. Precious things."

"Can you show me?"

Her eyes took on a cautious slant. "I'm the only one they let inside."

"But I'm their friend too," said Sherwood, glancing at Harry, who rolled his eyes.

"What time is it?" the girl asked.

"Early morning," said Sherwood.

"They mostly come at night." She glanced furtively behind her. "You want to see?" A sly look came from beneath the stringy, golden hair.

Sherwood nodded, though Harry didn't look like he wanted to see anything, except the way out.

They followed the girl back the way she had come, trying to stay a few feet behind her odor.

"This is too weird," Harry said in a low voice. "How the hell did she get down here?"

"Well, she sure didn't come from our direction. All the officers and lights . . . they would have seen her. She must have already been here."

"How could she be down here? It's pitch black. She doesn't have a torch. What? You think she just wandered in here by accident? How likely is that?"

Sherwood just shook his head, concentrating on keeping the light pointed on the floor of the tunnel in front of the girl.

They walked for nearly twenty minutes, the tunnel continuing its gradual downward slope. Water dripped from the ceiling now, but they didn't see any more evidence of rats. In fact, there was nothing at all in the tunnel. They might have been the first humans to ever walk through it, except the girl definitely seemed to know where she was going.

Finally, she stopped, glanced back at them, then stepped to one side out of the light and disappeared.

"What the . . . ?" Sherwood spun the light in every direction. The girl had vanished.

"I think I see something," Harry said. "Bring the torch over here."

There was a boulder that jutted out of the wall. Behind it, as Sherwood played the light, was a tiny opening. They could hear the girl doing her singsong somewhere within. It was a tight squeeze for the two men, but they managed to force their way through.

They were in yet another tunnel, even more crudely built than the one they had just passed through. Ahead, they could see the girl. She looked back at them, then laughed suddenly and continued on. Harry and Sherwood kept after her, feeling more every minute like they were following Alice down the rabbit hole. A very dirty Alice.

After several more turns, the tunnel walls began to widen and then they were in a crude room carved from the heavy clay.

Harry exclaimed," Holy shit!" and stumbled backwards bumping into Sherwood, who dropped the torch. In the moment it took to find it again, they could hear the girl laughing, her voice seeming far away, fading. When Sherwood spun the light around finally, she was nowhere to be seen.

But the room held another surprise, the one that had made Harry cry out. The space was filled with coffins. A few boxes had been broken open and human skulls lay amid bits and pieces of clothing.

"Mother of God," said Harry. "What is this? Some sort of burial ground?"

"Looks like we've got more work for the boys upstairs," said Sherwood. "Let's get them down here. We'll need better light to examine this lot. And I want to find our little friend. She couldn't have gone far. She needs to answer some questions."

"That girl's as loony as a two-pronged fork," said Harry. "She's not going to tell you anything that makes any sense."

Sherwood shrugged. Nothing was making any sense. Why should the girl be any different?

4

Norwegian born RAF Flight Commander Gunnar Hansen turned his head as the air raid sirens started to go off. He'd heard them so many times that this was the only reaction they still engendered.

He'd been cooling his heels in a small room of the Ministry of Defense between Whitehall and Horse Guards Avenue for over an hour. It was the usual bullshit. He'd been ordered to make himself "available," then been picked up by special car from his air base on the Cornwall coast and driven here, arriving shortly before dusk. His driver could tell him nothing, but it wasn't the first time he'd been called in on a special assignment.

In April, 1940, as the Nazis marched into his homeland, Gunnar had become separated from his unit. Forced into hiding, he'd begun to work with the first resistance groups. Then, shortly after Norway surrendered on June 10, he managed to sneak onto his air base and fly his Norwegian Air Force plane to England, where he offered his services to the RAF. There was no way he was going to allow himself to be sidelined by the occupation, or worse, put in a concentration camp. His was not the only such decision. The entire elected social democratic cabinet of Johan Nygaardsvold also sought exile in London.

Since then, he'd undertaken a series of reconnaissance flights over his homeland, taken aerial photographs, participated in the sinking of a German battleship and air-dropped dozens of agents behind enemy lines. He was practically a one-man espionage transport system.

An army officer, probably a major, stepped out of a door and crooked his finger. Gunnar still had trouble identifying English insignia, though he found it a convenient excuse for ignoring brass when he felt like it. He got up and followed the man down a series of long corridors.

Blackout shrouds covered all the windows. Most of the staffers in the building had already begun to make their way to the shelters.

"Where are we going?" Gunnar asked.

"The underground war room," said the major without breaking stride. "But you'll see Mr. Sandys first."

They passed down several flights of stairs and then down more corridors. All of London seemed to be connected underground these days. Finally they came to a heavy door. A guard checked their credentials and let them through. Now they were in a dark warren of rooms, each busy with secretaries and military personnel going about the business of a nation at war.

He heard the distant booms of the first bombs falling as the major opened one final door, leaned in and said, "Commander Hansen, sir."

A balding, middle-aged man sitting at a desk studying aerial reconnaissance photos under a dim lamp looked up.

So this was Duncan Sandys, thought Gunnar. He'd heard about him, of course. Churchill's son-in-law, though no one seemed to know quite what he did.

Sandys threw the photo he'd been looking at to one side, stood and came around the desk with his hand out. "Hansen! It's an honor to meet you. Every one of you flyboys who've come over to fight makes a real difference in this bloody war."

"Thank you, sir."

"Here, have a chair. You're probably wondering what the bloody hell this is all about. You'll talk to the prime minister shortly, but my job is to brief you first."

Sandys watched him settle into the chair, then retreated behind his desk again. He leaned back, stared at the ceiling and tapped a pencil on the desk. "I head a committee called Crossbow. You won't have heard of it. It's top secret. We've been investigating the German rocket program at Peenemunde."

"Sir?"

"Hitler has staked the outcome of the war on his ability to develop a flying bomb. If he is successful, London will be at his mercy. Peenemunde is a village on the island of Usedom, just off the German coast in the Baltic Sea. The Nazis converted it to a rocket research site in 1937. Over 4000 skilled workers live there now. The program is headed by Werner von Braun."

Gunnar found Sandys's manner disorienting. His eyes seemed to dart everywhere except at him.

"It was slow going at first," he continued, staring at his shoes. "Many spectacular failures. The Third Reich was losing billions of marks. Hitler lost interest and diverted funds elsewhere. That was our good fortune. The führer expected to win the war quickly, before the rocket program was likely to offer anything substantial. Now, with the outcome of the war more in doubt every week, they have begun to build the program back up. About a year ago, in an operation codenamed Hydra, the RAF sent 500 heavy bombers to attack Peenemunde."

"I heard there was a big raid on at the time," said Gunnar. "But no one knew where."

"Even the pilots didn't know what we were after," Sandys went on. "They weren't told their targets until after takeoff. The attack was successful, to a point. Many of the installations and scientists were killed, including one of von Braun's leading assistants, Dr. Walter Thiel, head of engine development. But the flying rocket, the experimental V-1, escaped relatively unscathed. We've learned that the Germans have since moved part of the program to Poland, beyond the range of our heavy bombers."

"Do you really believe the threat is serious?" asked Gunnar. "Things are not going well for the Germans almost everywhere. The war may be over before much comes of this."

"Wishful thinking. We have intelligence that suggests the Germans have begun to work on a new, even more advanced rocket. It's called the V-2, the 'Vengeance Weapon.'"

"Colorful," said Gunnar.

"We believe this new rocket can hold up to one ton of high explosives and will be a serious threat. It has a greater range, can be launched by a mobile ramp, reaches an altitude of fifty miles and then falls straight down on its target at speeds up to 3000 miles per hour. There is no way to defend against such a weapon."

Gunnar whistled softly. "I'm beginning to get the picture."

Sandys shook his head. "You're not even close yet, commander. While the V-2 is a terrible weapon and would doubtless cause great carnage in London, it would not, in our opinion, alter the outcome of the war. However ... "

He stood and walked over to a map of Europe. "We have reason to believe the Germans are also working on another program. In Norway. A unit of the rocket research team there has begun to test a new weapon. One so potentially dangerous that they chose to locate it at the end of a fjord on the remote northern Norwegian coast."

"But surely that would place the rockets out of range for any part of England," said Gunnar.

"If the research is successful, they will relocate the rockets back to Belgium for launch."

"I'm afraid I'm not following this, sir. Why would they choose to go all the way to Norway for the research? What's so dangerous?"

"Hitler appears to have decided that the individual rockets would have a bad psychological effect but not do much damage to the British war effort. He is counting on this new program for something more potent."

"Potent?"

"The research being done in Norway is to determine the effectiveness of delivering, via rocket, a biological weapon."

Gunnar felt a cold hand grip his stomach. "They intend to send some . . . sickness . . . to England by rocket?"

"What they plan to introduce isn't known. But it must be pretty bad if they only dare test it as far from the Fatherland as they can get."

Gunnar stared at Sandys's desk. "I'm just a simple pilot, sir. But it would seem to me highly improbable that any sort of infectious agent could survive the fiery explosion caused by a rocket."

"Our first thought as well," Sandys replied. "But the consequences would be so dire, we cannot afford to dismiss them. The Nazis have shown how inventive their scientists can be. Perhaps they have figured out a way to deliver a V-2 payload without any sort of explosion. A simple delivery system straight into the heart of London."

"I think I'm beginning to see what you want with me," said Gunnar.

"Good. We intend you to fly a team of commandos into that base, where you will find out what it is they plan to do, bring back the agent—if it can be done so safely—or destroy it on site if it cannot. If you can manage to bring us back one of the V-2 rockets for study, that would be helpful too."

Twenty minutes later, his mind still reeling, Gunnar sat alone in a tiny room waiting to meet Churchill. A young woman entered and nodded to him.

"This way, please," she said.

He followed her down a long, dark hallway, then she opened a door and ushered him into a room filled with steam and cigar smoke. He stood rooted to the floor and stared at the prime minister of England sitting in his bathtub, looking like a large, pink, hairless bulldog.

"Ah, Commander Hansen, come in, come in. Don't let all this," Churchill waved a hand to encompass the room, "throw you. There is so much to do these days that I must make use of every spare moment. So you must see your leader in a very spare moment indeed."

Gunnar moved forward. "It's an honor to meet you, sir. Under any circumstances. I confess I had heard that the war room amenities were quite unique."

Churchill removed his cigar and placed it on a side table. He pulled a large sponge out of the water and began to splash his arms. "Uniquely cold and drafty, but one must keep clean. We can't allow the Hun to disrupt our daily routines. You've been briefed about the V-2 rockets?"

"Yes sir."

"Rockets we can deal with. By God, the spirit of the British people impresses me more each day. But Hitler and his Nazis," he pronounced it Naaazis, "will stoop to anything, including the murder of innocents by the millions if need be."

The prime minister picked up his cigar with a soaking-wet hand and took several puffs, then replaced the sodden lump back on the table. He peered closely at Gunnar.

"This dastardly business of rocketing some bloody infection into our midst has me worried, I don't mind telling you. Not knowing what they have in mind is unacceptable. Your experience as a member of the Norwegian resistance makes you an invaluable resource. And I will use every resource I have in this war. Are you with me, Hansen?" The bulldog face stared at him hard.

"Indeed I am sir. It's why I came to England."

"Good!" Churchill struck the bath with his fist making a huge spray of water. "You must destroy whatever infective agent they are using, but more than that, we need to know precisely what it is, so if they continue on after your attack or if they have another place where they are developing it, at least we may try to prepare for it."

"I understand sir, but I'm afraid I don't have the ability to identify any infective agent more devastating than the common cold."

"Ah—I was coming to that." He reached over and pushed a button. Gunnar heard a buzzer sound in the other room and the door opened immediately.

"Come in here, Natasha, and meet your future partner in crime."

Gunnar turned to see the young woman who had ushered him in. He had hardly glanced at her in his anxiety at meeting the prime minister. She wore a Home Guard uniform and advanced without the slightest embarrassment to the very side of Churchill's tub, where she picked up his smoldering cigar and stubbed it out.

The PM stared at the terminated faggot with a mournful eye. "I'm going to miss your meddlesome ways, Natasha," he said.

"Fire regulations ought to apply to everyone equally, sir," she replied evenly.

Churchill sighed. "Gunnar Hanson, Natasha Newman. She's a handful, commander. But she will be indispensable to you. Natasha is a nurse who has worked in the infectious disease unit of the Foreign Office. She speaks and reads German fluently. She will go along with you and help identify the agents the Germans are using. I expect you to take good care of her."

"I quite believe I can take care of myself," Natasha said, but she smiled at Gunnar and offered her hand. "I think we will have some excitement, don't you?"

Her hand was smooth and firm. Gunnar detected the smell of soap coming off her. Her dark hair was in a tight bun, which gave her a severe look, except it displayed her very long and delicate neck. He hoped she would not be too delicate for what lay ahead.

"So it would appear," he said. "Do you have any idea at all what the Germans are using?"

"None. There are too many infectious agents. It could be anything, but given their selection of such a remote site, I suspect they may be playing around with something quite lethal . . . plague perhaps. If it *is* something of that nature, Mr. Prime Minister, there is no way we should consider bringing it back to London. We might end up doing the Germans' job for them."

Churchill grunted. "Very well. I leave that decision in your hands." The prime minister began to play with a small battleship that Gunnar hadn't noticed in the tub. He struggled to keep from smiling at the bizarre sight.

"The Special Operations Executive has undertaken many commando operations in Norway since its fall, commander," Churchill said. "But I personally consider this the most important, perhaps of the entire war. And most urgent. You will study your briefing papers en route. Much of the information we have has been provided by your elected government in exile. London's getting to be quite a community of exiles these days."

"Uh—en route, sir?"

"You leave for Scotland by train within the hour. There's a ferry waiting to deliver you to the Shetland Islands. From there, you fly to Norway." The PM motioned to Natasha. "Where are my glasses?" he said, and Gunnar thought he must be asking for his reading glasses.

Instead, she stepped over to a chest and poured scotch into three glasses, then handed one to each of them.

Churchill raised his. "I believe every important mission should be launched with a toast. Godspeed to you both and may the Hun meet his end with equal haste."

Gunnar hesitated, then swallowed the strong whisky in a single gulp. It would be one to tell his grandchildren. How the greatest statesman of the twentieth century had toasted his health from his bathtub. He only hoped he would live long enough to have those grandchildren.

5

Gunnar had just thirty minutes to gather his personal effects. Then Sandys placed a briefcase containing reconnaissance photos and what intelligence they had in his hand and wished him luck.

Now he sat with Natasha in a private compartment poring over aerial photos of Ofotfjorden, above the 68th parallel on the northern Norwegian coast. The green hills of the Cotswolds flowed unseen outside their window.

"About as remote as you can get," said Gunnar, "but I know the area. I used to fish those waters with my grandfather."

"Is there any place to actually land a plane up there?" Natasha asked.

"Unlikely. Unless the Germans have built an airstrip." He stared at two more photos. "I don't see any evidence of it. But you see this rail line here? That's new. It wasn't there two years ago. I'd bet that's how they move the rockets in and out. It might be done more quickly by sea, but they wouldn't want to risk losing their new toy to an enemy submarine. We'll have to land on the ocean or be dropped by parachute. A sea landing would be difficult, as the waters are very rough year round."

She stared at him. "I've never done a parachute jump."

"Well, you know what they say."

"What?"

"It's not the jump that's the problem. It's the landing."

She sat back and looked at him. "That sounds like something the PM would say. You sure you're not related?"

He laughed. "My ancestors were catching codfish and hake in the Norwegian Sea while Churchill's were leading men into battle for king and country in the 1700s. Not much opportunity to mix the bloodlines, I'm afraid."

She had dispensed with the tight bun and now wore her hair down to her shoulders. Also gone was the Home Guard uniform. In civilian clothes, he thought she looked very good indeed.

"I'm curious," he said. "How long have you worked for the prime minister?"

"You mean how long did it take before I was allowed in the same room with him in his birthday suit?"

"The thought never crossed my mind."

"Mmm-hmm. The fact is: there's no ulterior motive with him except to save time—time for England. I've seen him run an entire cabinet meeting from his tub."

He shook his head in amazement. "That would be something to see."

"I met him two years ago when he toured a bombing site near Charing Cross Station with a number of officials. I'd been with the foreign office working on infectious diseases. A lot of our boys came down with some pretty nasty stuff in Burma and other places. He asked me several questions, which I apparently answered to his satisfaction. Before I knew it, I'd been ordered to Whitehall. I think he enjoys my company and he relies on me for some of his medical information. When intelligence started to come in on Hitler's potential biological weapons program, we began to have extensive conversations about what it might mean."

"Not to belittle your experience, which sounds pretty impressive, but couldn't the PM get the best medical minds in Britain?"

"He could and he does. The very best. But he's an interesting man in that he believes fully in personal relationships. He came to trust me and to use me as a sounding board for many things."

The train entered a tunnel, causing the lights to flicker. When they re-emerged, the stars had come out. Soon, they were crossing the great barren moors of Scotland.

"I've never been to Scotland," Natasha said, gazing out the window. "Guess I'm not going to see much of it on this trip either."

"Nor have I. But I've heard there is great climbing here. Do you like to climb? Perhaps . . . once this is over . . . "

She smiled. "That sounds like an invitation, Gunnar. My father and brothers used to take me climbing in Wales. And the last summer before the war, we all went together to climb in the Alps." Her face grew sad. "It seems like another life now. I haven't seen my brothers in over a year. One is in North Africa, the other in the navy."

He nodded. "I haven't seen my family either, since I left home. For all I know they may think me a traitor for leaving. A regular Quisling. War is not good to families."

"Did you ever meet him?"

"Quisling? No. I'd give a lot to, though. Even before he helped the Germans stage their coup d'etat and he became Norway's puppet premier, we in the underground wanted to kill him. He was a fascist and a toady." He made a fist. "Someday . . . "

"Did you know he was made a commander of the British Empire? For his services in supporting the interests of Britain in the Soviet Union in 1929."

Gunnar looked stunned. "Quisling a CBE? I can hardly believe it."

"Well, not anymore, thank God. The House of Commons revoked the appointment in 1940."

The compartment door opened and Major Duncan Osborne entered balancing an armful of sandwiches and six bottles of stout.

"I'll be damned, major!" said Gunnar. "I didn't think there was a bottle of stout left in all of England."

"Had to trade a bloke for them. The last of my American cigarettes, but it was worth it." He handed them each a bottle and spread the sandwiches out on the seat. He glanced at the map. "My lads are asking where we're going. Kind of curious myself, given that we're heading away from any war zone I know of."

"I was under orders not to divulge the information until we reached our point of departure," said Gunnar. "But I guess this train qualifies as a point of departure. No reason to keep you in the dark any longer. We're going to Norway to investigate the German rocket program that has been relocated there."

Osbourne whistled softly and leaned over the map. His group consisted of just eight men. Inconspicuous enough, SOE believed, to slip into Norway and save western civilization. Gunnar wasn't so sure. But Duncan had been a welcome surprise. He was a happy go lucky redhead with a sense of humor and a muscular build that generally gave him his way in whatever pub he entered. He was also one of Britain's most intensely trained special operations soldiers.

They studied the maps and photos for an hour, until the stout made them drowsy. Natasha and the major left for their own rooms and Gunnar opened his seat into a sleeper.

He lay in bed listening to the repetitive sounds of the train and staring out at the stars. He had not imagined he would set foot in his homeland again until the war was over and hadn't realized how strong his homesickness was. His reconnaissance flights had only served to deepen his sense of longing for his native forests and fjords.

There was a soft rap on his compartment. He slipped out of bed and went to the door.

"Who is it?"

"Gunnar, it's Natasha. Can I come in?"

He opened the door. "Is something wrong?"

She slipped in and closed the door behind her, leaning against it. She wore a robe and slippers.

"Yes. I can't sleep. The major and his men are in the compartments surrounding mine. They're partying and making too much noise. I don't have the heart to ask them to stop. I wonder . . . can I sleep here?"

He looked at the fold down bed. There was only one.

She put her hand on his arm. "War leaves no time for things. We may not live another week, Gunnar. And I like you."

6

London — Present Day

The small creature proceeded purposefully through the drain pipe. This was its normal route, and as it passed from one of the primary tunnels into a lesser passageway, caution was the main order of business. More so than usual. Following the incident where one of the noisy things had put a limb into the pipe, the animal now took more care.

Lucky for the noisy thing that it had the bright light. Otherwise, it might be missing that limb. Noisy things were hard to come by, though surprisingly good eating. The light was annoying. Eyes so long underground were sensitive, meaning light was to be avoided; though a vestigial eyelid offered protection to the inner eye.

The animal raised its snout and sampled the air. It was hungry.

The creature was always hungry. It had a deep stomach churning and endless gnawing at its insides. It could not remember a time when it had not been hungry. And the grinding sense of longing for nourishment was so intense that it made it not only miserable, but angry. So angry it wanted to lash out. At anything.

It reached the end of the drainpipe and dropped softly to the tunnel floor. No longer alone, the animal's stomach growled in anticipation.

Ahead, another passage branched away and the creature's incredibly sensitive ears picked up the sound it had been searching for. The sound of something chewing—pausing— chewing again and then making a tiny squeaking sound.

Dinner!

Now it moved with great stealth. Years of living in the silent depths had given it the ability to proceed soundlessly, while simultaneously being able to hear prey from a great distance.

At a bend in the tunnel, the animal hesitated, gathering itself, for it knew that what it wanted was just a few feet away. A low, sucking sound emitted from its mouth. Then, in a blur of speed, it raced forward and clamped savage teeth and jaws onto the rat that had been gnawing obliviously on a bone. A single crunch of those powerful jaws and then the creature leaped onto another rat and another. It managed to kill or disable three before the others fled in terror.

Then it settled down to eat. Blood, flesh and bone. All were crunched and swallowed. It seemed no more than a moment before the rodents had disappeared right down to their tails and fur.

The instant the rats had been consumed, the awful hunger began again. The longing for food was persistent, like a machine that needed a constant running fuel supply in order to operate.

The search for prey began anew.

7

To save time, Carmen Kingsley cut across Coram's Fields, the great space dedicated to sporting grounds for the people of London. The northwest corner of the immense area had been cordoned off for months, the result of an archaeological dig being undertaken by the British Museum. When Roman ruins were discovered two years previously, the Museum administration swooped down and commandeered the site, relegating Philip Trimm, the archaeologist in charge, to a secondary role. No one else was going to oversee a dig of such national importance just a few blocks from the world's greatest museum.

It was the sort of jurisdictional bullshit she hated, but as the administrator in charge of greater London projects for the museum, she had to bow to the wisdom of the move. This was going to be a big one, much too important for Trimm to handle on his own. He was a good enough archaeologist, a specialist in Roman ruins, particularly Hadrian's Wall. But as the site expanded, it became clear that he was no administrator. Furious at his demotion, he retreated to studying his rocks and bones. There remained an undercurrent of hostility, however, that Carmen sensed whenever she came near him, as though somehow it had all been her fault.

Her ability to detect such feelings was limited, however. She wasn't very good at telling what others were thinking. It was one aspect of the AS, or Asperger's Syndrome, she suffered from.

She paced jauntily along the dirt path, wishing she was running the route, as she tried to do several times a week in her generally clumsy running style. The day was dark and overcast with a fine mist in the air. Good running weather, but she was more than tired of this strange, September gloom.

Her running had suffered lately, for it was always hard to get out of the office in the fall months. She got precious little site- time of her own these days. Her duties ran to budgets, government oversight and personnel issues. She was a whiz with numbers and computers. The personnel side took a lot more effort.

The path was lined with orange construction netting. And for good reason. Great gaping holes fell away on all sides, many connected to underground passageways, a few carefully sectioned off with gridlines; the bowed heads of students and professionals poring over what looked for all the world like nothing more than piles of dirt.

A cluster of middle-aged American tourists stared into one of the pits. As Carmen passed, a woman in a green velour pants suit said, "Did you see that? That was the largest rat I've ever seen anywhere, even in Manhattan. You'd never get me to go down there."

A balding man with a stoop laughed curtly. "We saw a rat that size next to a trash bin across the street from Bloomingdale's. You managed to go in there all right and spend two thousand bucks."

"Barbara spent two thousand dollars in a trash bin?" said another man and they all laughed loudly.

There *were* a lot of rats. Her friend Julia, nominally in charge of the site, worked side by side with Trimm. There were so many rats they had to call in an exterminator.

"Carmen. Hey Carmen!"

She stopped and peered down at Julia, who stood calf-deep in muddy water, holding a heavy construction flashlight. She wore gum boots, torn jeans and a baggy shirt. Carmen almost never saw her friend in anything except the filthiest clothes. But even the raunchiest garb couldn't hide the fact that she was stunningly beautiful, with long auburn hair and a firm, runner's body. Carmen would gladly trade her jet-black hair for Julia's any day. It gave her a softness that men loved. Every man at the site had hit on her at one time or another, which was fine with Julia. She loved men.

A gloved hand reached up and opened a section of orange fence. "Come on down here, Carmen. I want to show you something."

"Are you crazy? I'm on my way to a meeting. I've got my work clothes on. I'm not climbing down into that mash pit."

"Come on—it'll be worth it. I'll show you something no one's seen for a thousand years."

Carmen hesitated, staring at her new shoes. She never could resist anything old. Her parents had traveled all over showing her the temples of ancient Greece and Turkey when she was a child. They wanted to pull her out of the repetitive, tightly controlled world view in which AS children lived. And they hoped the contact with different cultures would help her open up to others. The fascination with ancient civilizations, at least, had stuck. All through college and graduate school, she'd chosen to take her vacations in places with the most interesting ruins—Angkor Wat, Machu Piccu, Pompeii. She never tired of it.

When she was hired by the British Museum a dozen years ago, she thought she'd died and gone to heaven. She reveled in the dusty, old workrooms piled high with uncatalogued treasures that had been stored, sometimes for more than a century. Her fascination with all things ancient led to long work days and several significant discoveries that paved the way for her rise in museum hierarchy.

Increasing administrative duties had come at a cost, however. She had no romantic life at all, had virtually not even dated since college. Julia nagged her constantly about her wasted youth. She also had fewer opportunities to get her hands dirty. Sometimes she missed that part so much it was like a physical craving.

Julia smiled knowingly. She was well aware of Carmen's AS and also of her other weakness—her inability to resist a mystery. "Here." She held up a pair of yellow rubber boots. "You can put these on right over your shoes." She took her friend's briefcase and put it on a worktable, then led off down a sloping tunnel lit by a few hanging lightbulbs.

"I better not lose those papers," Carmen said, looking back at her belongings.

"Will you relax? Whattya think, we've got thieves down here who've been waiting all week for you to arrive with a stack of financial reports?" Her voice changed from annoyance to excitement. "We've uncovered a previously unknown section of the Great Conduit."

Carmen stooped under a hanging wire. "Sounds like something you'd find in a sex shop."

"It's *medieval*, Carmen. Part of the system built in the 1200s to bring water to London from springs beside the Tyburn—that's near Bond Street Tube today. It took thirty years to build the system."

"Oh. I've heard of it. London's answer to the Roman aqueduct."

"Same principle. Gravity feed. The Great Conduit entered the city at Ludgate, climbed the hill north of St. Paul's and ran along Cheapside until it emptied into a huge underground cistern near Old Jewry that was discovered about ten years ago. No one expected to find a section in this part of the city, though."

"You're sure that's what it is?"

"We've found pieces of lead pipe and the location and alignment match contemporary map references for the Great Conduit's route. The system supplied water until the Great Fire of 1666." She stopped abruptly. "Behold!"

Carmen stared at the wall beside them. It appeared to be lined with clay tiles of great age.

"This was the first piece we found. We've made exploratory holes for almost a quarter mile. It goes a long way—we're not sure how far. But the best part is still ahead."

They walked another hundred yards until they came to a place where the mud path began to angle down steeply and Julia held out a hand to stop Carmen.

"This is as far as we can go," she said. She flipped on her flashlight and the beam seemed to be swallowed up by an immense cavern directly in front of them. Carmen stepped back in surprise.

"This is another cistern, previously unknown. It's immense. See across on the other side—all those tunnels emptying into it? It's a maze that's going to take a long time to explore." She grinned. "Job security. Provided we can get the funding."

Suddenly there was a scurrying sound. Julia swung the lantern toward a nearby tunnel and Carmen gasped. The passage literally crawled with rats. Emerging from amongst them was a bulky figure that hardly seemed human in size and form.

"What in the name of God . . . "

"Relax. It's just Norman. The guy we hired to get control of the rat problem down here. Hi Norm."

The man was short and a bit pudgy. He wore filthy coveralls. On his back was some sort of canister with a hose that snaked over his shoulder to a nozzle that he held like a six-gun. His eyes were covered with thick goggles. He looked like a diminutive Lloyd Bridges.

Norman stuck his nozzle into his belt and raised the goggles onto his forehead, revealing twinkling eyes and a ruddy face. "Did I hear someone mention job security?"

"From the looks of things," said Carmen, "I'd say you're good for a thousand years." Then she added, skeptically, "Can you actually do anything against all those?"

"Go ahead, Norm," said Julia. "Give her some rat facts."

Norman looked pleased. "There are an estimated three rats for every human in London. There are tens of millions of rats. You are probably never more than three feet from a rat at any time. There are 4000 rats born in London every hour. They are incredibly prolific. One rat can produce 2000 babies in a year. The largest concentration of rats is beneath the Houses of Parliament, which may not be all that surprising. When you pick up a rat by the snout—"

"All right, all right! Stop!" said Carmen.

Norman turned to Julia. "Seen the Germans?" he asked.

"Last time I saw them, our junior Nazis were consulting with Dr. Trimm in the main staging area. Why?"

He grunted. "I keep running into them. They manage to get into some pretty tight spots. Don't know what they're supposed to be researching, but if I didn't know better I'd say they were after my job."

"No one else wants to do what you do, Norm," said Julia, patting his arm. "And no one else is as good at it."

He smiled contentedly, pulled his goggles in place, drew his hose and disappeared down an adjoining tunnel. Julia said, "He's unattached. I could fix you up if you're interested."

Carmen groaned. To change the subject, she said, "What was that business about Nazis?"

"They're a team of German graduate students who volunteered to work here for free over the summer. They pretty much stick together and don't socialize, so some of the other workers make fun of them. Easy enough to do. They're a pretty tight-assed bunch, if you ask me."

Carmen looked at her watch. "I've got to get to my meeting, if you want to be funded for next year, that is." She turned away, then stopped. "I have absolutely no idea which way to go."

Before Julia could reply, light suddenly filled the underground space and several young men emerged from another tunnel. One of them carried a clipboard thick with paper. Another held onto a metal detector, while a third carried a strange instrument that emitted a beep every few seconds.

The man with the clipboard stopped in front of Julia. He was tall, blond and good looking. He smiled and said in perfect English. "We have finished this sector, Julia. Now we're going on to another." He gave them a little salute and the men disappeared down yet another tunnel.

Julia stared after them.

"I take it those are your Germans," Carmen said. "I notice you didn't offer *that* hunk up for my consideration."

"That's Hans. He is kind of cute, isn't he? A perfect Aryan specimen. But you can't start at the top, girl. Got to work your way up. You sure about Norman?"

"Mmm-hmm. What are they doing with a metal detector? And that other thing. I can't even guess what that was for."

"I don't have a clue what they're doing and I'm supposed to be in charge down here. It's annoying as hell. The only one they really talk to is our munchkin, Dr. Trimm, and he hasn't exactly been forthcoming since you took his job away from him."

Trimm stood only five and a half feet tall. Both women, who were in the five-ten range, knew it irked him to have to look up whenever he spoke to them. It was probably why he avoided them as much as possible.

"I didn't take his job," said Carmen. "I had nothing to do with it. But he's been angry at me since I was put in charge of the overall project. Anyway, so far as I know, he's simply refocused on his personal research interests."

"That may be, but I can tell you, he's damned territorial down here."

"Territorial? Over what? This hole in the ground? I never could understand what he finds so absorbing. His main interests are bones and walls, the older the better. You don't have either down here."

"Walls, no," Julia said slowly. "But we did uncover some bones early on. If you ever left your desk and your abacus, you might have heard about it. I suggested we contact Scotland Yard. Dr. Trimm almost had a coronary when he found out. Said he was the one in charge of any bones to be found."

"What were they?"

"Who knows? Some poor slob who died during the ancient construction, or a derelict who got in here. Or maybe . . . "

"What?"

"Well, it *could* have been more sinister. The Yard sent an inspector down. He poked around and then bagged everything up and left. I never heard another thing about it. When I called to ask for a report, I was given the brush-off."

Carmen raised an eyebrow. "Jack the Ripper couldn't find a better place to dispose of bodies than this. The very thought gives me the creeps. Still, that's pretty strange behavior by the authorities. Maybe I'll inquire about it."

8

"I have an appointment with Inspector Peets," Carmen said to an intimidating-looking woman at the desk at New Scotland Yard.

"Second floor, third door on your right," she replied, already scowling past her to the next supplicant.

She found the proper door without problem and knocked. After a moment, a voice said. "Come in."

Sherwood sat behind his desk, long legs and stocking feet perched on the only corner of the edifice not covered with papers and files. He was deep into one of the files and glanced up after a moment with a frown. "Can I help you?"

"I'm Carmen Kingsley. I spoke with you on the phone."

He looked blank.

"About the bones at the Coram's Fields dig."

The legs came down. "Sorry. Yes, I remember. Have a . . . uh . . . seat." He swept a tweedy jacket and scarf off the chair, then stared at her for a moment after she sat.

"This is a little awkward, Ms. Kingsley. I'm really not at liberty to discuss the findings. They relate to an ongoing investigation."

"I understood that these bones were old, inspector. *Really old.* You're not going to give me that "ongoing investigation" routine for bones that could be medieval in origin for all we know. That's stretching the statute of limitations a bit, don't you think?"

"I'm sorry, but Dr. Trimm requested that we keep this information confidential for the time being."

"Dr. Trimm requested?"

"Yes."

"Inspector, Dr. Trimm works for me."

Sherwood looked slightly ill. "I . . . uh . . . didn't know that." He considered his shoes for a moment. "Under the circumstances, I don't see any reason not to tell you."

"Tell me what?"

"Very little, actually. The bones aren't as old as you suggested. However, neither are they what you might consider current. They are between sixty-five and seventy years old and represent the remains of two young females."

"Do you know how they died?"

"So far, we have been unable to determine that. There is no evidence of trauma of any kind. Lab results have not been reported yet."

"I suppose it would be too much to expect that you've identified the women?"

"We have some leads along those lines. There is dental work that reflects the technology of the period but we have been unable to track anything down so far. As you know, many records were destroyed during the war."

She looked puzzled. "I don't get it. Why all the secrecy? If you want to find out who they were, I would think publicity might help. There could still be someone out there who remembers two young women going missing."

She found the inspector's manner disconcerting. He looked at her only fleetingly and seemed overly nervous about something. She caught him staring at her twice when he thought she was looking elsewhere. Then his eyes quickly flicked away and he would stare at the ceiling.

"The remains date from the war," he said. "A lot of people disappeared during the bombings. Anyway, Dr. Trimm thought it would be best not to make a big public scene about it. He thought it might endanger the archaeological work. And it's true, as you certainly know, that things could come to a screeching halt if a full investigation were to be launched. So . . . " He spread his hands. "I've been trying to conduct our review without fanfare."

There was a commotion outside in the hallway. A moment later the door burst open and Dr. Trimm entered, followed by three tall men wearing almost comically identical suits. He looked strikingly like the short point guard for the Boston Celtics.

Trimm was fiftyish, sported a tight mustache and wore a rumpled, corduroy sports jacket. He had thick glasses that magnified his eyes, and he glared through them at Carmen.

"Philip? What on earth . . . " She started to rise from her chair, but one of the suited men put a hand on her shoulder and pushed her down.

Trimm ignored her and turned to Sherwood. "These men are from the prime minister's office." He laid an official-looking document on the table. "They are authorized to remove all papers you may have relating to the bones found at Coram's Fields. The bones themselves have already been seized. *All of the bones.* You are hereby ordered not to discuss any findings related to this case with anyone." He stared again at Carmen.

Sherwood stood behind his desk, fists clenched. He looked like he was barely controlling himself. He picked up the document and scanned it. Without waiting for further reaction from him, the men began to search the office, going through the inspector's files and drawers.

Carmen stood, this time pushing aside the hand of the man who had kept her seated the first time. "What on earth does Prime Minister Harris want with a pile of old bones?"

"I have something for you, too," Trimm said, handing her a piece of paper. "You are no longer in charge of the Coram's Fields dig. I am now in control of the site."

"By whose authority?"

"As you can see, it is signed by the director of the museum, Dr. Jessmer. I hereby inform you that you are no longer permitted on the grounds. If you appear there, I will have you arrested."

Carmen stood with her mouth open as the men finished their search. They stuffed three cartons with papers, nodded to Trimm and left. Trimm looked up at her, his large, amplified eyes boring into her. "I warned you not to mess with me," he said.

Then he was gone.

Sherwood and Carmen stared after him, then looked at one another.

"Have you any idea what that was all about?" asked Carmen.

He sat heavily in his chair. "I can tell you one thing. This isn't over. No one comes into Scotland Yard and rifles through my private files. Who the bloody hell knows what they took? They've compromised every one of my cases. The prime minister will hear about this, through one channel or another. He hasn't been in favor here with his high-handed approach. Worse than Tony Blair ever was."

She knew about the conflicts between the Yard and the new prime minister. They had boiled over onto the front pages of the tabloids. Now it looked like there was going to be a lot more fodder for that mill.

"I don't understand something," she said. "What did he mean when he said 'all of the bones'?"

Sherwood looked uncomfortable. He crossed his legs, drummed his fingers on the desk but said nothing.

Carmen watched him. Was he hiding something? Did he know more than he was letting on? Damn her inability to read people's emotions. His odd stares and long silences started to irritate her more and more.

Finally, he stopped looking around the room and focused on her. Her face looked hard, unforgiving, almost . . . frightening. There was such intensity.

"Were more bones found?" she repeated.

"I can't talk about that. It's classified."

Her face showed exasperation. "What is going on, inspector? Men from the prime minister's office seize your private files and you won't even comment? 'Classified'? It sounds more like some sort of elaborate cover-up to me, but who would want to cover up old, dead bodies—other than the person or persons responsible for murdering them, that is."

She leaned forward, her chin jutting a bit.

He considered her silently; his long face emotionless, at least to Carmen. Finally, he seemed to come to a decision. "Ask me about the two bodies we found and I'll tell you what I know," he said. "I can't go further than that right now."

She stared at the annoying man in front of her. He was obviously hiding something, but he seemed genuinely disturbed by what had just transpired. She let out a long breath.

"All right. You told me the bones dated from the Second World War and were female?"

He nodded. "Young women, probably in their twenties. I haven't been able to correlate them against any records of women who disappeared, though again, because of the war, the records are not good and have been shuffled around a good deal."

He hesitated, unsure how much to say, but he found himself wanting to trust this strange young woman whose brown eyes seemed to penetrate him. There was something about her unwillingness to be put off that appealed to him. An inspector's mentality, he thought ruefully.

"There is something else I found with the bodies," he said. "It wasn't in my report, the one your Dr. Trimm just seized along with the bones. In fact, I haven't been able to determine what it is, quite yet."

He reached into his pocket and pulled out a small plastic bag. "I don't know why, really, but I've had it on my person ever since I found it. I thought it was just an earring, but it's an unusual piece."

She took the little bag and stared at the object inside. She held it up to the light and saw a small metallic cross about two inches long. It appeared to be made of some crude form of pewter or perhaps a badly tarnished piece of silver. There was a thin piece of wire on one end that could have been intended for a pierced ear. It definitely looked like an earring. She felt her heart thump. She'd seen this design before.

"You say this was on one of the bodies that were found? That dated from the Second World War?"

"Not exactly *on* the body. It was on the ground beneath one of the skulls. Why? Do you know something?"

"I can't be positive without studying it more closely, probably needs a cleaning too. But this design is one I've seen before . . . in the museum's collection, actually."

"What?"

"If it's what I think it might be, it doesn't date from the war. It's considerably older."

"How old?"

"About five hundred years."

He uncoiled his long legs and stood up abruptly. "Five hundred years?"

"It's a design that was in vogue during the reign of King Henry VIII. I've seen a number of them. We've actually made modern copies that sell very well in the museum shop, but—"

"What?"

"We didn't start making them until just a few years ago. No one could have worn a set of earrings like this during the Second World War, because none of the originals had been discovered up to that time. If this object accompanied bodies that date from the forties, and if it's authentic, then the person who had it must have found it somewhere. Because I'd bet my last shilling this is an original Henry VIII-period earring."

9

Carmen was in Dr. Jessmer's office by three that afternoon. He had one of those spectacular museum offices with floor-to-ceiling windows that could offer bright sunshine when it was available. Now, they looked out on a courtyard that was dreary and damp. It was Friday and the museum was crowded with tourists and student groups. The chaos matched her thoughts perfectly.

Dr. Laurence Jessmer had been museum director for almost a decade. In his late sixties now, Carmen dreaded the prospect that he might soon retire, for he had been her strongest supporter. He was also a medieval scholar and an expert on the life of King Henry VIII. He met her at the door with a sympathetic nod of his head.

"I've been expecting you, Carmen. This is a nasty bit of business."

"I thought we had a good working relationship, Laurence, which was why you selected me to take over the Coram's Fields site in the first place. Now this. What is going on?"

"I wish I knew. Believe me, your removal was not my idea and I tried to resist it, but Trimm appears to have the full support of the prime minister's office. God knows what that is all about. There is more to this than meets the eye but what that might be baffles me completely. A couple of long dead bodies found deep underground hardly seems like something that would interest the government."

She slumped in her chair. Clearly, she wasn't going to get the explanation she had anticipated.

"Did you know I've been banned from the site?"

"I suspected as much, though I wasn't told."

She sat up. "I want to go down there one more time. I want to see precisely where those bodies came from."

He stared at her. "You can't be serious, Carmen. And anyway, what good would it do?"

"Trimm is hiding something. We both know that. Maybe I can get some idea what it is. Look, it's Friday. The dig will be closed up for the weekend in just a couple of hours. No one will be there except site security. Have you told them about the changes yet?"

He shook his head. "This all came down within the last twenty-four hours. I thought notifying security could wait till Monday."

"Good. Then let me go down. I'll take Julia to guide me around. If anything happens or we're confronted by anyone, I'll say you knew nothing about it. What can they do? I may have been relieved as director of Coram's Fields, but there's no reason why I should consider that to mean I'm not allowed on the premises at all. I'm still in charge of London projects for the museum. As far as I'm concerned, that means I can go where I want."

He thrummed his fingers on his desk. "I never could stand that man."

"Good." She reached into her bag. "There's one other thing I wanted to run by you." She pulled out the earring. Jessmer recognized it immediately.

"Where did you get that?" he asked.

Julia was less than thrilled at having her Friday night plans curtailed. "Give a girl a break, Carmen. I've got a date."

"You've got a million guys hitting on you, Julia. You *always* have a date."

"Sure, lots of guys want to get into my waders, but you'd be surprised how few offers I get from someone I'm actually interested in. This is one of those."

"It's got to be this weekend, Julia. And the sooner the better. Who knows when Trimm will force a lockdown on the place and me specifically. It's now or never. Don't you want to know what the hell is going on?"

She grumbled a bit more, but Carmen could tell she was just as pissed off at Trimm as she was. By nine o'clock that evening, as darkness settled over London, they stood, dressed in coveralls, caps and gum boots near the place where Julia had let Carmen through the orange fencing. By entering here, they could avoid site security at the main entrance. They might still run into the guards as they made their rounds, but there was no reason why they should be confronted. They were both well known to the men on duty.

Julia turned on her torch. It seemed to be swallowed up by the blackness. "We've got about a mile walk to the spot where the bodies were located," she said.

Carmen found the underground site intimidating at night. Her only visits had been during the daytime and then in areas where light filtered through openings to the surface. The sounds of London sifted down as well; Big Ben pounding out the hour, the never-ending blare of sirens omnipresent in every metro area on earth, trucks rumbling.

But after five minutes, it was clear they were going lower than she had been before. The silence grew heavy. They were beneath a city of more than eight million people, yet there was not a sound, except for the distant tinkling of water falling somewhere and the occasional scurrying of rats.

They quickly passed the section of Great Conduit Julia had showed her earlier, bypassed the cistern and continued through a bewildering array of tunnels.

"You sure you can find your way out of here?" asked Carmen.

"It can be confusing all right, but I've worked here almost two years. You get a feel for how things are laid out."

At one point, Carmen jumped as there was a distant rush of sound that receded as fast as it appeared.

"Subway," Julia said. "Probably Victoria Line. Usually can't hear it during the day because of background noise. It's pretty far beneath us."

They passed through several places where tunnels came together. The passageways seemed to be getting smaller . . . and damper.

"You *sure* you know where you're going?" Carmen asked again. "None of this is familiar to me. We haven't passed any work stations for the dig in quite a while."

"The bones weren't where most of the work's been going on. A couple of student assistants discovered a small opening in a sub-tunnel that had started to crumble. That's where they found the bones, almost like they'd been purposely bricked in." She stopped abruptly.

"This is it."

Carmen edged around her to see what the torch was illuminating. There wasn't much there, just the crumbling bricks and a gaping hole that disappeared out of sight. She took the light from Julia. "Any idea where this goes?"

"Nope. And I don't know that anyone checked it out. Finding the bones sort of sidetracked everyone."

"Well, nothing ventured . . . " She stepped over the fallen bricks and climbed down into the smaller tunnel. "Kind of surprising they used bricks," she said. "I thought most of the older construction was done with stone." She sloshed forward. "Boy, it's really wet in here."

There was dampness from one side of the tunnel to the other and a tiny rivulet of water trickled down the center. There was an unpleasant smell as well. "You don't think this could be sewage we're tramping through, do you?"

"Wouldn't surprise me," said Julia. "The Fleet River goes by somewhere down here. There are at least a dozen different rivers flowing under the city. The Fleet was the foulest of London's lost rivers, practically a sewer before they completely covered it over in the 1700s."

"Terrific."

"How much farther do we have to go, Carmen? You've seen the place where the bones were found. Can we go home now?"

"Shh!" Carmen held the light up high. "Did you see that?"

"What?"

"Something moved down there, where that opening is."

"Probably rats."

"I'm going to check it out. You can wait here if you want."

She moved forward. The amount of water on the floor had grown until it was nearly a small stream in size. She reached the junction with the other opening and pointed the light into it. Suddenly, she stepped back; arms flailing as she nearly lost her balance, the light swaying wildly in the tunnel walls. "Son of a bitch!"

"What is it?" asked Julia.

"Rats. You were right. Come look at this."

Julia picked her way to Carmen's side and stared into the opening. Filling the tunnel, flickering in the glow from the torch, were dead and dying rats. Hundreds of them. It was like something out of a Hieronymus Bosch painting. The bodies lay on their sides or backs with stiff legs sticking straight up. They piled on top of one another into mounds three feet high. Here and there, a few still moved feebly.

"What could do that?" asked Carmen. "Is Norman responsible?"

Julia shook her head. "I don't think so. He'd have to be using something really lethal to do this. We told him when we hired him that we just wanted to get a handle on the problem and didn't expect him to completely rid the place of rats. Because to do that he'd have to use poison at a level that would be dangerous to the people working down here."

"Well it gives me the creeps," Carmen said. "Let's get out of here." She started to turn away, then stopped and lifted the light again.

"What's that down there near the end?"

Julia looked over her shoulder. The tunnel sloped away sharply. At the edge of their beam of light was something, a sort of mound, an irregular lump on the cavern floor. "Beats me," she said. "A big pile of the critters, I guess."

"I don't know. It seems different. I'm going to go down there and look."

"Are you crazy? You'll have to walk through all those rats."

"I'm going to do it," she said stubbornly. Then, "You know, these couldn't have been dead too long. There's almost no smell at all. It's pretty strange. Anyway, I think I can sort of shuffle along, pushing them out of the way with my boots. I won't actually have to step on them."

"Who the hell cares about a pileup of rats?" But Julia could see that familiar look on her friend's face. Stubborn. Compulsive. Obsessive. "Look, whatever you do, don't let any of the live ones bite you."

That was definitely going to be priority number one, Carmen thought. She was not at all sure she wanted to do this. But something about that mound seemed odd. Sometimes she just couldn't resist her compulsive need to know. It was what made her a great researcher and administrator. She pushed ahead slowly, each foot covered with small bodies. Once or twice, a live rat raised its head and snarled at her, but they seemed to have little strength.

Finally, she reached the mound. Julia had been right. It was just a pile of rats several feet high. She poked her foot at them. Squish. And again. This time there was a distinct metallic clank.

Using her boot, she pushed away piles of rodents until she discovered the source of the sound. It was a metal cylinder, and she remembered precisely where she had last seen it. Several more pushes with her boot and there was no doubt.

"Well, what is it?" Julia called to her.

"Oh God . . . it's Norman."

"What—?"

"I'm sorry, Julia. I'm not going to paw through all these rodents, but I'd say he's pretty dead."

Julia stood frozen in shock, unable to speak.

"I can hear water down here," Carmen said suddenly. "Like it's rushing right close by. A lot of water." She took another step, and then she felt the floor beneath her give way. Both arms flailed upward. She must have hit the switch on the light because it went out. Then she disappeared into a hole in the floor.

10

Carmen had never been so cold in her life. Or so terrified. She was being swept along in some sort of stream. It was pitch black and there was no way to determine how large the watercourse was. Every now and then she bumped against objects floating along with her. The first one she fully investigated with her hand was soft and she knew it was the body of a rat. That moment of realization sent a wave of fear and nausea through her like an electric shock. She flung the bodies away from her face with wild contortions of her hands, until the fierce efforts depleted her energy, forcing a more measured, but no less panicked response.

There was a swift current, and it banged her against rock walls as she plunged along. She finally got her wits about her enough to realize she still held onto the torch. She managed to locate the switch and turn it on. The water had not done it any good. The light flickered constantly, only giving her surroundings an even more unworldly cast.

Like many AS sufferers, she was unusually sensitive to various stimuli. Smell, light, touch, taste and sometimes pain and temperature could seem almost unbearably acute, depending on the circumstances. Right now the primary circumstance was cold. The water was damn cold.

The current slowed. No longer fighting to keep from hitting the walls, she willed herself to think, to fight back the almost incapacitating fear long enough to wonder where she was headed. If this really was the Fleet River then she could be floating through a bricked over sewer that would only come out once it reached the Thames. If it was some other, smaller causeway, totally encased in pipes, as she knew some were, she might eventually come to a place where water filled the pipe and she would simply drown. Or she might come up against a grating where the water flowed out to the Thames, and there she would stay until the beating of the river against her pinned body sucked the life out of her. Just as the cold was even now sucking away her strength.

She lifted her almost numb hand and shook the light. It flickered weakly, revealing that she was now in a sizeable body of water. A cavernous space loomed overhead and there seemed to be a shoreline with steeply rising banks. She floated past a sort of archway and wondered if she might be in some long abandoned subway station. Then, suddenly, the banks of the river glistened, like dripping liquid mercury. The yellow of the dimming light glowed against the walls.

She must be hallucinating. The river shone on all sides, sparkling. Shadows filled the cavern. She imagined strange shapes. Was that a giant standing against one wall? A giant riding on a chariot? Were those horses? How could there be horses down here? Her heart pounded in fear and confusion. She wasn't thinking straight. If she didn't find a way out soon, she would lose consciousness from the cold and the pure stress of what was happening to her.

Then the light went out completely and though she shook it violently, nothing happened. It was dead. Reluctantly, she let it slip away. More darkness and cold engrossed her. She slammed against a rock and yelped, then continued floating, nearly helpless now.

After a time, she became aware she was staring at the roof of the cavern again. A faint light shining through. How was this possible? It couldn't be, she thought, so she must be hallucinating—or maybe she was dead. But the light grew. Then she was tumbling into the dull gloom of London twilight. The last thing she heard before blackness came over her was people screaming. Why are they screaming? She wondered.

"Carmen. Can you hear me? Time to wake up, girl."

Through a deep fog, Carmen heard the voice and it pulled her out of the cold, black memories inside her head. She opened her eyes to find Julia staring at her, concern lining her perfect features.

"Thank God. I thought you were never going to wake up."

"Where am I?" Carmen asked, surprised at the croak in her voice.

"In the hospital. Actually, you were resting comfortably in this nice warm bed, while I was still banging around down there in the dark trying to find my way out. You *could* have left me the light. Anyway, by the time I got out and managed to go for help, Dr. Jessmer was looking for me. He told me they'd picked you up already and . . . here I am."

"How long have I been here?"

"You've been out for twelve hours. They treated you for hypothermia. Your lips were blue—I'd kill for a lip gloss that color. They said there might be brain damage. I guess you slammed out of that sewer pretty darn hard. Scared the living shit out of a bunch of moms and their kids at a little playground next to the outflow."

Carmen reached up and felt the lump on her head. She had a world class headache. But she didn't feel brain damaged. No more than AS sufferers usually feel anyway.

"The mayor ought to give you a citation. First person to ride the Fleet River through the heart of London."

"I don't think it was the Fleet," Carmen croaked.

"Why not?"

"Because the Fleet was covered over on purpose, wasn't it, in the 1700s?"

"Yup. It got so full of mud, dung, dead things and general filth, the city decided to cover it over. The river has a foul history going back hundreds of years before that, to the 1300s I think. It flooded periodically and overflowed in front of the Fleet Street prison. It was said that prisoners died of the stench, and it even blew up a couple of times from the buildup of rancid gases."

Carmen felt nausea rise in her stomach. How much of that unspeakable filth had she ingested?

"What I mean to say, Julia, is that I saw something down there. Or maybe I dreamt it. It was as if the walls had diamonds on them. Who would brick up a wall of diamonds on purpose?" She closed her eyes, trying to see what was in her mind. "It could have been some other river."

Julia stared at her. "I think you hit your head too hard, sweetie. You were seeing stars. Why don't you take another nap?"

And she did.

The next time she woke up, her head hurt less and she had two new visitors. Dr. Jessmer and Inspector Peets stared down at her with long, sympathetic faces.

"You two look like you're staring into an open coffin," she murmured.

"You came pretty close to that," said Sherwood. His worried face was comforting, somehow. She couldn't believe how tired she was. Saying those few words seemed to exhaust her all over again. She felt herself drifting off.

When she woke again, there was yet another face hovering above her. She knew she was hallucinating this time, because the face was that of the newly appointed Minister of Health for the Commonwealth of England. She recognized him because the man's picture had been all over the papers leading up to his appointment following a sex scandal that had done in his predecessor.

The familiar face peered at her. "Good. You're awake. You've had quite a time, I gather."

She tried to raise herself up in bed. The minister, what was his name? Simmons . . . no . . . Simonson, put a pillow behind her to ease her into position. She stared around the room. No one else was present. She realized how absurd this was. She was alone in a hospital room with Britain's minister of health sitting beside her. Talk about National Health Care. Maybe she *did* have brain damage.

"Your friend . . . Julia? . . . told us what you were doing down there. We've retrieved the body of that poor man, the exterminator. At least we think that's who it is. Kind of hard to tell."

Carmen's eyes wandered to the inside of her elbow. The vein was bruised. He followed her gaze.

"They took quite a spot of blood, I'm afraid. There were a number of tests . . . " He hesitated, then appeared to come to a decision. "Your friend Julia is having the same tests now in another part of the hospital."

"Tests for what?"

"We don't know really. You remember seeing the dead rats down there, right?"

She nodded.

"Well, something is killing them, and I'm afraid it's not poor, old Norman. The truth is, we haven't been able to determine what is killing the rats, but it's happening all over London. At least all over the underground. Dead rats by the thousands have appeared in just about every tube station."

Carmen's thinking suddenly got very clear. "Could it be a gas leak?"

"Frankly, it could be anything, but the gas company assures us they are not the cause."

"Is that why you took over the site?"

"Yes, in conjunction with the prime minister's office. Something is going on down there, Ms. Kingsley. We need to determine what before news gets out and we have a major panic on our hands."

She stared at him. "I'm afraid I'm still a bit confused. If the government has taken over the Coram's Fields site, why is Dr. Trimm in charge?"

"In charge is perhaps a little strong. Dr. Trimm was the first to discover the dying rodents. He reported it to my office. I authorized him to do a study and to keep things quiet. He evidently enjoys being in control. He really did not have the authority to dismiss you from your overall role or to ban you from the site." He looked at his hands. "The truth is: we would very much like to have your cooperation on this. Dr. Jessmer seems to think very highly of you and we may have made a mistake empowering Trimm."

"I don't know what I can do for you in here."

"As soon as we get confirmation you haven't been infected with anything, you and Julia will be released." He stood up. "I hope that will be very soon indeed. And then I would like you to work closely with my office. You and Julia know as much about that subterranean site as anyone."

He squeezed her shoulder. "Get well," he said.

She didn't want him to go. There were still a lot of questions she wanted to ask. But perhaps the man understood her condition. She was already drifting off again.

11

Norway — 1944

Vidkun Quisling sat in his office reviewing a report prepared for him by Albert Hagelin, one of his old associates in the formation of Nasjonal Samling, the Norwegian fascist political party.

They'd had their successes in the party in the 1930s, and after Germany invaded Norway in 1940, Quisling declared a coup d'etat, creating an ad hoc government during the confusion of the invasion, hoping that Hitler would support it. But Quisling had little popular support and Hitler had no use for him. The Quisling government lasted five days. Power went to Josef Terboven who was installed as reichskommissar, the highest official in Norway, who reported directly to Hitler.

The relationship between Quisling and Terboven was brittle, but Terboven saw advantage in having a Norwegian in an apparent position of power. It would reduce resentment among the people. He named Quisling to the post of minister president on February 1, 1942, allowing him to reside in a mansion in Oslo.

During the course of the war, Quisling encouraged Norwegians to serve as volunteers in the Norwegian SS division, collaborated in the deportation of Jews and presided over the execution of Norwegian patriots. Though little more than a figurehead, he had grandiose plans and focused on ingratiating himself with Terboven and the Nazis.

Hagelin's report suggested that the Germans had begun to construct a research facility in the far north. To what end, they didn't know. But the Hagelin report also contained bits of intelligence gleaned from sources in London. Quisling had his own man, a mole, in the exiled Norwegian government. Through this shadowy figure, they had learned that the British intended to conduct an assault on the research facility.

"It doesn't make sense, Vidkun," said Hagelin. "What could the Germans possibly be up to in our frozen northlands that could have any effect on the war?"

Quisling shrugged his shoulders. "I don't know, but clearly it is something important. If we can uncover the British plan, it will do no harm to our stature in Hitler's eyes. Perhaps he will see that he made a mistake in putting Terboven in charge." His forehead wrinkled in thought. "I want increased surveillance along our coastline from Saltfjord to Altenfjord. Aerial reconnaissance and coast guard patrols. And alert the members of Nasjonal Samling to be on the lookout for anything suspicious and to report it directly to me. But only the members of the inner circle."

Hagelin looked uncomfortable. "If Terboven finds out you are withholding information from him and operating beyond your authority, we may find ourselves in front of a firing squad."

"He appointed me minister president," Quisling said stubbornly. "He may think I'm only a figurehead, but I intend to be much more than that. I am the forer, the equivalent in Norway of the führer himself. If I protect Hitler's most special secret plans, there will be further advancements for you and me before this war is over."

12

Gunnar stood in the tall grass on one of the barren headlands of the Shetland Islands and stared out at the North Sea. The sky was low and gray, with menacing bands of heavy rain marching toward him, the wind gaining strength by the hour. They had been sitting in their tiny rooms beside the small airstrip for three days, unable to fly anywhere. It was maddening. Churchill had stressed the urgency of their mission. But there was no telling how long the bad weather might continue. In this part of the world, it could be weeks.

Major Osbourne came up the hill behind him, pant legs flapping in the wind and stood silently for a moment contemplating the skies.

"We need to consider alternate transportation," he said finally.

"I've been thinking about it," said Gunnar.

"I took the liberty of opening negotiations with the owner of a fishing boat," Osbourne offered. "Crew of three. They're familiar with the seas we need to cross."

"What did you tell them?"

"Only that we're a group of Norwegians who wish to return to our country."

"And they believed that?"

The major laughed. "Not in a pig's eye. There's a war on, you know. The Norwegians have 400,000 Germans in their country and the people have been suffering terribly from food shortages. I think the captain believes we intend to smuggle food. It's been done before, apparently."

"He won't think that once he sees how little we bring with us, only what we can carry ourselves."

Osbourne shrugged. It was a detail that didn't concern him. "The pay is good, and they have no love for the Germans. If they knew the truth, they'd probably be even more willing to help us. I actually feel badly that we can't take them into our confidence."

The first heavy raindrops began to strike the headland. "When can they leave?" Gunnar asked.

"That's why I'm here. Captain Macintosh says the sooner the better. He believes the weather will hold for two or three more days."

Gunnar looked at him in disbelief. "He considers this," he waved a hand at the black skies, "holding?"

"Evidently—considering what they usually get. In any event, he says the bad weather will cut down on German patrols and make it easier for us to slip through."

Gunnar looked at his watch. "It's eleven. Do you think we could be under way by one?"

"Already got my boys checking their gear. They'll be ready on ten minutes notice. It's up to you and Natasha."

"I'll go tell her," he said and turned away.

Natasha had grown distant following their night together. He wasn't sure why and hesitated to make too much of it. Perhaps what she'd said, that in wartime one must move quickly, also meant that one must be prepared to take what happens lightly. He was drawn to her, but there seemed little point in pressing the issue now. One or both of them might not survive what lay ahead.

He found her packing. She avoided looking at him. "One of the major's men told me," she said. "I'm almost ready. Looks like it will be a pretty rough ride."

"The crew sounds experienced at least, and they know the waters. But you're right. It's not going to be a punt on the Thames."

She gave him a quick smile.

He picked up her heavy pack. "Take this for you?"

She nodded, gathered up the rest of her things and slipped a nine millimeter handgun into her bag. Major Osbourne's men were armed to the teeth and had brought two large satchels of plastic explosives. Gunnar felt positively naked with his regulation RAF pistol, though the major had assured him they had an extra machine gun for him if it was needed. The mere presence of so many weapons was sobering. The crew of the fishing boat would have little doubt that they were not food smugglers once they boarded.

The craft was a sixty-foot fishing trawler, the *Jenny*. She looked to be in good shape and well provisioned with sleeping space below for fifteen. Major Osbourne introduced them to Captain Macintosh, a red-faced, pot-bellied man of about sixty who spoke with a strong brogue. He eyed them skeptically.

"Yurr a might underr provisioned," he said. "S'pose yurr not on a fishin' expedition, eh?" He stared at Natasha. "Didna spect a woman. Ye surr ye've a mind to come along, lass? Thurr's a storm brewin' furr surr."

"Just so long as I don't have to cook."

The captain laughed abruptly. "No worries thurr, lass. My man Edgar's a firrst rate cook. He wouldna let ya nearr his galley."

Natasha shot him a smile. "Then it will be a good cruise indeed, captain."

Forty minutes later, they had gear stowed and bunks selected. Captain Macintosh ordered the anchor hauled, the engines sputtered to life and the boat rocked out of the tiny harbor and into the teeth of a growing North Sea gale.

Gunnar, who had an ironclad stomach when it came to flying, began to feel sick almost at once. He took a couple of pills that were routinely given to RAF pilots for airsickness. Then he joined the captain in the pilot's house upstairs. He could see the horizon up there, which seemed to have a better effect than being tossed around down below.

He hung on to anything he could to keep from being thrown about. The captain stood easily on his bridge, knees flexing slightly, in complete control.

"Quite a swell," Gunnar said.

"Aye, it's a bit of a roll. She'll be rright tossin' once we round Farrly's Island. After that, it's 500 miles up to the Narrwegian Sea. Naught 'tween us and the Narrway coast but the Gerrman submarrine lanes."

"Do they patrol regularly?"

"Not too bad. Haven't the boots to waste this farr from the real fightin'. If we'rre lucky, we'll slip right on by. Even if they see us, thurr used to seein' the Scottish fishin' fleet in these waters."

Major Osbourne joined them. "I've been thinking we ought to make some sort of preparations in case we're stopped by a German patrol boat."

"What did you have in mind?" Gunnar asked. "If we're boarded and searched, it will be pretty hard to explain all this armament."

"Precisely. I'll tell you what I've been thinking . . . "

Sleeping was nearly impossible on the tossing ship. Virtually everyone was glad to see the return of daylight. But shortly after, Gunnar heard the captain's voice over the loud speaker.

"All hands, all hands! Patrol boat on the porrt side."

Osbourne was on deck immediately, scanning the sea with binoculars. "I see her," he said to no one in particular, since they were all lined up at the railing.

The captain leaned his head out the window of the bridge. "Get yurrselves away from the rrail. They can see you plainly."

But it was too late. The boat turned toward them.

Gunnar stared at the craft, then at a fog bank half a mile away. He yelled to the captain: "Can we pretend we don't see them and try to make the fog before they close on us?"

"It'll be right close," he yelled back, but the boat picked up speed.

The patrol boat continued to close. She didn't appear terribly concerned that this small fishing vessel might be any sort of threat. But as the *Jenny* began to close on the fog, the German craft sounded her siren, followed by a voice through a megaphone telling them in heavily accented English to heave to.

"All right," said Major Osbourne. "Everyone to their stations."

His men took up positions around the boat. Several sat on deck with nets in their laps, as though repairing them. Two others took refuge beneath the rail on the side nearest the patrol boat.

The Germans sent a shell whistling through the air over their heads. It exploded on impact with the water.

Gunnar yelled to the captain: "Heave to, Macintosh. Let them come alongside."

The patrol boat eased in beside the *Jenny*, her gunner ready at the bow, as a boarding party prepared to come across. A man on the German boat threw a line over. The two crafts were now just ten feet apart, rocking in the waves.

Gunnar stood on the foredeck. Osbourne crouched out of sight looking at him. On the bridge, Captain Macintosh watched him as well. Then Gunnar nodded to Osbourne and simultaneously gave a sharp wave to the captain.

Several things happened at once. Captain Macintosh pushed the throttle forward all the way and the engines suddenly whined. Two of the major's men who were crouched by the rail stood up and tossed grenades at the patrol boat's gunner. The gunner yelled something, spun around and began to fire. The men sitting on deck with nets in their laps threw the nets aside and also opened fire. Gunnar spotted Natasha on the catwalk outside the bridge, holding her pistol with both hands and shooting steadily.

Before the *Jenny* had increased the distance between the two crafts by more than a few feet, Osbourne stood up and almost gently lofted a plastic charge that landed amidships on the patrol boat. The major and Gunnar both dropped to the deck as a horrific blast shook the German boat. It was followed almost instantly by a series of explosions as the charge set off the Germans' own store of munitions.

The patrol boat split in half and sank in less than a minute. There were no survivors. Major Osbourne's men turned to putting out flaming chunks of debris that had landed on the deck. The brunt of the blasts had gone skyward and there was only minimal damage to the *Jenny*'s side.

Gunnar yelled to Macintosh. "Take her into the fog, captain, in case there are any other boats around. She might have gotten a radio message off."

"Not bloody likely," said Osbourne. "It all happened too fast."

"She could have radioed her intension to board us before we attacked her," Gunnar said. "We need to go on that assumption, anyway. When she can't be raised, someone will come to investigate."

The *Jenny*'s engines roared as she powered into the fog, then Captain Macintosh throttled back and they motored slowly forward as night fell.

13

London — Present Day

It didn't like being this close to the surface. Generally, the creature stayed well below the noisy lifts and generators. Even the distant roar of heavy trucks and the blaring horns of emergency vehicles were painful to its sensitive ears.

But sometimes, the insistent hunger sent the animal higher. Its primary prey, the rats, had learned to avoid their tormentors by staying closer to the rumblings of the surface world. So gradually, it was forced to increase its tolerance of the painful lights and sounds, waging a constant battle between discomfort and the animal's voracious hunger.

It whimpered at the sudden rush of a tube station nearby. It had followed several weak rodents higher, curious as to what was wrong with them. They appeared listless and lacking in their normal fear.

The animal moved stealthily across the bottom of one of the large cisterns, leaped a dozen feet up to a tunnel entrance and padded silently through the damp passage. Then it came to a small hole in the side of the tunnel and sniffed at it. There were rats inside. A *lot* of rats.

It squeezed through the hole. Everything around the creature was blackness, yet it made its way unerringly through a combination of its incredible hearing and a sort of echo location that used the sucking sound to send out vibrations. The rats had learned to detect the unusual sonance. Its sudden appearance had been known to panic them.

This time, however, there would be no reaction from the rodents. The thing entered a much smaller tunnel and found that it was filled with dead and dying rats. Why they were dead was of no concern. They represented one thing only.

Food.

Still, the animal was a social creature, to a point. It was one reason its species had been so successful. The thing returned the way it had come until others of its kind were found. Then, through a bizarre set of movements, almost a sort of dance, it passed on to them the location of the prey. Soon, hundreds of its fellows arrived to gorge themselves in the hidden room.

In a very short time, all of the dead and dying rats were consumed. It had been a grand feast, but like others before it, it left the animals ultimately unsatisfied. They were hungry again.

They were also just a little more tolerant of the world of the noisy things.

14

Carmen stared at the roomful of solemn faces. She wished they would all stop treating her like an invalid. She was fully recovered from her experience.

"Look, everyone," she said. "I'm not made of glass. Thanks for your concern, but I'm fine."

Health Minister Simonson cleared his throat. "Uh, yes. We're grateful for that and that you've joined us, Carmen. Forgive us for staring, but . . . "

"But you were exposed to something all but unknown," finished Dr. Jessmer. "And we're probably a bit gun shy, though you certainly appear to be okay."

Carmen looked from one face to another. In addition to Jessmer and Simonson, Inspector Peets, Julia and Dr. Trimm were also in the room, an airless, suffocating office at the Ministry of National Health.

"I continue to protest bringing this . . . *administrator* . . . into our group," said Trimm. "She has no professional standing and I fail to see what use she will be to us. The fewer people who know about this, the better. And who's to say Carmen and Julia *haven't* been infected? What do we really know about this disease, anyway? There could be a lengthy incubation period."

Simonson took a deep breath. He'd heard Trimm's diatribe before. "We need all the help we can get, Dr. Trimm. Carmen and Julia found the body of the exterminator and may have been at the epicenter of whatever this thing is. They are the most knowledgeable first-hand participants we have."

Carmen ignored Trimm. "Dr. Jessmer, you said we'd been exposed to something all but unknown. That suggests there is something you *do* know."

He nodded. "The exterminator—"

Julia interrupted him. "His name was Norman. Can't we at least call him by his name?"

"Certainly," replied Jessmer. "You are quite correct, Julia. Norman's body was somewhat decomposed, or perhaps even partially gnawed on by rats. Nevertheless, the autopsy showed that he had significant internal lesions, especially in his lungs. There were also vascular eruptions. We found the body in a condition of partial undress, suggesting that he may have removed his clothing due to fever or irrationality. Similar lung lesions and eruptions of the blood vessels have also been found in some of the rats that were dissected."

"Are you saying Norman caught something from the rats? That it's airborne and contagious to humans?" asked Carmen, growing more concerned.

"We don't know that. You and Julia would certainly have been exposed if whatever it is was airborne. Perhaps a rat bit Norman and infected him in that manner. But if you will bear with me, I have a hypothesis about what we might be dealing with here. It's speculative, but the more I study the symptoms, the more sense it makes."

"The more sense what makes?" asked Sherwood.

"There was an unexplained illness that swept through London, other parts of England and Europe in the fourteen and fifteen hundreds. The only reason I know about it is because it occurred in the time of Henry VII and Henry VIII, both of whom I've researched extensively. It was called the 'English Sweating Sickness,' or just 'the Sweat.' It first broke out in August of 1485, at the very beginning of the reign of Henry VII. Its course was extremely rapid and fatal. It was said the disease could kill in as little as an hour. And with that came great mortality."

"Do you think Norman died that quickly?" Julia asked.

"We're working on a timeline for that, trying to determine who the last person was to see him alive."

"Was the outbreak connected to rats?" asked Carmen.

"Well, of course, the people of that period had no way of knowing where the sickness came from or how it developed. Real medical knowledge was virtually nonexistent. There were those who speculated that the cause may have been related to the general dirt and sewage of the time, which would also mean, of course, rats and other vermin."

"Could it have been plague?" asked Julia.

"Plague is caused by a bacterium called Yersinia pestis, which is usually transmitted to humans by fleas. Flea-infested rats caused the fourteenth-century epidemic that killed half of Europe's population. The bacteria invade the bloodstream, causing internal bleeding that in turn leads to shock and death.

"The Sweat was considered to be quite distinct from plague, malaria, typhus, the pestilential fever and other epidemics previously known, not only by the special symptom which gave it its name, but also by its extremely rapid and fatal course. Its first appearance at the time of the Wars of the Roses suggests that it may have been brought over from France by French mercenaries. Henry VII used them to gain the English throne. Interestingly, the French seem to have been immune. One possible candidate for the cause is relapsing fever, which is spread by ticks and lice. Outbreaks usually occurred in the summer months when such vermin flourished.

"There was a second outbreak in 1507 and a third in 1517, which was extremely severe. In Oxford and Cambridge it proved very fatal. In other towns, as much as half the population perished."

"Sweet Jesus," Sherwood said in a muted voice. "If something like that broke out in London, panic would be the least of our worries. The dead could number in the millions."

"You're all getting way ahead of yourselves," sniffed Trimm. "Only one man is dead, and we have no idea yet as to what caused his death."

Jessmer continued without comment. "In 1528, the disease recurred for the fourth time, with great severity. It first appeared in London in May and spread rapidly over all of England. Many people in the court of Henry VIII contracted it."

"How awful," said Carmen. "Those poor people must have had no idea what was happening to them."

"Disease of any sort was inexplicable to them. People put it down to a curse, the anger of the gods, even witchcraft," said Jessmer. "When treatment was attempted, it generally amounted to herbs laced with molasses or bleeding from various parts of the body. In any case, this fourth outbreak spread to the continent. Germany, Holland, Switzerland, Denmark, Sweden, Norway, Poland and Russia all suffered. France, Italy and the southern countries were spared. In each affected place, it spread rapidly with high mortality but lasted at most a fortnight. By the end of the year it disappeared entirely and never appeared on the continent again, though England suffered one more outbreak in 1551."

Carmen said, "So you're saying this sickness that hasn't been seen for almost five hundred years may have caused the death of Norman and the rats? Do you have any proof of that beyond the lesions and blood vessel irregularities you mentioned?"

Jessmer pursed his lips. "Diseases come and go, though the mysterious disappearance of this one is particularly perplexing. However, we have one lucky break with regards to the last outbreak. There is an account by an eyewitness: John Kaye of Gonville Hall, Cambridge, the president of the Royal College of Physicians."

He stared at the floor for a moment. "As described by Kaye, the disease began very suddenly. There was a sense of foreboding, followed by violent cold shivers, giddiness, headache and severe pains in the neck, shoulders and limbs, with great prostration. The cold stage might last three hours and was followed by the stage of heat and sweating. The characteristic sweat broke out suddenly, and without any apparent cause. After the sweat, there came a sense of terrible heat, headache, delirium, rapid pulse and great thirst. He described palpitation and pain in the heart as frequent symptoms. But there was no eruption of any kind on the skin. In the later stages, there was general prostration and collapse, or an irresistible urge to sleep, which was thought to be fatal if the patient gave way to it. One attack did not confer immunity and some people suffered several bouts before succumbing."

"I don't understand," said Carmen. "Where's the disease been all these years?"

"No one can say. It wouldn't be the first time a disease disappeared, or simply burned itself out. And don't forget, we're relying on the very incomplete records of the time. It could have resurfaced and not been recognized as the same illness. We're working under a handicap. We may never be able to say with certainty that what killed Norman was the Sweat, since we have little basis for comparison."

"Perhaps it went dormant within the rat or tick population," said Simonson. "Diseases have a nasty habit of hiding, like chicken pox residing peacefully in the body's cells for decades until a weakened immune system brings the onset of shingles."

"Except," said Jessmer, "There have been no known outbreaks of the Sweat for nearly five hundred years. That seems pretty unlikely. Something should have caused it to break out of its dormancy before now. We might want to consider exhuming bodies from the time of the Sweat to search for remnants of the infection. Such an action would not be unprecedented. Similar studies have been conducted on skeletons exhumed from the East Smithfield cemetery in London, where many victims of the Black Death were buried."

"An interesting suggestion," said Simonson. "But not something that can be done overnight."

Trimm had grown increasingly agitated. "If the British Museum hadn't insisted on taking over my site, I might have this thing figured out by now. I was working closely with Norman and we were aware that something was going on with the rat population. By turning the site over to the administrators, you effectively stifled our investigation."

Carmen suppressed a laugh. Trimm wasn't qualified to track down something as devious as this. Get him away from his Roman walls and he was nothing more than a very mediocre and pedantic academician.

"What about the two bodies we uncovered in the service tunnel?" asked Sherwood. "Maybe they came in contact with the disease somehow, were bitten by a rat or tick and died down there like Norman. Who knows, people may have been dying throughout the last five hundred years from this thing without anyone knowing about it. Isolated, unexplained cases never related to the Sweat. I certainly never heard of this disease before."

"I agree, those bodies should be examined again, but we also need to do more studies on the rats. They're an important link in all of this and they're dying in huge numbers. Maybe the dormant disease has broken out and the death of the rats is the first real sign of that."

Carmen felt suddenly tired. Perhaps she hadn't completely recovered from her experience after all. "So where do we go from here?" she asked.

"I've already ordered the archaeological site closed down," said Simonson. "We can't let people down there until we figure out what's going on. We're continuing our tests on the rats and will also re-examine the two skeletal bodies. We're trying to keep this away from the press, but it's only going to get harder. Dr. Jessmer has already had inquiries into why the site has been closed."

"You're not going to be able to examine the skeletal bodies," said Sherwood, "unless someone can get permission from the prime minister's office. They've taken everything." He stared at Dr. Trimm.

Trimm ignored the look and changed the subject. "I'd like to continue my investigations using the German volunteers," he said. "They know the risks and are eager to get to the bottom of this."

Simonson shook his head. "This must be kept under the auspices of the Ministry of Health. We can't have volunteers—and foreigners at that—investigating something this potentially explosive."

Trimm swore. He stood up and left the room abruptly, slamming the door behind him. The others looked at each other in surprise.

"What's his problem?" asked Simonson.

Julia was still staring at the closed door. "Trimm's very tight with the German volunteers," she said. "Almost as though they work for him, which they don't. He never shares anything with the rest of the staff down there. He just kind of operates as an independent entity with an agenda all his own. It's pretty strange."

Carmen added, "Didn't you say he was also the closest to Norman?"

Julia nodded.

"What I want to know," said Sherwood, "is what we're all supposed to do. What does the government expect of us, precisely?"

"You all have your areas of expertise," said Simonson. "I would suggest that you, inspector, continue to follow up on those bodies. Approach the federal authorities if need be. Carmen, you and Dr. Jessmer can further research the history of the disease. Julia can help you if she wishes. My office will coordinate plans to contain the disease if an outbreak does appear. We're continuing to try to eradicate the rats and incinerate the bodies. You all have permission, as needed, to go onto the site." He stared at the little group. "No one—I repeat—no one speaks to the press except for this office. Let's work quickly and discreetly, people. I want to know what the hell we're dealing with."

15

Sherwood stared at the sixtyish Mildred Swimm, personal secretary to his boss, Deputy Commander Bernard W. Jarvis. Swimm controlled access to Jarvis as though she were in charge of the pearly gates. As long as he could remember, no one had spoken to the deputy commander without first going through the redoubtable Swimm.

"I need to know the reason for your visit, inspector."

"It's confidential," Sherwood replied, playing the game.

"I am the deputy commander's *confidential* secretary. He's a busy man. He can't have every Tom, Dick and Sherwood coming in here demanding an audience." She pursed her lips, looking down at the day's schedule. "He has a meeting, in fact, in half an hour with the home secretary. Are you more important than that?"

Sherwood sighed. Before he could respond, the inner door opened and Jarvis himself leaned out. "Mildred, please have my car brought round for my meeting with Home Secretary Bates." He paused after noticing Sherwood, who had since stood up. "Inspector Peets? Did I have an appointment with you?"

"No sir. If I could just have a word though."

"I'll try to schedule the inspector in," said Swimm, smiling sweetly. "There is an opening next Tuesday, I believe."

"Forget that, Mildred. I've got a few minutes before I have to leave. Come on in, inspector."

Sherwood avoided Swimm's steely eyes as he strode past her. He knew this little episode was going to make it even harder for him to see his boss the next time.

The deputy commander was commissioner of police for the Metropolis of London. As the senior figure at Scotland Yard, he reported directly to the home secretary.

Jarvis waved Sherwood to a chair across from his desk. On the wall behind him was a picture of himself with the home secretary and Prime Minister Nevil Harris.

"I gather you're here, inspector, to discuss the outbreak of disease in the city's rat population."

"Yes, sir, I am. I believe we have a potentially explosive situation. This disease, whatever it is, has already killed one person that we know of and many thousands of rats. We are trying to gather more facts concerning the outbreak. I have personally investigated the cause of death of two sets of skeletal remains found in the same general area. If they also contracted the disease somehow, it may give us a clue as to its origins. However, we have met resistance that appears to emanate from the prime minister's office."

Jarvis's eyes widened. "And what would his interest be?"

"Frankly, sir, I have no idea. But his men ransacked—there's really no other world for it—my office and took many confidential files away with them."

Jarvis looked shocked. He had worked his way to the top from within the organization, rising from constable to sergeant to inspector to superintendent of the Criminal Investigation Division. He was known for supporting his inspectors against outside interference of any kind, Mildred Swimm excepted.

"That is very strange, indeed, inspector. Do you have any other high-level investigations going on? Anything to do with national security, foreign spies, international drug cartels, that sort of thing?"

"Nothing like that, sir. And the raid, which was coordinated by a Dr. Trimm, who works for the British Museum, was specifically searching for anything having to do with the skeletal remains found in the tube station. I should also mention that my sergeant and I discovered a roomful of additional bones down there . . . actually coffins. There may have been as many as several hundred. All of these remains have since been removed by the prime minister's office."

"Several hundred . . . that's extraordinary. What do *you* think is going on, inspector?"

"Well sir, I think the remains in question may relate to the outbreak of disease that we are seeing in the rats and perhaps in the poor man whose body was found. What I can't fathom is why the PM would want to suppress this investigation."

Jarvis drummed his fingers and looked out his huge window toward Westminster Abbey and the buildings of Parliament. "It could simply be politics, you know. It's the height of the theater season. We don't need dead rats and a potential epidemic disrupting the tourists. Perhaps the PM just wants to keep things tempered down and out of the press."

"If that's the case, he's taking a serious risk, in my judgment. If we're not allowed to get to the bottom of this and it does prove to be something contagious, he'll face a firestorm in the press. At the moment, it's a low-level priority investigation. But if whatever this is infects more people and it's found out that the PM's office was suppressing control efforts . . . well . . . to put it succinctly, he could find himself out of a job altogether."

"And what a shame that would be, eh?"

No one at Scotland Yard much cared for the new prime minister. Sherwood now realized just how far up the chain of command that sentiment went.

"All right, inspector. I'll broach the subject with the home secretary. Of course, he may know nothing about it."

"Or may say that he doesn't." Sherwood said, then feared he had stepped over the line, but he'd been put off before on important investigations, with disastrous results.

"We'll cross that bridge when we come to it," said the commander. "There have been no reports of human sickness?"

"It's really too soon to say, sir. In a city this size, dozens of rat bites are reported every day. If there's an incubation period, we could be sitting on a potential time bomb. The man who died—a rat exterminator hired by the museum—had lung lesions and vascular irregularities that certainly suggest he had something unusual. Dr. Jessmer, director of the museum, has an idea that this might be some medieval disease he's studied."

Jarvis gave him a hard smile. "Anthropologists and museum directors see evidence of their particular specialties everywhere they look. Makes them feel self-important."

"Yes sir." Sherwood had noted that bit of human frailty himself.

"In any event, whatever got to that exterminator must have come from direct contact with the rats. Almost certainly, he was bitten. If the contaminant was airborne, we'd have a rash of cases by now, don't you agree?"

"I do, sir. The two museum employees who found the body have been exhaustively studied and appear to not be infected. I do not believe it could be airborne, at least at this point. But I'm no expert in this area. Health Minister Simonson is looking into it. You should consult with him if you want details."

Jarvis stood and reached out his hand. Sherwood took it firmly. "Thanks for bringing this to my attention, Inspector Peets. I'll see what I can unearth from 10 Downing on the matter."

"Thank you, sir." He started to leave.

"Oh, and inspector? I want to be kept up to date on your investigation. Anything new develops, see that I hear about it at once."

"I'll certainly try to do that, sir."

Jarvis smiled. "I'll tell Mildred that you are to be brought in promptly if you say it's important."

"Thank you, sir." Though he suspected such a directive would put him in even less favor with the formidable Ms. Swimm.

16

Julia found Carmen sitting at her private carousel in the new home of the British Museum's Reading Room. Her friend often worked here as she tried to verify her discoveries culled from the undocumented wastelands of the museum. In this case, however, she was mining for details of the infamous English Sweat.

"You're working too hard," said Julia. "A few days ago you had a concussion, for Pete's sake."

"I feel all right. That is, aside from the fact that research isn't the same since they uprooted the old British Library Reading Room." She glared at their surroundings. "Look at this place. Why they found it necessary to relocate most of the materials I require for my work to this modern brick building on a busy road near St. Pancras railway station, I will never understand. It's madness!"

"Well, you shouldn't be here anyway," said Julia. "Besides, there are more important things for you to be doing."

"What things?"

"I happen to know that there is a certain Scotland Yard inspector pining away for you."

Carmen stared at her incredulously. "Inspector Peets? Get off it, Julia. He's a cold fish. And the Ichabod Crane reincarnate is practically speechless whenever I'm around. I can't even figure out how he became an inspector. He's so quiet. Don't they have to ask questions and stuff?"

"Well, naturally, he didn't want to be quizzed about this business when he first met you. Government secrets and all that. But

I wouldn't be put off by his being quiet. He's a thinker. I have it from the highest authority that he's an up and comer. Very well respected at the Yard. He's broken some big cases. Trust me; I've seen the way he looks at you when he thinks no one's noticing. It's not the look of a detective. More like a lovesick puppy."

Carmen's mouth fell open. Julia was always trying to get her men, usually of the most improbable sort. Like poor Norman. Peets was okay looking, she supposed, in a gangly, Sherlock Holmesian way. She remembered how she'd caught him stealing looks at her. She assumed he'd been trying to read her feelings regarding the whole power grab thing between her and Trimm. That he might actually be interested in her never crossed her mind.

"You need a new hobby, Julia, besides my love life, which doesn't exist for a very good reason: I don't have time for it." She hesitated. "You don't even know if he's single."

"Divorced, two years, and desperately lonely," she replied chattily, sitting in an empty chair next to her.

"How on earth do you know that?"

"I have an old boyfriend who works in IT for the Yard."

"You have more old boyfriends than . . . than . . . the Queen of England."

"Well. I certainly hope so."

"I can't be doing this now," Carmen said. "I'm supposed to be researching the Sweat."

Julia peered over her shoulder. The computer screen showed a picture of a river with a scroll of text beside it. The stream was called the Walbrook. "I see," she said. "And what's this darlin' little river got to do with our Sweat?"

"It's actually pretty interesting. This is one of the lost rivers of underground London. Walbrook played a key role in the Roman settlement of Londinium. It got its name because it flowed right through the old walled city and into the Thames. The Romans even built a temple to Mithras on the east bank. It was discovered and excavated during reconstruction after World War II."

"Mmm-hmm," Julia murmured, feigning interest.

"It now runs completely underground, paralleling a street called Walbrook. See, I found it on this map. It's near the Bank of England."

"I think you *did* hit your head too hard falling out of that sewer," Julia said. "What, pray tell, does any of this have to do with the Sweat?"

"Nothing, really . . . except . . . a series of excavations in the 1860s led to the discovery of a large number of human bones and skulls in the river bed. Maybe . . . maybe the bones found at Coram's Fields were from there. Peets wouldn't acknowledge to me that more bodies were found than just the two he dated from the war. But his attitude alone suggests there were. Maybe the Walbrook was the river I fell into."

Carmen stared at her friend fiercely, chin jutting forward.

"Girl, you're getting a fixation. I don't know if you fell into the Walbrook or into the River Styx. Who the hell cares?"

Carmen slumped in her chair. "It probably wasn't the Walbrook, okay? It empties near the Cannon Street Railway Bridge today. That's not where I came out at all. I . . . I just *saw* something down there, Julia. I can't get it out of my head."

She turned back to the computer and punched a few keys. Another river appeared. "Maybe it was this one, the Tyburn. It runs underground from South Hampstead through St. James's Park to the Thames at Pimlico near Vauxhall Bridge. That's not right either, but there could be fluctuations in the river course over time, or other streams coming in that aren't known. The Tyburn gallows was alongside the river. It was the principal place of execution in the county of Middlesex from the 12th to 18th centuries, before they moved it to Newgate Prison. Maybe that's where the bones came from."

Julia considered her quietly. "What did you see down there, Carmen?"

She closed her eyes, trying to see it again. There had been so much blackness and cold, but then there was a moment of sparkling light and strange shapes, flickering in her damaged torch. She pressed her hands to her temples. "I don't know," she almost cried. "Wait. Look at this."

She punched some more keys, entering a code. A series of names appeared, columned opposite a list of dates. "These are the people who have been researching London's underground rivers."

"What's so strange about that? I daresay lots of historians, city planners, teachers and the like have reason to look this stuff up from time to time."

Carmen pointed her finger to one name that appeared frequently on the list. Julia leaned forward and stared.

"Dr. Trimm?" she said, her eyes widening.

"He's been all over these rivers, Julia. The records go back almost two years. It's the only thing he's been researching."

17

It was a bitterly cold night. The *Jenny* tossed her occupants like so many fleas in a sack. When dawn finally came, Captain Macintosh appeared in the sleeping quarters to awaken the few lucky souls who had managed to fall asleep.

"Thurr's a lull in the weatherr, gentlemen," he said. "We'rre pushing full speed toward Narvik and should arrrive by evening. Howeverr..."

Major Osbourne and Gunnar moved to the edge of their bunks. "Is there a problem, captain?" asked Gunnar.

"Thurr's been a lot of radio traffic. My men only know a smattering of Gerrman, but they know the word furr U-boat and they've also hearrd them talking about the *Jenny*."

Gunnar swore. Osbourne stood up in his long johns, fists clenched. "They're looking for us," he said. "You were right, commander. The patrol boat must have radioed their intentions to board us before coming alongside."

"They'll be on to us quickly, then," said Gunnar. "The Nazis have U-boat bases all along the Norwegian coast. It's the main reason they invaded Norway, so their submarines could harass Allied shipping in the North Sea."

"Aye," said the captain. "That and to control the porrt of Narvik. Swedish iron orre is the backbone of Gerrman industry, and it's shipped to the Fatherland from thurr." He looked at them. "What do you want to do? We can wait till we reach

Ofotfjorden to put you ashorre, as planned, if you dinna think they'll be waiting."

"They'll be waiting," said Osbourne grimly. "With the disappearance of their patrol boat, they have to know we're serious and there's only one thing we could be after. Why else would we be so far north? If I were a U-boat captain, I'd heave to and wait outside the entrance to the fjord for us to walk right into their bloody arms."

Gunnar looked at the tense faces of the other men. It was a critical moment. He had to admire Captain Macintosh and his crew. They were brave men, and no one had ordered them into such a dangerous situation. They were being paid, but that alone wasn't enough for them to put their lives in jeopardy. Their distaste for the Germans played a big part in their presence here. "You'll have to put us ashore somewhere else," he said finally. "We'll get to the rocket base any way we can. Is there another port shy of Ofotfjorden that you can put us in?"

The captain nodded slowly. "The town of Svolvaer in the Lofoten Islands. It's a regular stop for the Shetland Bus."

"The what?"

"She's a Narrwegian naval attachment. Runs a transport route between the Shetlands and occupied Narrway. It's a risky enterprise, but she's made a habit of running the submarine lanes without getting caught. If I put you off near Svolvaer, you might make contact with her. With luck, she could slip you closer to Narvik."

Gunnar considered the information. Narvik wasn't their end destination. The rocket research base was at least sixty miles north of there, near a remote village called Finnsnes. Here, the Germans had decided they were far enough away from the Fatherland for their deadly experiments. But none of this had been revealed to the captain.

"All right," he said finally. "Svolvaer it is."

Captain Macintosh nodded and left for the bridge. Gunnar went to find Natasha, who had separate sleeping quarters near the bow of the ship.

He had to knock several times before a sleepy voice said, "What is it?"

"It's Gunnar. Can I come in?"

There was a moment's hesitation, which he duly noted. Then she said, "Just a moment."

When the door opened, she had on the same bathrobe and slippers she'd worn during her nighttime visit with him on the train. "What's wrong?"

"Change of plans. The captain is going to put us off near a village called Svolvaer. We'll have to make our own way to the base from there."

He could see her mind working. "How far will it be?"

"Sixty or seventy miles. Captain Macintosh picked up some radio traffic that strongly suggests the Germans are looking for us. We're sitting ducks as long as we're on this boat. Every German submarine and informant in every port on the coast will be searching for us."

"How soon?"

"We'll be there near dusk, the best time to drop us off. You can get another hour or so of sleep. Probably be a good idea. God knows when we'll get another chance."

She looked into his eyes. "Gunnar . . . I'm sorry about how I've been. I know it's been hard on you. I just . . . "

"Let's not get into it now," he said, more brusquely than he had intended. "A lot's going to happen in the next few days. We need to concentrate on that. We'll see where we are when it's over."

"Okay, Gunnar. Goodnight," she said, then closed the door firmly.

He stared at the door feeling like an idiot. It was the first time she'd opened up at all about what had taken place between them, and he'd seen fit to throw a bucket of cold water in her face. Well, what did she expect? She couldn't take him into her bed and then just shut him out immediately afterwards. He was angry and had a right to be. Maybe, he thought, as reason kicked in once again, he should re-channel that anger towards the Germans.

He went up to the bridge, where Macintosh stood at the wheel. The captain nodded when he came in.

Gunnar stared out at the sea. The gale had dissipated and the waters were relatively calm, but there was still heavy fog hugging the bays and inlets of the coast.

"Where will you put us off?" he asked.

Macintosh pulled out a chart. "I think here, aboot six miles from Svolvaer. Thurr's a bit of a bay I know. We'll sneak in afterr dusk and put you ashorr by dinghy."

Gunnar nodded. "It's an island you're dropping us on. What are our chances of getting a boat?"

"Thurr's a man, Thor Heyerman, member of the resistance. He lives on the outskirts of the village and is a contact farr the Shetland Bus. I'll give you a note farr him. If the bus isn't scheduled any time soon, he'll help you arrange farr anotherr boot."

Gunnar told Osbourne to have his men ready to go the moment the captain gave the signal. Then he went forward and stood watching the coast drift in and out of the fog. It was a barren place they were about to be deposited in, rocky headlands covered in saw grass. There were few inhabitants and only the occasional fishing or lobster shack. He thought again about their mission. It would be a miracle if they pulled it off, especially now that the Germans knew they were in the area. He stood for a long time—until darkness began to sink across the barren hills and he saw a sprinkling of lights in the distance.

Svolvaer.

He turned and climbed back to the bridge. As he entered, one of the captain's men burst in behind him. "Submarine off the port side," he said. "Three hundred yards. I think she's spotted us."

Macintosh swore and spun the wheel, turning the boat hard to starboard. "We'll head straight farr the nearrest bay," he said. "They'll be reluctant to come into shallow water. With darkness, they may not see us at all."

But it was a forlorn hope. The U-boat closed fast. Macintosh made the bay, then hove to. At once, his men lowered the dinghy on the side away from the submarine. Gunnar, Osbourne, Natasha and the major's men boarded it silently in the dark.

Gunnar looked up at Macintosh for the last time. "Thank you, captain," he said. "What do you think will happen?"

"They willna see you leave in this darrk. Maybe we can convince them we were fishing and simply wanted a safe haven for the night. They'll find naught on board to say you were here."

"They'll wonder why you have no fish and no dinghy."

"Aye, they may," he shrugged. "Good luck to you. Give the Jerrys one for us." He waved and headed back to the bridge to await the boarding party.

Several of Osbourne's men manned the oars. There were no running lights, and under the moonless sky, they were all but invisible. In just a few minutes, they ran up on a pebble beach and scrambled out.

In a low voice, Osbourne said, "Pull her up into that crevice and cut some brush to cover her. It won't hide her from a detailed search, but the longer we can keep them from knowing we were here, the better."

The last bit of brush was going on the dinghy when they heard a siren out on the water. Then floodlights from the U-boat began to sweep the shore.

"Grab your gear and find cover," Gunnar cried, as the lights passed over them. Everyone scrambled for what protection there was on the bleak headland. From where he'd taken shelter beneath a clump of saw grass, Gunnar watched as the U-boat pulled up alongside the *Jenny*.

Natasha was beside him. "Do you think they saw us?" she asked, worried.

"I don't know. There must be some reason they turned the lights on shore."

The two vessels were no more than a hundred yards offshore. In the harsh floodlights from the U-boat they could see men scrambling from the submarine onto the deck of the *Jenny*. Commands in German floated across the sea. Gunnar saw Captain Macintosh standing on deck surrounded by uniformed figures. He gestured far up the shore from where they were. Then the captain and crew were hustled onto the submarine, which churned away from the fishing boat and dove.

"I think we're okay," Gunnar said.

They gathered themselves, lifting their packs on their backs; the major's men hauled the guns and satchels of plastic explosives.

"Which way do we go?" asked Natasha.

Gunnar pointed toward the lights of Svolvaer. "We'll try to find Thor Heyerman. Lead out, major."

Just then, one of the soldiers yelled. "Look! On the water."

They turned to see a trail split the water of the cove. A moment later the *Jenny* blew to pieces as a torpedo struck her amidships. She split in two and sank.

"Damn them!" said Gunnar.

"At least they didn't leave Macintosh and his men on board. I wouldn't have put that past them," said Osbourne.

"What will happen to them?" asked Natasha.

"Interned for the duration—if they're lucky," Gunnar said grimly. "They were good men. I hope they make it through the war. If we come out of this, we must inform their families. They won't have any notion what happened to them."

The major's men moved quickly over the rough landscape. Gunnar and Natasha, unused to the effort, soon fell behind.

But Osbourne kept track of them, dropping back periodically to urge them on.

It was tough going. In the blackness, everyone jammed knees against rocks and caught feet in snags and clefts. Their progress was marked by a series of grunts and softly muttered curses.

Gunnar consulted a crude map Macintosh had given him delineating paths and the houses on the near side of town, including the one owned by Heyerman. As they neared town, they found a dirt road that made for easier going, though they kept to the side, prepared to jump into the brush if anyone showed.

Finally, Gunnar called a halt and consulted with Osbourne, using a tiny pen light to look at the map.

"That's got to be it," he said, pointing to a small stone cottage overlooking the bay and set back from the road.

Osbourne grunted. "All right." He turned to one of his men. "Edmunds, you scout it. See if anyone's home."

The moon had risen, and they watched as the soldier skirted the house and inched his way up to a window. He peered in for what seemed an interminable amount of time, then made his way back to them.

"A man and a woman, sir. They looked fairly comfortably settled. Not like company. More like husband and wife."

Osbourne looked at Gunnar. "Your call," he said. "If it's not Heyerman and we burst in on the wrong people, you know we'll have to kill them."

"No," Natasha said. "That's not necessary."

"If it's the wrong people, they'll report our movements to the authorities," said Osbourne. "We'll lose whatever small edge we have."

"If you kill them, don't you think the authorities are going to take that as evidence we're here?" Natasha replied. "It won't make any difference."

Osbourne stared at her for a moment. "They'll report not just the fact of our presence, but the size of our group as well."

Gunnar looked from the major to Natasha. "All right. Natasha and I will go in alone. We both speak Norwegian. I can make up some story about what we're doing here. They'll be less suspicious of a man and a woman. If it's Thor Heyerman, we'll ask for his help. If it's not him, we'll ask directions and leave."

"They're never going to believe you just happened to be out for a stroll in this barren bit of heaven," said Osbourne, but he could see the determination in Gunnar's face. "All right. We'll wait for you here. If it's clear, turn the lights off and on twice and we'll come in. Once you get inside, don't let them out of your sight for a moment. If they have a phone in there and aren't who we think they are, they could call all bloody hell down on us."

Gunnar nodded. He looked at Natasha. "We'll leave our packs here. Take just our pistols."

As it turned out all the precautions were unnecessary. Thor Heyerman was a powerful-looking Norwegian in his forties with a neatly trimmed black beard. The moment Gunnar and Natasha arrived at his door, he seemed to understand who they were, almost intuitively.

"I have been helping my countrymen escape from or make trouble for the Nazis since 1939," he said proudly. He looked at Gunnar closely. "You, I think, are one who will make trouble for them too."

Gunnar quickly called in the rest of their party and while Thor's wife laid out some bread and cheese, he explained that he could not reveal their mission but that they needed transportation to Finnsnes.

Thor stared at him and slowly a broad smile appeared on his face. "You go to destroy the rocket base," he said.

Gunnar exchanged looks with Major Osbourne. "So much for espionage," he said. "How do you know about the base?"

The big Norwegian laughed. "There are no secrets in this part of the world. The Germans light up the night sky with their buildings. It is unlike anything else up here. Everyone knows they have a base. We did not know why until they began to fire rockets into the sky. Then, everyone knows. But it makes no sense, I think, to have a base so far from everything."

Gunnar saw no need to frighten him or the rest of the people up here by outlining the dangerous experiments that were going on. To change the subject, he said, "Could you get the Shetland Bus to take us there?"

He shook his head. "The bus was here last week. She won't be back for some time, and it's impossible to know when precisely. No. I will have to take you myself. I have a small fishing boat."

Before Gunnar could respond, the phone rang. Their host picked it up, listened for a moment, said "Yah," and hung up.

"The Germans have put out an alert for you. They must suspect you are on the island. It is a small island and they will search it very quickly. We need to leave at once."

He took his wife aside and exchanged a few words with her, then he gave her a hug, grabbed a jacket and led the way out the door.

"A curfew has been issued," he said. "But there is no reason for the Germans to expect everyone will know about it so soon. It is mainly to give them the authority to stop and question anyone they see. A sham, of course, since they do that whenever they wish anyway. We call it a Quisling Sham—to give the illusion of German cooperation with the Norwegian government. When they come here, my wife will tell them I have been out fishing for two days."

He led them down a steep path to a small wharf that was loaded down with lobster traps and where there were two fishing boats tied up. His craft was small and very crowded once they were all aboard.

"A tight squeeze, that is how you English say it, no? But I am not so easy to see in my tiny boat, especially at night. We will take the inland passage through the islands to Andfjorden, then around the back side of Senja Island and down the Malangen Strait to Finnsnes. The Germans mostly patrol outside the islands in the main channels. With luck, we will not see any patrol boats."

Gunnar nodded and squeezed into his spot next to Natasha, sitting on the port side. The trip would take at least ten to twelve hours, and they would arrive at dawn. They'd have to lay low until evening before making their final move to the base. It was going to be a very long night followed by an even longer day. Natasha laid her head on his shoulder and was asleep in minutes.

18

It was not his favorite duty, but Vidkun Quisling believed the executions sent an important message. Norwegians proved to be a stubborn people, not realists like he was. The Germans controlled their country and would for the foreseeable future. He'd been smart enough to see the handwriting on the wall, and he firmly believed that it was through his efforts that Norwegians had managed to retain any control at all. He had to make an example of those members of the resistance movement who were captured trying to destroy that control.

He stared at the two men standing in the courtyard below. Their arms were tied behind their backs, their heads remained uncovered. They stared defiantly in his direction as the firing squad took aim. At the last moment, one of them shouted, "Long live a free Norway! Death to the traitor, Quisling!"

Vidkun grimaced as the guns roared and the men slumped to the ground. He turned away. In the future, he would order the men to be muzzled to avoid such unpleasantness.

His secretary told him that Reichskommissar Terboven was waiting for him in his office. Quisling felt a jolt of adrenalin. Terboven did not have authority over the 600,000 German army forces in Norway, but he commanded a personal force of 6,000, including some 800 secret police. Not controlling the army forces directly grated on the reichskommissar, for he enjoyed the perquisites of power. As soon as he had assumed command in 1940, he installed himself in the Norwegian crown prince's residence at Skaugum. He rarely visited Quisling and almost never without advance warning. Whatever prompted this visit, it couldn't be good news.

He took a deep breath and put a smile on his face as he entered the room. "Reichskommissar! A pleasant surprise. How can I be of assistance to you?"

Terboven was a dour-looking man with fair hair, oversize glasses and a perpetual frown. "Some of my U-boats report that Norwegian patrols have been unusually active along the coast in recent days. Also, we have detected more activity amongst coastal guard units. Why have I not been informed of these changes?"

Quisling felt dampness at the base of his shirt. He smiled engagingly. "Ah, it is nothing, reichskomissar. You may remember that several POWs escaped from Akershus Fortress last week. I reported it to you. The increased patrols were to try to close off avenues of escape and to recapture them."

In fact, this explanation had been manufactured for precisely such questioning by Terboven. Quisling had orchestrated the outbreak himself, allowing three low-level prisoners to escape. It was a perfect cover story.

Terboven stared at him with cold eyes. "Yes. I remember your report on the escape. If you cannot manage to control men locked in a prison, I wonder what else you are incapable of."

Quisling sidestepped the comment. "It is good that you are here, reichskommissar. I wish to clear another matter with you." He went to his desk and picked up a piece of paper.

"I have received a requisition for several miles worth of rails to repair the spur line that runs from Finnsnes to Narvik. I was unaware of the need and thought I should ask you about the request." He handed the paper to Terboven.

This was also a planned bit of manipulation. Technically, Quisling was not supposed to know about the new research center. But in this manner, he could test Terboven and perhaps learn something useful about the project the Germans had in mind. The more he knew the more likely he could guess what the British intentioned.

"Yes, yes. This must be provided immediately. An important project ordered by the führer himself." Terboven mentioned Hitler's name constantly as a way to puff up his own importance, as though he were in daily contact with the führer, which he most certainly was not. Married to Ilse Stahl, Joseph Goebbels's former secretary and mistress, Terboven's wedding in 1934 had boasted Adolf Hitler as guest of honor. But Norway was a sideshow in this war and with the deteriorating situations on the eastern front and in Africa, Hitler had very little interest in Norway, outside of his special project, which he was very interested in indeed. Terboven himself, however, barely registered on the führer's thoughts these days.

Quisling's face registered surprise. "Oh, why of course then. I was not aware of the führer's interest. Really, reichskommissar, if I am to be of assistance to the Third Reich, I should be kept better informed."

Terboven looked distracted. "One of the führer's pet projects. I am not at liberty to discuss it. But you may be assured it is of the utmost importance to the war effort. Norway may yet take the lead in winning this war, Mr. Minister President."

Terboven rarely used Quisling's title. He considered the man little more than a puppet, unworthy of bringing into any confidences whatsoever. Still, he could not resist showing off his own inner knowledge of the most important projects of the Third Reich.

Quisling's eyes widened. "The lead? This is quite wonderful news, reichskommissar. I assure you the government is at your disposal in this worthy undertaking . . . whatever it is."

Terboven stood up. "Yes, well, I have another meeting to attend. If there are any further changes or developments regarding the search for those prisoners, I want to be informed. Is that clear?"

Quisling nodded and felt a wave of relief as the man left. The moment he was gone, he called his secretary and told her to send Albert Hagelin in. When his old fascist friend arrived, Quisling could hardly contain himself.

"The escape of the prisoners worked like a charm, Albert. Terboven had no suspicions at all. But I have learned something new. Something very exciting. The research base the Germans are building at Finnsnes is one of Hitler's top priorities. The reichskommissar says it may even affect the outcome of the war."

Hagelin's bushy eyebrows rose. "Most interesting indeed." He stared out the window for a moment. "We should increase our efforts to find the British commando group."

"I agree, of course," said Quisling. "But we must take the utmost precautions. I have been ordered not to undertake any more security changes without informing Terboven. It will be tricky to circumvent his direct orders, but it must be done." He was practically vibrating with excitement. "This is clearly very important to the German war plans. If we can stop the British commandos, we may be rewarded by the führer himself."

Hagelin nodded. "I will order more patrols and activate every man we have in the northern area. It will be done discreetly, I promise you, Vidkun."

19

London — Present Day

"You've *got* to speed up your work. Too many people are becoming interested in this place. The minister of health has already declared the Coram's Fields site off-limits. I can still get you in here, but the window is closing." Trimm stared at Hans with an odd light in his eyes. They were standing near the entrance to one of the recently discovered tunnels.

"If this damn disease does decide to break out, the place will be crawling with investigators and health department types. You and your people have been working down here all summer. We need results. Spread your men out. Cover more ground."

"Perhaps if you had not reported the death of the rats to the health minister," Hans said thickly, "we would not now be denied access to the site."

It was a sore point. The countless bodies of dead and dying rats had unnerved Trimm. He was terrified of catching something from them. It had been agony making the decision to inform the authorities, but he believed he could keep control of the events. Clearly, he had been mistaken.

Once the minister of health got wind of things, it was only a matter of time before the intelligence head, Secret Intelligence Service Director Marcus Hopkinton, found his way into the loop. He applied pressure as only an intelligence man could, with the result that Trimm was now in league with Hopkinton. There was no other way to put it. The play of events and Trimm's need to share his secret infuriated him. But there was nothing he could do.

"In any event," Hans continued, his point made, "This whole place is like a gigantic Swiss cheese. The substructures are weak from centuries of people cutting away down here, long before anyone thought about a tube system. Old hand cut sewers and channels, Roman waterworks, catacombs, underground defense caverns connecting the Tower and other fortresses, the maze of bomb shelters and subsurface offices created by the government during the war. My men have gotten lost on a regular basis. Several have been hurt by cave-ins that seemed suspicious."

Trimm stared at him. "Suspicious? What the hell are you talking about?"

"I mean maybe some of those old underground defense works were booby trapped. You know, in case the enemy broke through to British soil."

"That's absurd. I've never heard of such a thing, and I've researched the underground exhaustively."

Hans shrugged. "Two of my men are overdue right now. That's why I'm here. We're getting ready to go look for them."

"Look for them, then. But look for more of these while you're at it." Trimm held up an enormous ruby.

Hans had seen it before. Whenever Trimm wanted results, he held the ruby up as proof that what they were searching for was real.

"I scuffed this little beauty up with my boot in one of the sub-tunnels," Trimm said. "There weren't any others around. Believe me, I looked. This must have washed out on its own somehow. I tell you there's a fortune down here."

Hans looked away. Maybe Trimm had found the ruby or maybe he'd simply purchased it to use as incentive. The man was single minded. Probably unbalanced. They'd met while doing research in Munich two years ago. Trimm had been evasive as to the nature of his work, and Hans's initial reaction to the man was one of cautious interest. Then, during a night of heavy drinking in a German beer garden, Trimm told Hans that he was searching for a lost treasure beneath London.

It was absurd, of course, and Hans had laughed. In an instant, Trimm turned coldly serious, insisting that he was on the trail of something big. The two men ended up talking long into the night. Trimm's enthusiasm was infectious, and Hans felt a certain pride that he had been taken into his new friend's confidence. It was not lost on either man that they were both researching the same underground maze, albeit for vastly different reasons.

Hans's research had to do with the war. His grandfather had been involved in the German V-2 rocket program, and had worked with Werner von Braun. He'd told stories about the V-2 research programs, and how some of the rockets that had been fired actually contained biological weapons.

It was an incredible story if true, one of the last untold stories of World War II. Hans saw his entire future laid out before him if he could prove his grandfather's allegations. There would be a book and maybe even a movie or TV series. Perhaps a documentary: *The Lost Rockets of the Third Reich*. The more he looked into it, and the more he contemplated his future fame, the more convinced he became that V-2s—armed with biological payloads—had been fired on London.

But what had happened to them? There were no records of such rockets ever producing any sort of disease. Scouring accounts of the thousand V-2s that had been fired on London, he'd found only one whose origins and payload were undocumented. However, there was no record of it from the English side, even though he had the exact date and location— from a site in Belgium—of the firing. Nothing had appeared in the British press about a missile landing in the city on that date.

Still, he'd uncovered tantalizing anecdotes. One obscure article in the *London Times* quoted an eye witness who swore he'd heard a rocket go overhead on the night in question. The obvious conclusion to Hans was that the rocket had misfired, not exploded and perhaps embedded itself in some unlikely place where it was never found.

An unlikely place like an old tube line, perhaps. It was against the odds, but not beyond the realm of possibility that the V-2 could have tunneled through a weak section of ground and entered some old walled-off section of the tube or other underground tunnel. On the other hand, it seemed unlikely that any rocket could have survived the impact. It would have been blown to smithereens. Nothing made any sense.

For two years, Hans watched Trimm become more and more obsessed with his treasure hunt. The man did not eat or sleep, so far as he could tell. While the search for a lost V-2 preoccupied Hans, he nevertheless worked with Trimm, poring over aging architectural blueprints of the old tube system and even more ancient records of the burying of London's subterranean rivers.

Trimm treated Hans as his subordinate, something that grated from time to time, but the German let it go for the most part because he found the good doctor's research abilities to be formidable.

"All right," Hans said. "We will continue our search here." He pointed to the blueprint he was holding. "There are a number of tunnels that appear to connect with sections of the Great Conduit—maybe even with the Great Cistern itself. Some of these certainly appear to be manmade and very old." He folded the map. "We'll see what we uncover. But finding my men remains my first priority."

Trimm put one hand on the younger man's shoulder. "You will see. We are going to be very rich men." He smiled. He liked the impulsive, young German. All Hans needed was direction. Who better to provide it than someone of his many talents?

Hans looked away, embarrassed at the familiarity. He switched on his torch. It picked out his two companions who were setting up a rappel line nearby to lower them into a steep, darkened tunnel—one of the ones they thought might connect with the Great Cistern.

With a curt nod to Trimm, he moved off toward the working men. One of them, Wolfgang, nodded as he approached. "We're ready," he said. "I'll go first, then you, then Kurt. It shouldn't be difficult, even for a non-climber like you. You step into this belt and snap on to the line here. Then you simply ease back on the release and down you go."

Hans nodded and arranged the gear. He put his torch into his backpack and used a headlamp instead. Then he followed Wolfgang down into the black, wet opening. The footing was slippery and treacherous, the tunnel sloping at an intimidating sixty degrees. They could not have done it without the line.

"How far down does it go?" Hans asked into the funnel of light thrown by his headlamp.

He felt Wolfgang shrug his shoulders in the dark. The man had massive, climber's shoulders and muscles that bulged at the back of his neck.

"The line we lowered is seventy-five feet long. If that's not enough, we'll try to screw in pitons and use this." He made a motion to an additional length of nylon that hung from his belt, then slapped his hand against the clay walls. "Bloody clay everywhere," he said in disgust. "Impossible to get a dependable piton in the stuff. I don't like relying on them, but we've no choice."

Hans concentrated on the task of operating the clamp, lowering himself in jerky movements that were very different from the smooth motions of Wolfgang and Kurt. Water dripped from the ceiling and got in his eyes if he looked up. He did so only once, seeing Trimm's stern face staring down at them in the flash from his headlamp.

As they neared the end of the first rope, the tunnel's angle decreased. A moment later, Hans felt his feet gain enough purchase to walk without relying on the line.

He ran one hand along the wall beside him. It was clammy and damp; a heavy, muddy clay. There were scallop-shaped cuts on the surface. He couldn't really imagine how they had been made, couldn't think of a tool that would do that.

The three men stopped when the footing became feasible. Ahead, the tunnel branched in three directions.

Kurt grunted, "Which way do we go?"

Hans glanced at his compass, but it was a useless piece of equipment down here. There must be magnetic disturbances.

"My sense," he said, "is that the left branch will take us in the general direction of the Great Cistern. That's where our men were headed, albeit coming from the other direction. We'll take that one."

"Damned if I can see why we didn't follow their route directly," Wolfgang said. "It would have been the fastest way to find them."

"If they'd followed procedures and left us a precise plan of their movements, we wouldn't be searching for them right now," Hans replied testily. He had tried repeatedly to get the men to take the risks involved in this place seriously. For most, however, it was something of a lark. They were young and adventurous. They believed in Hans's mission to locate a possible missing V-2 rocket. It was exciting stuff for young Germans to be involved with. None of them had been told about Trimm's so-called treasure hunt.

"What about the line?" asked Kurt.

"Leave it in place. If our progress is blocked anywhere, this might be our only way out."

The left branch proved hard going. The sides closed in until it was barely the width of a man. Hans began to wonder if it would peter out all together when there was a low rumble ahead of them. A moment later, a cloud of black, choking dust engulfed them.

"Cave-in!" shouted Wolfgang. "Go back."

The dust consisted of very fine particles, for which they had no lung protection. Almost at once, they were coughing and choking as they stumbled back the way they had come.

By the time they reached the branch connection with the other tunnels, the dust had settled enough for them to breathe once more. They continued on to the steep entrance tunnel and their rope. When they reached it they stopped and stared.

The nylon line was gone. At the base of the rising tunnel mouth laid a pile of frayed and worthless line, completely torn to threads. It was in a heap like a jumbled ball of twine torn apart by a kitten.

Wolfgang stooped over and picked up a piece. "This looks like it's been chewed." He took off his climbing glove and felt the material. "It's damp." He drew back, and a sticky line of mucus ran from the line to his hand.

"Let me see that," said Hans. He took the shredded material from Wolfgang with his gloved hand and stared at it, feeling the strange, gelatinous, almost gluey texture. It definitely appeared that something had dissolved—or eaten—the line.

"I don't understand," said Kurt. "What could do this?"

"Rats," said Wolfgang.

But Hans shook his head. "In the first place there wasn't time. We weren't gone that long. And this rope is made of nylon. Rats wouldn't be interested in chewing on it. I don't think they *could* chew it even if they had some reason to do so."

"Ow! Son of a bitch!" Wolfgang grabbed his hand.

"What's wrong?"

"My hand. It's starting to burn."

Hans shone his light on the hand. The skin was flaking and red where he had been in contact with the strange substance.

He looked down quickly at his own hand. His glove was disintegrating before his eyes, the material falling away. He felt a stinging sensation and quickly discarded the rest of the glove. It fell to the ground, where the fibers continued to deteriorate and a thin wisp of something rose from the little pile.

They looked silently at one another. "What the hell's going on?" said Kurt.

A strange, scraping sound came from the tunnel behind them.

"What was that?" Kurt said nervously.

"Take it easy," Hans said, but he peered with the others into the black tunnel next to the one from which they had just emerged. The sound continued, like someone rubbing sandpaper against the walls. But there was also a wet, sucking noise, like an elderly man sucking on a bad tooth.

"Christ!" Wolfgang said in a low voice. "We can't go back. We've got to go into that last tunnel. It's the only way out now."

The others didn't say anything, but they knew Wolfgang was right. They couldn't climb up the way they had come down, it was too steep and slippery and the tunnel they had first tried had been blocked by a landslide. There was only one way to go.

"Just take it slow," said Hans. "I'll go first. Try to keep all of our headlamps focused ahead of us, so we can see what's coming. All right?"

Slowly, they headed into the last tunnel. The sucking and scraping sounds continued, but whatever was making them stayed just out of sight. It was nerve-wracking not being able to see what was causing the noise. After ten minutes of this—their nerves taught as piano wire—they reached another branching tunnel.

"Take the new one," said Hans. "I think it goes back the way we want—toward the Great Cistern."

But Wolfgang had barely set one foot into the new tunnel when they heard another rumble like the earlier one, only louder. Again, a few moments later, the cloud of black soot billowed out of the opening. They had no choice but to move forward quickly to stay ahead of the unbreathable air. They approached still another tunnel and again, as soon as they stepped into it, the distant rumble came, followed by the cloud of dust.

"This can't be a coincidence," said Kurt, his voice as frayed as the nylon rope had been. "It's as if something is making our choices for us."

"Just another cave-in," said Hans. "We knew that was always a possibility down here. There's tremendous weakness in the supporting structures. We're lucky we weren't in that last tunnel when the ceiling went."

"I tell you there's something down here," Kurt said. "Something that wants us to go in a certain direction."

"Don't be ridiculous," said Hans. "Even if there was, what they just did saved our lives by keeping us from being in the tunnel that collapsed."

They continued on in the preselected tunnel. They were rising now; Hans thought possibly back to the original level from which they had lowered themselves. The sounds they'd been hearing had diminished and then stopped altogether. Relieved, they began to think that maybe they had simply imagined the strange sucking and scraping.

Wolfgang was in the lead as they rounded a curve in the tunnel. He stopped abruptly and the others had to come up beside him to see why. The tunnel had come to an end. They stood at the mouth of the opening, which now overlooked an enormous, gaping hole, at least twenty feet in circumference.

"The Great Cistern," Hans almost whispered. "I've never actually seen it before. Julia told me about it, though."

"What the hell is that?" asked Kurt.

"Part of the Roman underground waterworks system. Water from the Tyburn flowed through the Great Conduit to fall into the cistern. It provided steady water for the city even in dry years."

"The question," said Wolfgang, "is how do we get across it? It's too far to jump. And we can't go back."

"I suppose we could just wait here for someone to come along," said Kurt.

"No," said Hans. "They closed the site. It might be a long time before anyone happens by. And we're not supposed to be here anyway. I don't want to have to explain what we're doing."

Wolfgang crouched down, studying the cistern, shining his light into the enormous opening. It was swallowed up before finding the bottom, but the walls looked rough and climbable.

"We'll have to climb down into it and then back up the other side," he said. 'It shouldn't be too difficult. Good thing I have another section of rope and plenty of pitons."

All three men stood silently for a moment, contemplating Wolfgang's scheme. Clearly, they had no choice. But the recent memory of the strange sounds now came back to them.

"We don't know what's down there," Kurt said uneasily, voicing the same concern they all had.

"No point talking about it," said Hans. He motioned Wolfgang to go ahead, and watched as the great knots of muscle in his shoulders pounded two pitons into the clay at the lip of the cavern.

Across on the other side of the opening, they could see another tunnel heading off into the gloom. It seemed to beckon them forward.

One after the other, they followed Wolfgang over the edge.

20

Sherwood stood at the entrance to the British Museum's Reading Room and shuffled his feet. He wasn't so sure this was a good idea. Julia suggested that he come here and look at what Carmen was researching. It wasn't as if it was taking valuable time away from his explorations into the bones found at the Coram's Fields site. The truth was he had run up against a brick wall.

Though the remains had been taken by the prime minister's office, he had thought after his meetings with the minister of health and the deputy commander, that he would be given access. Or at least be told why not. But so far, he had not heard a peep about the case. He was beginning to wonder if he might be dealing with some sort of turf dispute between government offices . . . or possibly something more sinister.

In any event, Julia's suggestion had not been unwelcome. He liked Carmen. In fact, he hadn't been able to stop thinking about her ever since she first showed up at his office. Of course, she was pretty. But that wasn't it, or at least not all of it. There was something about her independence—her unwillingness to be put off by him—that had struck a chord. Though he had to admit, the fierceness in her face when she got angry was intimidating, to say the least.

His ex-wife, Adria, had been the clingy type. He couldn't blame her. Her declining mental state made her more and more dependent on him. But there was no question he had felt stifled by her demands. Carmen was clearly not that sort.

Unfortunately, her career focus made him sense that she had no time for him at all. And certainly no interest of the kind he was thinking about. She was deeply entrenched in the same sort of internecine, bureaucratic conflicts that he, from time to time, also faced. He found himself fantasizing what it would be like to be able to share all of that with someone.

He asked directions from a woman sitting behind a desk and she pointed him to the private research carousels. He wandered down the aisle until he saw her, then stopped and just watched her for a moment. She was concentrating on her computer screen, one hand twining its fingers in her hair. She wore a skirt and had one foot up on the edge of the railing of the carousel. He stared at her bare calf and felt his heart lurch. When he looked up at her face, she was regarding him with a puzzled look.

Christ! What was wrong with him? He moved forward and stopped beside her. "Um, hello. I was just coming to look at you—I mean to see you."

She gave him a smile. She'd seen what he had been looking at. Maybe Julia wasn't completely crazy after all.

"Pull up a seat." She pointed to an empty chair in the next carousel.

He did so and then looked everywhere except at her. "I used to go to the old Reading Room when I was studying for my Yard exams. Don't get the time anymore."

"One of the things that got me interested in this job was being able to work in the old space. I used to think having my own carousel in the British Library's Reading Room was just about the coolest thing anyone could possibly have. But it's not the same anymore."

"Julia said I should come see what you're researching. Found anything interesting?"

So . . . Julia *was* behind this little visit. Wait till she got her hands on her so-called friend. She looked at his long face. It certainly wasn't handsome. But he had a dimple in his chin. And his eyes were close set and there was something going on behind them. She decided they were warm eyes.

Shit! Stop it. She didn't have time for this sort of high school nonsense. Her face turned angry at the thoughts and then she realized Sherwood was staring at her in perplexity.

"If this is an awkward time . . . I didn't mean to interrupt your work."

She gave him a weak smile. "Sorry. I was thinking of something else. It's all right. Really."

He leaned in to look at her screen. "She said you were studying the underground rivers."

She hesitated, looking at the telltale screen. But then those eyes focused on her and she felt the strangest sensation. She wanted to tell him what had happened to her. Maybe it was a knack that all Scotland Yard inspectors had. Maybe they all had to pass some sort of test where they made people spill their deepest confessions.

Ten minutes later, she couldn't believe that she'd told him everything. What it had been like to ride that cold, subterranean river; what she'd seen—or thought she'd seen; and how crazy it had been making her ever since.

He never once removed his eyes from hers. He seemed to literally drink in her words like some sort of huge, sympathetic sponge. When she finished, she looked away, embarrassed at how he had stripped her emotions clean. It felt like being violated. Except, she realized, she enjoyed the sensation.

"I think I can understand how it might upset you," he said, slowly. "Maybe because it's a lot like what I do. In an investigation, you pick away at things that nag at your subconscious until something clicks and you find a connection. I think that's sort of what your mind is doing. Trying to find something that will make sense of what you saw."

She stared at him. "That's exactly what it's like."

He nodded at the computer screen. "Have you been able to determine what river you were in?"

"No. It's incredibly difficult. There are a dozen subterranean rivers under London, but none of them seem to intersect with where I was. Maybe I merged with another river or followed some newly carved out course. It just seems impossible to pin it down."

He contemplated his shoes again. A nervous habit, she decided. "We could run the river again," he said softly.

She stared at him. "Are you crazy? I almost died."

"I know. But maybe we could do it in a more controlled way."

She was curious in spite of herself. "How do you mean?"

"Well, it's just that you did come through. And you never ran out of breathing room. There was always space above you, right? So why couldn't we take a boat and do it all over again. Only this time we'd have torches that worked."

"What about at the end? I don't want to go spilling out of that sewer again."

He thought about it. "How fast do you think the current was?"

"It sure felt fast, being in it. But I *was* able to sort of direct myself and even swim upstream away from an obstacle once, so it must not have been too swift."

He nodded. "I'll talk to someone I know at the Department of Public Works. If we could install a winch to the boat, we might be able to control our rate of descent, even be pulled back if it became necessary. And maybe they can arrange to widen the outlet so that it would be possible for us to exit more easily."

She stared at him with wide eyes. "You're serious. How would you explain it to them? What we were doing, I mean?"

He smiled. "One of the small perks associated with being a member of Scotland Yard is that people don't often question

your motives. They just assume you're involved in an investigation and leave it at that."

Despite her lingering horror of that black, watery nightmare,
she felt herself being drawn in by the plan. It might be the only
way to find out what had happened to her—what she had seen.
She realized she was at the point of being willing to do almost
anything to figure that out.

"Could we really do it?" she asked, her eyes sparkling.

"It will take a few days to get everything organized. But the
answer is yes."

Without thinking, she reached out and squeezed his hand.
He tensed and then relaxed, smiling at her with those big
brown eyes.

21

Norway — 1944

Gunnar gave a final wave to Thor Heyerman, then watched as the diminutive fishing boat disappeared into the fog.

They settled themselves into a deep draw where they would spend the day out of sight from any passersby or planes, even though either of those was unlikely. A sentry was posted on a bluff under an overhang. Natasha moved down the slope from the men and sat on a mossy bit of grass. Osbourne laid his map on a flat rock and consulted his compass. "It's that way," he said, pointing. "About half a dozen miles by my calculations. If we leave at dusk, we should reach the base in two to three hours, depending on the terrain."

"Not much dusk in this neck of the woods," said Gunnar. "And your estimate may be optimistic. This is rough country, with deep fjords and rugged headlands. We might stumble on a road, but I wouldn't count on it. In any case, we'd have to avoid it. Not too many people live around these parts. Once with my father when I was a boy, I put in at one of these lonely bays to make repairs. Took us three days and we never saw a soul, even though I went hiking for miles in every direction."

"What on earth did you live on?" asked Natasha.

He gave her a look. "We were a fishing boat and we were near loaded. We could have survived for a year."

The day passed slowly. The only sign of life was a small plane that passed to the north about mid-afternoon, too far

away to be a concern. Most of the men slept. Their training had taught them to take advantage of any down time.
Gunnar always found it difficult to sleep in daylight. So he
sat with Natasha.

"Do we have any idea what to expect when we get there," she
said in a low voice, not wanting to disturb the others.

He shrugged. "No. But my sense is the base won't be terribly
extensive. We're about as far off the beaten track as you can get.
Bringing anything into this place would require enormous effort.
You'd need to construct roads, probably a rail line too, and some
source of power would have to be established. My guess is they'll
rely on the area's remoteness for security. At least that's our hope."

She looked uneasy. "You're probably right, but after the sinking of their patrol boat, they have to know we're here." She
brought her legs up and leaned forward, hugging her knees.
"You know, this is my first real field assignment, Gunnar. I hope
I don't panic and do something stupid."

He wanted to put his arm around her but knew it would be
the wrong thing to do. This was the way she wanted it. At least
for now.

"To begin with, this will not be your first action. That came
when we attacked the patrol boat. And I saw you firing your
pistol. You weren't curled up in a corner somewhere."

She smiled weakly. "Thanks. I don't know what came over me.
I just sort of reacted without thinking."

"They spend many months training men like Osbourne and
the others to do just that, especially when something unexpected comes up. You'll be OK."

She changed the subject abruptly. "It's beautiful here, in a
bleak sort of way, but I don't think I could get used to the lack
of darkness."

"It's not as bleak as it seems to outsiders. Or maybe . . . to people about to risk their lives. The coast tends to be stark, with

3,000-foot-high mountains rising straight from the sea, but there are also forested valleys, lush river banks and small farms. It's the world of the midnight sun, of northern lights, Laplanders and reindeer." He smiled. "It's also the land of insomnia. With round the clock daylight, people simply forget to go to bed. I've never gotten into a regular sleep schedule here and it's my home. I sleep better in London."

"How on earth are we going to sneak up on the base and destroy it without the cover of darkness?"

"There are compensating factors. The light can play tricks up here. Displays of the aurora can last for hours at a time and it distorts what people think they see. Also, workers and soldiers get distracted when their sleep rhythms are upset. That will all play to our advantage." He stared at the overcast sky. "We might even get lucky and have a snowstorm. That would give us some real cover."

"You make it sound like a walk in the park."

"No. I don't believe that at all. I think some of us will be dead twenty-four hours from now."

She leaned into him, and he felt his arm go around her. They sat together, neither speaking.

There was no darkness, but the sun moved lower in the sky and visibility took on a sort of twilight quality. It was the best they could hope for.

About nine o'clock in the evening, Osbourne roused himself. "Time to go," he said.

There was little cover other than rocks and the occasional tree or clump of brush. But the major's men made the best of what they had, keeping to the shadows with uncanny efficiency.

They made good time, and as they crept up a final ridgeline that overlooked the base, a few snowflakes began to fall.

"There's a bit of bloody good luck," Osbourne said. "A blizzard would be just the ticket." He and Gunnar lay stretched out on the barren rocks, studying the base through binoculars.

The camp was more elaborate than Gunnar had expected. It covered perhaps four acres and consisted of half a dozen buildings surrounded by a ten-foot barbed wire fence. There was a watch tower, but he could only see two sentries patrolling the outside of the fence. The entire place smacked of utter isolation, and he doubted the sentries would be terribly alert. On the other hand, if an alarm had been raised due to their battle with the patrol boat, the sleepy demeanor of the base might be an elaborate ruse.

At the far end of the compound was a gate that ran across a rail line that then disappeared into the hills. The track led into a long, low building, then out the other end to a circular turnaround for the engine. Nearer to them was a launch test pad with a single rocket already in place.

Gunnar lowered his binoculars. "Our mission is not just to destroy the base," he said to Osbourne, "but also to learn how far advanced their program is and precisely what sort of biological agent they're using. As much as I'd prefer that your men go in guns blazing and take the bad guys out, Natasha and I need to get inside their laboratory somehow."

The major nodded. "Understood. I have a diversion in mind. Two of my men will circle the camp and retreat half a mile or so, where they'll set off a couple of small explosions and engage in some gunfire. That should make the camp security nervous enough to send out a patrol to see what's going on. It will also concentrate the sentries and the men in the tower on the far side of camp." He took another study of the compound.

"The question is where do you concentrate your search? See those two long buildings near the far fence? I'd bet those are sleeping quarters for the scientists and guards. The building with the track and the smaller one next to it are obviously a warehouse and unloading area. That leaves the three buildings near the launch pad. My guess is those are the laboratories and test buildings."

"So how do we get in?"

"Once the diversion begins and the guards move to the far side of the compound, my men will cut an opening in the fence and move to the target buildings. With luck, there will be no one but scientists inside and we can secure them without firing a shot. Then you and Natasha can do your investigations. I'd guess you'll have at least thirty minutes from the time the diversionary explosions start. It should take that long for the camp commander to figure out what's going on, organize a patrol and get to the site of the disturbance and back again."

"What about your men who set off the commotion—won't they be exposed?"

"They'll fire their weapons to get people's attention, set two explosions to go off on a ten minute delay, then hightail it back here to prepare to offer cover fire if we need it once we're ready to leave."

It was a simple enough plan and might even work, Gunnar thought, with one possible problem.

"Suppose there *are* guards remaining in the buildings we target and your men have to shoot them. It will alert everyone that something's going on inside the compound."

"It's a risk," said Osbourne. "There's no guarantees. If that happens, then we'll have a real firefight on our hands. But given the size of this place, I'd be surprised if there are more than fifteen or twenty guards. And they won't be as well trained as my men; that I *can* guarantee you. Hitler's got his best soldiers at the front. We can handle this lot."

Gunnar hoped the major's confidence was justified. But he couldn't think of anything to add to the plan. They retreated down the ridge and the major gave instructions to his men. The two selected for diversionary action loaded up and headed out, giving the camp a wide berth. The rest of the party slipped silently over the ridgeline, keeping well hidden, and reached a point less than thirty yards from the outer fence. Here they would wait.

Gunnar huddled with Natasha and checked his watch repeatedly. "You think thirty minutes will be enough time?" he asked.

"You mean can I search three buildings, locate and identify any biologicals, secure them to take with us or destroy them in that time? I'd say the odds aren't particularly good."

"Well, we may have to enlist one or more of the scientists to speed things along." He stared at her. "It could mean some unpleasant tactics."

She met his eyes squarely. "There's nothing more *unpleasant* than plotting to kill thousands of innocent people in the most horrible way imaginable. Anyone willing to engage in such activity—even with the sort of detached, intellectual attitude common among some scientists—will get no sympathy from me."

Her face showed she meant it.

"Get ready," said Osbourne. "The diversion will begin any minute. Once it starts, we'll watch to see what movements occur in the camp, then move out quickly, cut the wire and push through to the buildings. There are nine of us, three for each structure. I'll stay with you and Natasha. We'll take the closest building to the fence, then proceed to the others if we don't find what we're looking for. Remember," the major took in all of his men, "if you encounter any resistance, attempt to dispatch it without firearms, if at all possible." He gave them a casual salute. "Good luck!"

A moment later, Natasha and Gunnar both jumped as the first gunfire split the northern silence. It continued for almost a minute, nearly continuous machine gun blasts, as though a fierce firefight had broken out. Then there was a moment of silence, followed by the first blast. Gunnar had to admit, if he were one of the guards below, he'd be running right now toward the far end of the camp.

Sure enough, they watched as the sleepy camp burst into life. Soldiers erupted from every building, racing toward the commotion. The floodlight in the tower came on and was pointed in the direction of the supposed firefight. In the perpetual twilight it hardly made a difference. Gunnar counted only a dozen soldiers. Maybe the camp was more lightly guarded than they had supposed. They wouldn't know, however, if any had stayed behind until they breached the buildings.

They could hear commands being shouted in German below. Then Osbourne said, "Let's go!" and they were off, running crouched over to the fence line. It wasn't until this moment that Gunnar wondered whether there might be any mines around the camp. But it was too late to worry about that.

The nine attackers fell to the ground beside the fence. Two of the major's men produced wire cutters and in less than a minute they were inside the compound. Gunnar watched as the men split up—three to each building—and disappeared inside.

Then he, Natasha and Major Osbourne were inside the first building. The doors had not been locked, and they stood inside the entrance, which contained a small foyer and an office. There was no one around. Natasha pushed open a door leading out of the office and found what appeared to be a repair shop of some sort. Electronic equipment and hardware were everywhere. Pieces of what looked like rocket parts were lined up for assembly. Another small, glassed-in room, was filled with blueprints and schematics. Natasha went through them quickly, then shook her head.

"It's all mechanicals," she said. "Stuff to assemble and make the rockets work. The payload—the biologicals—must be in another building."

Osbourne swore. It was never easy. He removed a bundle of plastic explosives from his pack and quickly set a long fuse.

"All right," he said. "Come on." He retreated to the office and out the door. They would have to run across twenty open feet to reach the second building.

One by one, they crossed the space and burst inside. They found Osbourne's soldiers holding half a dozen bewildered looking men at gunpoint.

"The building's secure, major," said one of the men. "It appears to be a laboratory. All kinds of equipment, microscopes, test tubes, reactive agents and refrigerated compartments."

Natasha went up to one of the men being held. He was in his fifties, a heavy-set fellow with an incongruously thin, neatly cut goatee, the only hair on his bald head. She spoke to him urgently in rapid German. When he shook his head, she turned to Osbourne. "He refuses to talk, major."

Osbourne moved forward. They had no time to waste on this. He took out a knife and held it in front of the man. "Tell him he has three seconds to reply."

No translation was necessary as the man shook his head no. Without hesitation, Osbourne thrust the blade into the bald man's chest. He fell to the floor without a sound.

"Ask another one," said the major.

This time, there was no hesitation. A younger man in his thirties, nervous and sweating profusely, began to babble the moment Natasha looked at him. He quickly led the way into the laboratory, opened a refrigerator and pointed to several glass vials.

Natasha put her gun down, scooped up one of the containers and took it over to a microscope, where she prepared to open it to place some of the contents on a slide. But the nervous, young man grabbed her arm and shook his head violently.

"Is it in a dangerous form?" she asked him.

He nodded, already backing away from the work area. "Show me the latest reports on this substance," she said.

The man quickly led her to a filing cabinet and took out several folders. Natasha sat and began to work her way through them, her face growing longer by the minute.

Osbourne stood at a window, looking outside. "We're using up a lot of time," he said to no one in particular.

"What is it?" Gunnar asked Natasha.

"It's complex," she said. "These reports are from Dr. Alexis Carrel. I know of his work. He won the Nobel Prize in 1912 for devising surgical techniques to cut and connect blood vessels. He performed the first primitive coronary artery bypass surgery on a dog before the First World War and later worked with Charles Lindbergh. They were both interested in eugenics and the perfection of the species. I remember reading about one of Carrel's experiments at the Rockefeller Institute in New York. He bred a large colony of mice to create 'heroic' supermice— very large, very fit and very savage."

"Well, what the hell is he doing here?"

"I don't know. He disappeared from sight early in the war. He'd been forced out at the Rockefeller Institute and supposedly returned to Paris where he collaborated with the Vichy government. There's something else here. See this notation. It's on many of the pages."

Gunnar leaned over and stared at the letters. "Look like initials," he said.

"Yes. Perhaps one of the scientists working with Carrel. You know, I don't think Carrel, for all his faults, would necessarily work on such a project unless . . . "

"What?"

"Unless he was forced. These initials occur all through the work, as though it's another scientist checking on the work, overseeing it."

"Someone else was in charge?"

"Possibly." She read as rapidly as she could. The notes were in longhand and difficult to decipher. "He keeps referring to the agent in these vials as the 'Sweat.' I don't know what that means. I've never heard of it. But apparently he had great respect for it—for the care they needed to take. It looks like they were tinkering with it somehow, combining it with something else, trying to make it even more lethal." She rifled through another notebook. "They've done a lot of work with rodents here . . . "

She read for several more minutes. Osbourne looked ready to burst with impatience. Finally, she looked up, something indiscernible in her eyes. "I think Carrel or the people who controlled him were attempting to combine his early experiments with supermice with this other agent, the thing they call the 'Sweat.' To create some sort of extremely effective mode for transmission of the disease."

She stood up. "Gunnar, this could be incredibly lethal. There's no way we should take it with us. We may be in danger just by being here."

"What do you recommend?"

She looked at Major Osbourne. "Blow it up. All of it, in as fierce a conflagration as you can muster."

"All right," Osbourne said, with obvious relief. "Blowing up stuff is what we do best. You men," he said, "take the other buildings and set your charges. Spread any accelerants you can find before you leave; gasoline, lab supplies . . . anything."

The men grabbed their packs and left instantly. Osbourne began to set his own charges, at the same time knocking over shelves of various lab supplies onto the floor, though he was careful not to disturb the lethal vials Natasha had been handling.

For her part, Natasha gathered the notebooks that would be crucial back in London for deciphering the agent being used and to develop an antidote, if possible.

"What about our friends here?" asked Gunnar, who had taken over holding a gun on the scientists.

"Soon as I'm ready, let them go. Once the charges go up, we don't need to worry about being quiet anymore."

Gunnar looked out the window. The compound appeared deserted, but just as he turned away, he caught a flash of movement. His mouth fell open as soldiers appeared, running between buildings. There were a lot of them, more than just the guards. Had the whole thing been a trap after all?

In a steely voice, he said, "You about ready, major?"

Osbourne looked at him questioningly, but nodded. "All set."

Gunnar said to Natasha, "Tell these fellows that I'm going to open the door and they are to run as fast as they can away from the building. Make sure you tell them that if they don't run fast enough, I'll shoot them."

Natasha looked puzzled but translated the message.

Then Gunnar opened the door and let the men go. As instructed, they ran like hell. All but one. The nervous young man who had spilled the beans to Natasha slammed the door behind his comrades and turned to face them, hands upraised. In perfect English, he said. "Please. Do not kill me. I know what will happen to the others."

Gunnar kept his gun pointed at the man. "Set a two-minute fuse, major. We've got company. Lots of it." Just then they heard cries and heavy machine gun fire. Natasha peered out the window in time to see the scientists being shot down by the soldiers.

"We're going out the back door," said Gunnar. "Now!"

Osbourne lit his fuse and then led the way. Gunnar shoved the last scientist ahead of him, then turned back suddenly, long enough to swing the door the scientists had gone out wide open. Inviting.

Then they were out and running for the fence. The major's other men were already there, spread out, waiting for them with guns ready. In a moment, they were through the fence and running back into the protective rocks of the ridge.

Natasha looked back once they had taken shelter in time to see half a dozen soldiers burst through the laboratory doors. They were inside no more than a few seconds before the building went up in a terrifying blast of smoke and flames. Almost at once, the other buildings followed suit until half the camp was boiling with thick, sooty smoke and flames.

They could see other soldiers now. Gunnar estimated as many as fifty, but they were no longer interested in whoever had just penetrated their defenses. With buildings exploding on all sides, they fled, panic stricken, in all directions. Major Osbourne and his men, including the two who had returned from creating the diversion, fired indiscriminately at the Germans.

Natasha put a hand on Gunnar's shoulder. "Is it necessary to kill them all?" she asked. "We've achieved our goal."

It was Osbourne who answered. "This was a setup. Those fifty soldiers were hiding somewhere close by, waiting for us. Any we don't kill now will be coming after us."

Then the launch pad and rocket went up, apparently set off by the heat of the other explosions. The rocket actually blasted into the sky, turning in corkscrews of motion, trailing a streamer of vapor before it hurtled into the hard Norwegian coastline and exploded.

"All right," Osbourne said, after the last visible soldiers had either been shot or taken cover from the withering fire. "Our work's done. Let's get the hell out of here."

"What about him?" asked one of his men, pointing at the still visibly shaking scientist. "He'll slow us down."

"He's a bloody scientist who tried to kill thousands of innocent people," said another. He raised his gun at the man. "I'll kill him where he stands."

The terrified fellow raised his hands. "Wait," he said in a shaky voice. "I can tell you something . . . You got here too late."

22

"Boss? I'm at the morgue. You better get down here."

Harry refused to say anything more on the phone. Sherwood found him in the viewing room, watching a forensic assistant perform an autopsy on the body of a woman. She had long, stringy, blonde hair.

Harry nodded at the body as Sherwood came in. "Our young friend from the tunnel," he said. "The one who showed us the room of coffins."

Sherwood leaned forward, remembering when those locks had rested against his hand. What a hard life and what a waste of one so young. He felt angry . . . and very tired. "What happened to her?"

"She was shot. Single round, nine millimeter, in the back of the head. Like an execution." He tapped the side of his head. "At least she won't have to argue with her demons anymore."

"Where was she found?"

"Alley off Coventry Street, not far from Leicester Square. She was in a dumpster. Trash man thought he saw a pretty good coat in the bin and went to look before he attached it to the hydraulic lift. The coat had a body in it. If he hadn't wanted that coat, we might never have found her."

Sherwood stared at the sad creature in front of them. Such a harmless character. Why would anyone want to kill her? She had nothing of value.

"Was she sexually assaulted?"

"Preliminary says no," said Harry. "She still had all those layers of clothes on. Whoever it was didn't even want that coat. I got my own idea."

"What?"

"Way I see it, the only thing of value she had was information. She knew about those bodies down there."

Sherwood was silent for over a minute. "Those bones were removed by officials from the prime minister's office, Harry. Do you know what you're suggesting?"

Following the removal of papers from Sherwood's office and Trimm's sneering comment that they had removed *all of the bones*, Harry had gone back to look. Sure enough, the secret room with the coffins had been swept clean.

"What I'm suggesting is that someone killed our sweetheart here just to clean up a loose end. This thing stinks of a cover-up, boss."

Harry's words rang in Sherwood's head throughout the day. Everything seemed to go back to the bodies, the first two that had been positively dated back to the end of World War II. It seemed like a good place to start.

He used his ID to swipe his entrance into the Yard's research library. He already knew that records more than sixty years old were not kept here. He was looking for Darryl Spencer, chief research assistant.

"Hi Darryl, how's your soccer champ?" he asked.

Spencer was a research packrat. He had pale skin from too little time in the sun, oversized glasses and always wore the same white shirt and baggy pants. Sherwood figured he must have a dozen sets of the same outfit. If not for his twelve-year-old son—who kept him busier than the wife who'd left him ever did—Darryl would rarely leave his hallowed stacks.

"He still talks about that signed ball you gave him last year, inspector. David Beckham! Gawd! How you ever got that I don't know, but it's one of Ritchie's prized possessions."

"Truth is: I got it before anyone knew who Beckham was. He used to play pickup with a few of us at Coram's Fields years ago. Check out the other signatures on the ball, you'll find a bunch of unknown has-beens like yours truly. Uh . . . I wanted to ask about the records concerning unsolved cases dating back to the war. Where are they kept now?"

"In the annex 'cross town," replied Darryl without hesitation. "We ran out of room here back in the '80s. They took thousands of evidence boxes and files and threw them in there. Not much organization to it, either. Never had the funding to do a proper job. If you're going to look for something, you better take me with you. I might be able to point you in the right direction at least."

"That would be terrific, Darryl. When could you do it?"

He looked at the wall clock. "Almost four o'clock. I can slip out a bit early if you'd like."

It took nearly an hour to drive to the annex, a plain, boxlike structure near Holborn. London was awash with late-September tourists clogging the streets. Most of them had that tired, dragged out look of people who'd been fighting the rain for a week. Sherwood wondered what most of them would think of the great city if they knew about the piles of dead rats and human bones just beneath their feet. Inside, a clerk met them and nodded to Darryl.

"Bernard here is the organizer-in-chief, inspector," Darryl said. "How's the cataloguing going, Bernie?"

"I figger 'nother thirty years and I'll have a handle on't," said the wizened little man, who looked like he'd be twenty years in the grave by then. "That is if they ever stop sending more over."

He led them into a long room filled floor to ceiling with shelves crammed with evidence boxes and files. Sherwood had to admit, there appeared to be little organization other than an occasional alphabetical letter on the shelves. The rooms smelled stale, like the odor you get from the spine of a fifty-year-old book.

He sighed and took off his coat. "You got time to give me a hand, Darryl?"

"Hell, I can stay all night if you want. Ritchie's got an overnight with a friend. You order pizza and we'll see what's what."

"Thanks. I owe you."

"Well, we'll see . . . any idea what we're looking for?"

"Start with missing or unidentified from the war years. We had two bodies found near Piccadilly Tube Station—above it actually. Women. I want to know how they got there and what killed them. If we can ID them, that would be a start."

Darryl opened the boxes and went through them, pulling those files that indicated unsolved deaths or missing persons. He stacked them beside Sherwood, who sat at a long table going through them as quickly as possible, looking for any similarities to his two bodies and the location where they had been found. Missing persons reports filed by relatives could contain clues that might help ID the women. He kept an eye out for any instances of two women reported missing at the same time, though he had no way of knowing if the bodies had met their fates simultaneously. He no longer had the results of his own investigation—which had been taken by Trimm—but he remembered enough details to make a connection, if it was there.

By ten o'clock, they had plowed through a huge pile of files, along with two medium pizzas with extra cheese, pepperoni and mushrooms. Most of the material seemed to be completely ordinary, unsolved cases. During the war, there wasn't a lot of time to investigate murders or unexplained deaths. And there were a lot of them. Thousands of people were killed in the Blitz.

Bernie came in, said it was time to close up, but that if they wanted, they could stay and keep working. He showed them how to lock up when they left.

"Fun, in't?" he said. "Like finding a bleedin' needle in a bleedin' haystack. I get to do this stuff all the time. As if I don't have enough to do, the bleedin' prime minister's office sent over another truckload just yesterday."

Sherwood stopped what he was doing. "What's the PM's office doing sending records to Scotland Yard? Shouldn't they go to the Public Records Office?"

"Beats me. Good way to bury stuff you don't want no one diggin' into'd be my guess. The stuff was completely undocumented. No record sheets. Classification undetermined. Probably political—you know—they din't dare destroy it but want it lost. Wouldn't be the first time. This's as good a final resting place as you'll find."

"Show me," said Sherwood.

They followed Bernie to a warehouse-like receiving area, where there were oversize garage doors and mounds of boxes laid out, roughly organized into separate piles. Darryl indicated several score boxes in a corner.

"That's the new lot from the PM's office. Most of it from the '40s. Men who brought it in said to just store it and not worry 'bout it. How d'ya like that? Not worry 'bout it? Like I'm just some sort of bleedin' caretaker here." He took out a handkerchief and blew his nose loudly. "My job's to be able to put my hand on somethin' when some bloke like you needs it. But nobody cares 'bout my troubles."

Sherwood felt his heart skip a beat. "That's the period we're looking at. Mind if we take a gander at the new stuff?"

"Help yourself. They din't put no restrictions on it. Course, why would they? Nobody knows it's bloody here. Hope you got nothin' better to do for a few days."

Darryl looked skeptically at Sherwood after Bernie left. "What's this lot from the PM's office going to have to do with old Scotland Yard cases?"

"A lot of what the Yard did during the war was overseen by the home secretary and, indirectly, by the prime minister," Sherwood said. "The war mixed up a lot of lines of authority. It just might be that if something turned up no one wanted anything to do with, it might have got shunted aside or buried on purpose."

"So—what? We're back to looking for the bodies of your two young women?"

"It's a start—a lot of this stuff won't be relevant. Just padding to hide something more serious . . . "

Sherwood's cell phone rang. He picked it up, listened for a moment and then swore. "All right I'll be there as soon as I can." He looked at Darryl. "We've got thousands of rats coming out of Holborn Station, if you can believe that. Scaring the living shit out of the tourists. I've got to go. Can you keep on this for a while?"

Darryl nodded. "Rats, huh? Never a dull moment working for the Yard."

23

Holborn Station was just around the corner and Sherwood knew something unpleasant was happening the moment he stepped out of the annex. He could hear cries and saw people running. When he turned the corner, there were police units everywhere, with men standing around in riot gear holding nets, looking ridiculous and useless.

The streets were alive with rats running in every direction. It was hard to know for sure who was more frightened: the people or the rats. He saw Harry standing beside two officers holding a net. A very large rat ran over his partner's feet and Harry jumped about a yard in the air, cursing a blue streak.

"What on earth are you doing, Harry?"

"Damned if I know! How the hell do you catch a million fucking rats? We can't shoot 'em here on the street. Too many civilians around. Look at them. It's like they're panic stricken, running every which way, right on top of one another. Makes a guy wonder, what are they running from?"

It was an incredible sight, Sherwood had to admit. There were rats climbing up telephone poles, jumping onto gutters and roofs, snaking under parked cars. Many were ferociously fighting other rats, and the squeals and howls of pain when one was bitten echoed through the streets.

The entire neighborhood was in an uproar. Residents stared out their windows in disbelief. Fire trucks arrived and firemen began using hoses to try to contain the outbreak. But there was nowhere to corral the rodents, so the high-pressure hoses simply gushed through the streets, while rats that didn't move quickly enough were picked up and sent flying through the air. It was the most bizarre scene he had witnessed in his nearly twenty years on the streets of London.

"Come on. Let's see where they're coming from." He headed for the Holborn subway entrance.

"We're not going down there?"

"You got a better idea, sergeant?"

"Can we at least take some men with us?" Harry pleaded.

Sherwood glanced at the mayhem all around them. "They're going to need every man on the streets. You!" He yelled at the men who had been holding nets and staring wide-eyed at the chaos. "Block off this street and get rid of the civilians. Tell those people inside to close their windows and doors. And call Animal Health. Tell them to get their people down here. Maybe they'll have some idea how to handle this."

Then he grabbed Harry by the arm and pulled him toward the subway entrance, where hundreds of rats continued to emerge.

"Hang on," said Harry. He paused at his car, which was pulled up with two wheels on the sidewalk, and grabbed a torch. Holborn station had its lights on, but they might need it if they went onto the tracks.

They inched their way down the steps, sidestepping rats or just kicking them out of the way. Harry shuddered. "They don't pay me enough for this crap."

The rodents were large and aggressive, but they seemed more bent on getting out of the underground than attacking them.

When they reached track level, the numbers finally began to diminish and they watched as a few stragglers emerged from the tunnels.

"It's like something's chased every rat in London out through these tunnels," Harry said.

"I doubt that," said Sherwood. "There're a lot of rats here, for sure, but London's got tens of millions of rats. We're seeing only a very small fraction. But I have to agree that something's spooking them. Rats avoid light, especially sunlight. They're sensitive to vitamin D, which can kill them. I'm pretty sure they would avoid the bright lights of central London too, unless something forced them up."

Harry stared at him. "How the bloody hell do you know all that?"

"I've been reading up on them. Here, give me your torch. Let's check down this tunnel a ways."

"Subways are still running, you know."

"We'll be able to get back if a train comes. I just want to see where these critters are coming from."

They worked their way thirty yards into the tunnel, where Sherwood paused and shone his light into a sub-tunnel entrance. There were still rats coming out the opening, and it appeared to be the source.

"Whatever's panicking them must be down there," he said.

Harry looked at him, eyes almost pleading. No way did he want to go down into that hole.

"Look. You can stay here in the dark or come with me," said Sherwood. Without waiting for an answer, he started to climb down to the sub-tunnel.

The tunnel was similar to the one where they had first found the bodies. It was narrow, damp, crudely cut and ran straight off until the light dimmed.

"Look at that," said Harry.

There were no more live rats. But the sub-tunnel contained numerous bodies of dead rodents, most of them seemingly chewed on and a few moving about slowly and desperately.

"Friggin' cannibals," Harry said. "Eating their own."

"I don't know," Sherwood replied. He stared down the tunnel where something was moving at the edge of their light. "What's that?"

They stared into the darkness. Something was there, hunched over. They could hear crunching sounds. Whatever it was, it was eating. They watched as it shuffled forward a few feet, then grabbed one of the dead rats and began to gnaw. The creature was several times the size of the dead rats, but they couldn't make out its features.

"Mother of God," said Harry. "What *is* that?" He crouched down slowly, picked up a stone and hurled it at the thing, striking it head on.

There was a ferocious hissing sound and then the creature headed straight for them at unbelievable speed.

Harry stumbled backwards, hitting Sherwood and making him drop the light, which went out. Sherwood managed to locate it, pick it up and turn it on the animal just as it reached them. He barely had time to thrust the lantern at the thing as it leaped into the air. There was a crunching sound as the creature hit the light, then fell back to the ground and for an instant they saw something unbelievably ferocious literally chew the light to bits before they were plunged once again into darkness.

They stood, silent and unmoving, and completely stunned, as they listened to the lantern being eaten.

"Don't move or make a sound," Sherwood whispered.

It was all they could do. The blackness was complete, and they couldn't retrace their steps without making a great deal of noise as they stumbled blindly back toward the sub-tunnel entrance.

For what seemed an eternity—but was probably less than a minute—they heard the animal moving about just a few feet from them. The sounds it made were the most awful either man had ever heard. A series of sucking, squelching, wheezing and chomping noises, punctuated by what could only be described as a sort of horrible lip smacking.

Then the noises retreated back down the tunnel and gradually disappeared.

"I think it's gone," Sherwood said. "Let's get back to the main tunnel."

"What the hell *was* that, boss?"

Sherwood shook his head, then realized Harry couldn't see him. "I don't know, sergeant. It sure as hell wasn't like any rat I've ever seen. It sounded something like a rat, but it was way too big. And aggressive, coming at us like that. I've never known a rat to do anything but run away from humans."

When they reached the entrance to Holborn Station, they found the street had settled down somewhat. The number of rats had diminished, not from the efforts of the police and fire-men but simply because the creatures had evidently dispersed into the neighborhood.

Sherwood corralled several men and told them to close the Holborn Station doors and allow no one to go in. Whatever they had just seen had to be contained. That was the only thing he was sure of anymore.

24

Norway — 1944

They gathered in a rocky defile several miles from the camp. Osbourne had insisted they put as much distance as possible between them and the scene of the attack. Once word got out, all hell would break loose. There had been no chance for Gunnar to follow up on questioning their captive. When the major finally allowed a rest, Gunnar turned at once to the German.

"All right, we're listening," he said.

The scientist with the suddenly excellent English spoke eagerly. "The first experimental rocket—the armed V-2 with the new biological payload—is on its way to Germany right now by rail, where it will be fired on London."

Osbourne, Gunnar and Natasha exchanged dumbfounded looks. If true, this was their worst nightmare.

"The impression I got from reading Carrel's notes," said Natasha, "was that they weren't ready for that yet. There were still too many unknowns."

The young scientist nodded. "Yes . . . Carrel himself thought it was a big mistake to send the substance back to Germany in such an unstable form. But he was not in control. The orders came straight from the führer." He shrugged. "The war goes badly."

Gunnar swore. All their efforts had been for nothing.

"When was this shipment made?" asked Osbourne.

"Two days ago," the man replied.

Gunnar realized with disgust that the weather delay in northern Scotland had cost them their prize. He moved away from the scientist to consult with Osbourne and Natasha. "We have to go after it," he said in a low voice. "It will take a week for the rocket to get to Oslo by rail. Then they'll have to load it on a ship to take to the Fatherland. We still have time."

Osbourne looked doubtful. "They've got a two-day head start. Only way we can beat it to Oslo is by plane. You got a Messerschmitt hidden away somewhere, commander?"

"We'll have to find one. Churchill's orders were to take whatever steps are necessary to stop this threat. That's exactly what I intend to do." He stared hard at the major. "We need to split up our forces."

"What do you have in mind?"

"Your men will return to England via boat, however they can manage. They'll take the notebooks and our scientist friend here. You, Natasha and I will find a plane and continue this mission."

Osbourne stared at his feet. "Even if we can find a plane, we don't have any idea where the train is, commander. With a two-day head start, it would be easier to find a dory in a shipyard."

"I don't think so. I'm familiar with the Norwegian rail system. The most direct route if you intend to move something to Germany is through Oslo. Rail traffic all goes there for transshipment to the continent. If we get to Oslo first, all we have to do is wait for the rocket to come through. And who knows? Maybe we'll get lucky and spot the thing en route if we follow the main rail line south."

"Still a long shot, if you ask me. But you're in charge, commander. I'll tell my soldiers."

The major's men were not happy at being left out, sent home babysitting a handful of notebooks and a German scientist most of them would gladly have shot. But they were professionals and accepted their orders.

Gunnar thought there might be another benefit from splitting up. Once the remaining, disoriented German soldiers in the camp regrouped, they would likely search for the British commandos along the coast. That would free the three of them to escape inland by plane if—a very big if—they could locate an aircraft.

Goodbyes were said quickly. Gunnar shook hands with all the soldiers, wished them luck and stressed the importance of getting the notebooks back to London. If they failed to locate the rocket, those notebooks, along with whatever intelligence could be extracted from the scientist, would be Churchill's best chance to help London survive the treacherous attack.

Natasha went to each of the soldiers and thanked them personally on behalf of the prime minister for their service. She gave each a kiss on the lips and told them to take it back to their sweethearts and expand upon it. They all laughed heartily at that.

"One last thing," said Gunnar. He went over to their German captive and drew his pistol. The man's eyes grew wide. "You've got one chance to get this right. Understand? How can we identify the train carrying the rocket?"

The man was frightened, but he drew himself up. "You will not believe me, but I have never liked this project. I am just a scientist ordered to serve my country at the point of a gun. But I do not wish to kill innocent women and children. I did not think the research would be finished before the war ended. As to the train, I can tell you only that they intended to follow the main line to Oslo. The fastest route, per the führer's orders. The rocket is too large to fit in a box car. It will be on an open flatbed, though covered. That is what you must look for. Also, there is a red cross painted on the boxcars that bracket the flatbed. That is so enemy bombers will not be tempted to strike."

Gunnar looked at the man speculatively.

"Something else I want to know," he said. "I've never thought it likely that a biological agent sent by explosive missile would have a chance of surviving. Is it possible?"

The scientist didn't hesitate: "Yes. This V-2 has been modified. Very innovative stuff. Of course, there is no explosive payload that might destroy the agent, but this was not considered foolproof enough. Perhaps the agent would survive and be spread on impact, but we could not know for certain. So the rocket was made with super hardened steel over the usual thin skin, and a very unique delivery system was developed."

"What system?" asked Gunnar, knowing he wouldn't like the answer.

"The rocket is designed to come in on a lower trajectory than normal. Once its engines cut out over London, instead of plummeting to earth at full speed, parachutes will deploy to greatly reduce the impact, allowing the contents an excellent chance of survival."

Gunnar sighed deeply and waved his pistol at the man dismissively. The scientist and the major's men slipped silently into the rocks, leaving the three of them alone.

"All right, commander," said Osbourne. "Where's our bloody plane?"

"Narvik has a small airport, but it would take a couple of days just to walk there. We don't have time for that. I'm putting my bet on Finnsnes."

"What? That tiny fishing village? You must be joking."

Gunnar shook his head. "I don't think so. There has to be some way for the officer in charge of this camp, and maybe some of the scientists as well, to get in and out of here quickly. As urgent as Hitler views this project, I'm sure he'd want faster communications with Berlin than that rail line. We'll head for Finnsnes."

"God help us if you're wrong," said the major.

But in fact, they found the makeshift airport quickly. It consisted of a small, grassy field on the outskirts of Finnsnes, literally the only place big enough and flat enough to serve such a purpose. From the piles of brush and rocks pushed up along the sides of the field, it had obviously been hastily and recently constructed. It was not guarded, nor were there any fences. Again, the isolation of the place had given the Germans confidence that they had little to worry about.

The three of them crouched in the bushes across from a small, open hangar—the only one. In it was a lone aircraft.

"That's a Stuka," said Gunnar, with grudging admiration. "Junkers series. It's a good plane, well built. She's sunk a lot of Allied ships with the bombs she carries under her wings and fuselage." He stared at the plane. "I don't see any bombs on this one.

"Not much defensive armament and not much for speed or maneuverability. She was no match for our Hurricanes and Spitfires during the Battle of Britain. We don't want to be under attack in her, that's for sure. Looks like she has a rear 7.92mm machine gun and a couple of 37mm cannons under the wings. Think you can figure them out, major?"

"If it shoots bullets, I can figure it out."

Gunnar squinted at the plane. "The Stuka has a belly tank, you see it? It's fueled separately and then attached to the plane. We won't be able to fuel it ourselves, so let's hope it's loaded. There are also wing tanks. Those we can fuel, supposing we can find a source. Both wing and belly tanks each provide about ninety minutes of fuel. At a top speed of, say, 225 miles per hour, that won't take us too far. But we won't be going that fast."

"I wouldn't think so," said Natasha. "If the rail tracks are as poorly maintained as you say, our target is unlikely to be going much over thirty miles an hour."

Gunnar nodded. "I bet the camp commandant flies in on this. Probably a pilot himself, though he seems to be pretty casual about leaving it here unattended. They used to fit the Stuka with wind-powered sirens on the undercarriage, so when she went into a dive it would frighten the enemy. But I don't see them on this model."

They circled the hangar, searching for any activity. The place was completely deserted.

Finally, they shouldered their weapons and moved in. Gunnar climbed into the cockpit and began to study the instruments. "She's fully fueled," he said with relief. He hadn't relished seeking out petrol.

Natasha squeezed into a small seat behind the cockpit. "This will be exciting," she said. "I've never been in a fighter."

"The Stuka carries a two man crew: pilot and gunner. The extra seat you're in must have been a modification to allow space for the camp commandant. Hope you don't get airsick. She's a lightweight aircraft, and she'll bounce around a lot if we hit any weather."

Osbourne clambered into the rear gunner's seat. He swung the guns around and studied them. "Piece of cake," he yelled. "Bring 'em on."

"Let's hope not," said Gunnar. "None of us are skilled with this aircraft. We meet up with an ace who doesn't like our look, I'd say we're toast. Churchill will have put his money on the wrong soldiers."

He wound up the 1400-horsepower engine, and they taxied out of the hangar down to the end of the grassy field. There wasn't a soul around. The nearest house was half a mile away. As he pushed the throttle forward, he wondered if they were finally going to have a bit of luck. If the aircraft went unmissed for a day or two, they might make the trip without interference. He wondered how likely that was, given the havoc they'd caused at the camp. Someone would want to get out of here quickly and make a report. On the other hand, who would want to be the one to tell Hitler that his pet project had just been destroyed?

"Not me," he said out loud as the engines roared and they began to move down the uneven field.

25

Carmen hadn't seen Sherwood in two days, though he had called her twice in that time, just to talk. More and more she found she enjoyed talking to him. He was intense about his work, like her, but he had a sense of humor and seemed genuinely interested in what she had to say.

He'd been busy arranging their underground boat ride. Though the prospect frightened her, she felt her nightmares about the river would never go away until the many questions about it were finally answered. She'd been afraid, until his first call, that she might have scared him away with her strange, distant and cold looks. It wouldn't have been the first time.

Dr. Jessmer suddenly appeared in her office door.

"Laurence?" she said.

"I want to show you something." He came in and closed the door behind him.

Carmen looked at the impish grin on his face. "What are you up to?"

Without saying a word, he held out his hand and deposited on her desk an emerald over an inch long.

She stared at it for a full half minute without moving. Then she picked it up and turned it over in her hand. It was beautifully cut, the facets shining brightly.

"This is the biggest emerald I've ever seen," she said. "As big as anything in the Crown Jewels."

"Everything's relative, dear girl. They discovered a 12,000-pound emerald in Columbia recently. Course, it'd be a bitch to cut."

"Where did you get it?"

"You wouldn't guess in a thousand years, so I'm going to tell you."

She looked at him, waiting. She knew from past experience that when Laurence had something momentous to expound, there was always a buildup. Today was to be no exception.

"We've already examined this in depth. The craftsmanship of the cutting is exquisite and quite unique. There really is only one period where emeralds of this size and quality were found and that were cut in such a manner."

"And that would be?"

"The ancient Aztec Empire. In the 1700s, the descendants of Cortez sent a Spanish galleon to Queen Isabella that contained a hundred chests of emeralds, gold and jade death masks of the Aztec Emperors. There were golden idols, mysterious crystal skulls and instruments of human sacrifice. The ship was lost at sea. In my own studies, I have found clues . . . tantalizing ones . . . that there may have been much earlier galleons from the New World, dating to the early 1500s."

She looked at the emerald, then back at Dr. Jessmer. "I know you're going to tell me where you got it sometime this week, right?"

"Ahem, I was just getting to that. The Ministry of Health has been conducting autopsies on some of the dead rats, trying to determine what may have caused their aberrant behavior." He reached out and took the emerald from her. "This little beauty was found in the gut of one of the autopsied rats."

"In the gut . . . ?"

"Amazing really, but rats will eat anything, especially if it's shiny, though I suspect this gem may have actually caused the rodent's demise. Simonson asked for my opinion of it, then said it might as well go into the museum's collection. Which is why I have it."

"But if this was eaten by a rat recently . . . it must have been located somewhere under London, unless the creature managed to burrow into a Tiffany's showroom."

"I can assure you that Tiffany's has no such gem in its rather tawdry collection," he sniffed.

"So where did it come from?"

"What crossed my mind, dear girl, was your description of seeing shining things during your rather damp passage through our city's vast underground network."

Carmen gaped at him. She tried yet again to replay those fading images in her mind. Shining things, yes. But she also remembered strange figures, giants and horses . . . but always, sparkling things on the walls and ceilings.

"Do *you* think there could be something down there, Laurence?"

"I'm beginning to believe it might be a distinct possibility. Weren't you the one who told me that Dr. Trimm had been researching the underground rivers?"

"Yes, though I hardly see how that would be relevant, unless . . . "

Jessmer raised one bushy eyebrow.

Her mind raced. "Unless he knows there's some archaeological treasure down there. But if he believes that, why not announce it to the world? He would become instantly famous, something I'm quite sure he craves and believes to be his due."

"Ah, but what is fame," said Jessmer with a sad shake of his head, "compared to riches beyond one's wildest dreams?"

He left then, cradling the emerald that was headed into the British Museum's permanent collection.

Carmen felt her mind going into that strange, focused mode it sometimes entered. She recognized this trait of AS. One that could be useful on occasion.

She thought about Trimm. It had seemed to her that he always disliked her, right from their first meeting. She'd dismissed the notion as simply her inability to ferret out people's true emotions. But emotions or not, she felt she had him pegged when it came to his work. He felt unappreciated. Not quite paranoid, perhaps, but certainly closing in on it. Being dismissed from the Coram's Fields site had rubbed salt into that wound.

She got up from her desk and went round to a bank of filing cabinets. Trimm had been hired not long before she was. She realized she knew little about him other than his supposed specialty: Hadrian's Wall.

When she became administrator of museum programs for greater London, she moved into her present office, which contained personnel files on all the thousands of British Museum employees.

She opened the file drawer marked S-TU, pulled Trimm's folder out and returned to her desk. His education was impressive enough. Undergraduate studies at Cambridge, then studied abroad in Spain before returning to begin his work on Hadrian's Wall. He had published a number of monographs on the wall, as well as a surprising number of popular articles in magazines like *Archaeology* and even *National Geographic*.

She flipped back to the page on his graduate work in Spain.

November, 1986 – June, 1987 — Engaged as research assistant at the Alhambra, Granada, Spain. Extensive study of early stone architecture, including the massive outer walls, towers and ramparts of the Alcazaba, or citadel. Also research on early 16th century gem mining, pottery, amphorae and Spanish galleons.

Well, that explained where he got interested in the stone architecture that led to his professional focus on Hadrian's Wall. But the bit about gem mines was certainly interesting. She knew little about the museum's gem collection. Jewelry in general had never interested her very much. Maybe it had something to do with her unease around the topics of engagement rings, marriage and boyfriends. She was always too busy, too serious for that stuff. Now and then, she felt a little maudlin, that she might be missing something, especially when she saw the men flocking around Julia. But always work absorbed and redirected her thoughts.

She stared at the page and began to tally up. Gem mines. Spanish galleons. Trimm's research on the underground rivers of London. His secretiveness and possessiveness concerning the Coram's Fields site. Could her colleague's research have led him to evidence of some hidden treasure from the New World? But where? Beneath the city of London? Such an idea was preposterous. Impossible.

There were too many questions. But the more she mulled it over, the more convinced she became that Trimm believed there was *something* valuable down there, and he was looking for it.

Could it possibly be what she had seen when she floated down that awful river? Could she have floated past some ancient treasure trove? Her thoughts whirled at the implications. She needed to talk to someone about all of this. Julia, maybe . . . or Sherwood.

She was surprised that she thought of him so quickly. She didn't want to talk to Julia. Not at all. She wanted to talk to Sherwood.

How odd.

26

Carmen sat at a corner table of a small Thai restaurant a block north of Piccadilly. Sherwood had recommended it when she called and asked if she could talk with him.

Now he was ten minutes late and she was just beginning to consider whether she should be annoyed, when he walked in. She watched him speak to the receptionist, noting how much he had to lean over to talk to the tiny woman. Then he looked up and met her eyes. She saw sudden uncertainty in them and realized that she still had her "preparing-to-be-annoyed" look on her face. Damn! It seemed every time she met up with Sherwood, she was scowling like an old woman. I'll have to tell him about myself, she thought, or he'll give up on me.

Give up on her? What on earth was she thinking?

"Hi," Sherwood said, as he came up to the table and took off his jacket. "Sorry I'm late. It's been quite a couple of days." He hesitated. "You all right?"

She made a concentrated effort to smile. It felt terribly fake to her, but he seemed to relax.

"I'm fine, Sherwood. Thanks for coming."

"I like this restaurant," he said. "Though usually I eat alone. It's a treat to have company. Would you like a drink?"

"I'd love a martini."

He ordered two and asked for the menus, which they perused casually while they chatted.

"So—what have you been up to?" asked Carmen. "I take it you've been busy."

He proceeded to tell her about the rat outbreak at Holborn Station and about the strange creature he and Harry had encountered underground.

"That's scary, Sherwood. What do you think is going on?"

"I wish I knew. Something seems to have driven the rats crazy with fear, and I think this strange creature we encountered may play a part in it."

"What was it?"

He shrugged. "We only got a fleeting look at it. It certainly *could* have been a rat, but if so, it was the largest and most aggressive one I've ever seen. I talked to my boss the other day and he's going to see what he can pry out of 10 Downing. Someone over there knows something about all of this, but I'm not holding my breath that the home secretary, my boss's boss, is in the loop. Whatever the prime minister's interest, I suspect they are going to keep their actions as close to the vest as possible." He took a long sip of his martini. "To tell you the truth, I'd enjoy not thinking about it at all for a while."

"All right. You're on." She tried to relax her face into something approaching a non-threatening grimace. "How long have you been an inspector?"

He looked at his watch. "About three weeks. I'm supposed to get my new car tomorrow. Then it will feel official. But seriously, I've been working toward this for nearly twenty years. Started out as a constable on the beat and here I am, having worked all the way up to rat patrol."

She smiled and saw the positive effect it had on him. He answered her back with a sheepish grin of his own.

"Sherwood," she began. "There's something I want to tell you about myself . . . "

His face clouded. "Don't tell me. You're married, or seeing someone or engaged or . . . just not interested." His face had such a look of pathos that she felt her heart twang.

"No. None of those things. I just wanted to apologize for any strange looks that I may have sent your way in the past week. I have a condition called Asperger's Syndrome. Have you heard of it?"

He shook his head.

"Well, it's something that's usually diagnosed when one is a child, and there are many aspects to it, but suffice it to say that aspies—what we call ourselves—are characterized by unusual social interaction and communication skills. We sometimes display behavior, interests and activities that can be restrictive and repetitive and are sometimes abnormally intense or focused. It's a mild form of autism. When you look at me and see a bizarre expression, it's almost always because I'm thinking of something else and not you at all."

He smiled broadly. "Well thank goodness for that. I'd been thinking you just didn't like me."

"I've had to struggle with this my whole life. It's a big part of who I am, Sherwood, and I want you to know about it. All aspies have a certain degree of obsessive compulsive behavior. Did you notice what I'm wearing this evening?"

"You look lovely," he said.

"Thanks, but that's not what I meant. Everything I'm wearing is purple, from my shoes to my sweater, even my lip gloss has that tinge. When I was a child, I went from the age of twelve until I was almost sixteen before I would wear anything that wasn't purple. Since then, I've managed to branch out. But I still have moments when, unconsciously, I'll revert to character. Especially when I'm nervous. Like this evening."

He leaned forward and in a somber tone said, "I'm *crazy* about purple."

"Good. I also have trouble telling what's going on with people, specifically with their emotions. I misread them and it gets me into trouble. It's something of a triumph that I've been able to hold down this job at the museum. If you'd asked me when I was in college if I thought I'd make a good administrator, I would have laughed at you. Administrators are supposed to understand people. I've only done it through incredibly focused, hard work, which is another aspect of my problem."

"So far, I don't see it as having held you back a whole lot. You're bright, accomplished, verbal and pretty. I even see another positive aspect to it, from my point of view anyway. If it's turned off other men who might have been interested in you, I feel lucky indeed. Like I got here just in time. It won't turn me off." He hesitated. "There. I guess that's as clear as I can make it. I like you a hell of a lot, Carmen."

She blushed and looked down, then back up and met his eyes.

"I hope that's a real emotion," he said. "Because it's one I want to see more of." He leaned forward until he was just inches from her face, paused for a moment, then closed the remaining distance and kissed her.

She responded. The kiss went on. She felt his hand caress her hair and when he pulled away finally, she felt the strangest emotion ever. Utter contentment. She hadn't been kissed like that since college.

"I liked that, Sherwood," she said softly.

The rest of the meal flew by, as they drank each other in. She told him more about Asperger's. He told her about his ex-wife and how his work had been a lifeline since they split.

"That's something I can understand," said Carmen. "I've been so focused on my work these past twelve years that almost nothing else has intruded. That day Dr. Trimm came into your office, I was more surprised than you, I think, because I just never would have expected it from him. If I thought about him at all it was in simple, stock phrases . . . Hadrian's Wall scholar, secretive and reclusive, *such* an asshole!"

They both laughed.

"Trimm's simply not someone I would have thought forceful enough to do what he did that day," she continued. "If you had asked me, I would have said he'd be the last person on earth I could imagine working with the prime minister. That is incomprehensible to me. It's just part of my inability to see through people."

"From what limited exposure I've had to Trimm, I'd say you've got him pegged spot on. He's a pompous, egotistical ass with power hungry tendencies."

"Actually, Trimm is the reason I wanted to meet with you."

"Damn. I thought it was because of me."

She laughed, delighted. "When I thought I'd discovered something about Trimm, I realized the one person in the world that I wanted . . . needed . . . to talk to about it was you, Sherwood."

His eyes enveloped her. "Tell me," he said.

She proceeded to tell him about Trimm's research interests as a graduate student, about his uncommon interest lately in the underground rivers of London and about Dr. Jessmer's incredible emerald.

"The emerald was found *inside* a rat?" he asked incredulously.

She nodded. "I can only think of one explanation for Trimm's research, his attitudes and his obsessive interest in the Coram's Fields site. He believes there is something down there, something worth a lot of money."

He stared at her, thinking hard. "It makes sense, in a weird sort of way . . . except for one thing. Why would the government be involved? It stretches credulity to think Trimm would risk losing any so-called treasure by informing the authorities. He'd risk having the whole thing turned over to some government bureaucracy."

"I know. I thought of that, and it doesn't make any sense to me either. It's really why I wanted to get your input. See if maybe someone who can see through people better than I can ... someone with your professional skills ... might figure out what Trimm is up to."

He considered her words for several moments. "OK. Here's what we're going to do. We're going for a boat ride through the heart of London. Something I always like to do on a first ... make that second ... date. Though usually it's *on* the Thames, not under it."

She felt her heart race. "You've set it up?"

"I have. We'll be using a rubber raft, but it will be a good size, very stable. It will be attached to a winch set up in the sub- tunnel and manned by a couple of guys I know from the Department of Public Works. They'll be off duty and the whole thing will be unofficial. I want to keep this as quiet as possible. It will be you, me and Harry. We may not be able to go the entire distance you floated, because the cable has a set length of just under a mile. Hopefully that will be enough to get us to wherever you saw whatever you saw."

He took a sip of his drink. "But first, I'd like you to meet someone who can give us some background on the underside of London. A friend who teaches a course on the subject at King's College."

Her face showed excitement. Maybe they *would* decipher this riddle. She reached out her hand and ran her fingers lightly over the dimple in his chin. "Has anyone ever kissed you right there?" she asked.

27

Sherwood's friend from King's College was named Braidwood Humphries. His friends called him Brady, and in addition to teaching, he also led tours into historic underground London.

They met at the Green Man Pub near the corner of Oxford and Berwick Streets. After Carmen was introduced to the elderly and tweedy looking gentleman, they sat in a corner booth with large pints of stout in front of them. Humphries wore oversized, black-rimmed glasses that magnified his eyes when he opened them wide for emphasis, which he did frequently.

"Sherwood tells me you've seen a bit more of underground London than most," Brady said, taking a long swallow of lager that left a brownish rim on his upper lip, which he fastidiously wiped with his napkin. "Frankly, I was fascinated to hear of your ravine journey. It makes you a most remarkable woman. I know of no one else who has ridden . . . or shall we say floated . . . the Fleet. Quite remarkable, indeed. Tell me," he leaned forward intently, "how did it smell?"

"Smell?" Carmen said. "I . . . uh . . . wasn't really thinking about that. I was mostly trying to keep my head above water, not drink any more than necessary and keep the rats out of my face."

"Yes, yes, of course you would be. It's just that I've been reading up on the odor of London's rivers during the nineteenth century and thinking that things may not have improved all that much, given our modern petrochemical and pharmaceutical industries. The Thames really did flow 'sweetly' centuries ago, you know, filled with salmon and swans. But things had grown frightful by Victorian times."

He took another sip of his stout, again wiping his lip with excessive care. "Hardly surprising, of course, for a river that served so many purposes. Residents of our fair city thought nothing of emptying their chamber pots out the windows to join the bodies of dead animals, rotting vegetation, garbage, fish market offal and so forth. Cattle, sheep, pigs and horses deposited 40,000 tons of dung on London streets every year. Sewers were primitive, restricted to surface water and were quickly overwhelmed by a quarter of a million overflowing cesspits."

Carmen stared at her drink and began to feel slightly nauseous. But Brady, unnoticing, plowed ahead.

"In the 1840s, there were ninety-eight miles of covered sewers in Holborn and Finsbury with no access to the Thames. The foul effluvia that accumulated raised such a fermentative stench that the sewer running beneath Fleet Street had to finally be reconstructed in 1849. The best addresses in London, Westminster, Belgravia, Grosvenor, Hanover and Berkley Squares all smelled like the rankest offal, due to stopped up house drains. Buckingham Palace was one of the worst offenders, with sewers in some cases hundreds of years old and crumbling."

"I've seen the remains of some of those old sewers in the excavations beneath Coram's Fields," said Carmen. "Mostly constructed of brick and literally crumbling to dust."

"Precisely. Things got to such a terrible state that London's very first Metropolitan Board of Works was established in 1845. A new scheme was set up to divert those sewers that emptied directly into the Thames or its tributaries so they ran parallel to the river until they were far downstream of the central city. The old sewers had to be traced and charted because no one knew where they ran, which gives you an idea of how often they were cleaned.

"The new tunnel system was well under way by the 1860s. They were built beneath the city streets by what was called the 'cut and cover' method, digging down thirty feet and then covering over the sewers. All done by horse- and steam-driven cranes of course. A remarkable achievement."

Carmen had no argument with him there, but she was beginning to wonder what all this history had to do with their impending trip on the Fleet. Was Brady just here to prepare her for the impending obnoxious odors?

Sherwood saw the look on her face. "Uh . . . well . . . this is all fascinating, Brady, but we were sort of wondering if you could tell us anything at all about whether there have been any . . . unusual . . . discoveries along the old route of the Fleet River."

His friend looked blank. "What sort of discoveries?"

Carmen said, "While I was floating down there, I came to a place where there seemed to be something shiny lining the sides of the river. Would you have any idea what that could have been?"

He looked from Carmen to Sherwood and back. Then he shrugged. "In some places, bricks were replaced with tile. I suppose some of these, if they were glazed, might have reflected your light. A very small section of tunnels was actually illuminated by gas lamps, usually for purposes of inspection. There was one such section in the sewer at Old Ford in Hackney. But that was a 150 years ago.

"A pair of pumping stations were built, magnificent edifices they were, complete with minarets," he said, warming up again. "The Prince of Wales actually visited the opening of Crossness Pumping Station. The band of the Royal Marines played as his royal highness and his entourage of archbishops, princes, dukes and earls examined the boiler house and were taken into the culvert that connected to the sewers. It was constructed of superb brickwork and lined with rows of colored lights. One can just picture that august assemblage strolling where there would soon be sewage up to their eyeballs. You can still visit these stations, you know. It's actually one of my most popular tours."

"What about bones?" asked Sherwood. "Have you ever come across anything about bones or ancient remains down there?"

Brady gave him another long look. "Bones? Bones are everywhere in old London. Cemeteries, prison gallows, hospital plots, pauper burial grounds. The Pauper's Cemetery at St. Bride's Church had been in use since Charles II's day. Bones were piled up in heaps. Once a week, the remains of paupers were thrown into a hole fourteen feet deep. A clergyman said a few words and the grave received a slim covering of loose soil. The next week, the ground was opened up and a new lot interred. The whole neighborhood reeked with the smell of death."

Brady finished his pint, wiped his mouth and said. "You're beginning to sound dreadfully Scotland Yardish, Sherwood. What's going on?" He made a show of looking over his shoulder. "Let me tell you something."

Carmen and Sherwood both leaned forward.

"There was a rumor 'mongst us tour guides that there was a hidden burial site beneath central London. Hundreds of bodies. Story was an old-timer saw them after a cave-in. Some said it was bodies buried during the Blitz that no one bothered to recover. Others . . . " He paused and raised a hand to signal the waitress for another pint.

"What?" they both said in unison.

"Others said they might have been backwashed up the river on the tide. You know, from one of the notorious prisons of the fifteenth century, though that wouldn't explain how they came to be closed in. But it was all just rumors. You'd be surprised how some of my colleagues can run on after a few pints."

Sherwood sighed. What Brady was talking about could have been the bone field that he and Harry had found. But there was nothing new here. They still had no idea where those bones had been taken or how old they might have been.

Their next step would have to be a watery one, as dank and depressing as one of Braidwood's tours.

They parted company with Humphries and strolled down Wardour Street all the way to Shaftsbury Avenue. It was early evening and had stopped raining long enough for the tourists to emerge from their hotels.

They turned toward Piccadilly Circus, which was bright with lights. Near the tube entrance, they stopped beside a railing and watched the teenagers who inevitably sat round the statue of Eros in their baggy blue jeans, eyes and ears sporting earrings by the cartload.

"I love this place," Carmen said. "To me, it represents the very heart and soul of the British empire. The romantic center. The place to which boys serving in foreign lands like Natal and Jalalabad and Sierra Leone dreamt of returning one day, of meeting their girls and taking them out on the town." She pulled up the collar of her jacket and pushed her hands deep into its pockets. "God, I love history," she said.

Sherwood felt the tug at his heartstrings that he'd been experiencing ever since he had kissed her. He thought she was a pretty romantic character too, just like all those soldiers serving in foreign lands. Only she served in the middle of the richest bit of history in the world, the British Museum.

"I'd say you've found your true calling," he said. "I envy that certainty and passion you bring to your work every day."

She leaned back against him and looked up at the lights. "You can't fool me, Sherwood Peets. You feel the same way about what you do."

"Maybe you're right. It just seems difficult to remember sometimes on a hard day when people are killed or hurt. I want to help them and that's the best part, the most fulfilling. But often I can't help. I can't make it better or make it go away. That's when I envy the solitude of what you do."

She laughed. "And here I am wanting to go out into the world and have *real* adventures and take risks."

"Lately, I'd say you've found enough adventure and risk right beneath your feet."

She turned toward him. "Maybe we complement each other. What do you think?"

He thought if he didn't kiss her at that moment, his heart might break. So he did.

28

Norway — 1944

Albert Hagelin sat in the minister president's office and matched Quisling's sour expression with one of his own. He had just told his old friend about the disastrous British commando attack on the camp at Finnsnes.

"Wiped out?" said Vidkun. "It can't be true. Our best chance to win the führer's confidence, gone. Hitler will have less interest in Norway now than ever. We will never win back his support for our country."

Quisling could not have cared less about Hitler's interest in his country. It was his own career that he feared could now be in jeopardy.

Hagelin looked thoughtful. "Perhaps all is not lost, Vidkun. Yes, the camp was virtually destroyed and it appears the commandos escaped. It was a brazen attack. But I have learned from several of our men in the area that there was a shipment out of the camp two days before the attack. They were not certain what the movement entailed but did say that one of the experimental V-2 rockets was part of it."

"Good!" Quisling slammed the desk with his fist. "If they got one of the test rockets out intact, the program may yet go forward. Hitler will simply build another camp to continue the work. Do your contacts know where the rocket is being taken?"

"No. However, it was moved by rail, which means it has to be headed south. There is only one main line from the far north."

He considered. "They must intend to return it to Germany to continue testing or perhaps even for launch."

"We *must* find it, Albert," said Quisling. "The commandos could still be after it." He felt hope rising again. "We may yet be able to win the führer's favor if we stop the British from doing further damage. I want all of our planes up and searching for that train."

"Such a thing would be certain to get back to Terbovin."

"To hell with the man. This is too important. If he asks, say that we continue to search for the escaped prisoners. We must find that train and protect it." He looked out the window and grew quiet. "You know, my old friend, if the commandos are not still after the rocket, we may have to arrange for an attack on the train ourselves."

Hagelin raised one eyebrow. "I don't quite follow you, Vidkun."

"What better way to assure the führer's gratitude? We stage an attack on the train, then swoop down with our men and save it." His eyes took on a far off gaze. "We may yet be called to Berlin to receive the Iron Cross, Albert. Our future will be assured within the Thousand Year Reich."

29

Gunnar eased back the stick, and they rose gracefully into the Arctic twilight. The plane responded to the slightest adjustment of the controls. Being unfamiliar with the aircraft, he made only the smallest of corrections.

It was past eleven in the evening. As he banked and set a southern course, the sky lit up around them with a jaw-dropping display of northern lights.

"My God," Natasha said. "It's beautiful."

"Yes. But also disorienting. More than one experienced pilot has been fooled by those flickering lights into flying straight into the sea."

"But you're much more experienced than that, right?" she asked hopefully.

He laughed but didn't answer. Into his headphone he said, "Major, you ready on those guns if we need them?"

"I understand how they work," came the reply. "But I won't be able to count on my accuracy until I get to fire them a few times."

"Well, let's hope it doesn't come to that."

"How about banking out over the ocean so I can try them out?"

"Nope. We can't waste the time or the fuel. We've got one load of gas and a belly tank that can't be refueled. Even if by some miracle we find a fuel supply somewhere, we're only going to be able to fill the wing tanks. That won't get us far."

It was a simple matter to locate the rail line. It wound through the mountainous terrain, staying close to the valleys and passes. It followed a circuitous route; one Gunnar hoped would mean a train would have to move slowly. There was only one line this far north, but he knew once they reached the more populous areas of southern Norway, he would have to select from several possible routes. Then it would become a guessing game, though in the end, most lines would lead to Oslo.

"What's that?" Natasha asked suddenly.

He looked back to see her pointing below. He saw it at once. A train moving in the same direction they were going.

"Let's check it out," he said and pushed the throttle forward.

He lined up with the back of the train and they came in above it at no more than a hundred feet in altitude. A man stepped out the back of the caboose and stared up at them, then waved at the familiar looking Stuka.

"Might as well be friendly," Gunnar said. He waggled the plane's wings as they passed over the train.

"No red crosses," said Natasha. "Not our train."

"It's too soon. They've got to be hundreds of miles ahead of us. But we'll catch up. Then we'll see."

"Have you given any thought to how we're going to destroy the rocket? We don't have any bombs on board, you know."

"Don't remind me. We're sure not going to be able to do much damage with the major's guns, even if he does figure out how to hit the broad side of a barn. If we actually spot the thing, we may have to fly on ahead, land somewhere and figure out how to sabotage the rail line."

"That's not going to be easy."

"And it won't get any easier the farther south we go. Up here, there are practically no towns or houses. If we get too far south before we find them, it will be much harder to avoid people and villages." He turned around and gave her a dazzling smile. "You said you were looking forward to some excitement, right?"

She nodded. "You know what Winston likes to say."

"What?"

"I like a man who grins when he fights."

300 miles south of the remaining commandos in their Stuka, a military train of seven cars, including one flatbed, chugged along at barely twenty miles an hour. Maintenance of the rail lines had suffered during the war. There was no extra iron for rails or skilled laborers to effect repairs. Everything had been diverted to Germany. So the train rocked along, tilting back and forth from side to side as the rails beneath groaned and squealed from the weight.

The middle car of the seven held a mysterious cargo, long and narrow, covered with heavy tarpaulin and tied down on all sides against the elements and prying eyes. On either side of the load—hidden under camouflage netting—was a pair of machine gun nests, each manned by three men who kept a wary eye on the sky. The boxcars fore and aft of the mysterious load had large, red crosses painted on their roofs.

Hours ahead of the Stuka, another plane, flown by a Norwegian pilot under the orders of Vidkun Quisling, spotted the flatbed and prepared to fly lower for a closer look. Moments later, the pilot was back at altitude and radioing his command that he had made contact with the target. Coordinates were quickly given and then just as quickly relayed to forces of the minister president on the ground. Within the hour, a bridge along the intended route of the train was declared dangerous and closed. Two men, dressed as railway workers flagged down the train and waved the engineer onto a side spur.

As the train rocked slowly to a halt, the two engineers jumped down to go see what was happening. Suddenly, armed men burst out of the woods. They were dressed in unfamiliar uniforms that— as they drew closer—the engineers realized were those of the British army. The two stunned engineers gaped as gunfire erupted. The men in the machine gun nests on the flatbed car were dispatched before they realized what was happening. The engineers dove to the ground, hands over their heads, waiting to be killed as well.

But before that could happen, more men, dressed in the regular army uniforms of the Norwegian military, appeared out of the tundra and quickly surrounded the commandos who laid down their arms, almost as if on a prearranged signal. Not a shot was fired. The engineers were then hustled forward to have what had just happened explained to them in detail.

The magnificent forces of the Norwegian army, under the command of Vidkun Quisling himself, had thwarted a British attempt to destroy the führer's most secret new weapon. It was likely that the very war itself had just been saved for the Fatherland. At that moment, radio messages were being sent to Berlin to inform them of the brilliant work of the army and to assure the leaders that their special weapon had been saved and would soon be on its way to Germany once again. The radio messages made sure to mention the importance of Minister President Quisling's role in the operation.

Once the military maneuvers were safely over, Quisling appeared. Driving up in his personal car, he strutted about shouting orders for a few minutes, then went to the flatbed car and stared up at it approvingly. He would accompany the train the rest of the way to the port of Oslo, situated at the top of the hundred-kilometer-long Oslofjord, where he would personally turn over the V-2 rocket to the captain of the ship sent by Hitler to receive it. There would be no mistaking who was behind this brilliant military success.

The entire operation had taken less than two hours, including disposing of the bodies of the poor machine gunners who'd had to be killed for the benefit of the charade. All in all, a very precisely run timetable.

One that had the unintended outcome of delaying the special train long enough for Gunnar and his companions to quickly close the gap on their own intended target.

30

London — Present Day

Wolfgang pounded two pitons into the stone that lined the top of the cistern, strung a line through them and tossed it over the edge. There was a long moment before they heard it hit bottom.

"Fifty feet if it's an inch," said Kurt, staring nervously into the pit. "Who's going first?"

Wolfgang didn't say anything, so after a moment, Hans stepped up to the lip of the opening and strung the line through his harness as he'd been instructed. He backed over the edge and hung there for a moment, adjusting himself. His torch was in his backpack. He would rely on the headlamp again.

"Here goes," he said, and began to lower himself in small increments. He descended some twenty feet, then paused and tried to see below with his light. "Still can't see the bottom," he yelled up to the others.

"Take it slow," said Wolfgang.

Another twenty feet and Hans thought he saw something sticking out of the side of the cistern directly beneath him.

"There's something down here," he called out.

"If it makes a sucking sound," said Kurt, "I don't want to hear about it."

"No, it's not that. Wait a minute."

The sides of the cistern were roughly cut and uneven. Hans wondered how long it had been since there was actually water in it. He lowered himself until his feet rested on a protrusion from the wall. It actually seemed to be sticking out of another tunnel in the side of the cistern. He eased himself lower until he could look into the tunnel.

The protrusion extended back into the opening. It was black in color, curved slightly and gave the appearance of considerable age. He felt a sudden chill grip his insides. He knew what it was! He reached over his shoulder and managed to remove the torch from his pack. He banged the instrument against the protrusion and smiled as he heard the metallic echo.

Staring into the tunnel with his light, he saw a worn but still legible series of numbers on the side of the object. His heart raced.

"What is it?" cried Wolfgang.

"What we've been looking for," Hans said in a low voice.

"What? I can't hear you."

Taking a deep breath, Hans turned his head up to the distant opening above. "It's the V-2," he said.

His words were met with astonished murmurs.

"Are you certain?"

"No question. I can see the identifying numbers on its side. It looks to be caught in the tunnel. It must have penetrated the ground and somehow found this passage, following it all the way to the cistern before it got stuck."

"Go on to the bottom," called Wolfgang, "and we'll come down."

Hans placed one hand flat against the rocket, feeling its coldness. How long had he been searching for this bit of history? Nearly four years. Now it would only be a matter of time before they managed to open it and determine what the payload had been. They would have to get cameras down here, document everything. Reenact the moment of discovery. Soon he would know if his grandfather had been right. It would be the crowning moment of his life.

He stepped off the protruding missile and dropped to the cistern floor, hitting the bottom with a sickening crunch. He looked down to see his feet resting in a thick mulch of bones. The crunch had been the result of crushing several human skulls as he hit bottom. He swore loudly.

"What's wrong?" came Wolfgang's distant voice.

Hans shuddered but determined not to say anything to the others. Kurt, especially, was nearing a state of extreme anxiety.

"Nothing. I'm off rope. Come on down."

First Wolfgang and then Kurt descended, each of them pausing at the protrusion to marvel at its smoothness and metallic hardness before continuing on to the bottom, where they gaped at the piles of bones and skulls. Once they had absorbed this mystery as well, they just stared at one another for a moment.

"You did it," said Wolfgang to Hans, clapping him on the shoulder.

"We all did it," Hans said. "It was a team effort."

Kurt continued to stare up at the incredible sight of the rocket sticking out of the side of the tunnel. "Do you think we'll be able to figure out a way to get it out of here?"

"The first thing," said Hans, "is to try to figure a way to get *ourselves* out of here. We've still got to climb up the other side."

Kurt, the last one down, detached from the line, which hung against the side of the cistern. Suddenly, they heard the strange sucking sound again. It was coming from above them.

"What the hell . . . ?" Kurt backed up until his shoulders were against the wall of the cistern. His headlamp flashed back and forth, searching in every direction. The others were also looking all around. The effect was almost psychedelic, as the three headlamps whipped back and forth.

"There," cried Wolfgang. "On the missile."

Their lights coalesced on the black, protruding hulk above them, where they could make out . . . something . . . sitting on the V-2. It was at least three feet long, perhaps a foot and a half tall; a sort of dirty off-white color. But what they all focused on was the creature's head. It seemed to occupy close to half of the body length. There was a short snout, large round eyes and a mouth that dripped some sort of mucus from teeth that even at this distance, looked to be more than an inch in length.

"Mother of God," said Kurt. "That's no rat."

The creature appeared unconcerned by their presence or the flashing lights. With deliberate and seemingly intent movements, it pulled the hanging nylon rope upwards, hand over clawed hand, in almost humanlike fashion. Then they watched in astonishment as the line was quickly chewed to bits, the horrible sucking sound echoing in the enclosed chamber.

Though the men couldn't see the top of the cistern, they could hear an answering, sucking cry from above. A moment later, the remainder of the rope fell, chewed through at the top. They watched as the rest of the nylon line was chewed down until nothing remained but a pile of pulped nylon fuzz, which the creature allowed to drop at their feet.

"They're communicating with each other," Hans whispered.

"How many of them do you think there are?" asked Kurt.

"Only two that we know of," said Wolfgang. "But if these things are the reason for all the panic and dead rats up above, then there are probably a lot more of them."

The sucking sounds, which had continued up to this point, suddenly stopped. They looked up in time to see the rodent—if that was what it was—jump off the missile and land a few feet from them on the cistern floor.

Kurt cried out and tried to crawl up the near vertical wall behind him in an effort to get away. Wolfgang picked up a large rock and threw it at the creature. Showing incredible agility, the thing dodged the rock and then closed on Wolfgang in a blur of speed, leaping onto his torso and clamping those terrible teeth into his ribs with a crunch that made Hans shiver to his core.

Wolfgang screamed and fell to the ground, tearing at the thing that held him. Hans heard ribs cracking, saw his friend's muscles ripple with the effort of pulling at his attacker. Wolfgang was incredibly strong, but he was unable to dislodge the creature.

Hans grabbed another rock, almost a boulder, raised it over his head and smashed it down on the rodent with every ounce of his strength. There was a crunch and then a sort of release of air from the thing's mouth, as it let go of Wolfgang and rolled over onto its side.

Wolfgang was in agony. "God, it burns," he cried, wiping helplessly at the wound in his side. Hans knelt beside him. He could see the action of the strange mucus, as it bubbled and frothed in a mixture of Wolfgang's blood and flesh. There was almost a searing of the wound going on, as though Wolfgang had been all at once branded by a red-hot poker.

Hans pulled his pack off and searched through it for their first aid kit. He pulled out some antiseptic and poured it into the gaping hole in Wolfgang's side, his friend crying out in agony at this new, stinging pain. Then Hans took some dressings and pressed them against the wound to stop the bleeding. Wolfgang stopped yelling and eased himself up so he could lean against the side of the cistern. He breathed heavily, his whole body heaving up and down. Hans imagined the pain from the crushed ribs must be excruciating.

"Is it dead?" asked Kurt, staring at the strange beast lying on its side.

Hans looked at the thing. "I think it's still breathing," he said. "But I don't think it can hurt us anymore."

"Oh holy Christ," said Kurt.

"What is it?"

Kurt slumped to the ground, but Hans followed his eyes.

What he saw nearly stopped his heart.

The rim of the tunnel surrounding the missile had filled with more of the creatures. They sat at the edge, their claws protruding over the rock. Others kept arriving until there must have been forty or fifty of the strange rodents. They seemed to be in no hurry. It was almost like a social gathering.

But then one of the things began to make the strange, sucking sound. Others joined in. One by one, almost playfully, they leaped into the pit.

31

Prime Minister Nevil Harris had a lot on his mind. He was due to leave for Washington this very afternoon for a two-day conference on the environment. He had a cabinet meeting scheduled before he left and his wife insisted he stop by to say a few words to her arts group. But the secret gathering in his private study was potentially the most explosive matter on his docket. Or at least that's what Marcus said.

Settled into easy chairs around the fireplace were Minister of Health Simonson, Deputy Commander Jarvis, Home Secretary Howard Bates, Secret Intelligence Service Director Marcus Hopkinton and Deputy Prime Minister Rachel Forrester.

They had just finished listening to Simonson give his report on the rat infestation in central London.

"You say the rats that came out of Holborn have dispersed? Then I don't see what the problem is," said Hopkinton.

Deputy Commander Jarvis sighed. "The problem is we don't know what's causing them to act so strangely. If they have some disease, medieval or otherwise, there could be an epidemic. The fact that they've dispersed only means they will spread whatever it is throughout London. My office has begun to see an increase in reports of rat infestations and attacks."

Hopkinton was a lean man with a sharp nose and close-set eyes. He gave off an aura of intensity and danger. Since he was probably the second most powerful man in England, after the prime minister, that aura was best taken seriously. At the moment, the SIS director looked skeptical. "What you really mean is a few people have been bitten, don't you?"

"Actually, some 200 citizens have reported rat bites in the past seventy-two hours. That's a huge increase over the norm. Many have reported that the creatures seemed agitated, easily frightened and aggressive."

Jarvis turned slightly in his seat to face the prime minister. "Sir, I wish to bring up another matter."

Harris nodded curtly. His face exhibited, in addition to its usual vacuity, storm clouds that none of those present wished to see descend upon them. The prime minister was known to blow his stack when he didn't like someone, or when he didn't understand something, which—his aides had quickly come to learn—was often.

"One of my inspectors reported that your security men entered his office at New Scotland Yard and took confidential files concerning an investigation relating to the remains of bodies found underground near Piccadilly."

Jarvis saw the prime minister's eyes flick briefly to Hopkinton.

"I was hoping, sir, that you might tell me something to ease my inspector's concerns about his caseload, which has been compromised. He would also like to have the files in question returned to him or be given an explanation as to why they will not."

Home Secretary Bates said, "If I might weigh in on this, Mr. Prime Minister. We have checked the bodies in question through HOLMES. We did not find any hits on them."

Deputy Prime Minister Rachel Forrester looked annoyed. She was a brilliant, newly arrived, some said arriviste, politician from academia. In actuality, she'd had to be coaxed into accepting her position. "I can't keep all these damned acronyms straight. What on earth is HOLMES?"

"Sorry," said the home secretary. "It stands for Home Office Large Major Enquiry System. It's the Yard's crime database."

"I was unaware that HOLMES had been accessed for such a purpose," said Jarvis, a bit indignantly.

"We had the permission of the prime minister, Mr. Deputy Commander. I did not mean to step on any toes. I realize that, strictly speaking, we should have gone through your office. In any event, as I said, we still cannot identify the remains."

"Identifying the bodies is of secondary importance," said Simonson. "Though it might give us some clues, the fact remains that we may be dealing with a contagious disease. The Sweat was highly lethal when it swept across England and the continent five centuries ago."

"How certain are you that we are dealing with this . . . 'Sweat'?" asked the prime minister.

"Not certain at all, sir. Dr. Jessmer of the British Museum seems convinced we are dealing with the Sweat. He's an authority on the time period involved and of the sickness, but really, we do not have anything definitive. Both the rats autopsied and the body of the only person to die so far, showed unusual symptoms. I have ordered my office to have anyone reporting a rat bite brought in and examined thoroughly. If they become ill, we will know about it. But it will be devilishly difficult, if not impossible, to confirm if we are dealing with this particular medieval sickness. We have little basis for comparison, except for the weak eyewitness accounts of the period."

"This needs to be kept as quiet as possible," said the prime minister, leaning forward. "If news leaks that some awful disease is on the loose, there will be a panic that would make a terrorist threat pale by comparison."

SIS Director Hopkinton nodded. "I think the minister of health needs to continue to monitor the situation. But the prime minister needs to strike a balance. There are other matters at hand here."

"Sir," said Jarvis, "May I tell my inspector that his confidential files will be returned?"

Nevil Harris turned again to SIS Director Hopkinton, as though there were an invisible chain connecting them.

"For the time being," Hopkinton said, "I do not believe that would be wise. We may need to act quickly. It's important that we have any information relating to the disease close at hand in the event conditions change on the ground."

Jarvis stared incredulously. "Surely you've already examined the papers?"

"There are political considerations as well, deputy commander," said Harris. "The effects on the general populace are of paramount concern. There are also national security implications."

The prime minister stood, signaling the end of the meeting.

But Jarvis was not one to be put off, even by the prime minister. "I take it then, sir, that if something more happens with this outbreak, your office will assume full responsibility, since you will have all the 'information at hand,' as Mr. Hopkinton put it."

Harris's face turned red. "Scotland Yard will perform as I direct. Your function is to report to the home secretary, that is, to my cabinet. If there is any further need for you to know anything pertinent to this investigation, you will be so informed. Is that clear?"

Jarvis and the others were stunned at the outburst. Not because they had never seen one before, but because only one other member present, the SIS director, had any real knowledge of what was going on.

Hopkinton stepped between the prime minister and Jarvis deftly and put one hand on the deputy commander's shoulder.

"I'm sure we're all a little frayed right now. Let's just do our jobs and we'll come out of this without any further trouble."

The others had all left. Hopkinton, the prime minister and Deputy Prime Minister Rachel Forrester remained in the PM's office. Harris eyed Forrester cautiously. Her impressive academic credentials intimidated him. He didn't trust her, didn't like having her around showing off her intellect, and most of all, he hated having to confide in her. But she had to know certain things. The very deepest secrets of his administration. For what if something happened to him? What if he were to become sick? What if he were assassinated? He believed in the ship of state, that it must keep sailing on, no matter who had to be thrown over the side. It was probably his one truly honest political feeling. There had to be someone who would keep his secrets for him once he was gone.

Forrester was just thirty-nine years old, still very attractive, with dark hair and jet-black eyebrows that made her eyes stand out. She worked out regularly, running across Horse Guards Row and down to Buckingham Palace and back every day, security detail in tow. She'd never married or had children, so her body was firm and tight. So far as Harris knew, she didn't even have a lover. What a waste. He wondered from time to time if she might be a lesbian.

But whether she was or not, she used her beauty to great effect. Even opposing members of Parliament enjoyed having her around. The prime minister suspected some of them would just as soon see her in the top job. Even if they disagreed with her, at least they could enjoy looking at her.

Rachel stared at the two men with distaste. Their secrecy had compromised her, and she hated it. But from the first, she could not figure out a way to distance herself. As deputy prime minister, she had initially felt a surge of triumph as they took her into their confidence. These were the two most powerful men in England, after all. Only gradually, had the things they told her begun to seem a bit too unseemly, too risky. Secrets kept from the people, "for their own good," Hopkinton assured her. She no longer believed that but now realized she was caught in the trap of her own insider knowledge.

She took a deep breath and began. "We can't keep this locked up any longer. Think of the risks. If this outbreak in the rat population really is the Sweat and it sweeps through the city and country, everyone will blame us. It was one thing to try to protect Churchill's little secret for so many years, but now his secret has become ours. Besides, we need to get our medical people on this."

"They are on it, Rachel," said the prime minister. "Minister of Health Simonson is testing anyone who comes in with a rat bite. He has exhaustively autopsied the body of the exterminator. He knows all there is to know, which frankly is that even if this is the Sweat, we can't really prove it."

"They might make a better stab at proving it, sir, if we released the autopsies and reports of those two women's bodies from the war."

"And how do we explain Churchill's decision?" said Harris. "Granted, he acted in what he felt was the nation's best interest. And maybe it was at the time. But to reveal his actions now, especially after the rat attacks and disease outbreaks—well—it could lead to outright panic. And who do you think would get the blame then? Not Winston, I can assure you. It would be me."

Rachel cursed inwardly. Once again, she was trapped by the secrets of the past. Somehow she needed to break free from this awful triad. She needed to confide in someone. Maybe she should go to the press. But the thought of the British tabloids having such a story made her almost physically ill.

Hopkinton said, "Let's not jump off the deep end. We don't know if there will be any sort of outbreak. We've got public health care, state-of-the-art sewage systems and clean water. This so-called Sweat is going to find London a lot harder to take over than it did five hundred years ago, or even sixty-five years ago."

Rachel shifted uncomfortably in her chair. "We've also got a free press, freedom of information laws and independent-minded doctors and nurses who will raise the alarm if they get even a whiff of a cover-up once the disease begins to spread. I tell you, Nevil, if you keep this to yourself and it breaks anyway, you won't have a friend left in Parliament—or anywhere else."

"That include you, Rachel?" He eyed her suspiciously. "Maybe you're looking to move up."

She stood up. "Damn it, Nevil! Not everything is about politics. You have a responsibility to the people of this country."

She stormed out past the surprised secretaries in the outer office. She went down the hall and out to her waiting car. She was furious with herself for acting so stupidly, so . . . irrationally. Just like a woman. She could imagine Hopkinton and Harris chuckling at her display. She stared out the window of her car all the way back to her office. She needed an ally somewhere in this government. Someone who didn't trust the PM either.

32

He had too many pans in the fire. Sherwood's thoughts flicked from rats to emeralds, from strange medieval diseases to the inexplicable actions of the prime minister, from a woman lying dead in the morgue to his pending trip into the underground sewers of London and to—more often than not—his sudden infatuation with Carmen.

Their dinner and especially the kiss at Piccadilly Circus had reawakened feelings he'd long ago put away. It had been years since he'd felt about his ex-wife what he was now feeling for Carmen. He hardly knew what to do with the emotions.

He finally gave up trying to concentrate and slipped out of his office to take a stroll along the Embankment. He often walked to Cleopatra's Needle when his thoughts were muddled. There, he stared up at the imposing monolith, then down to the black waters of the Thames. The flow of the great river always had a salutary effect upon him. These waters had seen so much. He could imagine himself transported five hundred years into the past, yet the waters always remained the same. All around, London bustled and progressed, yet there was something constant about the city; a hidden, internal life, almost . . . like a soul.

He grimaced. Perhaps that internal life had not so much to do with a soul as it did with underground rivers, ancient bones and a large, emerald-eating rat.

Slowly, he came out of his funk and remembered that he hadn't followed up with Darryl, whom he'd abandoned when rodents began to tumble out of Holborn Station.

He found his research rat—an unfortunate turn of phrase—still buried at the annex, where he had apparently been holed up for two days.

"You're dedicated; I'll give you that, Darryl. Find anything?"

Darryl looked like something one might find in the basement of the Salvation Army. His clothes were soiled and moist-looking, as though he'd spilled coffee on them and rubbed it in. The workspace was covered with papers, spilling out of files, falling onto the floor. If there had been any order to the boxes from the prime minister's office, it had long since departed.

"If I'd known you were going to leave for days and days . . . " he grumbled, but he thrust the feelings aside at once. "You could say I've found some interesting items. Sit down." He pushed a chair at Sherwood.

"To begin with, you might recognize the contents of these three boxes." He pushed the boxes, which were on the floor, toward Sherwood who leaned over and flipped through the contents of one of them. He knew what they were in an instant.

"My files!" he said. Darryl smiled.

"But I thought what's his name? . . . Bernard? . . . said this stuff was from the '40s?"

"Most of it is, actually, and some pretty interesting stuff at that. Clearly, your boxes were placed in here along with everything else as a way to get them good and lost. Incredible bit of luck, really, that I came on them after just two days. I'm still only a third of the way through this pile."

He stood up and shuffled over to a long library table on which he'd been sorting papers removed from boxes. Everything was divided into categories . . . more or less.

"Found something else here. Those two bodies you were looking for—you know, the women whose bones turned up in the subway? Evidently it isn't the first time they were discovered.

They were actually found during the war and given at least partial autopsies at the time."

Sherwood stared at him in astonishment. "Autopsies?"

"Yes. I thought it was rather surprising myself. Here, you can read the findings. Both bodies had symptoms similar to those exhibited by your exterminator fellow. Norman, wasn't it?"

Sherwood leafed through the autopsy material. The evidence was clearly dated, without many of the modern tests that had since been developed. But there it was in black and white. The two women had had lung and vascular lesions, just like Norman and the rats. But even more surprising was how the files were marked. Each was labeled TOP SECRET—OFFICE OF THE PRIME MINISTER.

"I don't understand," Sherwood said. "If Prime Minister Harris wanted to keep this under wraps—deciding to bury the files—why would he label them as coming from his office? That's just stupid."

Darryl rolled his eyes. "This stuff is from the 1940s. The prime minister who had it labeled wasn't Harris. It was Winston Churchill."

"Churchill?" Sherwood couldn't get his head around the incredible thought. "Churchill classified this information?"

"So it would seem. What's more, I can't prove it yet, but I'd be willing to bet he's also behind having the bodies returned to the sub-tunnel where they were found."

Sherwood remembered how unlikely it had been that the bodies were discovered, how they had actually seemed to be bricked into an undocumented sub-tunnel. "But why?" he said more to himself than Darryl. "Why would Churchill want to hide the bodies of these poor women?"

"It does give one pause," said Darryl.

Back in his office, Sherwood stared at the wall. He found the evidence of Winston Churchill's involvement in his case utterly baffling. What possible reason could the wartime prime minister—his hands so full dealing with the Nazis—have to hide not only evidence but the actual bodies of two citizens in the hidden chambers beneath London?

No matter how he looked at it, the facts would simply not come together in any sort of comprehensible fashion.

When his phone rang, he was so distracted it took a moment to realize it was his boss, Deputy Commander Jarvis.

"Inspector, I wonder if you could come up to my office at once." It was not a request.

"Yes, sir," said Sherwood. "I'll be right there."

As he made his way down the long corridor to the bank of lifts, he wondered if this might have something to do with his impending subterranean journey with Carmen and Harry. He'd gone to lengths to keep their plans secret, but it was still possible one of the Public Works men had managed to spill the beans.

He realized he was facing something more when Mildred swept him through without so much as a word. Sitting next to the deputy commander was the prime minister's second in command, Rachel Forrester.

"You haven't met, I believe," said Jarvis. "Madame Deputy Prime Minister, one of our talented and upcoming young inspectors, Sherwood Peets."

Rachel stood and offered her hand, appraising him. "Bernard speaks highly of you, inspector. We may be in need of someone with your talents and discretion."

Bewildered, Sherwood sat across the desk from both of them. "How can I be of help?" he asked, with real curiosity.

Jarvis took a deep breath and ran one hand through his thinning hair. "The deputy prime minister—"

"Please," said Forrester, "things will move a lot more quickly if we stop using all of these ridiculous titles, don't you agree? Rachel will be fine."

Jarvis nodded, began again, slipping up at once. "The deputy pri—uh, Rachel—has brought some disturbing and, I believe, quite relevant information to my attention."

Sherwood regarded her with interest. She was an intriguing figure in the government. The youngest, first woman and certainly best-looking deputy prime minister in the history of the nation. She wore a tight-fitting, black-wool suit; the dress fashionably cut above the knee. Her face was as nearly perfect as could be and Sherwood found himself enjoying looking at it, despite his nervous anticipation.

"What I am about to tell you, inspector, is top secret. I do not actually have the right to reveal this, but I fear our nation may be looking into an abyss with this potential disease outbreak. I firmly believe that the people who must act for the good of the nation need to know the relevant facts."

Sherwood felt his antenna going up. If there was one thing he distrusted, it was politicians who claimed that they had to do something for "the good of the nation." The statement was nearly always followed by something utterly self-serving.

Forrester crossed her legs and Sherwood glanced down at them. It was only for an instant, but he recognized that she had done it for his benefit. Frankly, he thought Carmen's legs were better.

"In September of 1944, inspector, two young women's bodies were discovered in the underground. It was not considered unusual. They were both members of the Home Guard and were assigned as staff at the stations being used as bomb shelters. However, the manner of their deaths was not clear. The bodies had obviously not been trapped in an explosion or cave-in and for that reason, they were sent for routine autopsy."

Sherwood cleared his throat. "Yes, I've seen their autopsy reports."

Forrester and Jarvis both looked startled.

"How . . . ?" Jarvis began.

But Rachel waved a hand. "I think your assessment of the inspector was correct, Bernard. He has been continuing his investigations, despite the interference from the prime minister's office. Am I correct?" She smiled at him.

"The point is: inspector, what was found as a result of those autopsies, and I suspect this was not in the reports you have seen, because they were immediately redacted by the prime minister, is that those two women died from symptoms that were identified at the time as being related to the English Sweat."

It was Sherwood's turn to be astonished.

"There was an outbreak of the Sweat during the war?" he asked.

Forrester nodded. "There were many top secret meetings with health officials and others at the time. The prime minister was in the loop. There was a real fear that the disease might break out into the populace at large."

"But I never heard anything about it," said Sherwood. "And I've read a great deal of WWII history."

"Churchill quashed all evidence of the disease, ordered a blackout on information to the press and even had the women's bodies reinterred in the underground. Their families were told they were lost in an explosion and that no remains were found."

Sherwood was stunned. "But why . . . ?"

"It was at the height of the war. The British people were under tremendous pressure. No one knew where the disease had come from and so far as anyone was aware, there was no treatment available anyway. Churchill feared that the prospect of a devastating epidemic striking London would be the last straw. That it would cause panic and quite possibly undermine the resolve that was needed to finally confront and defeat the Nazi menace. Those were very nearly his exact words in diary entries that have been kept secret since the end of the war."

"So what you are telling me is that Winston Churchill kept the first appearance of the Sweat in nearly five hundred years . . . a secret?"

She nodded. "It's hard to know how people today would react to learning of such a thing. Especially now that we may be facing another outbreak. Prime Minister Harris made the decision, with the counsel of SIS Director Hopkinton, I might add, to quash the discovery of those poor women's bodies for the second time in sixty-five years. That was why your files were taken. Dr. Trimm was the perfect foil, used by the prime minister as a front for the action."

"And Trimm," said Sherwood, "has his own reasons for not wanting national attention focused on the underground."

"Again, you appear to be well informed, inspector. We too have learned something about Dr. Trimm's obsession with certain . . . valuables he believes to be hidden under London. Frankly, my feeling is the entire thing is patent nonsense, but it made him useful to us." She hesitated. "I say 'us' advisedly. I only gradually became aware of all of this and I am going out on a limb telling you. But I believe all the secret doors need to be opened if it will help us deal with what we now confront."

33

Norway — 1944

Gunnar felt Natasha's hand on his shoulder.

"You awake?" she asked.

He realized he'd been drifting off again. Four hours at the controls had taken their toll. He rubbed his face with first one hand, then the other and tried to stretch in the tight confines of the Stuka cockpit.

"I'm all right," he said. "But thanks for keeping track of me."

"I wish I could help," she said. "But you're the only pilot we've got."

It was very early in the morning, not yet six o'clock, but the sun had grown stronger in the sky as they made their way south. Ahead of them lay a dark front. The weather would soon change, making both flying and looking for the train more difficult.

Gunnar checked his fuel gauge. The belly tank was empty, and the wing tanks were less than a quarter full.

"We've got to find a fuel depot," he said over his shoulder.

"I think I saw something about ten miles back," Natasha said. "There were round tanks and a fence line beside a small airport. But do you think we can risk landing there?"

He shrugged. "We either land there or we'll land in a field somewhere when we run out of gas. And that will be the end of the line."

He banked the aircraft and began to retrace their route along the rail line. In a few minutes he saw what Natasha had described. He flew low over the field. There were only a couple of airplanes, which appeared to be civilian in nature. A small, block-type building stood off to one side. Next to it, two large tanks squatted on the ground. He pulled up, turned and came in low again.

"What are you doing?" Natasha yelled at him.

"If there's anyone down there, they'll come out to see who's buzzing them." He swooped low over the compound three times. No one appeared.

"Maybe it's too early in the morning."

"We can hope." Into his headphone, he said, "Major? You awake back there?"

Osbourne yawned audibly. "Just barely. Christ, it must be around five. Riding in this thing is like having someone rock you to sleep."

"Well wake the baby up. We're going to land in that field down there and steal some petrol. Get on the guns and be prepared if anything develops. I'll taxi right to the tanks and we'll try to do this fast. Maybe no one is home."

"I'm awake now," came Osbourne's crisp reply.

The landing was rough, on a field that evidently was not well cared for. They bumped to the end of the strip, then Gunnar turned and taxied to the tanks. He idled the engine, detached from his restraints and lowered himself to the ground.

The two tanks were obviously old, rusted and poorly maintained. He had a sudden fear in the pit of his stomach that this was an abandoned airstrip and there would be no fuel. He approached the first tank and rapped on its side. An empty echo rewarded his efforts. He swore and moved to the second tank. This one also sounded hollow but with a slightly lower pitch. Maybe . . .

He unwound the hose at the side of the depot, pulled it round to the wing tanks and stuck the nozzle in. Then he returned to the squat reservoir and began to pump up the pressure. Soon, he heard the heartwarming sound of moving petrol.

He climbed back into the cockpit and stared at his fuel gauge.

It moved up slowly. A third of a tank, then half.

"Is it working?" asked Natasha.

"Seems to be."

When the gauge read almost full, he climbed down again, topped off the wing reservoirs, rewound the hose and placed it back in its cradle. No point in leaving visible evidence they had been here. A moment later, they were taxiing back to the end of the runway. The engine sounded rougher to Gunnar. Probably the fuel was of poor grade or quality. Maybe it was even contaminated. They would just have to hope it didn't damage the engine before they found their prey.

As he wound up the engine and began to move forward slowly, he felt Natasha's arm on his shoulder again. Only this time she gripped him fiercely.

"Look." She pointed past him.

He turned and saw three vehicles roaring toward the entrance to the gated compound. Two were army trucks and the third appeared to be some sort of police vehicle. He swore.

The little convoy careened through the gate and turned at once to intercept the course of the plane on the runway. Gunnar heard the sound of small weapons firing and winced as a bullet ricocheted off the fuselage.

"Major! You awake back there?" He shouted.

"I've got 'em," Osbourne replied. Then, after a moment's pause, they heard the deafening sound of the 7.92mm machine gun. Gunnar watched a line of bullets tear up the side of the grass runway. Osbourne's rear mounted guns wouldn't be able to fire on the vehicles if they got in front of them.

The Stuka was almost at full speed now, its powerful engine whining. The front wheels began to lift off the ground, but two of the vehicles angled in to intercept them and Gunnar wasn't sure he would be able to clear them.

"I'm losing them!" Osbourne shouted. "They're getting too far in front of us."

Gunnar turned the plane more towards the tree line. It gave them less runway but the angle would allow Osbourne to keep firing. The trucks were now heading straight for the side of the plane.

"Gunnar," Natasha cried. "They're going to hit us!"

He pulled back on the controls with every ounce of strength he had. The plane seemed sluggish. The new fuel was undoubtedly contaminated, weakening their thrust.

"Major!" Gunnar yelled into his headset. "You need to move them out of there."

Osbourne didn't answer but the guns fired relentlessly, chewing up the grass and then settling, finally, witheringly, on the trucks. One driver leaped from the cab as the truck veered, then fell over on its side, spilling soldiers out of the back. The other took the brunt of the major's fire directly into the driver's section. It careened wildly, and then took a bullet in the gas tank.

There was a deafening explosion. Gunnar felt the Stuka get a lift from the blast as it rose above the truck into the sky. He turned and glanced down in time to see the police vehicle pull to a stop. A man stepped out of the door and stared skyward as the Stuka disappeared into the early morning mist.

"Well, that ties it," Gunnar said. "So much for our stealth approach to refueling. Every Nazi and Quisling toady in Norway will know where we are within an hour."

"What can we do?" asked Natasha.

"Not a damn thing. We'll continue along the rail line. Our only hope is that we find the train before they find us."

"What about that?" She pointed at the black clouds ahead.

He grunted. "Our window's closing, that's certain. In more ways than one."

34

Julia listened to the phone message for the fourth time. It was from Hans.

"Julia, sorry I couldn't locate you. Two of my men have not returned from their exploration of a new sub-tunnel near the Great Cistern. I'm organizing a search for them. Dr. Trimm also knows about this. I'll call you later. I miss you."

Hans was the date she'd been looking forward to when Carmen diverted her into exploring the underground. She and the young German had begun seeing each other shortly before all the excitement began. When Carmen had asked why Julia didn't offer up Hans for her consideration as date material, Julia had been less than forthright with her friend. She liked Hans herself, even though the secrecy around his work was annoying.

Aside from being hunky, she'd discovered a sense of humor in him that she found herself drawn to. They'd even had a couple of elliptical conversations about Trimm, in which she had detected more than a hint of discomfort from Hans.

Now there was this message. She was worried about him. If Trimm knew what was going on, that was all the more reason to be suspicious as far as she was concerned. She didn't trust Trimm as far as she could throw the owl-eyed, little man.

She stood up, suddenly certain of what she needed to do. She was going to go find Hans and help him in his search. No one knew the underground better than she did. She could help, she was sure of it. Maybe Hans didn't realize the dangers that existed from the Sweat. And Carmen had told her, in strictest confidence, about the unusual creature that Sherwood had encountered. It made her blood run cold.

From Hans's message, she had a pretty good idea where to look for him, in a section of newly discovered tunnels that coalesced at the Great Cistern.

She stuffed her backpack with a few pieces of extra clothing and checked that her torch was fully charged. On her way out the door, she hesitated, then returned to the bedroom closet. In a box on the top shelf was something her father—an ex-special forces veteran who had served in the Falklands War—had given her. A nine-millimeter handgun. He'd taken her out to his farm in the Wye Valley and taught her how to use it.

Her dad had been nervous about all the men Julia dated. It was ridiculous of course. What did he think? That she was going to pack heat when she went out dancing? The miniskirts she wore left precious little room for a sidearm. The truth was: she didn't like guns. And getting a license to carry one in Great Britain was all but impossible. Still, she wanted to humor her father, so the weapon sat on the shelf in her bedroom. She would be in serious trouble if anyone ever caught her with it.

She considered throwing a box of ammunition into her pack but settled for thrusting a handful of extra shells into her pocket instead.

It was early morning and London continued its damp and dark September. The gloom fit her mood, but it felt good to be doing something. She couldn't just sit at home and worry about Hans. It wasn't in her nature.

Coram's Fields was dismal and deserted. A few rats darted between trash barrels. They seemed disinterested in her and certainly nothing like what Sherwood had reported to Carmen. She still found the whole story unbelievable. It must have been a very large rat, plain and simple. What other possibility was there?

She headed for the same place where she and Carmen had entered the week before. Despite Dr. Jessmer's closing of the site, security was still haphazard at best for such a huge area, and she didn't expect to be confronted.

As she stepped through the orange netting and pulled out her torch, a sudden, almost paralyzing chill overtook her. She tended to be impulsive. Maybe she should have brought someone with her. Or at least told someone what she was doing. But the moment passed and she began the trek down the long, gentle decline toward the Great Cistern.

She was less than a hundred yards in when she heard an unusual sucking sound.

35

Sherwood pulled his bright, new patrol car to a halt in front of Carmen's apartment. He enjoyed driving his new car so much that Harry had been relegated to the passenger seat whenever they were together. His sergeant did not like being chauffeured by the boss.

"It's not proper for a sergeant to be squired about by an inspector," he sniffed.

"You'll get used to it. Why don't you use your freed-up brain capacity to think about what we're going to do."

"What we're going to do is get ourselves drowned." Harry hated the plan Sherwood had concocted for exploring the underground river. He could think of a thousand things that might go wrong and he'd already told Sherwood at least nine hundred of them.

"Now if this little slip of a girl," Sherwood nodded at Carmen who had appeared at her apartment door, "can handle it, I think we two great bruisers should be OK."

Harry just snorted, but he got out of the car, opened the door for Carmen and then got into the back.

She was in a cheery mood. "Was that a ray of sunshine I saw this morning?" she asked.

"If it was, it was the first one in the month of September," said Harry, grouchily.

Sherwood looked at her carefully. He was getting used to her mood swings. "You still all right about this?" he asked, putting one hand on her shoulder for a moment. "We don't have to do it."

She gave him a brilliant smile. She'd been practicing. She was determined not to always be scowling like an old harridan whenever Sherwood was around. It took real effort, but seeing him actually did make her feel like smiling more these days.

"I can't tell you how ready I am, Sherwood. All the delays have been driving me crazy. Now that we're finally underway, I feel positively relaxed and excited at the same time."

He nodded, looked over his shoulder and pulled the car out into traffic. If he'd done more than glance behind them, he might have noticed the black sedan that pulled out after theirs and stayed half a block back as it followed them.

They parked at the Piccadilly tube maintenance entrance where Sherwood and Harry had first entered the sub-tunnel system. Sherwood got out and spoke briefly to one of the Bobbies standing guard. The man confirmed that two Department of Public Works men had already gone below with a generator and winch setup. Sherwood had given instructions to let the men pass without explaining the nature of their mission. Bobbies took orders from Scotland Yard inspectors without question.

They descended the gritty steps and entered the sub-tunnel, following the lights set up by the transportation workers. Both Harry and Sherwood were armed with revolvers. They rarely carried firearms, but after seeing the strange creature, Sherwood did not intend to place Carmen in any more danger than necessary.

They worked their way down the gloomy tunnel to where the men waited. One of them grunted as Sherwood came up. "Glad you're the one taking responsibility for this," he said. "Craziest damn scheme I've ever been part of."

"I appreciate you taking it on," said Sherwood. "And keeping it to yourselves." He surveyed the setting. They were crammed into the tunnel where Carmen had fallen through the floor after discovering Norman's body.

Carmen stood back a little, remembering again how it had felt to fall into that black river. Sherwood gave her arm a squeeze. "You OK?"

She just nodded, not trusting her voice to come out in anything more than a squeak.

"We had to use sledges to enlarge the hole enough for the raft to fit," said one of the men. "I don't mind telling you it was dangerous swinging those mallets in here. There's no telling whether this whole floor might subside. But it's set now. You see? It's already in the water and we've attached the cable fast to one end of the boat. It runs back to the winch, which operates off the generator down here."

Sherwood examined the setup closely. The winch itself was anchored solidly with lag bolts drilled into the stone floor. It looked solid enough to hold an elephant in place. "How much line do we have?"

"Just under a mile." The man handed Sherwood a wireless radiophone with a three-foot antenna. "This is how we'll communicate. Cell phones don't work down here. Too much rock and clay between us and the surface. Tell you the truth: I don't know what the range of this thing will be either. When we reach the end of the cable, if we haven't heard from you, we'll wait five minutes, then reel you back in. That's the way you want it, right?"

Sherwood nodded. "You've done a great job. I'll put you both up for a commendation if the time ever comes that we can tell people."

"Just don't screw up," said the man. "I don't want to have to explain what the hell we were doing down here and how we lost three people."

"All right, let's go," Sherwood said.

They followed the cable line thirty feet down the tunnel.

"What do you think happened to all the dead rats?" asked Carmen. "This tunnel was full of them when I came down before."

In fact, there were only a few bones left here and there.

"Looks like something ate 'em," said Harry. "Bones and all."

No one had anything to say to that.

The raft sat in the hole, several feet below the tunnel floor. They could see water flowing beneath it at a good clip. Once they were all aboard, Sherwood looked up at the man staring down at them.

"You sure you want to go through with this?" he asked once more, shaking his head. "You couldn't get me to do this for a commissioner's salary."

"We'll be all right," Sherwood said, more for Carmen's benefit than because he actually believed it. He was having serious doubts about this cockamamie scheme. He picked up the radiophone. "Go back down to the winch and make sure this thing is working."

They confirmed that their communications were good. Then the sound of the winch began as it slowly let out the cable and Carmen watched the opening above them disappear.

Almost at once, a dank, rich smell assaulted them; a mixture of mold, sewage and perhaps bat dung. Harry and Sherwood each held torches and though she was nervous, Carmen couldn't help being fascinated at actually seeing the place which she had hitherto only experienced through brief strobe-like interruptions as her torch had faltered.

They moved slowly, the workers letting out the cable steadily but cautiously. They could feel the bite of the current as it licked beneath the raft, trying to pull them downstream faster.

Harry shone his light on the water, and they saw the bodies of dead rats floating by. Carmen shuddered, remembering how she had brushed the creatures out of her path and the mouthfuls of that foul water she had swallowed. Her stomach nearly heaved.

The torches surrounded them in a cocoon of light that reflected off the walls and ceiling above them. After proceeding

for perhaps two hundred yards, Sherwood picked up the radio
to make sure they were still in communication.

"Can you hear me, gentlemen?" he called, then released the
button and listened. There was no reply.

"Shit," said Harry. "I knew we couldn't trust those things."

Sherwood tried again. This time, they heard what sounded
like several voices all talking at once.

"I can't understand you," he said. "Say again."

But the voices only grew louder and more contentious. Then
they heard two loud claps, which Sherwood and Harry recognized instantly as gunshots.

"What's going on?" Sherwood yelled into the device. Again,
they heard multiple voices. Then, suddenly, the boat lurched
and they stopped their forward motion.

"What's happening?" asked Carmen.

Sherwood spoke again into the wireless. "We've stopped moving. Are you having trouble with the equipment? Pull us back if
that's the case."

But nothing happened for almost five minutes. They were
stopped, the water rushing beneath them. Then, suddenly, the
boat leaped forward and Sherwood looked down at their cable
attachment to see the line hanging limply in the water.

"The cable's broken!" he said.

They grabbed the sides of the boat which now careened along the
river. Their lights showed that they had passed into a larger cavern.
Then they came to a place where they saw water rushing towards a
large boulder that seemed to split the river into two channels. The
raft had a rudder, which Sherwood grabbed uncertainly.

"You remember any of this?" he shouted to Carmen. "Do you
know which way you went?"

"No," she said in a tightly controlled voice. "I think there may
have been branches but I couldn't see anything most of the time.
I don't know which way I went."

He nodded grimly and steered their little craft into the larger of the two channels. Now they were in uncharted territory. They could no longer be certain they were going in the direction Carmen had traveled. They might once again be at the mercy of whatever channel they were in, waiting for the roof to close in around them or for the water to simply fill the channel completely, drowning them.

"What's that?" Harry said suddenly.

They listened and heard the sound of falling water.

"Sounds like a bloody waterfall," said Sherwood. "You never came on anything like that, did you?"

"No. At least not till I fell out of the damn sewer," Carmen responded.

Sherwood and Harry shone their lights ahead and could see that the current had picked up discernibly. They were now in near white water and the sound of a falls ahead grew louder.

"No way this little rubber boat will stand up to going over a falls," said Harry. "We're going to be in the drink in a minute."

Then their lights picked out what appeared to be the end of the river. In fact, it was the water disappearing over the edge of what seemed like a great cavern. The water roared, echoing through the underground chamber. They were bathed in a cold mist.

"Son of a bitch!" Harry cried, grasping the sides of the boat. They were hurtling straight for the unknown drop-off, when suddenly the boat lurched and stopped moving.

Their stop was so abrupt Carmen fell forward and almost out of the raft. She picked herself up and had to yell so Sherwood could hear her over the roar of water that now tumbled about them, bubbling and foaming in small whirlpools.

"What's happened?" she cried. "Why have we stopped?"

"Maybe they reattached the cable," said Harry. But they all knew that was impossible.

The boat slapped repeatedly against the side of the channel, threatening to capsize at any moment, as they hung on for dear life. Sherwood looked around desperately for a way out of their dilemma. There was a bit of rock above them in their wildly gyrating torch light.

"Quick," he said. "Carmen, I'm going to lift you up onto that shelf of rock. I think the cable we've been trailing must have snagged on something. That's what stopped us. But we can't expect it to hold for long. We've got to get off this thing."

She clambered over to Sherwood and with him pushing her up, she managed to grasp the edge of the shelf and pull herself onto it. Harry followed. Then the two of them pulled Sherwood up just as the cable broke free. They watched as the rubber boat disappeared over the edge of the falls, the trailing cable snapping viciously through the air.

Sherwood cursed.

"What is it?" asked Carmen.

"I forgot our pack with the food, water and extra torch." He looked around. "Looks like we lost the radio too."

"No great loss there," said Harry. "Piece of junk. But I've still got my torch."

"Good. Turn it off. We need to conserve them."

Sherwood used his own light to explore the limits of their new home. There wasn't much to see. The shelf of rock was wet from the mist in the air and slippery. It was no more than a meter wide and perhaps three long. The water rushed less than a meter beneath their feet. They were unable to see the opposite side of the channel.

"We're dead meat," said Harry. "They're not going to have a clue where to look for us. If someone finds the raft five miles downriver at a sewer outlet, they'll assume we're dead."

"No," Sherwood said, firmly. "They'll look for us. But we may be stuck here for some time."

Carmen shook her head. "I don't think so, Sherwood. You heard the same thing I did. Those were shots coming over the radio. Someone attacked your men and cut us loose. It had to be deliberate."

He was silent. He'd had the same thought but hadn't wanted to express it for fear of scaring the others.

"Bloody hell!" said Harry. "This is a bleak bit of God's earth to die in." He shivered. "If we don't starve to death, we'll likely get hypothermia. When we get thirsty enough, we'll drink this water and it's anyone's guess what that will do to us. I'd rather catch the Sweat. At least that's supposed to be quick."

Sherwood stared at the water flowing below them. There was another possibility he'd thought of. The water level might rise from all the rain that had come down this September, covering the ledge they were on. Then they would be washed over the falls.

How long should they wait here for help that might never come? The falls might well be their only avenue of escape. He certainly saw no other. Perhaps they should just trust their bodies to the water and pray they would survive and float out somewhere. If that was their best bet, they should take it while they were still strong and not wait until the cold sapped their strength. He was hit with the reality of how stupid this whole operation had been.

"Some great inspector I am. Didn't even last a month. Now I've put the lives of two of the best people I know at risk. I'm sorry," he said glumly.

Carmen moved over and curled her body into his. She was shivering from the cold. "If anyone's at fault, it's me. It was my stupid need to understand what happened to me that got us here."

Harry put his hand on Sherwood's shoulder. "We'll work it out," he said. "I wouldn't have wanted to be assigned to anyone else in the department." He leaned back and stared at the ceiling. "At least there aren't any rats around."

They were silent for a while. Sherwood turned the light off to save the charge. The blackness was total, like ink. The roar of the falls had a disembodied quality to it in the dark that was frightening, like a huge monster baying at their feet. After a few minutes, he turned the torch back on and could feel the shudder of relief run through Carmen's body. She had obviously not counted on being down here in the dark again.

He gently uncoiled from her, stood up and played the light across the water. The roof of the cavern was some twenty feet above the flow. It was black and dank looking. He swung the torch along the ceiling to where it met the walls of the tunnel, then back down to their ledge. Nothing. He played the light along the other side, again slowly following the curve of the ceiling and then down the wall.

He stopped, the light frozen on a section of wall above the farthest end of their platform.

"What's that?" he asked.

Harry and Carmen looked up. "I don't see anything," said Harry.

"There where the light is. Is that a darker section of rock? Or something else?"

Harry stood up and moved along the ledge as far as he could go. Then he stared at the darker bit of rock.

"I'm not sure, but it could be another tunnel."

36

Hans stared in horrified fascination as the giant rats, or whatever strange monsters they were, fell into the pit. Half a dozen made the initial leap, and they milled about, seeming in no hurry, a few feet away.

He thought they looked like some sort of parody of a rat, like something someone who had never seen one might make up. Even in his terror, he thought of the early drawings made by men of creatures they had never seen, polar bears and whales, which were often given human faces, oversized bodies and small, humanoid hands where the forelegs or flippers should have been.

The faces of the beasts were short, with snout-like noses. They had small, close-set eyes that hovered above an enormous mouth filled with needle-pointed teeth. It was a face that was very nearly all mouth. The ears were short and pointed, sticking straight up. The fur was tight to the body and nearly white in color, though constant contact with the earth due to incessant tunnel digging had turned them more off-white than anything.

The bodies were mesmerizing: very muscular and lean, perhaps three feet long, standing a foot and a half high with a curled, furless tail. For the first time, Hans watched one of the creatures make the strange, sucking sound, which appeared to be created through a compression of their lips. When the sound occurred, it seemed to trigger the creation of the strange burning mucus that dripped from their jaws.

"Mother of God," whimpered Kurt. "We're dead men."

Hans could hardly argue with him. He and Kurt stood with their backs to the wall. Wolfgang lay on the ground a few feet away, one hand holding the blood-soaked bandages against his side.

More of the creatures began to fall from the tunnel lip to join the others. The strange sucking sound spread until nearly all were dripping mucus from their mouths, like some awful, contagious, acid reflux disease. They appeared to be building themselves into a frenzy. Suddenly, without warning, one large, super rat darted in and clamped its teeth onto the downed man's leg.

Wolfgang let out a scream and before either Hans or Kurt could react, the rats piled onto the hapless climber and began to devour him alive.

There was nothing they could do but watch in horror. Hans was the first to shake the terrible image from his head long enough to think clearly. He grabbed Kurt.

"They're not paying any attention to us," he said. "Wolfgang's blood has got them in a frenzy, like a pack of feeding sharks. We've got to get out of here."

Indeed, the animals were completely ignoring them, as though the remaining men were simply tomorrow's dinner, stored in upright, mobile form perhaps, but certainly not going anywhere until it was required.

Kurt stood frozen, incapable of movement, staring at the feeding rats swarming over their friend. Hans turned him away from the drama in front of them and slapped him across the face as hard as he could. Kurt's glassy eyes focused on him.

"You've got to fix pitons in the side of the pit and climb out of here. You're the climber. I can't do it by myself. We've got some time, until they finish eating, anyway. Do it!"

Kurt broke his eyes away from Hans and looked up at the wall. It was not technically difficult for a good climber, but the height was almost fifty feet. It would take time.

He grabbed his hammer and thrust his hand into a pocket, pulling out a fistful of pitons that he clipped onto a shoulder strap. "Be a miracle if the damn things hold in this clay," he muttered, then, "Lift me up."

Hans made a cradle with his hands and lifted Kurt onto his shoulders. From that height, he pounded in a piton, grasped it tightly and lifted himself up, clamping his harness into it. Then he placed another as high as he could reach, pulled himself up until he could stand on the first and began to repeat the action over and over.

Hans, helpless, with nothing to do, faced the rats and watched them eat his friend. Already there wasn't much left. The meat had very nearly been stripped from Wolfgang's bones. The white of his skull gleamed through the stains of blood. A large strip of deltoid muscle dangled from one shoulder. Hans stared at it in fascination. He'd always admired Wolfgang's incredibly muscled arms and shoulders. Now he was staring at those very muscles themselves.

He tore his eyes away long enough to look up. Kurt was almost at the top. When he looked back, he saw that several of the creatures had stopped chewing at the pitiful pile of remaining bones that had once been Wolfgang. They were looking at him with what he could only consider renewed interest.

Without taking his eyes off the drama, he said, "Hurry up, Kurt."

A moment later, he felt Kurt's rope hit him on the shoulder. Slowly, he coiled it around himself. Then he eased up off the ground. Using a foot loop to stand in, he could raise himself two feet at a time.

The rats continued to stare at him. He wondered how high they could jump and what was stopping them. Maybe they were no longer hungry.

When he was ten feet above the mass of rodents below, he began to feel for the first time that he might make it. At twenty feet, he relaxed even more and that, evidently, was when one of the creatures suddenly decided it was hungry again.

The thing leaped upward. Hans stared, dumfounded, as it jumped flatfooted from the ground to a height of almost fifteen feet. It fell back and tried again, this time reaching within a few inches of Hans's feet. It was the most powerful jump he'd ever seen, and it gave him all the impetus he needed to climb much higher more quickly.

The rat stopped after its first two attempts. But then it did a strange thing. It jumped up, grabbed onto the nylon rope dangling below Hans and began to climb up the line, grasping it with all four of its sharply clawed feet.

"Son of a bitch!" Hans cried. He redoubled his efforts, finally feeling Kurt's hands pull him over the top.

"Cut the rope," he yelled, but Kurt didn't need to be told. He could see what was happening. The giant rat was just half a dozen feet below. He sliced the line cleanly and they watched the rodent fall back into the darkness.

Fifty feet was a long fall even for the creature. While they couldn't see the bottom, they heard it hit with a sickening splat that almost certainly killed it; the next instant, they heard the sucking sounds once more as the thing's comrades tore it apart and devoured it.

They stared at one another.

"Thanks," Hans said. "You did that climb fast."

"What now?"

It was a good question. As Hans looked around, he realized he didn't recognize where they were.

"This isn't the Great Cistern. It must be another one. Maybe even one that hasn't been documented yet. I could have sworn that's where we were, but these tunnels aren't familiar. The creatures must have directed us here when they caused the landslides."

"So you *do* think they were causing them?"

"I never would have believed it, but you saw what those things are capable of. They certainly acted like animals in that feeding frenzy and in their bloody attacks. But they also seem to have some way of communicating between themselves. And they worked together. If I didn't know better, I'd almost say they were intelligent."

Kurt looked nervously at the tunnels that stretched away before them. "You think there could be more of them?"

"I don't know, but the ones we've seen are enough. They may know another way to get into this tunnel system. We need to move on as fast as we can."

"But we don't know where we're going."

"I don't know about you, but any direction away from those things down there is fine with me."

37

Trimm stared at the papers lying on his desk, leaned back in his chair and stroked his chin. Damn, he was one hell of a researcher!

He had filed a freedom of information request in the United States to examine the papers of Dr. Alexis Carrel during the time of his research at the Rockefeller Institute prior to WWII. Carrel had done extensive work devising surgical techniques, but his longest-running experiment had involved breeding a large colony of "heroic" supermice. After learning about Carrel's work from Hans, Trimm began to think about the strange behavior of the rats beneath London. Dr. Jessmer's lecture on the origins of the Sweat and the possibility of the rats being a vector for the disease led him to wonder what other interests Carrel might have had.

Like Carrel—a short man—Trimm found the scientist's fascination with breeding a superior race of animals completely understandable. He had long had his own inferiority complex when it came to his height. To have to look up at Carmen—his administrative nemesis—tortured him every time. What he would have given to be able to have controlled the development of his own growth.

He already considered himself superior intellectually, but his physical shortcomings had tormented him all of his life. His hatred of anyone taller bordered on the pathological. People he interacted with: coworkers, acquaintances, even family rarely understood this motivation and simply assumed he was antisocial to an almost irrational degree.

Hans had been a rare exception. Though he, too, was taller, Trimm had taken a liking to his fellow researcher and explorer. There were so few with whom he could relate. He felt a bond with the German, one only partially reciprocated, at best.

After examining the papers at great length, he became convinced that Carrel had gone further than his original experiments. In addition to the mice, he believed the man had also attempted to breed super rats. From his talks with Hans, he knew that it was highly likely that biological weapons developed during the war by the Germans had been placed in V-2 rockets for firing on England. At least that was what Hans was trying to prove.

He regretted he hadn't paid more attention to Hans's work. He'd simply been too focused on the treasure. Being the richest man in the world—even if he had to share the wealth with Hopkinton—could go a long way toward making other people forget about his height. But the appearance of the Sweat, along with the strange behavior of the city's rat population, now threatened to derail his search if public officials closed off the underground. Hopkinton—as powerful as he was—had also begun to feel events beginning to slip out of their control.

Information was always the key to unraveling mysteries, and it was the reason he had begun to expand his research into Dr. Carrel's activities. Everything would go into the mix that would one day make him one of the world's wealthiest men.

He mused about what else Carrel could have been up to. Might he have tried to create a super disease to go along with his super rats? But what sickness would he have used?

The answer was obvious. Carrel had figured out a way to insert the Sweat into his rats. Super rats carrying the Sweat inside them. The disease had not appeared in five hundred years, there was no treatment for it and scientists would likely not even recognize the sickness—certainly not in time to prevent its spread or develop a serum to fight it.

It would be the ultimate biological weapon. Deadly beyond conception. Rats were the perfect vector to spread disease, and super rats that viciously attacked anyone they came in contact with would spread the illness all the more quickly.

He realized suddenly that Hans and his men might be in serious danger. If they were to encounter such a vicious and deliberately created adversary, they ought to be warned. They ought to be armed.

But who would do it? The thought of going into that underground alone was hardly appealing now that he thought he understood what they were up against. Still, if he was to find and secure the treasure, he needed to act quickly, before the authorities took complete control. Then the riches of King Henry's Spanish galleon would likely end up in the British Museum. Under the control of Jessmer and Carmen, no less.

The very thought made his blood boil. The treasure belonged to him! He was the one who had spent years uncovering its existence. He was the one who had sunk every penny of his money into the search. He was the one who had recruited the Germans to look for it. He would never let it be taken from him.

But he would not go unprepared into that dark underground. He needed to protect himself. It was time for Hopkinton to earn his share, God damn it! And there was no time to waste.

38

Minister of Health Simonson emerged from the Waterloo tube and stared up at the looming hulk of St. Thomas' Hospital on Lambeth Palace Road. As the leading emergency care hospital in London, it was open 24 hours a day, 365 days a year and treated 100,000 patients annually.

Parking was limited near the hospital, which was why he had taken the tube. As health minister, he had his own parking space, of course, but sometimes the tube was the fastest way to get around traffic-clogged London.

Inside, he found the waiting and emergency admit areas filled with people. He had never seen such crowds before. He paused outside the glass-fronted doors to the quarantine section and stared at the chaotic scene within. Overnight, the city had exploded with rat-bite victims. They were coming in by the hundreds, overwhelming health authorities who had to examine each one for signs of the Sweat, many cases of which had begun turning up.

He had instituted the tightest need-to-know controls around the disease. Only a handful of medical professionals knew about the existence of the sickness. Even the technicians doing the testing didn't fully understand what they were looking for. Simonson had serious doubts that this level of secrecy could be maintained for long.

He believed the torrent of rats that came out of Holborn Tube were to blame for their predicament. Those rats had spread across the city and were almost certainly the source of the rat bites now being reported. He suspected most were not infected with the Sweat or else there would already be a virtual city-wide epidemic by now. But something was causing the disease to appear and rats were the primary candidate.

Damn the authorities for not containing the infestation! Of course, Scotland Yard was hardly to blame. His was the ultimate authority when it came to public health.

He had three laboratories working secretly on the Sweat—on specimens taken from the exterminator, from infected rats and from bite victims—trying desperately to develop a vaccine, or at least to increase their limited understanding of the disease. But he was painfully aware that such results could not be found overnight. The chance that something could be developed, manufactured and distributed within days or weeks was close to nil. They were working to control future outbreaks, not this one.

With a heavy heart, he turned away from the quarantine section and made his way to one of the laboratories where his people were carrying out their investigations. He found Dr. Eric Westerling in his office, poring over a pile of reports. Westerling was a brilliant scientist but an MD with less than ideal interpersonal skills. To put it bluntly: he didn't get along with people. In the lab, he had found his niche, alone with his test tubes and reports. A robust man with a bouffant of hair like Jimmy Swaggart, a perpetual frown and half-raised eyebrows, his demeanor gave new meaning to the word imperious.

Simonson stared enviously at the huge floor-to-ceiling windows that offered spectacular views of the Houses of Parliament, Big Ben and the serenely flowing Thames. His own office was not nearly so grand. "I've never seen so many people admitted for black rat bites," he said, grimly. "Have you learned anything?"

Westerling gave him a long-suffering look, laid his file on the desk and said, "We are not dealing with black rats or *rattus*.

They were the cause of the London plague of 1665 and a number of earlier pandemics, as a result of their harboring of fleas. Your *average* health minister would probably know that."

Simonson said nothing. He was prepared for this. If he was going to get anything useful out of Westerling, he had to expect at least three good insults first.

"Today," Westerling continued, "*rattus* is virtually extinct in London. Present day rats, the brown rat, *rattus norvegicus*, arrived in England in the late 1720s. They do not have such a poor reputation as *rattus rattus*."

"I stand corrected," Simonson said, hoping to hurry him along.

"However," Westerling went on, ignoring him, "today's rats are probably more prolific. A single rat can produce thousands of offspring in a single year. *Rattus exulans*, for example, the Pacific rat, was brought to Easter Island by the Polynesians. It multiplied quickly, eventually numbering in the millions and wiping out the island's palm trees.

"Plague and this latest menace aside, rats certainly have a reputation for killing in innumerable ways. Their urine sometimes carries a water-borne bacterium that causes liver or kidney failure. Then there is Eosinophilic meningitis, Leptospirosis, Rat-bite fever, Murine Typhus, Hantavirus . . . the list goes on."

He stared at the ceiling as if searching for divine guidance, since there obviously was none to be had from his uninformed visitor.

"God help us if these rats infected with the Sweat decide not to die faster than they can breed or spread the disease. Then, I fear, we may be looking at a possible Armageddon situation.

"As you are *possibly* aware, one of the ways we have been protected from outbreaks of Ebola, for instance, is because the disease progresses so rapidly that it kills all the potential targets in an area, running out of new victims to infect. This result has been much more likely given that Ebola has appeared primarily in remote African areas. An outbreak by your Sweat in the heart of London will not have the benefit of a limit to the potential supply of victims."

Simonson groaned inwardly. It was not *his* Sweat. "How many confirmed cases do we have?"

Westerling picked up a piece of paper. "We have seventy-six supposedly confirmed cases of the Sweat, though we can't really confirm much of anything other than symptoms, since we know so little about the disease. There are another 200 suspected. And we have several hundred more rat bite victims in the quarantine section. If they keep coming, we'll have to start putting them on the roof."

It wasn't a facetious remark. Simonson knew it had been done before.

"How many dead?"

"Only sixteen so far. Our care facilities—poorly funded as always by you bureaucrats—are still vastly superior to those of the sixteenth century. We appear to be able to treat most patients with some degree of success, provided we find them before the disease has progressed too far."

"Thank God for that, at least."

"God has nothing to do with it," Westerling said, clearly believing he and his colleagues deserved the credit. "Presently, this thing does not appear to be airborne. We're still unsure, however, if that was the case during the initial outbreaks of the 1500s. Direct contact—a bite by a rat or perhaps fleas carried by rats—appears to be necessary. But if it should mutate to an airborne form . . . " He shrugged. "Our days on this planet may be numbered."

Dramatic claptrap, thought Simonson. The man was a fool. Nothing so dire could or would happen on his watch.

"There's another issue," Westerling went on. "A reporter from *The Times* has been pestering me. The scoundrel thinks he's got his teeth—pardon the pun—into something with all the rat bites being reported. Despicable ambulance chaser. Trying to make a name for himself off the suffering of others. He's not going to let it go. And there will be others."

Simonson gave him a tired nod. "The government's policy thus far is to deny the existence of the disease. That's a mistake. Someone's going to pay for it."

39

Julia moved confidently through the tunnels. She was thoroughly familiar with this section after her years working at Coram's Fields. Her feet echoed in the underground silence, but she remained curious about the strange sucking sound that always seemed to hover at the edge of the darkness behind her.

The whole thing was beginning to make her a little nervous. She knew about the strange creatures Sherwood and Harry had encountered, though Carmen hadn't said anything about a noise. Anyway, she was sure they were just rats. Big ones, to be sure, but rats had never scared her.

Still, it was a really strange sound. Like a cross between someone smacking their lips and making a tsk-tsk sound.

She reached the Great Cistern and stood at the edge, peering in. Her light didn't reach to the bottom but it seemed as if the unusual sound was louder here. She edged around the opening and into another tunnel. After a hundred yards or so, she stopped and thought how ridiculous this was. How could she ever find Hans in such a maze?

During the entire summer, she had almost never run into him by accident. The one time with Carmen had been it. He could be anywhere. He could be lost. If she wasn't very careful, she could become lost too.

There was a sudden, distant rumbling sound. It echoed down the corridor and flowed over her like a living thing, the shock wave making the hairs on her neck stand up. Cave-in! A minute later, a fine black cloud of soot drifted down the tunnel towards her. She started to move away from it, then realized that wherever it had come from, it had likely blocked her from retracing her steps.

Well, that was no problem. There were connecting tunnels ahead, and she still knew where she was. But where was Hans?

She continued onward, walking slower now, trying not to breathe in the soot which continued to drift along with her. What nasty stuff it was, gritty and fine at the same time. She increased her pace to keep ahead of it.

At another branching of tunnels, she hesitated, a little confused. Was the right branch the one she wanted? Uncertain, she started into the left branch. At once, she heard another distant rumble. Again the soot came down the tunnel, forcing her back and into the other branch.

Now she was definitely concerned. This branch didn't seem right somehow, but it was the only option left open to her. She increased her speed again to keep ahead of the soot.

What a little fool she was. She wasn't going to be able to help Hans. All she was going to do was get lost herself. Then others would have to come look for her. It would be the ultimate humiliation for the person in charge of this place to be the subject of a search. She should have told someone where she was going, damn it. But who could she tell? She hadn't wanted Carmen to know her feelings for Hans. Not yet anyway. And the site was supposed to be closed off. Simonson had given them permission to go in, but not to do so in a foolhardy manner, which was precisely what she'd done.

The tunnel went deeper. Already, a small stream of water ran down the center. She tried to avoid it by walking on the sloping sides. Moisture dripped from the ceiling in an almost constant drizzle.

Then the sucking sound grew suddenly louder.

She froze, trying to determine where it was coming from. It seemed to be up ahead, but the sound was difficult to pinpoint in the close confines. Then she heard it behind her as well.

Now she was scared. Even more than if she knew she was lost. She could deal with that. But what the bloody hell was making that awful sound?

"Is anyone there?" she yelled into the gloom.

The words echoed back at her, sounding for all the world like someone laughing at her predicament.

"Hans?" She cried.

The echoes died away until she could hear the sucking again. It seemed to be closer and definitely behind her now.

She began to walk as quickly as she could away from the noise. It wasn't easy in the wet tunnel; her feet kept slipping on the steep edges of the side, as she tried to avoid walking in the water. Finally, she gave up and committed herself to getting her feet soaking wet, walking down the middle of the little stream. She slipped once, and fell to her knees, getting her pants wet almost to the waist. The water was frigid.

She came to another opening, stopped and stared. It was another cistern. Only one such cavernous well had been discovered by the scientists. She realized she must be in completely new territory. Could the cave-ins be opening up new passageways? In spite of her growing consternation, she examined the gaping hole as much as her light would allow. One part of the cavity appeared to have recently subsided. Perhaps it was one of the rumbling cave-ins she'd just heard.

The collapsed earth continued to settle down into the cistern, creating a slope that was steep and treacherous looking. Not that she had any intention of going down there.

She edged around the cistern until she could reach yet another tunnel opening. But as she prepared to enter it, there was another rumble. It was louder than the others, and almost at once the familiar soot came floating toward her.

She swore out loud. This was enough, damn it. Now there was nowhere for her to go.

Then the sucking sound became more intense. It was very close and seemed to have taken on almost a sense of urgency.

She stood at the edge of the cistern and looked all around. Then she saw it; at the entrance to the tunnel she had come down.

It looked almost comical. Like an oversized, stuffed rabbit with those ears sticking up and the whitish fur. And it just sat there, looking at her, its cheeks and lips compressed, making that strange sound.

"You don't look all that scary," she said out loud. "Why, you're almost cute."

Then the creature spread its lips, the sucking stopped, and she saw the teeth for the first time.

"Oh my God!" she whispered.

She looked quickly behind her. The black soot was still coming out of the tunnel and it probably meant the passage was now blocked. The strange animal or rodent barred entrance to the other tunnel, which was blocked in any event. The only way open to her was to go down into the cistern. A certain dead end.

Still, she hesitated. Maybe she was making too much of this. The thing didn't seem to be threatening her exactly. It just sat there, sucking its teeth, like some toothless old Harpy.

She eased her backpack off and lowered it to the ground. Slowly, she reached inside and pulled out the gun. When she stood back up, she felt better. She wasn't helpless . . . just in case something should happen.

She looked across at the other side of the cistern. There was another tunnel over there, but it might as well have been on the moon. There was no way she could reach it.

Then the creature began to make louder sounds, almost like smacking its lips. She could see a strange mucus dripping from its mouth. Slowly, it began to move towards her. She felt a cold trickle of sweat run down her lower back and nestle between the cheeks of her rear end. She began to back away from the animal, in the only direction she could—down the steep slope into the cistern.

She descended twenty feet, slipping and nearly losing her balance several times, as the earth threatened to slide under her. The creature, on its four feet, had no difficulty following her. It was almost as though the thing were playing with her, directing where she went.

"Go away!" she shouted, waving her arms. Then she took the pistol and fired a warning shot into the dirt near the animal's feet.

There was a loud blast, the dirt sprayed up into the animal's face and the sound reverberated like a crack of thunder through the tunnels. The creature paused and shook its head at the unaccustomed noise. Then it made a low, guttural growl and sprang at her in a leap that covered fifteen feet. In an instant, it was standing at her side, its wide mouth displaying the incredible rows of pointy teeth, mucus dripping from them in an almost constant stream.

She stared at the thing through horrified eyes, her feet nearly slipping out from under her as the dirt—aggravated by the impact of the beast's landing—subsided beneath both of them. She flung the gun up and fired as the thing leaped at her again.

She leaned to one side and watched it fall to the earth, a bullet through that horrible face. It started to roll down the slope, then caught on a rock and stopped. It was dead, half the face blown away, those needle like teeth sprayed all over the ground.

Cautiously, she knelt beside it and stared. She'd never seen any living thing like it before in her life. The blood and mucus from the mouth seemed to coalesce on the ground, where it bubbled and sizzled, emitting a wisp of something. She reached out a finger and touched . . . whatever it was.

"Ouch!" It burned. She rubbed the finger on her pants, but it continued to sting for several minutes.

She collapsed beside the body of the strange rodent, adrenalin coursing through her like a freight train. She gasped for breath and gradually felt her heart rate return to something like normal.

"What the *hell* are you?" She wondered out loud.

As if in answer, she heard the sucking sound again.

Terrified, she stood up and swung her light up to the top of the cistern. Two more of the creatures sat on the side of the opening, their claws hanging over the edge, lips pursed, as though they were watching a movie in a theater.

"Oh, mother . . . someone help me," she almost whimpered.

Then the new arrivals slipped over the edge and moved down the slope.

40

Rachel Forrester waited impatiently in SIS Director Hopkinton's outer office. She doubted he was meeting with anyone else this late in the day and fumed that he was probably making her cool her heels on purpose.

Finally, his secretary, who appeared more than a little embarrassed, bless her, picked up some unheard directive through her headphones and smiled weakly at her.

"You may go in, Madame Deputy Prime Minister. I'm sorry for the delay."

Rachel smiled at her. "Not your fault," she said and proceeded to push her way into the inner sanctum. And that's what it was, all right. Few people actually got to see the secretive SIS director's office.

"Rachel. How good to see you." Hopkinton smiled like he hadn't been expecting her. "To what do I owe the pleasure?"

She looked around the office. Hopkinton was a hunter and dead animals lined the walls: an enormous rhino head—she'd thought they were a protected species, something that looked like a musk ox and several impala-like things. Two enormous hunting rifles hung on the wall behind his desk, along with a number of African wood carvings, spears and clubs. The African motif continued even to the colorful Swahili fabrics that covered the chairs and sofa. Rachel thought the whole place looked ridiculous, like some pre-teen's idea of a James Bond set. She half expected him to ask her to take off her clothes and stretch out on the bearskin rug in front of the fireplace.

Instead, she sat tiredly in a wing chair. "Some things I'd like to clear up, Marcus."

He sat across from her. "That's why I'm here," he said condescendingly.

"When I first came to this job, I was told certain things that I didn't really understand. I'd like to understand them now."

He nodded, patiently. "You're a good woman, Rachel."

"Then why do I feel like I'm being used." She stared at him.

He met her gaze, then leaned back. "You've been around. Politics is the art of being used . . . usefully."

"Like those two poor women's bodies that have become pawns in all of this?" She sat forward in her chair but tried to control her anger. "You people think you can do whatever you want. Churchill is a hero of mine. I still believe in him. His reasoning made sense, to avoid a public panic that might have turned the course of the war. By denying those two poor women's families the right to bury them, he may have saved the free world.

"But you and the prime minister have denied their existence all over again, for the second time. And you didn't do it to save the world, God damn it. You did it to keep a sixty-year-old political secret that nobody gives a damn about today. Why, Marcus? Why did you do that?"

He stood up, crossed to the fireplace and leaned against it, staring into the artificial flames. "When we accept positions of authority, we don't do so in a vacuum. We inherit the history that came before. The Sweat was there during the war. They fought it the only way they could."

"By ignoring it; by lying about it?"

"No. By burying it."

She stared at him. "What are you saying?"

He returned to his chair. "The prime minister wants you to know this, Rachel. He feels you need to know it."

She felt cold. "Know what?'

"When the Sweat broke out, Churchill realized there was nothing they could do about it. For a time, they thought it might mean the end of everything, the war, the Allied effort, the royal family, our very way of life. The whole nine yards. You have to understand the level of fear that existed. There were no solutions; there was nothing they could do to fight it. So . . . they buried it, along with hundreds of those who had died from the disease."

"Hundreds . . . ?"

"Yes, the infected got sick almost immediately. The progress of the disease was incredibly rapid. That's ultimately why they were able to contain it. The government quarantined the stricken quickly, secretly and effectively. Once they died, they were interred beneath the city. It wasn't difficult to hide. London was in an uproar; bombs falling, fires everywhere, uncounted dead. People disappeared all the time."

"I don't understand what you're saying."

"Churchill didn't just bury those two women. He buried hundreds, brought in heavy equipment and sealed off half of underground London. Just dozed it over. They didn't know if it would prevent the disease from spreading, but it was the only thing they could think to do."

"And it worked?"

"Yes. The Sweat died out. It never spread. But one of my predecessors decided to take things a step further."

She raised an eyebrow. "What things?"

"He was not the most distinguished of my predecessors, and his name is unimportant. Indeed, the SIS was overshadowed during the war by several other intelligence agencies, including MI 5 and the cryptanalytic work of GC and CS, the bureau responsible for interception and decryption of foreign communications at Bletchley Park. But this intriguing fellow thought the Sweat might be used as a weapon. Maybe even to win the war."

Her mouth fell open. "You're saying they thought they could use it as a biological weapon?"

"Astonishing idea, wasn't it? But the SIS at the time felt a need to reassert its importance in the intelligence world. The Sweat struck them as a potentially useful and unique disease. Very lethal. No known treatment. No one even knew where it came from. The perfect weapon—if they could figure out a way to control it and deliver it to Germany."

"So . . . ?"

"So the SIS constructed an underground research laboratory beneath the city where British scientists worked to find a way to use the Sweat. Very secret. Even Churchill was unaware of it. Nothing came of the program during the war, but the work continued on long afterwards, financed secretly through the SIS budget. They developed some pretty advanced methods to keep the disease under tight control."

Rachel's astonishment was written on every line in her face. "You're not saying it's still going on? That they're still working on the Sweat?"

"No, no. It got out of hand. The program was finally halted in the late sixties. Everything was closed down, sealed up tighter than Churchill ever did. Too bad, really. Some of the techniques they developed would probably be useful today, but of course there was no way the work could be revealed. Original science can't just appear—poof—out of nowhere. Everything was lost." He sighed. "We don't know how it got out again, Rachel. You must believe that. But there was something else."

She couldn't believe there could possibly be anything else. What she now knew would tie her to the Harris administration forever.

"No one ever figured out where the Sweat came from during the war. There were rumors, of course, that returning POWs from Burma brought it with them, that the Nazis somehow introduced it into London. But no one could explain it. In the sixties, however, something else began to happen."

"What?"

He spread his hands, shrugged a little. "People began to die in the research laboratories. Not just die. They disappeared. All that was ever found were a few bones, like the two young women whose bodies rekindled this mess. Some felt they must have been killed by the Sweat, the bodies largely disposed of by rats. But no one ever really knew. And there was no evidence of another outbreak of the disease. Eventually, the laboratories had to be abandoned. They were sealed off and those who knew about it no longer spoke of it. You have to understand, in the intelligence world, people are not allowed to talk about things. They sign confidentiality agreements. It was kept secret, like the whole Sweat research program."

She felt ill, nauseous. It all sounded like some fantastic science fiction tale concocted by Hopkinton as a joke. But when she stared into that cold face, she knew it was no joke.

"Anyway, when the Coram's Fields site archaeologists began to expand their research into areas close to where the original underground laboratories were, we were afraid they might unearth some embarrassing historical artifacts best left buried. Or conceivably, they might even release the Sweat all over again. That's when we decided to remove the coffins and stifle the investigation by Scotland Yard. And we were right to do it, Rachel. Because clearly, the Sweat is upon us once again."

"Where are the coffins now?"

"Reburied in a secure, remote place. We used extreme measures to ensure there would be no contamination."

She found the presumption of the entire business exasperating. "If you and your colleagues didn't have such incredible paranoid delusions, Marcus, you might have realized you could never keep such a thing secret forever. It should have been revealed, allowing scientists and doctors to figure out a way to deal with the disease. Instead, you tried to bury not only the Sweat but any information about it that might have helped to develop a vaccine. My God! You people never learn. The cover-up is always worse than the crime."

He stared at her for a long moment. "You're a part of this now, Rachel. If you decide to come clean . . . go to the press . . . who's to say you haven't known about it all along?"

All she could do was look away. She knew he was right and she knew she didn't have the fortitude to fight such a battle all alone. For the first time, she really understood what it meant to be deputy prime minister to Nevil Harris.

41

They'd been sitting on the cold, sodden ledge for two hours, the mist from the falls soaking everything. Carmen thought they looked like three wet rats—the normal kind.

For the third time, Sherwood stood up, shook himself to dispel the damp, a fruitless exercise, and edged along their small platform to stare once again at the dark spot on the cavern wall. That it was another tunnel was no longer in question. They'd thrown pebbles at the opening and watched them disappear into the black void. It was definitely not simply a discoloration of the stone.

What it was, however, was out of reach. Twenty feet above them and just off the end of their ledge, it was as inaccessible as the other side of the falls that rumbled and roared beside them.

Sherwood turned to Harry. "Didn't you tell me you used to be a rock climber?"

He snorted. "In the army, I did some climbing. But we've got no equipment, boss. No pitons and most of all, no bloody rope."

"Come look at this."

Harry lumbered over, shaking from the cold and wet.

"It's only twenty feet. See those knobs of rock? They go all along there. Do you think you could use them to climb up there?"

Harry looked at him as though he'd lost his senses. "Those little knobs are wet, slippery as a seal. And most of that wall is made up of clay. Pieces could break away anywhere I tried to get a hold. Maybe if I had some chalk for my fingers, I could do something. But like this . . . " He shook his head.

"Well, if you don't think we should try, then I guess we can just curl up here and freeze to death," said Sherwood.

Harry gave him a disgusted look, but he peered at the wall again, using the torch to follow every inch of its course up to the opening. Finally, he looked at Sherwood.

"Maybe . . . maybe I could do it. It'll be a miracle if my hands don't slip right off those wet knobs. But even if I make it, then what? Without a line, how could I get you two up there?"

"Twenty feet," Sherwood repeated to himself. "We could make a line almost that long by tying the legs of our pants together. Say three feet per leg, six legs. That'd give us almost eighteen feet. You're strong enough to pull Carmen up. She doesn't weigh much. Then the two of you can pull me up." He placed the light of the torch on Harry's face. "What do you think, Officer Forsyth?"

Harry looked back at the wall, then at Carmen shivering beside them. He shrugged. "What the hell? We're probably going to die down here anyway."

"Good." Sherwood looked at him. "We'll . . . uh . . . need your pants before you leave, officer."

Harry glanced at Carmen and sighed. "Would you mind not looking, miss?" he said.

She smiled a shivery smile but turned away.

Harry took his pants off and dropped them on the ground. "Actually feels warmer without the soddin' things on."

Carmen said, "Why officer, you have nice legs. Very muscular."

"You peaked," said Harry, embarrassed. "But while we're in this mode, I'll need to take *your* pants with me."

Sherwood and Carmen stripped their own pants off. Then they tied them together, one leg at a time, until they had a good fifteen foot length. They pulled on the knots with all their strength to make them tight.

"Seems pretty strong," said Carmen.

Sherwood looked at her legs, which were very slim, very shapely and very pink from the cold. He felt his heart tug again at the danger he had placed her in.

Harry wrapped their makeshift line around his waist and tied it off.

"Come on," said Sherwood. "I'll give you a boost." He made a sling with his hands.

Harry stepped into it, then hoisted himself onto Sherwood's shoulders. Carmen held the torch so he could see where the knobs of rock were. He studied the wall for a minute, getting its shape clear in his mind, because once he began to climb, he wouldn't be able to see much farther than the next hold.

"OK," he said finally. "Here goes nothing."

He grabbed hold of the first knob and began to pull himself up. Sherwood helped, lifting his feet until he held them above his head. They swayed a bit, then Harry caught the next hold and Sherwood felt the weight disappear.

They stood watching his progress. Harry did indeed have muscular legs, and his squat body seemed made for climbing as he pulled himself ever higher. The rocks were slippery though and he lost his grip and nearly fell twice. He looked down once and grunted, "Don't you be looking up my knickers, miss."

"Harry," she replied, "if you manage to get up there, I can assure you I will dream about your fine legs every night for the rest of my life."

With that bit of encouragement, he lunged for the last knob, held on for an instant, then slipped free. As he started to fall, he kicked himself out from the rock and disappeared into the water below with a loud splash.

"Damn!" said Sherwood. He fell to the ground at the edge of their platform. But when Harry emerged, the current had already carried him toward the falls. Carmen was closest to him. She threw herself down and reached out a hand, catching him just before he was swept past. In a moment, Sherwood was beside her and together they pulled him onto the ledge, dripping and cursing.

"D-d-damn water's cold!" He spit and wiped his mouth. "Tastes like a bloody sewer."

He rested for a minute, then stood up. "I'll get it this time," he said.

Sherwood lifted him again and again they watched him climb with their hearts in their mouths. When he finally pulled himself over the top into the tunnel, they let out a whoop. "Let me catch my breath," he cried down to them. Then he lowered the line and Sherwood caught the end of it. It reached just to his shoulders.

"Harry, I'm going to tie the torch on. Take a look in the tunnel. Make sure it doesn't just peter out after a few feet. Not much point pulling us up if that happens."

Harry pulled the light up and they watched the glow reflect off the top of the cavern as he explored. The light disappeared completely for two or three minutes. When he returned, he peered over the edge.

"Well, it goes quite a ways. I went to where it branches off, so it connects with something. Anyway, it's a hell of a lot better option than what you've got going down there."

Sherwood tied a loop in the end of the pants line, then picked Carmen up in his arms, lifting her easily until she could slip it over her head. She looked at him with a smile. "I kind of like being in your arms, inspector. You've got a firm grip."

He blushed. He had hold of her bare legs and though they felt cold as ice, they felt damn good too.

He maneuvered until he could grab her lower legs, then her feet, as he lifted her the same way he had Harry. He gave a final shove and held his breath as Harry pulled her confidently up hand over hand. He untied her and they threw the line down for Sherwood.

It was harder getting him up. He was heavier and there was no one to lift him up a third of the distance. But they pulled and struggled and he used the knobs of rock for support until he finally joined them in the tunnel mouth.

They untied their pants, which were soaking wet from Harry's fall into the water. Putting them back on was decidedly unpleasant, but they would dry off eventually from their body heat.

Sherwood turned the light on their new tunnel and they moved forward without a word.

42

The two rodents proceeded slowly down the steep slope toward Julia. They no longer struck her as cute, bunny-like creatures. The needle teeth had disabused her of that notion. Those white barbs weren't intended for carrots. She found their bodies fascinating in a horrid sort of way. As they padded along, in catlike fashion, she could see the muscles rippling in their sides.

She kept ahead of them, slipping down the steep landslide of earth, her feet buried in the soft, sandy soil. She was painfully aware that going down was a dead end. Once she reached the bottom of the cistern, she would have to face them.

The animals appeared to be in no hurry. When they reached the body of the creature Julia had killed, they stopped.

She watched as they sniffed at it, then began to drool that horrible mucus from their mouths. A moment later, they were tearing into the remains with gusto. It was an awful sight and she turned away, but only for a moment. She couldn't bear not knowing precisely where they were.

When she glanced back up, she felt her knees buckle as she saw more of the animals appearing and slipping over the edge to join their feeding comrades. She had no doubt now what lay in store for her. Once they finished the dead rodent, they would turn on her. She felt in her jacket pocket and counted the extra shells. There were seven left in her gun and eight more in her pocket. Fifteen. Make that fourteen, she thought. She needed to keep one for herself. No way was she going to be eaten alive by these horrible creatures.

She was now only ten feet from the cistern floor. She could see by the light of her torch that the bottom was covered in bones and human skulls. In one corner, she saw evidence of a more recent kill. There was still blood on the skull and more splattered over the piles of bones. She shuddered. The pitiful remains could be Hans or one of his men.

As she reached out one arm to balance herself in the softly settling sand of the landslide, she felt cold metal. Startled, she turned to see what it was and found herself staring at a smooth, black, metallic surface. The object stuck out of the side of the cistern, and she could see that it appeared to have arrived at this spot by way of yet another tunnel.

She had no idea what it was, but the prospect of another tunnel brought new hope. The cistern wasn't a dead end after all. Perhaps there was another way out . . . if she had time to explore it.

But there wasn't going to be any time. Half a dozen of the creatures were now smacking their mouths and making the strange sucking sound around their dead companion. The small body was almost completely gone, eaten down until there was nothing left but a nub of tail, some teeth and fur. Several of the remaining rodents now eyed her, mucus dripping from their mouths like a runny nose. They began to move forward eagerly.

She was astonished at how quickly they covered ground. There wasn't going to be time to even contemplate a move into the tunnel. She did the only thing she could think of. She raised her pistol and shot another of the beasts. The explosion boomed across the cistern, echoing back and forth, hurting her ears.

The animals flinched at the sound as though in real pain. They retreated briefly, turning their heads in almost rabbit-like fashion from side to side, noses twitching. But when the sound was not repeated, they returned and began to tear into their newly dead comrade.

Their appetites seemed insatiable. She had only a minute or two before they would turn on her again. And she could hear more of the creatures slipping over the edge of the cistern.

With one hand holding the pistol and the other her torch, she slid alongside the metallic protrusion and into the tunnel. It seemed to curve away, and there was a pile of debris farther into the opening. She struck the object lightly with her pistol and was rewarded with an empty sounding echo. When she reached the pile of debris, she was astonished to discover that most of it consisted of various mechanical components. Old pressurizing tanks and pumps, wiring, piles of an insulating material and metallic plates, all seemingly ripped from the strange, oblong object. She had no idea what the thing was, except that it was obviously manmade and very out of place down here.

The sucking sound erupted behind her. She turned to the entrance where the rodents now milled about, pursing their lips and smiling their horrible, tooth-filled smiles. By now, most were covered in blood that streaked their white fur.

She knew her time was almost up. She lifted her pistol to shoot another of the things when she heard more sucking sounds behind her. She whirled about and saw a mass of the rodents approaching from the other end of the tunnel. She'd hit the mother lode. They were all around her; mewling, sucking, hissing, smacking their lips. Her blood ran cold. There were many more than she had bullets for. She brought her gun up, prepared to shoot herself. The horrible end staring her in the face made such an action not only justifiable, but logical.

She had her back against the metal object, her head turning in first one direction and then the other. She wasn't crying out loud, but tears were running down her cheeks. She would never see Hans again. Probably no one would ever know what happened to her. She would disappear as utterly and inexplicably as the two women whose bones were first found in this cavern sixty-five years ago.

She turned the torch one way and then the other, mesmerized by the fate slowly enveloping her. The creatures paced stealthily towards her in an eager, lip smacking, mouth drooling fashion. She edged along the side of the metal object and felt her jacket catch on something, holding her fast. She jerked and it ripped away, pulling out a piece of the cylinder.

Swinging her torch to see what was holding her, she saw that she had pulled open a hatch. She stared at the interior—of something. There was no time to determine what. In her mind, it was one thing only. A possible haven.

She glanced one last time at the beasts approaching on all sides. They were only feet away now. She stepped over a metal frame and into the cylinder, swinging the hatch closed behind her. There was a latch, which she turned. Then she saw that there was a wire wrapped around the latch running back to a metal bolt. She quickly wrapped the wire around and around the bolt.

She could hear the animals outside, milling about the hatch, clawing at it, hissing and sucking. They were clearly frustrated. After a few minutes, they seemed to go away. But she was nowhere near ready to contemplate leaving her safe haven. She slumped to the floor, utterly exhausted, as much from the stress she had been under as from her exertions.

Turning the light on the cramped interior, she stared in wonder at her surroundings. It was definitely some sort of flying projectile. For half a moment, she contemplated that she was inside an alien space ship, but the foolishness of that thought made her reject it instantly. Whatever this thing was, it was of the earth.

The inside of the projectile was in shambles, yet she had the overwhelming sense that someone had been here before her. In one corner was a pile of blankets and a piece of insulating foam, as though a bed had been fashioned. There were odd bits of things stashed all around. Wooden boxes, clothing, cans of food and soft drinks, a pile of what appeared to be kitchen utensils, several books.

Someone had lived here.

Great pieces of the mechanism had obviously been ripped out to allow space for the precious belongings of whoever had been here before her.

She picked her way through the piles and lay down on the blankets. She was suddenly very tired and very hungry. She picked up a can of some kind of beef stew and pulled back the tab. Using a wooden spoon she'd found, she began to eat the gelatinous substance ravenously. She opened a bottle of Pepsi, one of several stashed about the messy interior. It was refrigerator cool from the frigid confines of the tunnel. She drank deeply. It tasted like nectar.

Then she lay back on the blankets and wondered what strangeness would come next. She feared she might never have the courage to leave this place; that she'd die here before submitting to those awful things outside.

Beside her was a book; a children's story: *Charlotte's Web*. She opened the cover. On the inside, in a wavy, childlike handwriting, someone had written: Lila's book.

43

Norway — 1944

Gunnar eyed the front ahead of them with unease. The temperature was falling rapidly and he could see fog beginning to drift inland from the sea. The rail line ran close to the coast here, passing between low, fir-covered hills. The deep fjords that struck far inland provided avenues for thick coastal fog to move into the interior.

Osbourne, glued to his guns, still had a clear field of vision, though it would not last much longer. "Train below," he said suddenly.

They all strained to see it—a long, slow-moving snake appearing and disappearing in the fog.

"We'll have to go pretty low to check it out," said Gunnar. "Hold onto your hats."

He banked the Stuka and took them in sharply, then leveled out half a mile behind the train.

"Those cliffs are awfully close," Natasha said nervously.

"I see them. It's the ones I can't see in this fog that worry me."

As they approached the train, he nudged the plane lower still until they were less than a hundred feet above it. They roared the length of it before he pulled the Stuka up steeply and banked again.

"Anyone see anything?"

"Not me," said Natasha.

"For a moment, I thought I saw something on one of the boxcars," said Osbourne. "But I lost it in the fog. Take another go around."

Again the plane began its descent. It was raining now and they were about to enter the dark front. Visibility was decreasing rapidly. Gunnar crept lower, barely fifty feet above the slow-moving train. He could sense Natasha gripping her seat fiercely.

Then the major's voice came across their radio loud and clear.

"That's our baby! I see the red cross on two box cars. There's a flatcar between them and it's got something covered on it. Got to be the V-2."

Gunnar nodded, concentrating on winding through the hills. He regained altitude and began to fly ahead of the train, following the tracks.

"What do we do now?" Natasha asked.

"If we're going to be able to do anything to stop them, we'll have to do it on the ground. They aren't going more than twenty miles an hour on those rickety tracks. Probably giving Hitler fits. We'll keep to the line and look for someplace to land far enough ahead to give the major time to perform some magic with his bag of tricks."

It was late afternoon and they were now far enough south for nightfall to become an issue. The front continued to tease them, seeming to hover just offshore, rain spitting and then stopping continuously. They had, at most, four hours of good light left and probably not enough fuel to fly half that distance. Sabotage was best done in darkness, of course. But spotting some feasible place to land and then carry out the tricky maneuver would require either daylight or a lighted field. And they weren't likely to get the latter.

They flew for almost ninety minutes, keeping to the tracks. Gunnar stared grimly at his rapidly depleting fuel supply. It was a lonely piece of country, raw and beautiful, but almost completely lacking in human settlement, other than a few fishing villages hugging the coast. These were connected to the rest of the country only by boat.

The drone of the plane was mesmerizing, and Gunnar talked to Natasha to stay alert.

"Tell me more about this guy Carrel, the scientist," he said. "Do you think he could have been coerced to do the research? If so, maybe he also sabotaged what he was doing, so it wouldn't work."

"A comforting thought," Natasha replied. "But I wouldn't want to count on it. Human intelligence can sometimes take on a bizarrely particulate nature, allowing scientific genius and moral idiocy to exist side by side."

"Dr. Jekyll and Mr. Hyde?"

"Yes, though I suspect in this case, the moral side may have simply taken a backseat to utter absorption with the science. There are plenty of examples of scientists becoming so fascinated by what they're doing that they forget to eat, sleep or even bathe. I'd bet Hitler's fantasy of world domination is something Carrel hardly gave a passing thought to."

"Our talkative friend back there at the camp certainly wanted us to believe *he* would never do anything to hurt innocent civilians."

"He was trying to save his hide, and I don't believe him for a minute. But I think Carrel was a more complex man. His research into surgical techniques actually saved lives. Even when he and Lindbergh began to collaborate on eugenics and the perfection of the species, they were always talking about the betterment of mankind. You know, in one of their experiments, they removed a cat's thyroid gland and attached it to a pump Lindbergh had designed. It perfused the organ with nutrients and oxygen and forestalled infection. It lasted for weeks, still producing thyroid hormone."

"Sounds more like Frankenstein than Jekyll and Hyde," said Osbourne, who had been listening in.

"You may not be far off, major. They went on to maintain many other organs, including a cat's ovary that continued to ovulate on the pump."

"Phew! That's pretty amazing stuff," said Gunnar.

"Amazing enough to get them some serious publicity. You may remember some of the newspaper articles at the time: *One Step Nearer to Immortality* was a pretty representative headline."

"Well, you've given me new respect for Carrel," said Gunnar. "Maybe he really didn't want to do this work for Hitler."

"I wouldn't get carried away. Carrel wrote a best seller in 1935 in which he argued for the establishment of biological classes. The weak and sick at one end, and the strong and fit— receiving new organs as needed—at the other."

"The master race, huh?" said Osbourne.

"Something like that."

"And who decides where any individual gets placed on the continuum?"

"That's the nicely convenient part," said Natasha. "The sorting was to be done by a council of scientific experts like Dr. Carrel himself."

"So much for the Jews, I suppose, if Hitler and his ilk were doing the choosing," said Gunnar.

"Hey," said Osbourne, "Look down on your port side."

They looked out and saw a relatively level, grassy meadow running between two low hills. The rail line ran on the far side of one of the hills.

"See any buildings or towns?" Gunnar asked.

"Nah. I haven't seen any settlements in a while," Osbourne replied. "I bet that open spot was caused by a fire."

"Great. If we try to land, we'll run into a blizzard of leftover burned trees and downed limbs."

"I don't think so," said the major. "Before the war, I used to go camping in the Adirondacks with my American relatives. Way out in the back country there'd be meadows like that one down there. No one really knew where they came from, though fires were suspected. The fires either burned everything down to the ground or else happened so long ago that nothing was left of the remains. It was smooth walking through those grassy fields."

"OK, major. It's the best option I've seen. We're running out of both daylight and fuel. Buckle up everyone."

Suddenly, Natasha and Gunnar felt the hair stand up on the back of their necks as the major's guns burst into fire with a shockingly loud staccato. In between bursts, they heard him yell, "We've got company at ten o'clock! They're already diving on us."

Gunnar spun around and looked. Two planes had begun approaches on them. He recognized them instantly. They were Norwegian Air Force, almost certainly flying under the command of Quisling.

Without hesitation, he took the Stuka into a steep dive. He could hear Osbourne swearing a blue streak, as he tried to keep firing on target while the plane spun down.

Gunnar headed straight into the low valley and the advancing front. Their only chance was to lose the attackers. He'd once flown for the air force that now saw him as an enemy and he understood both their tactics and level of skill, which were very high.

Bullets danced across one wing tip, just missing the fuel tank. No serious damage was done, but it further emphasized their predicament, if that was necessary.

"Look over there," said Natasha, pointing. Heavy coastal fog hung above the shoreline.

"That's our escape hatch," Gunnar said.

They barreled straight down into the fog, so steeply that Natasha feared they were going to crash into the sea. But Gunnar knew what he was doing. One thing pounded repeatedly into the heads of new pilots by their trainers was to avoid flying into low lying fronts or fog banks. It nearly guaranteed disorientation and disaster. No way would those pilots follow them.

He dipped into the fog bank, which rose less than a hundred feet above the sea, and quickly leveled off. Their attackers would expect him to hug the coast to allow at least a minimal visual target to orient himself. Instead, he turned straight out to sea, keeping a close eye on his altimeter.

The guns silenced once they entered the fog. Gunnar said, "What were they doing before you lost sight of them, major?"

"What the hell do you think?" came the annoyed reply. "They were shooting at us. If you weren't driving this thing like one of the king's bleedin' race cars, careening all over the place, I might have gotten a clear shot at them."

Gunnar smiled in spite of himself. Osbourne certainly had confidence in his marksmanship. But he knew their only real chance was to hide. He had never flown a Stuka before and though he was a good pilot, their foes would be highly trained in their craft. He couldn't hope to outfly them.

He flew straight and level, hands gripping the controls tightly. They had to be flying on fumes at this point. He'd thrown the flight manual out the window. What he was doing was nearly guaranteed suicide, only slightly less so than staying in a dog-fight with the enemy. He looked at his watch. He would main-tain this course out to sea for two or three minutes, then rise above the fog and hope they were alone.

Neither Osbourne nor Natasha spoke to him. Intuitively, they understood that it was in their best interest not to distract him. Gunnar hoped they didn't know enough about flying to realize just how much danger he had put them in.

Finally, he rose above the fog. Out of the heavy mist, but still in the middle of the darkening front, visibility was not good.

"Anyone see them?"

Necks careened in every direction.

"Nothing," said Natasha.

"Same here," said the major.

"You think it was an accident that they stumbled on us?"

"No way. They were looking for us after that refueling debacle. And we have to assume there are more around, maybe patrolling up and down the rail line. They have to know what we're after. It's going to make our job that much more difficult."

"So what do we do now?"

"Pray like hell we have enough fuel to get back to our meadow and they don't find us before we land. It'll be dark soon. We'll have one chance for the landing. If we make it, they won't be able to find us in the dark."

They dipped back into the fog until they neared the coast, then Gunnar brought them out and they made a dash for the meadow. He circled once. The open area looked much shorter than his first impression, but there was nothing he could do about that. Visibility was almost gone. In addition, the engine had begun to sputter from low fuel.

He came in low over the trees and dropped suddenly, touching down with a comforting solidity. At least it wasn't a hidden quagmire; but they raced toward the trees much too quickly. He applied the brakes as hard as he dared. They hit a dip and the plane gave a sickening crunch, then elevated again momentarily before settling back to earth.

"We're going to hit the trees!" Natasha cried.

He tried to turn the craft, but the wheels handled sluggishly in the tall grass. Then they were into the trees. Branches scraped and pounded the airplane. They bounced over some sort of stone wall, then one wing was torn completely off by a dead tree and they came to a stop in a thick clump of brush and alders.

They all sat, momentarily stunned, not quite believing they were still alive.

"Everyone all right?" Gunnar finally managed to say. But their internal communications no longer worked. He turned and located Natasha, seeing that she was shaken up but not hurt. Then he called back to the major.

Osbourne was also unhurt, but practically immobilized by the crumpled side of the plane. It took half an hour to disentangle him. Then another half hour was used up gathering their gear and, most importantly, the explosives. By then, the moon had come out allowing them to see haphazardly, at best.

Standing beside their little pile of equipment, Natasha said, "Thank God those explosives didn't go off when we crashed."

"Not bloody likely without the caps," said Osbourne, "but we're lucky everything wasn't torn apart and made useless."

Gunnar surveyed the wreckage in the moonlight. "At least no one is going to find the plane in this brush, even come morning." He used his flashlight to check his watch. "We've got to move quickly. The train will be approaching in two, maybe three hours at the outside."

Osbourne consulted his compass, then they each gathered up some of the crucial supplies and headed up the hill between them and the tracks. There was a lot to do and not much time to do it.

44

London — Present Day

They were being watched. Hans could sense it. They'd seen no more of the strange creatures that had killed Wolfgang, but he had little doubt that he and Kurt were still in danger.

Kurt trudged along in front of him, head down, as though he didn't want to see any more of the awful things, even if they were to suddenly appear. He had never been the strongest member of their group. The estranged son of a major German industrialist, he'd been brought up in luxury and neglect at the same time. He dropped out of university in his freshman year and drifted for a while, refusing all attempts by his parents to rein him in. He had begun to get embroiled in the drug culture when, almost miraculously, he had been brought out of his downward spiral by the climbing community. His passion for the sport soon took him around the world, working for professional guides who took rich clients up mountains they had no business being on.

The two men met and struck up a friendship during a trek in the Hindu Kush. When Hans began to recruit his team to investigate the V-2, he thought Kurt's contacts through his family might prove useful, estranged or not. But now, he was worried. Though Kurt had performed well enough in climbing his way out of the pit, the need to shake him out of his fear and into action was not a good sign.

They came to yet another branching of the tunnels. Kurt halted in frustration. "We're never going to get out of here," he said. "We could be heading straight back into the clutches of those things."

"Take the left branch," Hans said quietly. "The main thing is to keep moving." He didn't add that simply moving would help keep Kurt focused on the task at hand. He hoped.

"Did you see what they did to Wolfgang?" Kurt muttered for the tenth time. "Ate him alive. The same thing's going to happen to us."

"No, it's not, Kurt. Not if we keep our heads. And keep moving. We're lost, but we're bound to run into someone sooner or later. The authorities are going to send people down here by the truckload. It's only a matter of time."

They had to select between two more branches in quick succession. The tunnels seemed to be getting more primitive, with those strange sculpted sides and increasing dampness as water fell from the ceilings. But then, finally, things began to look up. The tunnel widened and they came abruptly to a set of steps.

"I'll go ahead," said Hans, as Kurt hesitated.

He climbed the dozen steps cautiously. The stairway seemed to be crafted out of marble, he realized, incredulously. And it led to a much larger space, where he stood, mouth open, turning his torch in every direction.

"It's an abandoned tube station," he said.

They hiked along the raised platform above the tracks. Everything was obviously old and long unused. But just being out of the smaller, stultifying sub-tunnels was a relief.

"Look," Kurt said suddenly.

Hans turned and followed the beam of his friend's torch. High on one wall was the well-known symbol for the underground, a circle with a slash through it. Above it were the words: Down Street Station.

"Down Street," said Hans, thoughtfully. He'd researched London's underground as thoroughly as anyone. "That's the station that was reconstructed for use as a bunker by Churchill before the Cabinet War Rooms were built. It's part of the Piccadilly Line. Or was. I think they closed it as a tube station back in the '30s, or thereabouts."

"Only thing I care about," said Kurt, "is whether it gives us any idea where in the hell we are."

"Down Street was located between Green Park and Hyde Park Corner. We're not far from Buckingham Palace . . . as the bird flies anyway."

"He'd have to fly straight up through a hundred feet of solid clay," Kurt muttered.

They continued along the platform and then stopped. The tracks disappeared behind a wall of cement blocks. The entire end of the station had been permanently closed off. Hans went up to the wall and struck it with his hand. It was rock solid.

"We're not getting out through this," he said.

They made their way back down the platform and came to a similar obstruction at the other end of the station.

"We can't get a fucking break!" cried Kurt.

But Hans stared at what appeared to be a small depression at one end of the sealed entrance. "What's that?"

Kurt followed his light. There did indeed seem to be an indentation of some sort.

They approached and saw a steel door. It was old and obviously in rough shape. It still had an ancient padlock on it.

"Hold my light," Hans said.

He put his shoulder to the door and shoved. The hinges creaked but the padlock held tight.

"Give me a hand."

Kurt put their lights on the ground and together they slammed the door repeatedly until it felt like their shoulders might fall off. The padlock held tight, but finally the hinges gave way and the door fell in, hanging only by the lock.

Kurt rubbed his sore shoulder and picked up his light. He shined the beam into the darkness beyond.

"Surprise," he said, sarcastically. "Another damned tunnel."

"At least it's a modern one," said Hans. "Relatively speaking, anyway. And there are tracks. I think we should follow them. Who knows, maybe it will lead to Churchill's Cabinet War Rooms."

"What the hell good will that do us? They're probably walled off too."

"Some of it may be. But the war rooms covered almost three acres in underground London. They had steel reinforced ceilings and housed a staff of more than 500. There was a canteen, hospital, shooting range, dormitories, not to mention the cabinet and map rooms. Churchill even had a telephone scrambler system concealed in his private lavatory that allowed him to speak directly to President Roosevelt in Washington."

"Terrific. Maybe we can call the American CIA for help," said Kurt.

Hans ignored the remark. "The point is, at least part of the complex is now run by the Imperial War Museum as an exhibit open to the public. If we can somehow find our way into that, we should be able to get out of here."

Suddenly they both froze. The one sound they had hoped never to hear again was coming from somewhere behind them. It was an orgy of sucking and smacking, like something being eaten with great gusto.

"Jesus Christ!" said Kurt, his eyes like two saucers. "They're back."

45

Carmen shivered. Her wet pants were plastered to her thighs and felt clammy and frigid. She doubted they would dry out down here even if she tramped around for weeks. Sherwood's arm came around her shoulder, and she leaned into him for a moment, his own warmth—little that was there—was a haven.

"You OK?" he asked, his worried face hovering over her. "Aspies have a hard time with cold?"

"Yes. Cold, wet, dark, enclosed places. But who's complaining? Do you think we'll ever get out of here?"

"Absolutely," he answered without hesitation.

"I wish Julia was with us. She knows her way around down here better than anyone."

"Maybe so," said Harry. "But I don't mind telling you this place gives me the creeps. Can't tell up from down, left from right, backward from forward. You'd think the blokes who built all this would have seen fit to put in a few helpful signs . . . you know, like 'This Way Out,' or something." He scratched his belly. "Gawd, I'm getting hungry."

His words made Carmen realize that she too was starving.

Sherwood gave her a final squeeze. "No good talking about food," he said. "Just makes it worse. Let's keep moving."

They followed the tunnel a long way. Carmen worried that they must have left any part of the Coram's Fields site far behind. They could be anywhere beneath central London by now. She tried to listen for subway trains, but heard nothing.

Then the tunnel began to narrow, the walls closing in on them until there was barely room to move forward in single file.

"This is no good," said Harry.

Sherwood stopped and looked at the others. "I agree," he said. "It looks like it's going to peter out. Maybe we should turn back, take one of the other branches."

Carmen shrugged and turned around. There was no room for the others to pass her, so she led the way. She had gone only a dozen feet, when they heard a loud rumbling and felt a blast of air hit them.

"Cave-in!" Sherwood cried.

They stumbled backwards, feeling the shock wave of the collapse in the tiny space left to them. Then the air began to fill with soot.

"No choice, now," Sherwood coughed, holding his arm over his face. "We'll just have to see where this tunnel goes."

Their path continued to tighten until they were literally pushing themselves through. Finally, they were reduced to crawling on hands and knees in a space no larger than a sewer pipe.

Sherwood, in the lead, stopped to rest for a moment. He could hear Harry swearing softly behind him.

"Buried alive, that's what we are," he said.

Carmen had never been so terrified. Even her underground river journey now drew only a close second. She could literally feel the weight of thousands of tons of earth pressing in on them like something alive, something that wanted to entomb them. She fought against panic with every fiber of her being.

"Listen," said Sherwood. "We're not done yet. I can feel a breeze in my face. It's got to come from somewhere."

"Well, if this bleeding tunnel gets any tighter," said Harry, "it won't make any difference. Instead of suffocating, we'll just lie here till we starve . . . or go mad."

The urge to retreat was overwhelming. Just to return to a place where they could at least stand, where they could see each other would have been reward enough. But turning around was impossible. So, too, was crawling backwards. Moving forward, they could use their hands and arms to pull themselves against the heavy clay walls of the tunnel. But retreating without the use of their hands was not an option.

Sherwood said nothing to Harry's mention that they might starve. He believed now that they were probably as good as dead. He berated himself constantly for having led them into such a predicament. But he pushed forward, pulling with his hands, pushing with his toes, fighting back the sense of panic.

Then he was stuck fast. He couldn't move. He forced one hand out in front of him and felt cool air blowing on it. His light showed what he thought was a slight widening of the tunnel ahead. It might as well have been a hundred miles away.

"What's wrong?" asked Harry. "Why did you stop?"

"I can't move," Sherwood said. "But it looks like it might widen just ahead. See if you can use your hands to push against my feet."

He heard Harry grunting as he maneuvered himself into position. Then hands grasped Sherwood's feet and pushed. The sergeant was a strong man. It was fortunate he was the one behind Sherwood and not Carmen. He grunted and struggled, kicking with his feet, while Sherwood pulled himself forward inch by desperate inch.

Then, miraculously, he was through, popping out of the tight confines of the tunnel like a cork out of a bottle.

"I made it! I'm through," he said. He still couldn't stand up but at least he could turn around and look back at Harry. "Can you get through?"

"Don't know," Harry said. "I'm wider through the shoulders than you."

Sherwood could hear him struggling. If Harry couldn't get through, then Carmen wasn't going anywhere either. He reached back and grabbed his friend's hands and pulled while Carmen pushed from behind.

Harry cried out as his shirt ripped and the skin on his shoulders was literally flayed against the rock solid clay.

But then he was through, breathing like a wounded whale, while Carmen easily pulled her slim body after him.

They sat for a few minutes, regaining their composure. It was a relief just to be able to sit up and look at one another.

"There won't be any going back through that," said Sherwood. "We're committed to whatever lies ahead."

Carmen gave him a squeeze. "Like you said, that air has to come from somewhere."

They moved on slowly, still on hands and knees, but with room to move more freely. Then the walls began to pull back, the ceiling gained as well, and in a few minutes they were once again standing in a normal size sub-tunnel. The sense that they had been pardoned from a horrible fate was almost overwhelming.

Sherwood kept them moving. The tunnel here was dryer than the others they had been in. The floor had soft sand on it. He couldn't imagine where sand had come from or how it had gotten down here.

They reached the first branching of tunnels since squeezing out of their bottleneck. It didn't matter which way they went. They were hopelessly lost anyway. But the branch they started down ended after a dozen yards.

They stopped and stared, transfixed. The tunnel opened into a room, a cavernous space, really, with water dripping from a great height somewhere. The entire room was filled with human bones. There were scores of bodies. Some of the remains still held remnants of clothing.

"Jesus," said Harry. "What is this? Some bleedin' burial ground for disease victims?"

Carmen knelt beside the remains. She reached out and turned over several skulls.

"Oh my God," she said.

"What's wrong?"

"These people didn't die from disease. Look."

The skulls had been crushed. They examined more of the remains. Every single one had had its skull crushed by some crude, heavy object. There were no other signs of struggle. The bodies were stacked neatly in straight lines.

"This was deliberate," Carmen said. "Like a ritual killing or sacrifice of some kind. Look how orderly everything is. Every one was killed in the same way, with a blow in exactly the same spot on the skull. Then they were laid out in straight lines. I'd guess no one resisted, and I don't see any sign of them being restrained or tied up in any way. It's as if they expected to be killed."

"What would be the point of bringing them all the way down here just to kill them?" said Harry. "That would take a lot of work."

"There's something else," Carmen said. "These remains are old. I know enough about bones and how they deteriorate. And look at this bit of cloth. That sort of weave is definitely sixteenth century, maybe even earlier. These bodies are hundreds of years old."

Sherwood looked at her in the dim light of their torch. "Maybe . . . " he said, "from the time of Henry VIII?"

She glanced up with a shaken expression. "Possibly. If they suffered from the Sweat, perhaps they were killed to put them out of their misery, though the course of the disease was generally so rapid, I can't believe there would have been time for such a ritualized set of murders."

"What's the difference?" said Harry. "It's just more damned bodies. I'm beginning to think there are more dead people beneath London than there are live ones upstairs. The point is: we've got another dead end, no pun intended. We've got to return to the other branch and try to get the hell out of this charnel house."

There was no argument.

The other tunnel continued in winding fashion and seemed to be trending lower. The floor grew increasingly damp. Before long, they heard the sound of water rushing.

"That's all we need," said Harry. "Another damn waterfall. You're not getting me to take my pants off this time."

But the water wasn't falling. It was flowing. And when they emerged at the side of an underground stream, Harry rolled his eyes. "Terrific, another bloody river," he said.

"Or the same one," said Carmen. "Maybe we've been going in circles."

The walls of the tunnel had pulled back, revealing a wide area beside the river. Overhead, were a series of heavy arches. Carmen began to think it looked familiar. And then she knew for certain, as her torch started to pick out shiny things—wonderful things.

Sherwood could hardly contain himself. "Look, Carmen. You didn't imagine it."

Stacked against the cave wall beside the river were indeed many, many incredible things.

There were crude wooden boxes and baskets filled with gemstones, including emeralds of a size none of them had ever seen before. There were crystalline skulls rimmed with gold, boxes of worked silver, candle sticks, plates and jewelry. Exquisite pieces of Chinese porcelain lay side by side with chests of pearls, an enormous bronze cannon and gold ingots stacked ten feet high.

Many of the baskets had deteriorated, spilling rubies and emeralds and all manner of exquisite gems onto the floor. This must have been how some of the incredible stones had been found by rats and people. When the waters of the river rose, they washed precious stones out and took them on a subterranean journey.

Carmen wandered about as though in a dream. For the first time in her career, she understood how Howard Carter must have felt upon opening Tutankhamen's tomb, achieving the goal of a lifetime.

Only she had not had to wait a lifetime for her discovery. They passed beneath an arch and into another roomful of treasure.

"Good Lord," Sherwood said, his voice incredulous. They stared at silver and gold bullion, coins and ingots, gold doubloons and pieces of eight. The silver piled higher than any other. "There must be ten or twenty tons of silver here."

Carmen gaped in disbelief at great statues of horses and a carriage that seemed to be made entirely of gold. These were the giants she had seen in her dazed state as she floated, helpless, through the cavern.

Her eyes flowed over the treasures and life-size statues. Who could have hidden such a treasure in such a place? And why? There were life-size figures of men and women crafted in pottery and others dressed in coats of arms. She returned to the first room and knelt beside the bronze cannon.

"Can you tell anything about where it all came from?" asked Harry.

"I don't see any markings on the cannon. But I recognize the type. It would have come from a Spanish galleon, probably sixteenth century."

Sherwood stood over a chest of pearls and ran his hands through the marble-sized, flawless pieces.

"A galleon?" he said, disbelief in his voice. "I thought pearls came from the orient."

She shook her head. "The Spanish discovered pearl oyster beds in the Caribbean in the fifteen and sixteen hundreds. They enslaved native divers and Africans to retrieve them from the ocean floor. God knows how many poor souls died to fill that single chest."

She hesitated, her mind putting together possibilities the way she had done for so long in examining the riches of the British Museum. "I've got a strange thought," she said. "Someone obviously hid this treasure here a long time ago. It would have taken many men to carry everything down here. I think those bodies in the other tunnel . . . they were the ones who did the work."

"And the poor bastards were murdered for their trouble—to keep the secret," said Sherwood.

Harry held up an enormous ruby. "Some things never change, boss. There's enough wealth here to justify killing an awful lot of people."

As Carmen stood, mesmerized, by the incredible riches, she felt her AS suddenly kick into gear. One of the statues was moving. She shook her head. She had to be hallucinating. Still, the form moved. Then there were others.

She cried out, stumbled backward and was caught by Sherwood, who also gaped at the figures moving toward them.

As the strange visions moved forward into the direct light of their torches, one figure, shorter than all the others, spoke in an all-too-familiar voice.

"We meet in the strangest places, don't you agree, Carmen?"

Her eyes went wide. "Trimm?" she said.

46

Julia woke with a start. For several moments she had no idea where she was, the blackness engulfed her more completely than anything she experienced at home, even in her own bed at night.

Then everything came flooding back—along with a numbing fear—as she remembered the awful things that drove her here.

The silence of her tomb rivaled the blackness. What could have awakened her? The thought had barely risen to the surface of her thoughts when she heard it.

Something was scratching around inside the projectile. Her heart began to race. With one hand she slowly reached out and groped for the torch. It took every ounce of her willpower not to cry out in terror. Could one of those awful creatures be in here with her?

Where on earth was the damned light? She couldn't find it anywhere. Sweat began to run down her forehead and into her eyes. Her terror was absolute.

She lay still again; listening. The scratching continued and seemed to be moving. She concentrated as hard as she could, trying to determine where it was coming from. Was one of the things trying to gnaw its way in? No. It wasn't outside; it was in here . . . somewhere . . . close.

She rolled over onto one side in an attempt to put both ears on the sound. In doing so, she rolled on top of the torch, which had become ensnared in the blankets.

Slowly, she reached down, unraveled the light and turned it toward the sound. In the other hand, her fingers gripped the pistol so tightly they hurt. Still, she hesitated. She didn't really want to see the thing, and what if the light made it mad?

But nothing was worse than not knowing. She flicked on the torch. At first, she saw nothing. Slowly she panned the light around her compact space. The sound was still there, a scratching, like someone rubbing fingernails against the floor.

Then she saw movement. There. In the far corner, where the various bits of food and ancient wrappers had been piled. Her hand shook as she tried to keep the light focused.

A surge of adrenalin pumped through her body as something emerged from the pile of debris. She stared at it in disbelief. It was a rat. A plain, ordinary, run-of-the-mill barnyard rat.

She nearly swooned with relief.

"Well, hello, little guy," she said. "You gave me quite a scare."

The rat sat up on its hind legs and sniffed the air. It held a tiny bit of food in its forelegs, which it continued to chew on.

Julia sat up and leaned against the side of the missile. "I guess maybe we're both hiding in here, is that it?"

The rat hesitated, then went on eating.

"Who are those guys out there?" she asked, almost in earnest. "They can't be relatives of yours. Besides, all your friends have apparently been chased out of the underground altogether. You got left behind, huh? Well . . . me too, I guess."

She reached for the half empty soft drink and took a sip.

"Do you stay in here?" she asked her new friend. "There can't be enough food for you and what about water?"

She looked around and found a small, chipped saucer. She poured some of the soda into it and placed it on the floor, pushing it away from her with her foot.

The rat stared at it, then edged forward cautiously. It was almost comical. The poor thing was obviously frightened, but it was also very thirsty. One emotion clashed with the other, as the creature circled the saucer. Finally, after several minutes, it got up its nerve and took a drink. Then it settled in and drank the entire amount.

"Probably not what you're used to," said Julia. "But liquid is liquid." She stared around her tiny prison. "I may get as thirsty as you before I'm through."

She got to her feet, though there was barely enough room to stand upright. In the front of the projectile, she could see a pile of odd looking parts. She went over to look at them. At her movement, the rat jumped back into the pile of debris, but continued to watch her.

Not only did the electronics look very old, but incredibly primitive by modern standards. She pulled out a sort of drawer and stared at more ancient wiring. Whoever made this thing was not very advanced technologically. There was writing on a panel. She leaned forward to look at it. What she saw made her gasp.

Warnung! Stromschlag, the label read.

She knew only a little German, but the meaning was clear enough. "Warning! Electric shock."

She stepped back and contemplated the enormity of those two words. She was inside a German missile. Some remnant left over from the war? It was the only possible explanation. From the Blitz, perhaps. A bomb. She was living inside a bomb.

For a moment, she almost panicked. What if it was still capable of blowing up? But that was nonsense. It had been here for seventy years. For some reason, the thing had failed to explode and had lodged here in the tunnel.

Well. Lucky for her, she thought. Otherwise she'd be inside the digestive tracts of those awful things by now. She placed one hand on the metal sides of her abode. Good German steel. What a testimonial she could give. 100% rat-proof German steel.

Except of course, for her small friend across the room.

She went over and crouched beside the latched panel that had given her access to the missile and listened intently for several minutes. She heard nothing. It might be the only chance she would get to escape. Yet she found it nearly impossible to will herself to open the little hatchway. What if they were just sitting out there waiting for her? She stared at her new companion.

"What do you think?" she asked. "Are they gone?"

Hardly believing what she was doing, she began to unravel the wire that held the hatch shut. Then she put the torch in her left hand, held the pistol tightly in her right and cracked the opening.

Her senses were at fever pitch. She could hear the blood rushing through her veins, as she strained to detect anything at all that might indicate the presence of her awful tormenters. Slowly, glacially, she swung the hatch open and back on itself.

She leaned out and turned the torch to the right and then the left. Nothing. She glanced back at the rat.

"Good luck, little fellow," she said. "I hope we both make it."

Then she stepped carefully out of the hatch, taking care not to make any noise. She took a few small steps into the new tunnel—what she now thought of as the missile-delivery tunnel—and stopped. Turning back, she closed the hatch again. No point in letting the creatures into her hideaway or giving them access to her friend inside.

She proceeded down the corridor. The sides of the tunnel were blackened, as though something had squeezed through at considerable speed, causing great friction. Something like a missile, she thought with amazement. For all of her fears, she had enough of her wits about her to realize that the missile was an incredible discovery. A real piece of World War II arcana that would excite anthropologists and make war buffs sit up and take notice. She could see the ad on EBay: *For Sale: A living piece of wartime London.*

Well, she thought grimly, before anyone is going to hear about it, I've got to get out of here. The tunnel stretched straight away until the light from her torch dimmed. She walked more quickly now, determined to find a way out before the creatures returned.

But then she heard them. That terrible sucking. Her knees grew wobbly with fear. The sound grew louder and seemed to be just ahead. Frozen, but her mind racing, she tried to think of some way to escape. The pistol in her hand was literally shaking.

What was that?

At the outer limits of her field of vision, she saw movement. It was one of the creatures. No. It was a mass of the terrible things. A pile of them moving rapidly toward her, almost crawling over one another in their haste to reach her.

She gasped and cried out loud, the sound of her own voice jolting her into action. She raised the pistol and shot into the surging crowd of rodents. At least two of the things were killed or wounded. The rest stopped and began to feed.

She had only a few minutes. Despondent, she retraced her steps, opened the hatch and climbed back inside the missile, wiring it tightly shut behind her.

Her little companion sat in his pile of debris and watched her curiously, nose twitching.

"Looks like we may grow old together in here," she said tightly. She slumped into the pile of blankets that had been her bed.

47

SIS Director Hopkinton sat waiting for Prime Minister Harris to fully comprehend his words. The man could be incredibly obtuse sometimes. But he needed to get him to understand that they were at a critical moment.

"I don't understand, Marcus," Harris said uneasily. "You told me you'd explained the situation to Rachel and that you were sure she wouldn't dare go public."

Hopkinton sighed. "I don't believe she will. That's not the issue currently. The Sweat is beginning to break out. Simonson reports that the number of victims is almost at a tipping point. Not only are we going to get a lot more very quickly, but it's going to become increasingly difficult to keep what's happening secret from the public. Rumors about the number of rats and rat-bite victims are spreading. A few members of the press have begun to pick up stories of a strange disease not seen for five hundred years. They're practically drooling over it. You can hardly blame them. It's great copy.

"Once topnotch reporters begin digging into this seriously, well ... it's only going to be a matter of time before someone uncovers that there was another outbreak during the war."

"My God," said Harris. "If they figure that out, they'll know we and our predecessors suppressed information about the Sweat. The public will have our heads on a platter."

Your head, thought Hopkinton, not mine. He hadn't kept a low profile all these years for nothing. Few among the public had any idea who he was. But he said, "I'm working on a way to redirect blame away from the administration, Nevil. I've put Dr. Trimm to work on the problem."

"The British Museum archaeologist? What's he got to do with all this?"

Hopkinton had kept his dealings with Trimm as much out of the prime minister's orbit as possible. No need to fill his meager brain pan with details about the treasure. The SIS director hadn't believed it himself for a time.

But once Trimm went to the authorities with his information about the rats, Hopkinton had quickly discovered that the shady little character had much more up his sleeve than just anxious rodents. A master of the veiled threat, he soon had the good doctor babbling everything he knew. It *had* been unfortunate that Rachel Forrester happened to be in on the meeting where Trimm first spilled the beans, but she clearly didn't believe the nonsense about buried treasure. She refused to even mention it to the prime minister. More's the pity for her, Hopkinton thought. He had a greater imagination.

Trimm had been horrified that he would lose all access to his future riches. He needed Hopkinton and he knew it. For his part, Marcus had begun almost at once to see his own future—post Harris administration—as one of the wealthiest and most influential people on the planet. The two men had become codependent, Hopkinton for Trimm's knowledge about the treasure and Trimm for the SIS director's support and manpower. Forrester had been neatly shut out of the loop.

"I have supplied Dr. Trimm with our own highly trained men to undertake an investigation beneath the city to . . . uh . . . determine the extent of the infestation."

"I thought we already knew the extent—it's bloody out of control," said Harris.

"Perhaps. Perhaps not. Our scientists have accompanied Dr. Trimm. They will determine what—if anything—is out of control. And I control them. Nothing will be released to the public without my authorization. Meanwhile, we need to keep one eye on Forrester and another on Simonson. Neither of them must be allowed to bring the public in on this."

"But the longer we keep this from the people, the more danger I will be in once the truth is revealed," said Harris.

You bet your sweet ass, thought Hopkinton. But the longer he could keep a lid on things, the more time they would have to get the treasure out to a safe place. Then he could retire and leave this schmuck to deal with the consequences.

He smiled gently at the prime minister. "I think a press conference is in order. We need to reassure everyone that the government is firmly in command of the events." He raised a hand as the prime minister started to protest. "Trust me," he said, "I've got everything under control."

48

Mitchell Harrison III directed his tiny car across Vauxhall Bridge, turned onto John Islip Street and then slipped into a gritty parking garage set in the warren of streets behind the Tate Gallery.

He drove to the top floor, circled once to make sure he was alone, then pulled into a space that had grown familiar. The garage was nearly empty at seven in the morning. He turned off the engine and sat, nervously drumming his fingers on the windowsill.

This would be his fourth meeting with the mysterious woman who had first contacted him as he left *The Times* building one evening around suppertime. She had been bundled up against the September damp, had a handkerchief over her head and wore dark glasses. She spoke only a single sentence, telling him to meet her on the top floor of the garage the next morning at seven if he wanted the most important story of his generation.

Then she had disappeared into the busy night crowd, leaving him standing with his mouth open.

Harrison had been a reporter for almost twenty years and had his own byline, which was undoubtedly how the woman had picked him. It wasn't the first time he'd dealt with a mysterious source, though most generally proved to be unsubstantiated dead ends.

There was something about this woman, however, that intrigued him. Though he could see very little of her, and she had kept her face turned away throughout their conversations, her voice and demeanor suggested someone highly educated. Perhaps, he had mused, someone high up in the government.

In their previous meetings, she had given him statements that he'd managed to confirm through other sources. She clearly had access to high-level information. But she was cautious to a fault, and would only dole out bits and pieces of tantalizing details regarding the strange goings on of high-ranking public health officials.

His editors continued to treat the story as incomplete, but they pressed him to stay with it, based primarily on the strange behavior of rodents in the city in recent weeks. This rat thing definitely had all the elements of human interest if nothing else. People were fascinated by a good rat story. And the hundreds of critters piling out of Holborn Station had been one of the best.

The Times carried it on the front page for two days in a row. There was precious little real information, but the public lapped up the horrifying aspects of it. The paper kept the story going with interviews of homeowners who lived near the tube station, firefighters and policemen who had been at the scene, even Animal Health people who pontificated at length on what might have panicked the rats. Their primary rationale was sewer gas.

He looked down at his watch. She was late. He hoped that didn't mean she wasn't going to come. He had some things he wanted to ask her. He was getting tired of this cat and mouse game. What was she afraid of?

He had a view out his car window over the top of the massive Tate Gallery all the way to the Thames, where he heard the moan of a ferry whistle. Traffic was light along Millbank, but the hum of a huge metropolitan center never ceased.

Then, without warning, she was there, standing beside his window as she always did, face turned away from him, staring at the view.

"You're late," he said, annoyance in his voice. He was an important person too. He needed to let this woman know that she owed him something for his time.

"Did you get to Dr. Westerling as I suggested?"

"I've talked to the bloke twice. He gives a very good impression of a clam. Yes, there have been a few rat-bite victims, more than usual, perhaps. But London's a big city, don't you know. Millions of rats."

"Don't let up on him. He knows more than he's letting on. If you can get your hands on the medical records of any of those bite victims, they will tell you a lot. Follow the bites."

He stared at her. His own personal Deep Throat. Except the moniker was inappropriate. Her voice was more musical and refined. "They used to tell you in this business to follow the money," he said, dryly. "I must be the first reporter ever told to follow the bites. Now if this was a story about a passionate love tryst, maybe . . . or a vampire . . . "

She had no sense of humor.

"The government has great secrets," she said. "I will lead you to them, but I have to do it in my own way."

"*All* governments have great secrets," he said in a disgusted voice. "I need more than that. What the bloody hell is going on?"

He felt her tense. She hesitated, then said, "The people of this city are in grave danger. The Harris administration thinks they can keep it quiet. They are mistaken, but they are in too deep now to back away. If . . . when . . . the truth gets out—a truth that goes back to the Second World War—the government will fall. You must move quickly. There isn't much time."

"Then give me something to damned well work with. I need leverage. People like Westerling don't talk unless they have to."

She stared out at the river and seemed to come to a decision. "Ask Dr. Westerling what he's doing about the Sweat."

"I beg your pardon?"

But she was gone. He craned his neck and saw a fleeting movement across the parking ramp and then nothing. His phantom was gone till the next time. He hoped there would be a next time.

The Sweat? What the bloody hell did that mean?

49

Hans shook Kurt out of his terrified stupor. "Help me lift the door back into place. It's solid steel. Ought to slow them down, at least."

They propped the door back up. The ancient padlock still held, but the rusted and broken hinges didn't offer much protection.

Hans held the door in place. "See if you can find something to barricade this with."

Kurt stumbled back into the tunnel, his torch flashing back and forth. He found some old wooden scaffolding and began to rip boards from it. He brought them back to Hans and they propped them against the door.

The creatures were now just on the other side, mewling and sucking madly, their frustration palpable, claws scraping against the door.

"Jesus! Why don't they go away?" Kurt cried.

"More supports," said Hans, ignoring him. "We need more. It's got to be stronger."

For another ten minutes they propped and jammed boards against the door until finally Hans was satisfied. He stood back and stared at their work. The animals on the other side continued to claw and suck, but the door held.

"We're safe," he said.

"Safe?" Kurt laughed almost hysterically. "Those things are everywhere down here."

Hans just said, "We've got to keep moving."

They walked down the center of the rail line. This section had clearly not been in use for many years. After fifty feet or so, they

came to a steel ladder built into the side of the tunnel. It disappeared into an opening in the ceiling. They stared at it, filled
with indecision.

"I say we take the ladder," Hans said finally. "It goes up, and up
is the only way out of here."

Kurt shined his light at the opening. "I don't like the idea of
going into that tiny hole. Some of those things could be up there."

"And some could be ahead of us in this tunnel. We know
they're behind us. If they can't break through our blockade,
they'll eventually find a way around through the tunnels.
They're tracking us, Kurt, like a big-game hunter tracks a tiger
through the bush. They have the smell of our blood and they
mean to catch us."

It was the wrong thing to say to Kurt in his present state,
but he seemed resigned now and willing to do whatever Hans
suggested.

Kurt started up the ladder, which was so old that it rattled
loosely against the wall. Hans waited until he was up before
starting himself. Two on the rickety structure at the same time
would not be a good idea. Then they heard the sound of wood
splintering back down the tunnel.

"What was that?"

"I'll go see." Hans said.

He walked back toward the steel door until he was close
enough for his torch to illuminate it. What he saw stopped him
cold. The door was actually bent towards him. He could see
pressure on the wooden planks they'd stacked against it. Even
as he stared, several more planks snapped with loud cracks. The
door was now open almost six inches, and he could see some of
the creatures trying to get through.

He could also see what the animals were up to. They had
climbed on each other's backs, using their combined weight to
put pressure on the door.

He gaped in disbelief. The damn things were working together, forcing the door open. It couldn't possibly hold more than a few seconds.

He turned and bolted back to the ladder, hearing more boards splintering behind him. He leaped onto it and began to climb like a man possessed. Kurt looked down at him from above with a confused stare. Then he shined his torch down the corridor and saw a mass of the creatures, mucus dripping from their mouths, racing towards them.

"Hurry," he shouted needlessly.

Hans went up the ladder hand over hand. "See if you can find something to cover the hole," he cried.

He slipped through the small hole to the next level as the rodents reached the ladder and began to climb. They were incredibly agile and had no trouble with the rungs, climbing faster than Hans had.

He looked around desperately for something to cover the hole. Kurt was nowhere to be seen, and he wondered if his friend had simply panicked and bolted. The closest of the creatures was just a couple of rungs from the hole.

He picked up a stick, the only thing he could find, crouched over the opening and poked viciously at the animal. Surprised, the creature lost its grasp and fell back to the ground, but it was immediately replaced by another. The animal stared at him with cold, purposeful orbs, like the unfeeling button eyes of a doll.

He batted futilely with the stick, until the animal grabbed the weapon in its teeth, crunched it into splinters and tossed it aside. An instant later, it was through the hole and Hans scrabbled backward on his hands and knees, kicking at it with his feet. He was certain he was as good as dead.

Then, suddenly, Kurt was beside him carrying a huge slab of concrete, which he dropped onto the creature with a loud yell, splattering the thing, killing it instantly.

"Pick it up," he yelled. "It should cover the hole."

Together they lifted the thing which was twice the size of a manhole cover and dropped it over the opening, covering it almost completely.

They fell to the ground, breathing heavily. "Thanks," Hans said. "I thought I was done for."

"Couldn't find anything useful; not until I found that piece of concrete fifty feet back. Don't know how I lifted the damn thing. It must have been the adrenalin."

Hans turned his torch on the crushed animal, and they stared at it in wonder. Kurt poked it with his boot. It was their first chance to examine one of the things up close, without having to worry that its friends were about to eat them.

With a splintered piece of wood, Hans forced open the mouth so they could examine the teeth.

"They're like God damned needles," said Kurt. He reached out a hand to touch the point of one of them, but Hans grabbed him.

"Better not do that," he said. "That mucus, or whatever the hell it is that comes from their mouths, burns and it might infect us."

"Look at the claws," Kurt said in a hushed voice.

The nails were an inch long, scallop shaped with flat ends, like the teeth of a beaver. They were clearly designed for cutting and ripping . . . or digging. Hans wondered if they might be responsible for the scalloped cuts in the sides of many of the tunnels.

Kurt had the same thought. "Do you think these things could have carved out the tunnels down here? There are an awful lot of these smaller passageways connecting the tube lines."

"Hard to believe. They'd have to have been tunneling away for a long time." He hesitated. "Or else there are a hell of a lot of them."

He stood up. His legs felt wobbly from the stress they'd been under. "Let's go," he said, halfheartedly.

"Wait," Kurt said. He leaned over the concrete slab. There was a three-inch gap not covered by the block. He shined his torch through the gap.

"What are they doing?"

"Just milling about. They're . . . good God . . . "

"What?"

"Must be a hundred of the things. They've formed a kind of chain up the ladder and you won't believe this . . . "

"I'd believe anything about now."

"There's got to be half a dozen of them holding on to the top of the ladder . . . I'd swear they're trying to push the slab up."

"Do you think they can?"

"I don't think so. They don't have any leverage, and this thing is heavy. I think we're OK for the time being."

Kurt stood shakily. "Where the hell do you think these things came from?"

Hans shook his head. "I don't have a clue. It's like they're some sort of mutants or something. Like a branch of the rat family that evolved differently. The question is: why hasn't anyone ever seen them before? There are a lot of them and they're living beneath one of the biggest cities in the world."

They turned their backs on the hole and began to trudge down the new corridor. Almost at once, Hans realized that this tunnel was different. It was more finished, the sides more uniform. They came to a branch and stopped.

"This is as far as I got," said Kurt. "I thought I saw something down this side opening, but then I found the slab and came back." He put his light on the branch.

"What *is* that?" asked Hans.

They went a few feet down, stopped and stared. The corridor ended in a room filled with very old machinery.

Kurt entered the room and played the torch all around. "I think it's some sort of generator."

They stared at the thing. Cables ran out of it in several directions. They followed one until they realized it connected to an overhead line that continued out into the corridor, where a series of filthy, ancient bulbs ran off into the distance.

"These tunnels were lit sometime in the past," said Hans. "Maybe we've found Churchill's bunker."

They continued down the passageway, marveling that it now was straighter and actually lined with some sort of paneling. Soon, they found themselves in a maze of rooms. Some appeared to be offices or storerooms; then they entered into what could be nothing other than a series of laboratories.

Several large rooms were filled with shelving around the sides. There were work stations with sinks, lab equipment, racks of glass tubing and file cabinets.

Kurt moved forward to another room and exclaimed, "Holy Christ! Come look at this."

Hans joined him. The room was filled floor to ceiling with shelves that held cages of all sizes. Most of the cages contained skeletons. And most of the skeletons were obviously rats, though some were bigger, probably the remains of larger animals, Hans thought, like raccoons, foxes, cats or dogs.

"What the bloody hell were they doing down here?" Kurt muttered.

50

"What do you think of our little treasure?" asked Trimm. He stood over one of the baskets and picked out an enormous emerald. He seemed completely enamored by the jewel.

"How...how long have you known about this?" replied Carmen.

"I've known about the possibility for years. But I'm afraid there's little time to go into the details. And *you* have no time at all to worry about it."

He gestured to one of his men. Carmen focused on them for the first time. There were a dozen off them, including one who had evidently driven in on a small tractor with an attached trailer.

"How on earth did you get that down here?" Harry blurted.

Trimm contemplated him for a moment. He was on a schedule, but he couldn't help gloating over his triumph.

"There was a direct route, more or less. My research only just determined how to break through to it. We had to widen the tunnels in one or two places. Henry VIII didn't have the benefit of modern machinery. He used manpower, which I suspect you've seen the evidence of back there."

He waved a hand. "And that's where you're going."

One of the men came forward. He had a cylinder on his back and held a hose that snaked over his shoulder in front of him.

"Give our guests a brief demonstration," said Trimm.

The man set his feet apart, taking a firm stance. Then he pointed his hose at a section of wall and let off a blast of liquid fire.

Carmen gasped. A flamethrower.

"A useful bit of insurance against anyone else after my treasure." With a dismissive wave of his hand, Trimm said, "Put them in the bone room."

The man holding the flamethrower gestured with his head, and they began to move down the corridor, back to the room filled with the remains of King Henry's men.

"Trimm!" Carmen cried. "You can't seriously be planning to leave us down here. That's murder. You know the way out. You have to help us."

He turned back to them. "I don't *have* to do anything anymore. Not what Scotland Yard says, not what that fool Jessmer says and most certainly not what you say. I'm going to be the richest man in the world. I'll be telling others what to do from now on."

Sherwood said, "What do you other men think will happen to the rest of you? Because I can tell you that whatever Trimm has promised, he won't deliver. Once you remove the treasure, you'll all be expendable, just like us." He gestured back down the tunnel. "Just like those poor bastards down there."

The man holding the flamethrower said, "We don't work for Trimm, and we'll be taken care of all right. There's enough loot down here to buy our help many times over. Marcus will look out for our interests."

"Shut up," Trimm yelled. "I told you not to mention his name."

"What's the difference?" the man shrugged. "They're not getting out of here."

Carmen, Harry and Sherwood were forced back into the dead-end tunnel. Then another of Trimm's people knelt down and set an explosive charge. He lit a fuse and backed quickly away.

A moment later, the ceiling of the tunnel collapsed in a roar, sealing them in forever with King Henry's dead servants.

51

Norway — 1944

Major Osbourne led the way up the slope away from the meadow, away from their destroyed Stuka and toward a very uncertain next few hours. As they climbed through the rocky, snow covered terrain, sparsely treed with stunted spruce, Gunnar worried. He worried that they would not arrive in time, that they would become lost or disoriented and that they had no avenue of escape.

Natasha labored away in front of him. The climb was steep, and her breathing was harsh, but she didn't complain, even turning to give him an occasional smile in the moonlight.

"If we manage to get there in time," Gunnar said to the major, "I gather you plan to blow the tracks and derail the train. My question is: what then? If that's all we achieve, they will undoubtedly send another train and we'll have managed nothing more than a few hours, or at best days, of delay."

Osbourne grunted. "I've considered that. We have our guns and plenty of explosives, enough to blow up the missile. But we're not likely to have time to do that once she's derailed. There have to be armed men on board. Some may be injured after the derailment, but we've got to assume we'll be under constant fire once our charges go off. Frankly, I haven't figured out how just the three of us can pull this off."

He stopped to brush snow from his pants and gave them a grim smile. With his pale skin and strong, white teeth, he looked like some sort of Cheshire Cat in the snow-reflected moonlight.

"But if this wasn't an impossible mission, Churchill wouldn't have given it to us, now would he?"

Natasha nodded. "I've watched Winston send a lot of men off to near certain death on one espionage mission or another. He knows only a fraction will achieve their goals, yet he truly believes that each will be successful at the time he toasts their departure. He sees this war as a titanic struggle between good and evil, and he has absolute faith that good will triumph."

"Well that's bloody comforting," said Osbourne.

Gunnar said, "I don't suppose it would be possible to time your blast so it comes when the missile is directly on top of it?"

"I'm good, but not that good," said the major. "There are too many variables: the speed of the train, how much time I have to set charges, what our viewing point will be. It would just be the greatest stroke of luck."

On that sour note, they grew quiet; the only sounds were their heavy breathing and the occasional whiplash of a branch.

After an hour of labor, they reached the top of the hill and looked down on the tracks in the valley below. Another thirty minutes and they stood beside the rails. Osbourne removed his pack and began to organize the explosives, while Gunnar scouted for the best place to set their charges.

He explored a hundred yards in each direction, then settled on a sharp curve where the train would emerge from a stand of spruce. The curve would make derailment more certain and lessen the time the engineer might have to spot the damaged track. The nearby trees offered cover for them to fire from.

As Osbourne crouched in the snow beside the tracks, running his charges, they looked up suddenly as a train whistle sounded. In the vast, frozen landscape, Natasha thought it was the most mournful sound she'd ever heard. It was still far away, the clear night sky helping the sound to carry.

"That's the next valley over," said Gunnar. "We've got maybe twenty minutes. You going to be ready?"

"Almost done here. Doesn't take much of a blast to part these rickety rails." He hefted several smaller packets with short fuses. "These babies, lobbed onto the flatcar, are what I'm counting on to destroy the missile. Why don't you find a spot for us to watch the fireworks?"

Natasha stared uneasily at the small packets. "You know," she said, quietly, "if what we think is on the missile is really there, the major's fireworks may not destroy the lethal agent. It may release it."

If such a thought had occurred to any of them, it was the first time it had been brought into the open. They all remembered the look of horror on the scientist's face when he thought Natasha was about to open one of the lethal test tubes. They might very well be planning their own imminent deaths in a most unpleasant fashion.

Osbourne shook off the comment. "Our goal is to destroy this thing, or at least its method of deployment. Nothing we can do about possible side effects."

Suddenly, Gunnar had an idea. "Major, what if you set off the charges now? When the train gets here, she'll slide off the broken rails, but they won't necessarily think it's sabotage. They may think it's just another weak section of track. They won't have their guard up."

Osbourne stared at him. "It's a bloody good idea," he said. "We need to hurry though, before they're close enough to hear the blast. Pick your spot down the track and pray that once the engine runs off the rails, the V-2 will end up close enough to us that we can lob our smaller explosives right onto the damn thing."

Quickly, Osbourne lit his charge and they backed away into the woods. When the blast came, it was—as the major had promised—muffled and almost insignificant in the magnitude of the landscape surrounding them. As soon as the snow and rock dust settled, he ran to the spot and surveyed the damage. One side of the rail was completely severed, with pieces of wooden ties strewn about.

"You and Natasha kick snow over those pieces. I'll do the same to the broken track. With luck, they won't see a thing until it's too late."

Tasks completed, they came together behind a clump of boulders on a rise thirty yards from the tracks.

When the train emerged, Gunnar was surprised at how fast it was going. She might have carried close to thirty-five miles an hour of speed. It was sheer folly with the ancient, poorly cared for rail line. Hitler must have ordered it, or maybe Quisling. They were in a hurry to get their new toy.

As the engine ran out of track, Gunnar saw nothing for several moments. The speed carried the huge beast forward, plowing through the snow, almost without sound. But a whirlwind of blasted snow rose into the night sky and finally they heard the unmistakable crunch of metal grinding against bedrock.

Osbourne cursed as the flatbed carrying the V-2 flew past them, carrying on for another hundred feet before coming to a stop. The engine tilted over at a thirty-degree angle. Half a dozen cars had followed it off the tracks, but the V-2 remained intact and upright.

"Not good," said the major in a low voice. A sudden silence filled the night air, following the cacophony of the derailment. "They can send another train, tilt those derailed cars out of the way, repair the tracks and be back on course. A good crew could probably pull it off in less than a day."

"So let's throw your remaining charges and be done with it," said Gunnar.

Natasha grabbed his arm. "Look," she said.

Up and down the train, soldiers had climbed down. Clearly under orders to examine the track, they walked up and down in the cold, stamping their feet and making cursory checks under the cars. Many looked like they had been asleep only minutes before.

Gunnar observed them coldly. He recognized the uniforms of his own countrymen. Perhaps they had no idea what they were guarding, but they were doing the Nazis' bidding. The thought made him sick to his stomach.

The men carried machine guns, and there were too many to confront.

"Damn," he swore. "Now what do we do?"

Osbourne shrugged his massive shoulders in the moonlight. "Wait," he said. "They may let their guard down after a while when nothing else happens."

They settled back and watched the soldiers. Most of the men returned to the warmth of the train. It would be a fleeting warmth at best, as the source, the engine, was now silent and tilting in the snow.

"That's one small consolation," said the major. "They'll soon be as bloody cold as we are."

Two things were clear. No one was going anywhere until help came. And the few soldiers left outside to guard the train were more than enough to keep them from completing their plan. Gunnar wondered if those in charge really believed the derailment could be an accident, since the enemy certainly knew they were in the area.

The night passed slowly and bitterly. The three of them huddled miserably, unable to escape an almost uncontrollable shivering.

At one point, late in the frigid night, Natasha said to Gunnar. "I'm remembering how I felt when we were in bed on the train coming through Scotland. I felt warm and safe there with you, Gunnar."

He put his arm around her, but said nothing.

"I'm sorry for the way I've been since," she said. "I think that feeling of security scared me. I didn't want to rely on it, to think about something that might be lasting when we were about to head off into God knows what. So I tried to put it out of my head. It was wrong of me."

She wanted to see him, but there wasn't enough moonlight in the woods. Instead, she felt his warmth and how his arm hugged her more tightly.

"Thought maybe something went on between you two," Osbourne muttered. "Anyway, I'm bloody freezing and maybe you could hug me for a while."

They laughed, teeth chattering, as the major squirmed in beside them.

At daylight, they heard voices and struggled to their feet, shaking their arms to create some warmth.

A group of men, perhaps half a dozen, had descended from one of the rear cars and was making their way to the front of the train. It seemed to be another inspection party, determined to understand more clearly what had befallen them overnight. As the party approached the middle of the train, one of its members stopped and seemed to stare right at them. His eyes swept the tree line, searching for something.

Natasha felt Gunnar go rigid. "What is it?" she whispered.

He didn't respond but instead reached for his gun and put it to his shoulder. His heart lurched, finger toying with the trigger, squeezing. Just a little more . . .

Osbourne looked up just in time and nearly yelled out loud. Instead, he reached out his hand, pushing the gun down. "You want to get us killed faster than we're already trying?" he hissed. "What the hell's the matter with you?"

Gunnar resisted him for a moment, then stopped, falling to his knees. "That's Quisling," he said simply.

"What? Which one?" Natasha stared out at the men.

"The one in front with the glasses and dark uniform. I had no idea he was going to be on the train. I swore an oath when I left the country that if I ever got him in my sights, I'd kill the treacherous bastard the moment I saw him. Now, there he is and I can't do a thing."

"Not yet anyway," said the major. "Just give it a little time."

Time was something everyone in that cold Norwegian valley had plenty of. Evidently, the plan of the train's occupants was to sit tight and await the arrival of help. The day stretched on. Snow began to fall near midday and by three in the afternoon a full, raging blizzard had descended.

The increasing wind and heavy snow clung to them, even under the trees, turning their bodies cold as ice. Natasha seemed to suffer the most. She was nearly immobile from the cold as she lay in Gunnar's arms.

"I don't like this," Osbourne said finally. "Once help arrives, our chances will only decrease. We've got to act now, before we freeze bloody solid."

Gunnar had to agree. He was worried that Natasha might freeze to death if they spent another night out here. They didn't dare build a fire and had only a limited amount of food and water.

"Look," Osbourne said, "we can barely see the train in this snow and the guards must not be terribly worried about attack in this weather. We can make our move now, in daylight. It's a risk, but so is staying here and freezing."

Natasha murmured, "You've got to destroy the missile. Thousands of lives . . . " She pushed Gunnar's arms away from her, even as she began to shiver more uncontrollably. "Do it!" she said hoarsely.

He stood and moved a few feet away with the major.

"There's only one way to blow the missile up and save ourselves at the same time," said Osbourne. "We've got to use the cover the storm offers and the element of surprise to kill every soldier on that train."

Gunnar stared at him. "You know that's impossible," he said.

They were both covered with the heavy, wet snow. "Winston wouldn't think so," Osbourne said evenly.

52

London — Present Day

Mitchell Harrison III was spitting. As a reporter he was used to having to wait to see people, and God knew he waited forever to see his own doctor. But in his opinion, Dr. Westerling was nothing but a public servant. The asshole ought to be awaiting an audience outside *his* office.

In the inner sanctum, Westerling glanced at his watch. There was no way he could avoid the annoying little scribe any longer. He got up, ran one hand through his luxurious hair and opened the door.

"Ah, Mr. Harrison. Sorry to keep you waiting. What can I do for you?"

Mitchell resisted the impulse to deck the good doctor on his way through the door and settled into a leather armchair next to the window instead. He had a splendid view of tourists lining up for the Westminster tour.

Westerling went round and sat behind his desk. He left the door open. Maybe it would beckon to this annoying creature. "There's really nothing new to tell you. We've had a nasty rash of rat bites. Something's sending the creatures out of the underground but no one knows what. I admit it's a bit of an unusual scenario, but there it is."

"Come on, doc. Your halls are overflowing with patients. No reason a simple rat bite should warrant quarantine." He met Westerling's eyes. "Something's going on with the Sweat, and I want to know what it is."

It was a gambit, pure and simple. Mitchell had no idea what his informant had been talking about, but some days bluffing was ninety percent of his job. For an instant, he saw fear flash in Westerling's eyes. He covered it well, but not well enough. After twenty years of interviews, Mitchell could read a subject's eyes like tea leaves. There was something there. He was certain of it.

"I'm sorry. What was that you said?" Westerling pretended to gaze out the window serenely.

"You heard me, doc. I know all about the Sweat, so you might as well drop the act."

Westerling stared at him silently for maybe thirty seconds, then got up, went to the door and closed it firmly.

"All right. I knew someone in the press was going to get the story sooner or later. You'd be doing me and your country a service if you kept this quiet for the time being. If you'll agree to that, I'll talk to you. What do you call it? An exclusive? But you can only go with it when I say."

Mitchell's mind raced. He'd struck pay dirt. Even though he still didn't know what the hell they were talking about. The idea of allowing this imperious SOB control over when to release a story grated, but then he didn't *have* a story without him. He ought to wait, talk to Deep Throat some more, try to fill in the blanks, but he knew he was going to bite. A service to his country? It had to be something big.

"All right," he heard himself say. "I agree."

He held his breath, praying that Westerling had already decided he couldn't put the reporter off any longer, that the doctor had taken the bait, hook, line and sinker and wasn't going to further probe the level of Mitchell's knowledge.

He was not to be disappointed. Westerling took the hook and buried it in the side of his cheek like a bullhead on a diet.

53

Sherwood had placed himself between Carmen and the blast. Now he pushed her towards the back of the room, away from the clouds of rock dust that drifted in on them.

Harry coughed and rubbed his eyes. "I'm getting God damned tired of breathing this crap," he said. "When we get out of here, I'm going to thrash those SOBs, flamethrowers and all."

As the last particles of rock settled to earth, they were once again enveloped in the deafening silence. It was the silence of the dead and buried. Total, absolute and numbing. Only this time, they weren't alone. They were surrounded by the bones of King Henry's poor, doomed laborers.

Sherwood said, "You still have your torch?"

His sergeant answered by flicking on the light. "Still got this, too." He pulled out his pistol. "If I'd thought faster, I might have shot that little prick, Trimm."

"And gotten us fried for our troubles," said Sherwood. "You can't face down a flamethrower with that pea shooter. Besides, at least a couple of Trimm's men had weapons on us the whole time. Never mind. Let's look around."

The room was larger than their first impression, almost cavernous. The light from the torch didn't reach the ceiling, nor did it cast enough of a beam to penetrate to the far side. It was difficult to move about without stepping on bones, which they assumed had been spread about by rats. They made a sickening crunching sound wherever they went.

As they moved toward the rear of the space, Harry suddenly held up his hand. "What was that?" he asked, swinging the light back and forth.

The others listened. Then they all heard it. A strange sucking sound, the same one Sherwood and Harry had heard just before they were attacked by the bizarre creature in the Holborn Tube Station.

Harry looked at Sherwood. "Is that what I think it is?"

"What?" asked Carmen, who had neither seen nor heard the strange creatures.

"It's nothing good," said Sherwood. They began to move away from the sound, which now seemed to emanate from three sides.

The cavernous room started to narrow. They played their torches back and forth on the walls that were slowly limiting their range of movement. It was terrifying not to be able to see what was making the unusual sounds, as the source stayed just beyond the range of their lights.

Harry attempted to step off to one side to investigate what had seemed like an opening, but the sucking sound moved to cut him off.

"It's like they're herding us," he said. "Trying to get us to go in one direction."

Then Carmen got her first look at one of the animals. It had moved a little too far into the light, and she gasped as she saw the muscular body, the porcine nose and a Cheshire-like grin revealing needle-pointed teeth.

"Holy Christ. What *is* that?" she asked.

"Look over there," said Sherwood. He pointed his torch at a knob of rock that thrust out of the side of the room. Next to it was a bit of space that was blacker than the rest of the wall.

"An opening," said Harry. He glanced back at the creatures. Others were visible now, closing in on all sides.

"It's almost like that's where they want us to go," Sherwood said. "Not that I see any alternative."

He and Harry now held their pistols tightly in their hands. But as more of the strange things appeared, it became painfully obvious that the handful of rounds they possessed would be useless to stop them.

Sherwood reached the dark opening next to the knob of rock and stopped, dumbfounded.

Harry, unable to take his eyes off the creatures, said, "What is it, another tunnel?"

Sherwood shook his head, then moved into the dark space, not quite believing what he was seeing.

"It's some sort of a lift. But a really old-fashioned kind."

He was interrupted by the blast of Harry's gun. The animals had begun moving in rapidly on all sides. Now they halted less than a dozen feet away and began to tear apart the animal Harry had killed.

"Mother of God," said Carmen. "What *are* those things?"

"Never mind," Sherwood cried. "Harry, help me get this thing open."

The lift was obviously ancient. It resembled one of those tiny metal cages sometimes used in older apartment houses. He had no illusion that the thing might still work, but the metal cage could offer protection from their pursuers.

Together, they forced the doors open, which gave off a shrieking of joints that were long overdue for an oiling. Carmen stared at the animals just a few feet away. A few looked up at the noise, as though the sound hurt their ears. Then she turned and entered the cage with Sherwood and Harry. Again, the gates gave off an earsplitting sound as they forced them shut.

"Great," Harry said. "Now what do we do? Ring for the concierge?"

The animals had nearly dispatched the dead beast shot by Harry. Some were already turning towards the lift.

Carmen shrank against the back of their tiny shelter and Harry and Sherwood crowded her as the things reached the metal caging.

The spaces between the metal housings were just small enough that the beasts couldn't squeeze through. There was a horrible fascination in watching them mill about, mouths dripping their awful mucus, as they tried to force themselves through the openings.

Sherwood remembered reading somewhere how rats could compress their bodies so they could squeeze through holes the size of a shilling. He hoped these strange mutants, or whatever they were, hadn't developed that particular adaptation.

He put his light on the ceiling of their tiny haven and saw a small hatchway. He reached up and poked it with his torch. He handed the light to Carmen, then stretched up and pushed the hatch all the way open.

"That's our way out," he said.

He jumped up, grabbed the edge of the opening and easily lifted himself through. Harry boosted Carmen up until Sherwood could grab her hands. Then Harry followed. He took one final look at the animals below, then shut the hatch.

They were in a shaft that was as tiny as the lift itself, but the walls were lined with a metal framework that allowed them to climb without difficulty. The lift itself appeared to have been designed as just a one-level transport. When they reached the upper level, Harry and Sherwood had to work together to force the lift door open.

They found themselves in an odd warren of rooms that appeared to be offices and then, as they moved farther along, took on the feel of a series of hospital laboratories.

The rooms continued, one opening into the next.

"A bloke could get lost in this maze," said Harry, speaking what all of them were thinking. They had no way of determining which direction might best help them escape their underground prison.

After half an hour of wandering around, they finally collapsed on a disintegrating couch in an office. The stress they had been under for so long, combined with the shocks of seeing Trimm, finding the treasure and being attacked by the creatures had taken its toll.

"What do you think this place is?" asked Carmen.

"Some kind of research lab would be my guess," Sherwood said. "The equipment is pretty old. I don't see anything that looks more recent than sixties vintage and it may be older than that."

"Well it's got to be something that wasn't common knowledge," said Harry. "I sure as hell have never heard about any research laboratories underneath the city."

"Me either," said Carmen. "And I've researched everything I could find about subterranean London. There was no more mention of something like this than there was about Trimm's treasure."

"Could it be something left over from the war?" Sherwood speculated. "You know, some top secret program?"

"All that sort of stuff came out a long time ago," said Carmen. "Everyone knows about Churchill's cabinet rooms and so forth. But this isn't anything like that."

She stood up, went over to a wall of ancient, dust-covered file cabinets and began to open drawers. As a researcher, she had a knack for finding her way through bureaucratic verbiage to the often hidden nuggets of worthwhile information. Soon, she was deep into research files.

Harry and Sherwood spent the time poking around as well. They found what appeared to be an old, walk-in cooling unit. Inside they found all sorts of bottles of various agents, all of them long ago evaporated.

Sherwood examined the mechanism on the door. "This thing would make a good retreat if we need to escape from those things down below. It's built like a blockhouse."

They wandered back to where Carmen was sitting.

"Find anything interesting?" Sherwood asked.

"Like a map showing the way out of here," said Harry, only half joking.

"No maps," she answered slowly. "But maybe something more interesting than that."

They leaned over her.

"This office we're in?" she said. "It appears to belong to a man highly placed in the SIS during and immediately after the war."

"So this *was* part of the underground bureaucracy set up during the war," said Sherwood.

"I don't think so," Carmen said slowly. "Everything's labeled and coded, as though only selected people could know about it. But that's not the biggest part of what I've found."

She flipped through several files, then took out one page and placed it on the table in front of them. It was filled with a blizzard of incomprehensible figures.

"What are we supposed to make of that?" asked Harry.

"What I wanted to show you was the name at the top of the page."

"Dr. Alexis Carrel," read Sherwood. "Who was he?"

"A scientist from the early part of the century. Nobel Prize winner, if I remember correctly. A man who got famously sidetracked by his fascination with eugenics, among other things. He eventually went to work for Vichy France, and some thought he may have done research for Hitler. Somehow, his research papers made their way here, to an underground laboratory beneath the city of London."

"How the bloody hell could that happen?" asked Harry.

She shook her head. "It certainly raises some interesting questions, don't you think?"

"Eugenics," Sherwood mused. "You don't suppose your doctor would have practiced his little theories on rats?"

"I can't say," Carmen said. "I really don't know the science of it very well. But one thing I do know is that it's pretty strange that Carrel's papers came to be here, when my understanding was that he died in Vichy France towards the end of the war."

54

Norway — 1944

Major Osbourne removed two pistols from his seemingly bottomless pack and fixed them with silencers. Then he placed the smaller, bundled charges into the deep pockets of his coat.

Gunnar did the best he could to make Natasha comfortable. He cut branches from the tree to make a bed for her to lie on. The frozen ground was sucking the heat out of her already frigid body. He took the packs and stacked them beside her to cut the wind and drifting snow.

"We'll be back as soon as we can," he said, unable to meet her eyes.

But she knew. If they were killed, then she would die here in this barren, desolate place. Frozen to death. Another nameless agent lost in the war.

She grabbed his arm with stiff fingers, even inside her mittens. "D-don't d-die," she said. "But d-do what you have to." She tried to smile, but it came as a grimace.

Then the two men were sliding through the snow toward the train. Visibility was only a few feet in the blizzard and the wind was making enough noise that they probably could have yelled to each other without being overheard.

They reached the rear of the train and huddled on the ground, using the slope of the rail bed for a brief respite from the storm.

"Tell me you have a plan," said Gunnar, through chattering teeth.

"We're fortunate the cars remained upright when they ran off the track. It allowed the soldiers to stay inside. We'll enter the last car here," he said. "Turn your collar up and pull your hat down. Our coats aren't all that different from what those blokes are wearing, and we'll be covered in snow. They should think we're some of their own come in out of the storm. At least for a few moments. That should be all the time we'll need."

Osbourne stared hard at him. "I don't need to tell you that if you hesitate, even for an instant, it will mean death, not only for us but for Natasha and God knows how many on the ground in London."

"I understand," Gunnar said.

Still, Osbourne looked at him. "These are your countrymen," he said. "You're not going to be killing some nameless Germans from ten thousand feet, commander, by pushing a button. This is different. You understand?"

Gunnar nodded. He understood one thing very clearly. He wasn't going to let Natasha freeze to death all alone out there.

The first car was easy. There were just two men in it, sitting with their backs to the rear. They didn't even turn around when Gunnar and the major entered. One of the men said in Norwegian, "Tell me you guys have come to fix the heater."

Those were his last words. Osbourne shot both of them before Gunnar could even raise his gun. Then the major started forward toward the next car.

"Wait," said Gunnar.

The major turned toward him questioningly.

"We've got time," he said. "I'm going to give Natasha the best chance she can have if you and I don't make it."

Osbourne stared at him uncomprehendingly for a moment, then smiled in understanding. There was a desk covered with papers in the rail car and next to it a pair of coats hung on hooks; heavy, arctic survival gear. Gunnar took both coats, along with one of the men's warm fleece boots. He also grabbed a full canteen, some food the men had been eating and a flask he found in one of their shirt pockets that contained some sort of liquor.

Arms loaded, he headed for the door.

"Five minutes," said the major. "We don't know if someone may come back here to check on these guys."

Then Gunnar was out the back and running through the snow to the woods. Natasha's lips were blue and she didn't say anything when she saw him, just managed to raise an eyebrow.

He lifted her up and spread one of the coats out beneath her. Then he helped her put on the other coat and the heavy boots. He heard her sigh with the sudden warmth. He lifted her head and gave her some water followed by a sip of the alcohol. Then he laid her back down and arranged the hood of the parka over her head.

He showed her the food and put it and the canteen next to her. Her loaded pistol was by her side. He couldn't stay any longer. The time the major had given him was up.

He leaned down and kissed her. She responded, putting one hand on his cheek.

"Thank you," she whispered. "Good luck."

He slithered back across the opening and entered the last car, covered in snow.

"Just about given up on you," said Osbourne. "I reconnoitered the next car. There are eight men in it, sprawled all around. It's going to be harder. I'll go in first and move straight toward the front. You move slower and stay near the back. I'll shoot the first one once I get at least two thirds of the way forward. That's your signal to begin shooting the ones at your end. Remember, one shot each, dead center. No mistakes. And try not to shoot me, OK?"

It went as planned. Most of the men appeared to be sleeping or at least nodding off. Osbourne shot the first and the noise from the silencer didn't even waken the other sleeping men. But two others quietly playing cards in the middle of the car, reacted faster than anticipated.

One cried out and nearly got his rifle up before Gunnar shot him in the head. Osbourne shot the other.

They stood facing each other in the middle of the car. Ten men had been killed in a matter of minutes. Gunnar felt strangely calm and emotionless. Countrymen or not, these soldiers were guarding one of the most dangerous weapons of the war and were doing Hitler's bidding. As far as he was concerned they were the enemy. He only wished that one of them had been Quisling.

They passed through three cars that were empty and knew they had to be getting close to the V-2. In the last empty car, Osbourne paused.

"I'm going to go outside and see how close we are to the missile," he said. "Wait here."

Gunnar watched him disappear into the blizzard. After a couple of minutes, he returned.

"Just one more car between us and the flatbed," he said. "It's got to be the car with the gunner's nest. They'll be on duty, probably more alert than the others."

Gunnar thought for a moment. "Why don't we bypass them, go straight for the missile and blow it up?"

"Risky. If those guys with the big guns see us, we'll be toast."

Gunnar nodded. "Yes, but we're close enough to our target now to throw the charges. If something goes wrong in that last boxcar and we're killed, the mission will be a failure. I say we take our chances now."

Suddenly the door to the car opened and two men entered. It happened so quickly, there was little time to react. The men realized at once that something was wrong and cried out, pulling their pistols. Gunnar and Osbourne fell behind seats, as a fierce firefight broke out.

The noise quickly brought more soldiers until a dozen were crowded at the end of the car or firing through the rear windows.

"We're pinned down good," said Osbourne, who had substituted his machine gun for the silenced pistol. "And we can't match their firepower." He pulled one of the small charges from his pocket and looked at Gunnar, who nodded.

The major lit the fuse, waited a moment, then tossed the bundle to the end of the car. He and Gunnar ducked low and covered their ears. The blast in the enclosed space was deafening.

The entire back half of the rail car was peeled open like a can of sardines. Dead soldiers lay everywhere. A few were blown out into the snow.

In the moments that followed the blast, Gunnar heard the sound of more soldiers coming. The train must have contained a hundred men or more. Their plan to destroy everyone had been madness. A madness born of desperation and perhaps the cold that had blunted their thinking.

"We've got to blow the missile now," said Gunnar. "Another minute or two and we'll be completely overwhelmed."

Osbourne nodded. "Cover me." He gave Gunnar that funny, wry smile and then was up and moving quickly down to the end of the car. Gunnar was right behind him, firing almost blindly.

Shots came from everywhere. Some of the soldiers had formed a line on one side of the train and were firing into the car from out in the blizzard. It was impossible to see them. Only the flashes from their gun barrels penetrated the blowing snow.

Osbourne tossed his charge into the boxcar with the armored nest of soldiers. Again, a deafening blast shook the entire train. Before Gunnar could recover, the major had jumped onto the ground and was running forward to the flatcar, his last charge in hand.

Gunnar leaped off the train and began to fire on the muzzle flares out in the snow. It was a hopeless cause and he knew it.

Before Osbourne could reach the missile, he was shot down, his body contorting horribly, riddled with bullets. The charge fell forward out of his hand and exploded in the snow.

It was all over. He was alone and surrounded. He had no explosives to destroy the missile. They had failed utterly.

He wanted to keep shooting at the men who had just killed his friend. He was more than willing to die, but if he did then Natasha would die too. There was no sense in it. He wouldn't let her freeze to death in agony for nothing. He should give up. Surrender. They would become prisoners of war, but there were worse things.

He laid his gun in the snow and prepared to stand up to announce his surrender, when a voice rang out, yelling orders to the men to move in on the railcar.

Quisling.

Here was a reason to give his life, a way to salvage something out of all the failure. The traitor who had collaborated with the Nazis, who had tracked down and assassinated his own countrymen and who had ordered the executions of countless Norwegians. With Quisling dead, who knew what could happen? Norwegians might rise up and retake their country, thrust the Nazis into the sea and form a bulwark for the Allies on Germany's northern seaboard.

He grabbed his gun and crawled quickly away into the blizzard. Then he stopped and waited, listening for the commander's voice to appear again.

Men were running everywhere. Perhaps they thought they had killed all the saboteurs. Gunnar let the game play out. Slowly, the cries and shots died down. Things appeared to be returning to normal.

The blizzard began to let up. Visibility opened to a dozen yards, then fifty. He lay on the ground, his rifle pointed toward the train, legs and torso covered with snow. He was all but invisible.

Then Quisling was there, not thirty yards away, strutting about and shouting orders. Men were being sent up into the woods to make sure there were no more enemies hidden there. Gunnar realized they would find Natasha unless he distracted them.

He took careful aim at Quisling, his finger tightened slowly on the trigger, and then he fired. But at that instant, a soldier who had been leaning over adjusting equipment, suddenly stood up and took the bullet meant for Quisling in his chest.

Instantly, a barrage of bullets split the snowdrifts all around him. He saw Quisling flat on the ground, huddled behind the body of the man just shot, yelling at his men to return from the woods and save his worthless hide.

The last thought Gunnar had was that he had failed at everything. Failed to destroy the missile, failed to kill Quisling, failed to save Natasha and the people of London. He would never learn that Quisling's actions would lead to his conviction after the war for treason and to his execution by firing squad at Akershus Fortress.

Gunnar would die here in the snows of his homeland. Winston had chosen the wrong man for the job.

55

London — Present Day

Prime Minister Harris stared out at the enemy, otherwise known as the press corps, with a combination of distress and nervous anxiety. There was double the usual contingent, including representatives from all of the world's major news corporations and media outlets.

Normally the prime minister's spokesman, called the PMS, gave press briefings, sometimes called lobby briefings. But in this case, Harris felt the need to make his own appearance. Since the crowd was so large, it had been decided that the briefing would be moved outside, in front of the most famous door in the world, 10 Downing Street.

The dreary September gloom seemed a fitting setting, as an aide held a large black umbrella over the prime minister's head to keep off a light drizzle. Harris took some pleasure from watching the press corps slowly dampen in front of him.

He began with a statement confirming that there had been an unusual number of rat bites in the city and that some victims had even become infected, though he hastened to add they were being successfully treated with antibiotics. He was unable to complete his opening remarks before the questions started.

"Mr. Prime Minister. There have been reports that some people have died. Can you confirm that?"

"Uh . . . yes, there have been a handful of deaths. These have been primarily the elderly or very young or those with weakened immune systems. Despite the very best efforts of our health officials, there will always be a few such infections that do not respond to treatment."

A pretty young news woman from the BBC spoke up loudly. "Can you explain why the rats have been behaving so strangely?"

"Yes," said another. "We've all read the reports of the Holborn outbreak. Do you have anything more on why that happened?"

Harris's eyes flicked to Hopkinton who stood to one side, studiously avoiding the prime minister's attention. The SIS director had seen that deer in the headlights look from Harris before. The man was going to say something monumentally stupid, and Hopkinton couldn't wait to hear it.

"They're just rats, people," Harris said with a weak smile. "Though I sometimes can explain the motivations of my political opponents, I have a little more difficulty dealing with real rats."

"Are you saying your political opponents are rats?" asked the young woman broadcaster, scribbling rapidly in her notebook.

Harris looked stricken. "Of course I'm not saying that. Our health and animal welfare officials are trying to determine what has driven the rodents out of the underground. Present thinking is that it has to do with gas leaks or possibly some turmoil due to blasting being done on a new spur line near Kensington. There may have been some flooding that forced the animals to seek higher ground."

Mitchell Harrison had been biding his time. He'd agreed not to publish any of the information he'd received from Dr. Westerling, but there had been no restrictions about asking questions in public. He stood up and said in a loud voice, "Mr. Prime Minister, can you explain to us what the Sweat is?"

Hopkinton thought Harris was going to throw up.

"Uh . . . uh . . . excuse me, what did you say?" Harris managed to choke out.

"Many of the rat-bite victims have had similar symptoms, sir," said Harrison. "Lung and vascular lesions that in some cases led to breathing problems and death. Isn't that why there are currently hundreds of people quarantined at St. Thomas Hospital? There are rumors that a new disease may be emerging. I personally have been told by one of my sources that this disease may in fact not be new at all but rather a return of something very old and long suppressed. Don't the people have a right to this information, if true?"

"I want to state for the record here and now," said Harris, "that there is no such thing. Nothing of that sort at all. We are dealing with a simple rat infestation and I'm sure our officials will have it under control very soon."

Hopkinton's mouth curved upward in a grim smile. There it was. The absolute denial. When the truth came out about the Sweat, Harris would have no wiggle room after that statement.

Now other reporters who had not heard of the Sweat were looking to Harrison for more information. Mitchell reveled in his moment. This was what reporters lived for, to be the only one who knew a pivotal piece of information in a roomful of powerful people. He intended to milk it.

"My sources," he began, noting the devoted attention of the very pretty broadcaster in the front row, "tell me that the Sweat is in fact a disease that last appeared in this country during World War II. That prior to that, it had not been seen for hundreds of years. Can you confirm this, Mr. Prime Minister?"

Harris was virtually speechless. That someone actually knew about the Sweat's appearance during the war was more than he was prepared for. It was the final bit of information that, if openly revealed to the public, could very well bring down his government. He went immediately into complete denial mode, sometimes called the "full Blair sandwich" by reporters, two slices of white bread filled with baloney.

"It would be the height of irresponsibility to suggest such a thing," he said. "I have no knowledge of any such scenario. Let's keep to the verifiable facts, shall we, ladies and gentlemen? We have a simple infestation here and nothing more. Let's try not to go off half cocked and risk panicking our citizens."

With that, the prime minister's press secretary strode to the podium, leaned into the microphone and said, "That's all the time we have today, people. Thank you for coming." He virtually pushed Harris toward the door.

Hopkinton fell in beside his boss as they entered the building.

Harris said in a low voice, "How the hell did they know all that stuff about the Sweat, Marcus? We're in serious trouble here."

Hopkinton gave him a surprised look. "Why, I thought the press conference went very well, Nevil. Just the right touch. You're a master, you know."

56

The dust had barely settled from the charge sealing Carmen and the others in the bone room—as Trimm called it—when his thoughts turned to the matter at hand. The treasure had to be removed to a secure location as quickly as possible. Hopkinton had been adamant on the point. He wasn't at all sure how long the prime minister could remain in power, and once the government fell, his own access to resources would be sharply curtailed.

"Get that cart loaded!" he ordered. "Start with the gems and anything made of gold. Leave the silver until the end."

The man with the flamethrower stood by while the others piled baskets of gold coins and fabulous gemstones into the cart. As soon as the vehicle was filled to capacity, the driver began to maneuver back and forth until he managed to turn around.

Trimm was frustrated at the small amount the wagon could hold. At this rate it would take a week to get everything out. He told the men to gather the next shipment in one place, so it would be ready for loading the moment the cart returned.

The tractor slowly started down the tunnel and was out of sight when a loud rumble reverberated from deep within. A moment later, the driver came running back.

"Cave-in!" he cried. "Right bloody in front of me."

Before he could say more, black dust floated in from the tunnel. Trimm swore a stream of invective, grabbed his torch and ran into the cloud. Choking and spitting, he turned his light on the blockage.

It was complete. Tons of the weakened clay ceiling had fallen, releasing clouds of powdery soot. They had neither the time nor the tools to reopen the passage.

He emerged from the tunnel with wild eyes. The men watched him cautiously. As short a time as they'd known Trimm, they had not come to form any charitable opinions about him.

And their leader was obviously at a complete loss. With the passage blocked, they couldn't use the tractor and the quickest way out was no longer an option. In fact, there was now only one other exit, a branch that split off near the entrance to the tunnel that had suffered the cave-in. It was unclear where it led, but it wasn't as if they had any other choices.

Trimm stood, looking first one way and then another, indecision ruling his features. Finally, he said to the tractor driver, "Take it down there," pointing to the remaining outlet.

The man looked as uncertain as Trimm. "None of these other tunnels are big enough for the tractor," he said. "And the tires can barely get any purchase because of the slope of the sides. It won't work."

Trimm didn't want to hear it. They couldn't just sit here. They had to get his treasure out.

Then there came a sound that none of them had ever heard before, a kind of high-pitched sucking noise. It emanated from the collapsed tunnel.

"What's that?" Trimm asked, his voice several pitches above normal. He ran back behind the man holding the flamethrower. "Go see what it is," he said.

Uneasily, the man moved forward. The tunnel entrance was dark and the flashlight mounted on his weapon seemed to have little ability to penetrate the still-settling dust.

The sucking grew louder and the men were becoming nervous. There was a strange quality to the sound, almost like something smacking its lips. Except it seemed to come from more than one source.

The man with the weapon moved to the tunnel entrance. He stopped and shot a blast of fire into the passage, lighting it up suddenly, so that everyone could see the strangest sight they had ever imagined.

The tunnel was filled with pallid, muscular, rodent-like bodies. Except these were unlike any rodents any of them had ever seen before. They were many times the size of normal rats. A number of the creatures actually clung from the sides of the tunnel and seemed to be slicing at it with their claws, making it larger.

The animals produced a kind of high-pitched mewling as the flames bounced off the tunnel walls. Then, before anyone could quite believe what was happening, one of the rodents darted forward with lightning speed and clamped its jaws onto the leg of the man holding the flamethrower. The creature dragged him screaming into the tunnel. His cries lasted only a moment before they heard the crunching of bones and then silence. Almost immediately after they heard eating sounds and more smacking of lips.

The effect on the men was electrifying. Trimm, at least, had some idea that such monsters might exist. He hadn't bothered to inform the others, however, saying only that the flamethrower was for protection against other treasure seekers.

"What the hell were those things?" asked one of the men, his voice punctuated with fear.

But before anyone could reply, the animals began to emerge from the tunnel. It was a monstrous sight. They spread out, moving like oversized, albino cats. Their muscles rippled as they crept in a sort of bent-legged, stalking fashion, mouths half open, teeth like needles, mucus dripping onto the cavern floor.

They seemed to be enjoying themselves, as though this night-marish scene were a social outing.

The men scrambled backwards in the only direction left open to them, towards the now sealed bone room.

Only Trimm and one of the other men carried firearms— small handguns. He hadn't really believed they would need anything beyond the flamethrower to scare away a bunch of rats, no matter how oversized or vicious. And he hadn't trusted Hopkinton's people enough to give them firearms. Now their primary protection was gone—chewed to bits—along with the operator's body.

Two of the rodents managed to single out one of the men from the rest and encircle him. Seeing his predicament, the man cried out for help, but the animals worked quickly. With almost blinding speed, they sprang upon their hapless target, who managed only a brief scream before he was torn to pieces.

The other creatures moved in and joined in the feast, so that in minutes, their comrade was completely gone.

There was a stunned silence as they watched this drama unfold. Then, absolute panic struck the men. They ran blindly down the dead-end tunnel to the bone room until they reached the blockage. Several of them began to tear at the thick clay with their bare hands, Trimm among them. The clay was heavy and dense, coming loose in chunks that they thrust behind them as quickly as possible. In just moments, they were filthy from their labor, nearly black from the mud-like substance.

There was only space for three or four men at a time to dig at the top of the cave-in. The others stood holding the two pistols, prepared even to throw clumps of clay at the beasts, if nothing else.

Once they finished eating, the things moved into the tunnel. There were dozens of them now—sleek, vicious eating machines.

"Shoot one of them," cried Trimm. "It'll keep them occupied."

Both men with guns fired into the mass of beasts, killing or wounding several. The others, smelling fresh blood, turned on their comrades. Here in the close confines of the passageway, by the light of the torches, the men watched as the animals tore apart their own.

"There's a breeze coming through here," one of Trimm's people cried.

Trimm pushed the fellow aside and took his place. It was true. At the top of the pile of now caked, muddy clay, there was a small opening, and he could feel air moving through it. He began to throw pieces of debris back behind him in a frenzy.

One of the biggest rodents, a giant nearly four feet long from snout to tail, suddenly leaped more than ten feet and landed squarely on the back of one of the men with the pistols, clamping his teeth into the hapless fellow's neck. Quickly the thing hauled him back to where the others could begin to eat him, still alive and struggling, but unable to utter a sound due to the creature cutting off his windpipe.

The other armed man dropped his weapon in terror and turned to join his comrades who were now all tearing at the heavy clay with everything but their teeth. Slowly, the opening at the top widened.

Trimm was at the forefront, kicking at anyone who tried to take his place. He pushed half his upper torso through the opening and got stuck.

"Push me," he yelled, and the others pushed him because he was now blocking the only way out.

The beasts tore another man and then another from the rubble pile. Each time, they pulled the screaming body back to the others and began to eat him alive.

Finally, Trimm was through. He turned and immediately began to try to fill the hole up behind him, but the force of the other men was too much. They pushed Trimm back until three of them managed to clamber through. The fourth and last man alive almost made it, but one of the creatures grabbed onto his foot and wouldn't let go, slowly pulling him back as the poor fellow cried out for God, mother and anything else that might save him.

However, this lost soul gave the others a brief respite from attack and they used it to good effect, thrusting clumps of clay into the open space.

"More!" Trimm kept yelling. He wouldn't feel safe until there was a wall of mud between them and those awful things. He reached up to the collapsed ceiling itself and began to pull more clay down.

"You're going to cause another bloody cave-in," shouted one of the men. But Trimm didn't care. Maybe another cave-in was what they needed.

"More clay. More!" he shouted and the others became infected with his fervor, forming a human assembly line hauling thick clumps of the black substance up into the space.

At last, exhausted, dripping with sweat, every last drop of adrenalin in their systems spent, they fell to the ground and waited to see if it would hold.

They could hear the animals sucking and mewling about in the blackness, like demons from the darkest recesses of their minds. The beasts scratched at the sealed hole, but they appeared to not be terribly interested in pursuing the game. Perhaps, at least briefly, their hunger had been sated by the half dozen victims already consumed.

Slowly, the men began to breath normally again and to retrieve some of their sanity. Even so, it was hard to comprehend that so many of their friends were now gone, eaten alive before their eyes.

"Where are we?" asked one.

"Who the hell cares?" responded another. "Just as long as it's not where those things are."

"By all that's holy," said the first man. "Trimm—you brought us down here. You knew about those things, didn't you?"

Fear bubbled up once again in Trimm. If the men thought he'd led them into this fix, they were as likely to tear him apart as the beasts on the other side of the rubble.

"I had no idea such things existed," he said. "Hopkinton should have given us more weapons to defend ourselves."

"You're saying he knew?"

"I don't know. He seemed cautious about something. But he wanted to get the treasure out as much as I did. It wouldn't do him any good if we were killed."

There was silence as the men tried to take in all that had happened in such a brief time. Finally, one said, "So . . . what do we do now?"

Trimm seized the opportunity to divert attention away from the question of who was to blame for the turn of events.

"We're all right," he said. "They can't get to us in here, and we've still got one torch." He flicked it on. "Let's see where we are."

But then, for the first time, he *did* remember where they were. They were alone in the bone room with Carmen, Sherwood and Harry. They were four men to the other's two, but Trimm realized they had never searched Sherwood or Harry. As policemen, they would almost certainly have brought weapons into such a place. The treasure hunters' own guns had been left behind in the mad rush to escape.

"Quiet," Trimm said. "Be quiet and listen."

For a minute they listened in silence. Nothing. But they had to be in here. Where else could they have gone? They needed to join forces against the awful things that lived down here. His own treachery conveniently forgotten, Trimm believed it only made sense that they would now help him escape. Behind them, the treasure was sealed, inaccessible. For the moment, forgotten. Only a mad man would go back there. Now, the only thing was survival.

"Carmen?" Trimm called out hesitantly. "We can work together to get out of here. It's your only hope . . . *our* only hope."

Silence.

"Spread out," he whispered to the men. "We'll cross the room in a line. If anyone sees anything, shout out."

They moved across the cavernous space slowly. It was disconcerting to hear the crunch of bones beneath their feet, and the dark corners that remained unlit by their single torch offered flickering suggestions of things better not thought of.

When they found the lift, they were as surprised as Sherwood and Carmen had been. But at least they were not entombed. There was a way out . . . or at least a way . . . somewhere else.

Trimm ordered two of his men to lift him up through the hatch and then they all proceeded to climb to the next level.

57

Julia flicked on her torch. She only allowed herself to use it for a few minutes every couple of hours or so. Of course, she had no way to gauge the passing of time. There was only darkness and more darkness. She cursed the habit she'd adopted of not wearing a wrist watch.

Down in this blackest of tunnels, far beneath the bright lights of London, entombed inside a relic of World War II, she felt disembodied, as though she were experiencing some strange dream.

How long had she been here? She'd slept twice, which had served the function not so much of providing rest as simply increasing her sense of disorientation. Early on, she'd listened to the creatures clawing and probing her protective cocoon. But it had been some time since she'd last heard them.

With the light on, she explored her sanctuary. There was nothing else to do. But there really wasn't all that much to explore. Someone . . . Lila? . . . had torn out much of the interior equipment in order to increase the living space.

How long, she wondered, had this strange woman lived down here, and how had she managed to avoid the bizarre creatures outside? Was there some secret? Something . . . if she could just figure it out, that would make it possible to get out alive?

Of course, there was no sign of Lila. Maybe the rodents had finally gotten her. All that was left of her pitiful life was a few bits of clothing and food that she'd managed to hide down here. And her book, *Charlotte's Web*.

She was in something of a web herself, she mused. Stuck in the center of a web constructed of horrible things that wouldn't let her go. She sat down and turned her light off. In the dark, her frustration built until it was like a living thing. What was she going to do? She couldn't just stay here until she starved or, more likely, died of thirst. This missile had been here, undiscovered for seventy years. There was no reason to think anyone was going to find her either.

Perhaps a hundred years from now, someone would stumble upon the missile. There would be great excitement and stories in the papers. Everyone would wonder about the skeleton . . . hers . . . found beneath the city, inside a Nazi rocket.

No, damn it! She wasn't going to die that way. Better to be eaten alive and be done with it.

Not quite trusting her own resolve, she gathered a few bits of food and stuck a soft drink in her pocket. Then she sat beside the hatch for a long time, listening, building her nerve. It was quiet. The animals seemed to be gone for the moment.

Slowly, she undid the wire and pushed the hatch open silently. She had decided to do everything as quietly as possible. Maybe the creatures would be able to smell her, but there was nothing she could do about that.

Or was there? How could those things move about down here in the blackness? They certainly didn't use sight. They must have some sort of ability to use . . . what? Sonar? Some kind of echo reflection like bats? Maybe that horrible mewling they made had a purpose. But almost certainly, their sense of smell would be highly developed.

Suddenly she stopped. Her heart was racing. Quickly, she shut the hatch again and went back to the pile of food and general junk that Lila had accumulated. Early on, she'd found two jars that appeared to contain something too disgusting to even think about. She had pushed them aside.

But now she had an idea about them. She picked one up and removed the lid. The smell was terrible, nearly causing her to gag. The jar contained a mass of something, a combination of solids and liquid. She'd thought it was some disgusting preserve that had gone bad. But she wondered . . . could it be coagulated blood? Could Lila have somehow killed one of the creatures and then discovered that by putting some of the noxious remains on her, she could fool the rodents into thinking she was one of them?

She had no way of knowing, but if there was a chance . . .

Somehow, Lila had found a way to survive down here.

Turning her face away from the open container and trying to hold her breath, she dug into the jar and smeared the substance liberally over her clothing. She even spread some on her knit hat. She touched a drop to her bare skin but was met with a stinging pain. Whatever this stuff was, it was still potent.

She wrapped the remainder of the jar in a cloth and stuck it in her pocket along with her other treasures. Then she returned to the hatch.

This time, she felt a bit braver. She had no idea if what she was doing would work, but at least she had a plan.

She stepped out of the missile and stood beside it. Her light filled the tunnel. She began to move down the passageway. Thirty feet. She stopped, cupped her ears, trying to hear anything at all. She continued around a bend, another fifty feet. The tension was almost unbearable, to be facing death so totally alone.

Then she heard it. The mewling sound. She froze and flicked off her light. They were coming. For an instant she thought of turning and racing back to her haven as fast as she could. But she'd gone too far. She'd never make it. Either her plan would work, or she was going to be dead very soon

It was excruciating not to see them, but she didn't want the creatures to be able to rely on anything but smell. She felt, as much as heard, the padding of their feet. For what seemed an eternity she listened in the darkness as the things grew closer.

She was certain she was going to die. The impulse to flee was stronger than any she'd felt in her life, but she willed herself to stand her ground. She was done with running.

Then the creatures were all around her, moving right beside her, bumping into her, their damp noses brushing her skin. Her fear was like a living thing. The blood pounded in her ears. Goose bumps the size of marbles rose on her arms and legs. Her sphincter wanted to let go.

But the animals didn't attack. They didn't make the strange sucking sound. The creatures seemed almost placid.

It was working. She'd figured out Lila's secret. She was going to get out of here alive. Still, her heart beat so fast she thought she might have a heart attack and simply drop dead. She forced herself to relax, to fight back her fear.

Ever so slowly, she moved out of the path of the things as they parted and went around her. She put her back against the wall and waited for them to pass.

She was alone inside a living horror show beneath London. But she felt strangely elated and free. She could go anywhere she wanted now. Eventually, she would find a way out. She was certain of it.

58

Sherwood was exploring. He'd left Harry with Carmen while he tried to determine the extent of their confinement. The underground research facilities were extensive and had obviously been well financed at the time of their creation. No one had money to burn like intelligence agencies.

Yet everything appeared to have been suddenly and quickly abandoned. It was inexplicable, though the appearance of the rats might certainly have been one possible explanation. Could they have been around longer than anyone knew?

He roamed from one block of rooms to another. There were sleeping quarters with showers and toilets, more offices, storage rooms, a kitchen, a dining area, extensive laboratories and even what appeared to be some sort of secure holding cell.

One of the last rooms he discovered was the most fascinating—in a horrible sort of way. Shelves lined the walls and were filled with cages containing the skeletal bodies of various kinds of animals.

He got turned around several times in the complex but eventually made his way back to the others, where he told them of his findings.

Carmen, still surrounded by research files, listened as he described the underground facilities. "I'm not surprised at the caged animals," she said. "Obviously they were test subjects. It *is* surprising that they were left behind. Test animals are not easy to come by and can be incredibly expensive."

"Well what the bloody hell were they testing?" asked Harry.

"The Sweat," Carmen said without hesitation.

"What?"

"Dr. Carrel's papers make it pretty clear. He'd begun his work by creating advanced—if you want to call them that— mice. He called them "heroic" mice. They were smarter, bigger and more vicious than their forebears. He first worked on this at the Rockefeller Institute way back in the early part of the century. Then he apparently continued the research, progressing to rats, in France and later Norway."

"What's that got to do with the Sweat, and for that matter, how on earth did Carrel get here?" asked Sherwood.

"I seriously doubt he was ever here. But somehow his research papers found their way here. His work on rats seems to have been peripheral to his research on the Sweat. While under orders, what he was expected to achieve in Norway—as nearly as I can determine—was to find a way to introduce the Sweat via rocket for the Nazis."

"A biological weapon?"

"Exactly." She hesitated. "But I'm not certain he was quite as bad a character as this all sounds. Some of his comments and the way he set up various experiments suggest that he didn't believe in what the Nazis were doing. I think he may actually have been trying to slow down the work, send it off on dead-end tangents and so forth, hoping the war would come to an end before they were successful."

"So . . . what? We should give him a bleedin' medal?" said Harry, incredulous.

"That wouldn't be my inclination. But people got caught up in things during the war. And their lives were at risk. That he made any effort at all makes a definitive judgment more difficult."

"Bullshit!" said Harry. "Revisionist bullshit, if you'll excuse my English. He was just another longhair doing Hitler's bidding, without a whiff of conscience."

She shrugged. "I can't really argue with you, Harry. At least not until these papers are given a thorough review by people who understand the science."

"If Carrel delayed or sidelined the program," said Sherwood, "how do you explain the fact that the Sweat is here? And more to the point, how did his bloody 'heroic' rats get here too?"

"I said he may have been trying to slow down the research. I didn't say he was necessarily successful. Perhaps the Nazis did manage to introduce the Sweat into London somehow. I just don't know enough. One thing though . . . "

They both looked at her.

" . . . no way did the Nazis set up these extensive research facilities—practically beneath Whitehall for God's sake—in the middle of the Second World War. This place had to be run by the British government, or at least some branch of the government . . . maybe the military or intelligence."

"You're suggesting British intelligence was carrying on these experiments on the Sweat?"

"On the Sweat and possibly on the strange creatures that are living down here. Think about it, Sherwood. Why else would the prime minister's office try to stifle your efforts to examine the bodies you and Harry found."

He stared at her. "You might be on to something. They could have been afraid we'd find evidence of an outbreak of the disease during the war. That we'd blow the whistle on this whole research program going on down here for who knows how long. And if it ever got out that the prime minister *knew* about the Sweat without doing anything about it . . . well . . . it could bring down the government."

She picked up another piece of paper. "These laboratories were active for many years, through the fifties and sixties at least. There's another name here I recognize. Marcus Hopkinton."

"Our current SIS director?"

"The same. He held a much lower position then, of course. He must still have been in his twenties. But from what I've read, he had a certain amount of authority even then. He was very much in the mix, especially around the time they closed off the labs permanently in the late 1960s."

Suddenly there was a commotion in a nearby room. Sherwood and Harry had their pistols out in an instant. They were all thinking the same thing. The rats had found a way inside.

In a manner of speaking, they were right. The rats had arrived, but they were the human version.

Carmen's eyes widened as Trimm and several of his men entered the room. They were covered in dirt and filth, appeared exhausted and had fear firmly planted in their eyes.

"Thank God," Trimm said, going up to Carmen. "Are those the only firearms you have?"

"I ought to plug you right now," said Harry.

Trimm took a step back. "We . . . we have to work together," he said. "It's the only way anyone's going to get out of here. Haven't you seen those things?"

"We've seen them, Philip," said Carmen. "They're vicious, oversized rats."

"Rats?" Trimm looked incredulous. "I know about Dr. Carrel's so-called 'heroic rats.' But these creatures aren't just big rats. My God, they're three, four feet long, some of them. They move like cats, incredibly fast and strong."

"If you know about Carrel," Carmen said slowly, "then you know he talked about this in his notes. How the mice in his original experiments passed on their traits very quickly to other generations. After the Rockefeller experiments, he continued to work on his super rats for many years in France and Norway. There was something in their genetics that he thought might eventually speed up the evolution of the species. I think he suspected they would grow larger over time and more intelligent—more highly evolved."

"You suggested Carrel was never here himself," said Sherwood. "That he never knew the British carried on the work after the war."

"Yes, that's what I think. What confuses me," she said, "is why there aren't many more of these things. Millions more. They've had decades to reproduce, after all. I wonder if Carrel suspected that British intelligence would be unable to resist continuing the work. Like the Nazis he was used to dealing with. Maybe . . . "

"What?"

"There's no way to know of course, but I wonder if he could have done something to affect the rodents' ability to procreate, so the numbers wouldn't get out of control." She shrugged. "It's just idle speculation, but something's kept their numbers from exploding and moving to the surface where people would have encountered them long ago."

Sherwood met her eyes. He'd learned how to read her emotions much more clearly now from when they'd first met. What he saw now was the true aspie flush of mixed feelings— indecision, concern and fear.

"Sherwood, we've got to get out of here and warn people. It's going to take the full resources of the government to fight these things if they ever do get to the surface, no matter how many of them there are."

Suddenly there was another commotion from one of the hallways. Everyone looked at the door. Trimm's face registered panic, and his men were not much better. They'd only just escaped from the terrible creatures below and their nerves were stretched tight.

But then they heard voices.

"People!" Trimm shouted, nearly hysterical with relief. "We're saved. It must be the army," he added, absurdly. "Hopkinton's sent reinforcements to get us out."

But then two decidedly unmilitary looking souls burst into the room. It was Hans and Kurt.

"What are you all doing here?" asked Hans. And then, "Never mind. The rats are right behind us. They found another way in." He stared at Sherwood and Harry holding their pistols. "Those peashooters won't do any good. There are too many of them."

As if to prove his point, Kurt turned and shined his torch into the corridor. The entire space appeared to be moving. The hall was alive with dozens of the beasts.

"Shut the damn door," shouted Harry, even as he leaped to do so.

"That won't stop them," Sherwood said. "We need to barricade it somehow."

They pushed an assemblage of desks and worktables together in a line that ran across the room to the back wall. Anything pushing on the door would be pushing against the rear wall of the room.

The first of the creatures slammed into the door. They could hear them scratching and pawing at the wood, gnawing at it with their teeth.

"It's not going to hold for long," said Carmen. She could already see cracks in the wood from the beasts' terrible claws.

Without hesitation, Sherwood directed everyone out another door. "I know a place where we'll be safe," he said. "Come on."

Trimm—in character—was the first one out after Sherwood, pushing his way to the front of the line.

Sherwood led them down the corridor past research rooms on either side. Behind them, they could hear the rodents breaking through the barricade. They would be on their trail quickly.

Trimm looked over his shoulder and whimpered, "There they are."

The animals approached purposefully but without seeming haste, as though they knew there was no way their prey could escape. Even in her fear, Carmen marveled at how the animals moved. They were almost feline, sleek, graceful, their muscles rippling beneath pale fur.

Sherwood raced through a series of rooms until they came to a kind of central pod where the corridors coalesced. He'd been here before. He stopped, trying to remember which way to go.

"Sherwood," Carmen came up beside him. "There's no time."

He spun around. "They all look bloody alike," he said. "I don't remember which way to go."

Then the creatures were upon them, moving slowly, almost expectantly, into the central pod, pushing their prey back against one wall. Their noses twitched and seemed to be part of some sort of communication process, as they touched one another, making gentle snuffling sounds. There was no hurry, as though they wanted to play with their targets, like cats playing with a mouse. Perhaps the overwhelming hunger was diminished after eating so many of Trimm's men.

Sherwood put his arm around Carmen and held her tight. His biggest regret was that they would not have time to get to know one another. He turned her head into his chest and they waited.

"Let's at least shoot some," said Harry. "Maybe it will give us time to slip away." He brought his gun up, then stopped as he saw something moving in another of the corridors.

They stared as still more rodents appeared. These weren't as big as the ones that had been chasing them, but they were undeniably vicious. Their open mouths showed the same needle-like teeth and dripped the same burning mucus. But they had a slightly different color and body shape.

"They're not the same," Carmen whispered to Sherwood. "Maybe another strain—an earlier strain."

Suddenly, there was a roar from the bigger rodents that had surrounded them. The two groups of animals evidently held no love for one another. Whether they were prepared to fight over the prey or simply had some ingrained antagonism was not clear.

The little party of humans stood, dumbstruck, as the two groups of beasts sized each other up, their stupid, helpless prey forgotten for the moment.

Then one of the larger animals leaped into the middle of the smaller rodents, and the fight was on. The bigger rat grabbed one of the smaller beasts by the neck and shook it. But instantly, the other rats swarmed on the hapless attacker, literally tearing it apart with their needle teeth.

The smaller rats had the advantage of being faster and they could maneuver more quickly in the tight confines of the hallways. But the larger rodents were clearly stronger. They also appeared to have greater intelligence, working together to try to separate the enemy into smaller, more manageable groups.

It was the most awful, bloodthirsty battle any of them had ever witnessed, as the creatures tore into each other with incredible ferocity. Blood and body parts flew everywhere.

He made a decision. "Come on," he said. "Looks like they're going to keep each other busy for a while. This way." He led off down one of the remaining corridors not blocked by the carnage.

"How do we get out of this place?" a terrified Trimm said to no one in particular.

Sherwood wished he knew. London's underground was a maze of near biblical proportions: subway stations, research labs, WWII bomb shelters and government offices, sewers, river channels, rooms filled with bones and treasure. One of the world's great cities had a secret, subterranean life unlike anything anyone could have imagined. And all of it appeared to be inhabited by creatures straight out of a living nightmare.

But Sherwood kept on. Several more halls split off and each time he made an educated guess from his earlier explorations. Then everyone froze, as they heard once again that distinctive sucking sound behind them. Whoever had won, the battle royale was apparently over.

"They're coming," said Carmen in a tight voice, her hand squeezing Sherwood's until it hurt.

"Turn there!" he said. Then, "Yes! This is right. It's the next room."

They burst into the secure room Sherwood had found toward the end of his roaming about the facility.

"Into the cell," he said.

They crammed into the holding tank that was barely a dozen feet long by six wide. But as soon as Sherwood slid the bars shut, they felt a small margin of safety for the first time.

"We can't lock the door," he said, "but hopefully they aren't smart enough to figure out how to slide it open."

There were nine of them, Hans, Kurt, Trimm and his three men, Sherwood, Carmen and Harry.

As the animals approached and entered the room, they saw for the first time who had won the great contest. It was the large rats. Whether they had destroyed the smaller rodents or simply sent them packing, they could see evidence of the battle's intensity. All of the creatures had open sores and claw marks and many were bleeding. But one thing seemed evident. The fight appeared to have renewed their appetite.

The animals pawed about the room, staring at them with cold, vicious eyes. Their mouths hung open and the drooling mucus seemed to signal their hunger. One of the beasts hurled itself at the cell, crashing into it and causing the entire room to vibrate. Others moved more cautiously. Several attempted to push their heads through the bars but they were too big. Sherwood stood to one side, ready to hold the door closed if it should start to slide open.

"Good thing the smaller ones didn't win," said Harry. "They might fit between the bars."

It seemed like a long time before the creatures would accept defeat. But instead of leaving, one by one they lay down, licked themselves and each other, rolled about lazily and many slept. Periodically, one or another of the creatures cast a lingering eye on them, like rats contemplating a piece of cheese just out of reach.

"Maybe they'll all go to sleep and we can slip past them," offered Trimm, hopefully.

"It's what happens when they wake up that I'm worried about," said Harry. "They'll be rested and hungrier than ever."

It was a sobering thought, but there was clearly nothing they could do for the time being.

"Might as well try to get some rest ourselves," Sherwood said.

He sat down in a corner of the cell, and Carmen went over and sat beside him. The others positioned themselves around the tiny room, taking care to keep at least a rodent's length from the bars.

Carmen said to Hans, "What were you doing down here?"

He shrugged, looking at Trimm. "I guess there's not much point in secrets anymore. We were looking for two of my men who disappeared. Not much question what happened to them now. And we were searching as well, at Trimm's direction, for King Henry's treasure. Didn't expect these awful things, though." He stared at Trimm, seeming to consider something. "You didn't know about these creatures did you, Philip?"

Trimm looked greatly agitated. "Of course not," he said indignantly. "After you and Kurt and Wolfgang went down, I began to have suspicions once I read Dr. Carrel's notes. That's why we came down here, to warn you. It took us a while to arrange for additional men and a flamethrower for added security."

Of course, this was only partly accurate. What they had hoped to find was the treasure, and the extra security had been for Trimm's protection. Searching for Hans and his crew had been decidedly secondary.

Hans looked almost amused, fully understanding Trimm's obsession and what he'd really intended. "A flamethrower?" he asked. "And where would that be now?"

"Destroyed by the beasts."

"Anyone have a clue where these things came from?" asked Hans.

"Our current theory," Carmen said, "is that they represent some experiment gone wrong by the British government."

"That's patent nonsense," said Trimm. "Dr. Carrel was working with the Nazis and then Vichy France. He's behind it. I'd bet my life on it."

She considered what he was saying. "I've been reading Carrel's papers, Philip. And I think his ideas definitely contributed to the work being done down here ... on the Sweat and on the rats. What I don't understand is how the papers got here, or how the Sweat got here originally either."

"On the V-2 would be my guess," said Hans.

Everyone turned to look at him. Trimm's eyes grew round as saucers.

"You found it?" he asked incredulously.

Hans nodded. "It was embedded in the side of one of the cisterns. It must have hit the ground at just the right angle to enter one of the tunnels and make its way down into the underground. If it carried some biological weapon created by the Nazis, then that's how your Sweat got to London. As for how Carrel's papers got here, I have no idea."

They grew quiet, contemplating the many elements of their predicament. The creatures continued to rest, but were never all asleep at any one time.

Sherwood stood up periodically and paced around their cage like a trapped animal, which he most decidedly was. Carmen was right. If they didn't figure out a way to escape and reach the surface, he could only imagine the chaos that such creatures would bring to London. And if they were carriers of the Sweat, that chaos would be compounded many times over.

She held out a hand to him finally, and he slumped beside her.

"None of this is your fault," she said softly. "We'll do the best we can. It's all anyone can expect of us."

"I know. But what if our best isn't good enough?"

59

Carmen woke with a start. She could hardly believe she'd been able to sleep in the cold cell with the rats only a few feet away. Sherwood was lying on the floor next to her, his lanky body curled into a ball against the cold.

Reaching out a hand, she stroked his hair. He'd been a pillar of strength since their subterranean adventure began, refusing to give up, always ready with a new plan. They'd had virtually no time alone together since they had kissed, first in the restaurant and then at Piccadilly Circus.

He stirred, sat up and gave her a tired smile. "How are you holding up?"

"If you'd told this aspie a few days ago what she'd be going through during our little underground adventure, I'd have slunk off and found a hole somewhere." She shivered. "Well, maybe not a hole, let's say a mountaintop. An open, airy, big sky kind of mountaintop. I've had enough of holes."

They stared at the rats. Most were now awake. A few paced about, their eyes focused on the inhabitants of the cell with a cold intensity.

"They look hungry," Carmen said.

"Those damn things are always hungry," said Harry. He and the others were now awake also, at least those who had managed a few minutes of sleep under the stressful conditions.

Trimm stared at the rodents, his voice tinged with fear. "How are we going to get out of here?" he asked.

Sherwood hadn't a clue. They might as well be locked in a cell in San Quentin, he thought. The animals showed no interest in giving up. Their prey was too close, too helpless and too succulent to pass up.

Again, one of the biggest rats took a charge at the cell bars. The entire room shook from the force of its attack. Sherwood grimaced and grabbed the cell door to keep it from sliding open. At once, another of the beasts slammed into the bars near his hand, which he managed to withdraw an instant before its jaws closed with a crunch.

The ferocity of the two attackers seemed to rev up the others. Soon, they were all sucking and mewling and pressing in on the cell bars. Sherwood tried to keep close enough to the cell door to grab it if it started to slide open but not so close as to risk being clawed. It was a game of cat and mouse, and the inhabitants of the cell had no illusions as to who the mice were.

The standoff continued for over an hour, the rats periodically slamming into the cell, Sherwood struggling to keep the bars shut and the rest of the room's pitiful occupants remaining out of reach.

The tension in the room was palpable. Trimm, especially, was nearly catatonic from fear. They could all see how the bars of their haven were beginning to weaken from the constant assaults. Several bars were now loose in the sixty-year-old concrete that encased them, and it seemed only a matter of time before the rats would break through. Most of the cell's occupants could no longer bear to look at the creatures literally salivating for their flesh. They sat on the floor, their heads turned away.

This was how they were—only Sherwood paying attention to the beasts, as he fought to keep the cell door from sliding open— when they heard him gasp, "Oh, my God."

Carmen was the first to look. What she saw made so little sense that she thought she must be hallucinating.

"Julia?" she said slowly.

And Julia appeared before them, standing at the door to the room, looking more bedraggled and haggard than Carmen had ever seen her before.

"Julia. My God, run! Get out of here. They'll kill you!" Carmen couldn't bear to look and turned away from her friend who was certain to be torn to bits.

But there was a strange silence in the room. The rats continued to stare at them and pace about, but they showed no interest in Julia whatsoever as she moved across the room to the cell door.

"I can't believe I've found you," she said, looking at the bereft group in the cell. She put one hand on the bars and gave them a little shake. "Not a bad refuge, all things considered."

Sherwood stood next to the bars, not believing what he was seeing. "How . . . ?" he began.

Julia looked quickly at the rats which seemed to have quieted for the moment. "Why don't you let me in, Sherwood," she said.

Cautiously, he slid the cell door back two feet and then quickly shut it after she slipped through.

Hans was the first to greet her, hugging her tightly, then Carmen took a turn before she pushed her friend away.

"What on earth is that smell?"

"My new perfume. I call it 'Salvation.'"

"How did you get down here?" asked Sherwood.

"I came down to find Hans. I was worried about him, and then I stupidly got lost and trapped by those things."

"Trapped where?" asked Hans.

"In a missile stuck in the side of one of the cisterns. I found a way to get inside the thing to escape the rats and I discovered that someone else had stayed there also, a woman named Lila."

Harry snorted, remembering their encounter with the strange woman when they first were down here. "I *knew* she had to have some place. But how did she avoid the rats? And what in God's name is that smell?"

Julia held up a large glass jar. "Like I said. It's the smell of salvation."

They all stared at her blankly.

"I found this in Lila's little nest. I think it's a mix of body parts and offal. Somehow she figured out how to use it to mask her body odor."

"That would have to make it pretty strong stuff," said Harry, remembering Lila's indescribable smell.

"The point is, it works," Julia said. "I put it on and have been walking freely down here. The animals don't pay any attention to me."

"Give me some of that," said Trimm, reaching for the bottle.

Sherwood stepped in front of him. "We'll all use it," he said. "But it looks like there might not be enough to go around. There are nine of us here. Why don't you dole it out, Julia? Use as little on each of us as you think we can get away with."

So she did, carefully spreading each drop as economically as possible. Soon the cell stank like the inside of a slaughterhouse, and they had to fight the urge to gag. But as the noxious substance was divided up, the rats began to lose interest in the game.

"It's a God damned miracle," Harry said.

Slowly, one by one, the big rats left the room. Julia dipped the last drops from her jar and tossed it aside.

"I don't have any idea how long this stuff works," she said. "Or if I gave each of you enough to work individually. As long as we're together in a small space, I suspect the collective impact of the odor will protect us. But we probably shouldn't get too far apart once we start to move."

"Move where?" Trimm said. "We don't know where the hell we are. I don't want to go walking around down here side by side with those things, no matter how much we stink."

"I know a way out. I wandered around down here a long time, looking for Hans. I didn't know that you three cowboys were down here too." She looked accusingly at Carmen, Sherwood and Harry.

"Sorry," Carmen said. "Sherwood thought it best to keep our little river adventure a secret. But while we're on the subject, didn't you tell anyone where you were going?"

It was Julia's turn to look sheepish. "Nope," she sighed. "I guess we're on our own. But like I said, I found a passage to the surface. Not far from here. It looks like it only recently opened up from a cave-in. I wasn't going to use it until I found Hans." She squeezed his hand and Hans looked totally smitten. "Unfortunately, the rats have also found it."

Sherwood looked aghast. "The rats are on the surface? They're on the streets of London?"

She nodded. "And we need to get out of here too. I rather think Scotland Yard is going to need every one of its inspectors . . . and sergeants."

They moved out into the hallway. Using just a single torch so as not to draw any more attention than necessary, they followed Julia in a tight group. The rats were everywhere, scores of them. They paid no attention to the strange shuffling group moving through the hallways. It was terrifying to be standing right beside the creatures, seeing their dripping teeth, listening to their mewling and sucking.

They had gone only a short distance before they detected a dim light emanating from somewhere ahead. The rats seemed to be heading toward the light as well.

"It's the surface!" cried Trimm, whose nerves had been frayed to near collapse by being so close to the rats. Before anyone could stop him, he bolted ahead for the light.

"Stop!" Julia shouted. "We've got to keep together."

But there was no stopping Trimm. He hadn't gone more than a dozen yards before the rats began to show interest in him.

"You don't have enough of the smell on you," Carmen yelled. "Come back to the group."

Trimm stopped, suddenly aware of his mistake. The others could see the terror creep across his face. Several of the rats began to surround him, scratching at the floor and sticking their snouts in the air, trying to determine how this strange creature could have appeared so miraculously in their midst.

"Help me! What should I do?" Trimm cried, his back to the wall.

Sherwood looked at Julia. "Isn't there anything we can do?"

In a low voice, she said, "Without the smell, they'll be on him any moment." She pulled out her gun. "We can try to distract them by shooting one of the things," she said. "But it's risky. It could just get them in a frenzy."

Sherwood and Harry had also pulled out their guns. They stood, uncertain what action to take. The rats were now literally beside Trimm, sticking their noses on him, still not quite comprehending his smell. But the rank odor of Trimm's own fear was beginning to seep through.

One of the rats jumped up and took a nip at Trimm's hand, biting off two fingers. He screamed in pain. "For God's sake, shoot them," he yelled.

But it was too late. Even as they took aim with their guns, the rats went completely wild, leaping onto Trimm and tearing him to bits before their eyes. His cries ceased after just a few seconds.

In a shaky whisper, Julia said, "Let's move. We've got a few minutes at most until they finish eating him. There's no telling how much longer the smell will protect us."

They moved forward in an even more tightly compacted group than before. No one wanted to separate from the pack after seeing what had happened to Trimm.

The tunnel rose steadily into the light. They could see where a cave-in had opened up the new passage to the surface. The rats could be heard eating and smacking their lips behind them.

Then they were on the surface. It was evening, and the light they had pursued out of that awful darkness was from London's brightly lit skyline. They emerged in a park where a section of lawn had seemingly collapsed into a yawning opening in the earth.

"It's Russell Square," Carmen said in astonishment.

They could see the impressive Victorian facade of the Russell Square Hotel. It must have been late evening, for there were few people around.

"Where is everyone?" asked Harry.

Then they saw the rats. At least a dozen were lurking about the manicured lawns, keeping to the shadows. One curled up on a park bench and seemed to be chewing on something with the remnants of a backpack attached to it.

"Maybe that's why there are no people," Sherwood said flatly.

But Julia pointed to a street that still had traffic and a few people strolling about, unaware of the sudden danger that had appeared in their midst.

"They don't know yet," she said. "We should warn them. And we should get out of here ourselves. In the fresh air, our protection may have an expiration date."

"You're right," said Sherwood. "But no one is going to believe us if we go off shouting about giant rats. The whole city has got to be mobilized."

He stared at the rats. The bright lights and noise of the city had them cowed for the moment, but it wouldn't last.

"Come on," he said. "Let's get the hell out of here."

60

The first of October, as if to herald the end of London's gloomy and overcast September, dawned in brilliant sunshine. At Kew Gardens, the unusually cold September brought an early rush of autumn colors. Red and gold leaves speckled the still emerald green lawns. Holly berries hung in great clumps, mimicking the maroon of the cranberries floating on the lake.

By evening, as the full intensity of the sun began to dissipate, there crept from a hole in the ground several strange creatures that only vaguely resembled ordinary rats. They stayed beneath a thick covering of brush, avoiding the last vestiges of sun, as they contemplated the smorgasbord of tourists wandering about like mobile entrees.

No longer did the rodents have to scratch out a meal in the underground, searching for rats of the old variety. No longer did they need to rely solely on their ability to echo locate their dinners. This new prey was not nearly so skittish and their hearing was simply laughable.

The rats sized up a young mother walking with two little girls. The family had spent a lovely day at Kew and was now making its way home before dark. One of the children was quite attractively plump. It would hardly prove much of a challenge to the creatures' stalking abilities, but the gnawing hunger that never went away pushed the rodents to rub noses amongst themselves, stretch in a decidedly feline posture and begin to make a soft, sucking sound.

Stalking, the animals padded along the well-mowed lawn, their claws carving strange, scallop-shaped divots in the grass.

They were careful to keep the bushes and trees between them and their prey. No other people were around, and the little girls chattered noisily, as they ran back and forth exclaiming at the many specimen trees and pointing out the small, informative plaques that identified them to their mother. The sun had set, and it was growing dark.

The rats eased into position beneath a thick holly berry bush, muscles rippling. They gauged the distance, calculating, gathering for the lunge. Just at the last moment, the girls' mother looked up as she heard an unusual sucking sound.

Then, like lightning, the creatures burst from cover and flew down upon the unsuspecting child. In an instant, the plump girl was firmly ensconced in one beast's mouth. A moment later, they had all melted away into the bushes to enjoy their meal, leaving behind a stunned and then hysterical, screaming woman. The rodents were surprised at the amount of noise the tasty things could sometimes generate. They picked up their prey and dragged it down into their hole, where it was quiet and where even the last bits of sunshine could not penetrate.

In St. James's Park, an arrow's flight from Buckingham Palace, a caretaker arrived for his early morning shift to discover that the ducks, geese and swans had virtually all disappeared. The man followed a trail of feathers that dotted the pathways and lawns. They seemed to lead to a thicket of bushes.

At the edge of the thicket, he hesitated, uneasy. But what could there be to concern him? Clearly, a pair of foxes had simply had themselves a banquet. A pair? More likely a score. Still, he would be commended for solving the mystery quickly. They would have to put out traps for the predators. He parted the shrubbery and stepped forward.

A moment later, an enormous, unbelievably vicious-looking, rodent-like creature dangled from the caretaker's throat.

Unable to yell through his crushed windpipe, the man staggered and fell. The last thing he saw as he was dragged and then deposited almost gently amidst a pile of bird carcasses was the arrival of many more of the beasts, their thick jaws dripping moisture.

On the Embankment, a group of Japanese tourists approached the London Eye with growing excitement. The enormous wheel, magnificently lit against the dark night sky hung, seemingly without support, against the backdrop of the Houses of Parliament. Like the Eiffel Tower, the Eye had been promoted as a temporary structure in order to appease the traditionalists who were dismayed at the transformation of their beloved skyline. But Londoners and tourists had fallen for the Eye, and it was likely to remain.

The tourists had planned their visit for the final ride of the evening. The nighttime views of the city would be spectacular. A handful of houseboats and barges still plied the Thames, Big Ben rang the hour and a light mist rose from the river, giving everything a look of fantasy.

As the tourists lined up and the first gondola approached boarding level, the men, women and children surged forward to be first to enter. As the door opened, there was a moment of hushed disbelief as they stared at the interior of the gondola.

The floors and windows were awash in blood and body parts. They stared in incomprehension, until a few realized there was something else inside, something crouching in the corner, its white fur stained red with blood. The beast looked up from licking itself and issued a strange, lip-smacking sound. Then it leaped out of the gondola into the midst of the screaming Japanese, scattering them like birds chased by a dog.

The creature stood for a moment, disoriented by the noise, then it turned toward Westminster. In a few moments it had disappeared, climbing the superstructure to a great height, until it looked like nothing more than a blood drenched gargoyle.

At the London zoo in the corner of Regent's Park, curator Marie Gonzales arrived every morning before sunup. Her job was to see that all the creatures had survived the night without incident. She consulted with the night security staff who informed her that all was quiet. They had made their last rounds an hour before and were waiting, sipping their morning tea, to be relieved by the day shift.

Marie entered her notes in the daily log, then passed through the administrative offices, turning lights on and security systems off, opening those cages that shut animals in at night so they could move out into the courtyards and viewing areas. A handful of other zoo staff members trickled in, filling offices, preparing for the usual onslaught of tourists and regulars.

She passed through the reptile house where everything was calm and normal and steamy warm. Good. The problems with the heating system must have been fixed. There was nothing more pitiful than a shivering Gecko.

She climbed onto a catwalk that overlooked the bear pens. Here, she hesitated, surprised. None of the animals appeared to be outside. That was unusual. Then she saw something odd in one of the enclosures. It looked like a pile of red meat. It was too early for the animals to have been fed. She stared more closely. It was a very large pile.

Then she noticed that blood stained the ground. She glanced at some of the other enclosures and that was when she saw the first body. Or part of a body. She was pretty sure it was a bear, one of the males from its size. But it was hard to tell. Pieces of the beast seemed to be strewn all about. She could see the gleaming white of bones stripped clean of tissue.

She felt a sudden loosening of her bowels. Her eyes swept right and left, taking in many more bodies and body parts. Blood, she could now see was everywhere: all over the ground and on the imitation stone cliffs. She followed a trail of red up to the very top of the cliff house and froze.

A dozen enormous, rat-like creatures sat at the entrance to one of the darkened, faux caves. Pallid, muscular bodies appeared to be drenched in blood. A few of the animals still gnawed at bones. Their rodent-like heads had snouts and even at this distance, teeth unlike anything she had ever seen before. They seemed to be dripping some strange mucus onto the ground.

She watched, entranced, goose bumps rising on the back of her neck, as one of the creatures stood, stretched like a house cat, then suddenly leaped a distance of nearly thirty feet to land in the giraffe compound. Without pause, it bounded onto the back of Gerome, one of the zoo's oldest and most popular animals and with a single bite of those enormous jaws, brought the giraffe down to earth. The rest of the strange beasts then roused themselves and leaped into the adjoining compound to share in the feast. The destruction of poor Gerome took remarkably little time, though his legs kicked feebly for several minutes.

Gerome was completely gone in fifteen minutes, as if he had never existed, and Marie was gone too, screaming for security and running madly back into the offices, where her colleagues stared at her as if she had suddenly gone quite mad, yelling something about giant rats.

61

It was early morning, far earlier than usual for a meeting of important people. Only a handful of hours had passed since Sherwood and the others had emerged from beneath London, but word of the new threat to the city had yet to spread.

Marcus Hopkinton sat behind his desk. He was furious, and when the SIS director was in a foul mood, his employees knew to keep out of the way.

Things were not going as planned. Not at all. To begin with, he'd heard nothing from Trimm and the men he'd sent with him into the underground. Trimm had agreed to report the moment they found the treasure. Marcus didn't trust the diminutive archaeologist as far as he could throw him, which, when he thought about it, was probably a fair distance. It was why he'd ordered his own people to send one of their members back to the surface every day to report.

It had been three days now without a word. He wasn't used to his orders being ignored and was inclined to put the silence down to something having gone wrong. Perhaps monumentally wrong.

Meanwhile, things had been deteriorating for the prime minister as well. A reporter who went by the pretentious name of Mitchell Harrison III continued to ask about the Sweat, at press briefings, in his column and just the other day in an interview he'd given to the BBC.

The man had stirred up a hornet's nest, and the rest of the media had begun swarming around the potential new honey pot of information. Hopkinton was seriously considering getting rid of Harrison. Permanently. He'd done the same with Lila and with the men who'd helped Sherwood organize his river journey. By extension, he assumed that the inspector, his sergeant and the young woman who had caused all the trouble had drowned in the maze of underground waterways.

He had few qualms about using the power he possessed to kill people. He'd ordered the deaths of dozens of foreign operatives and terrorists during his time as chief intelligence officer. It came with the territory and no SIS director could be successful if he harbored any sentimental feelings about carrying out the ultimate sanction, if events so warranted.

What concerned him most was that he had no solid evidence whatsoever that he was about to become one of the world's wealthiest men. He believed the treasure existed. But he'd taken it on faith, on the archaeologist's passionate conviction, bolstered by the outrageous ruby Trimm had shown him. Now he was beginning to wonder. Had he been a fool? Had Rachel Forrester been right in refusing to believe the story?

He needed to know what was happening. The way things were going, he might soon be out of a job if the government fell. Which was why he now waited in his office for the three people who knew the most about the Sweat: Dr. Jessmer, Minister of Health Simonson and Dr. Westerling.

His grim thoughts were interrupted by the buzzer on his desk.

"Sir," his secretary said, "Your visitors are here."

"Send them in."

The three men entered with grim faces and took chairs in front of the fireplace. Not one of them paid the slightest attention to the African war clubs, the burnished, walnut hunting rifles or the many dead animals that shared the room with them.

Marcus got straight to the point.

"How bad is it?" he asked.

"We've had at least five hundred deaths," said Dr. Westerling. " . . . assuming they were all caused by the Sweat, which we cannot verify positively. Only a few have responded to treatment, which includes massive doses of antibiotics that were not available the last time around in King Henry's day. However, there is another issue that Dr. Jessmer can best address."

"Our primary problem," Jessmer began, "is that the disease progresses so rapidly. That is also one of the reasons we are quite certain we are dealing with the Sweat. There are many reports from the sixteenth century describing how quickly death came, sometimes in a matter of hours, or even a single hour."

"Our dilemma," said Minister Simonson, "is in providing treatment in a timely fashion. By timely, I mean within a few hours, preferably an hour or two after onset. Unfortunately, by the time most people suspect they are sick, it is too late. They go downhill rapidly and die quickly. Too late for antibiotics to help in most cases."

"Not all of the rat-bite victims who have flooded into hospitals across the city since the rodents emerged out of Holborn have the Sweat," said Westerling. "Many have a variety of other rodent transmitted diseases, most of which can be treated. But by the time we identify those who make it to hospital with the Sweat, it is nearly always too late." He stared at the floor. "I have to tell you, gentlemen, that the situation is about to get much worse. Just before I left my office, I received phone calls from three other hospital directors. They said they were being flooded with calls now that the press has gotten hold of the story about a potential disease. Most were from people saying their loved ones had suddenly become very sick or had even died."

"And I can confirm something else," said Simonson. "Those people were angry. They felt betrayed by the authorities, who until only recently had denied that such a disease even existed.

Those denials led many not to seek treatment, thinking at first that what they had was the flu."

Marcus felt a drop of moisture slither down the back of his neck. It was starting. He could sense the final days and hours of the Harris administration slipping away. "Is there anything at all we can do?" he asked quietly.

"I think our only real hope," Jessmer replied, "is in what history tells us. Most of the Sweat outbreaks lasted two weeks or less. Then it was gone. No one knows why. Our first cases began to appear just over a week ago. I suggest we all say a prayer that a week from today, this thing will have run its course."

"What we don't know," said Westerling, "is how many more will die before then. Hundreds? Thousands? Hundreds of thousands? I suspect even now there are dead people all over the city who haven't been found yet or whose families haven't had time to inform the authorities."

"It gets worse," said Westerling. "A handful of cases have begun to appear across the British Isles, and a number of reports have shown up on the continent. If we don't get a handle on it quickly, we could be facing a world-wide epidemic."

"How on earth could it spread so quickly?" Hopkinton said, bewildered.

"Rats go everywhere," said Simonson. "It's why they may have been selected as the vector for the disease in the first place. They've been found on ships, trains, airplanes, even cars crossing the border. The Chunnel is one almost certain avenue to the continent, regardless of safeguards."

Then several things happened at once. Hopkinton's phone rang, his intercom buzzed and the office door burst open, admitting a highly agitated Rachel Forrester, accompanied by a scholarly looking man carrying several heavy books.

Marcus started to rise, ignoring both his phone and the insistent buzzer on his desk. "Rachel . . . what in the world . . . ?"

Forrester strode over to the SIS director's desk and pointed at it to the man who was with her. He began to lay out his books on its surface. She turned and faced the men assembled in front of the fireplace.

"It's good that you are all here," she said. "It will save time, something we don't have a great deal of." She met Hopkinton's startled eyes with her own. "I suspect you have not yet heard . . . "

"Heard what? What the hell is this all about?"

"One hour ago, I received a call from the head of London's emergency terrorist response teams. There has been a sudden eruption of rodents from the tube station that serves the Houses of Parliament."

Marcus froze. If members of Parliament became infected with the Sweat, he suspected the Harris administration would be over just as soon as a vote of no confidence could be taken.

"I use the word 'rodents' advisedly," said Forrester. "Because the creatures that have been reported do not resemble our normal rats in any way, shape or form. These things are not the same rats that have been biting citizens." She turned to the man beside her. "Professor Ellis, if you please."

He had unruly hair, a tightly cut goatee and wore a rumpled seersucker suit. He picked up one of the books, perusing the page it was open to. "We have only word-of-mouth descriptions thus far," he began. "As alarming as these appear to be, you need to understand that confirmation will take time, and since those closest to the incident have . . . been taken . . . that will prove difficult."

"Taken?" Marcus asked stupidly. "What on earth are you talking about?"

"What he's saying is that at least three members of Parliament were last seen being hauled away by the rodents," Forrester said.

Marcus looked shocked. "You're not making sense, Rachel. Rats carrying away people?"

"The animals in question have been described by eye witnesses as being at least three to four feet in length, with nearly-white fur and three-inch-long teeth."

She paused to view the effect her words had. Every mouth in the room hung open. Hopkinton slowly sat down. He held the sides of his chair with white knuckles. Dr. Jessmer's head was bobbing like one of those dolls in a car window. Simonson stood and began to pace about in confusion.

"You're not describing rats," he said.

"The beasts in question were identified as 'rodent-like,'" said Forrester. "Dr. Ellis . . . " She motioned for the professor to continue.

Dr. Ellis turned the book in his hand around, displaying a picture. Everyone leaned in to see it. "This is just an example of the sort of thing we may be talking about. It is *Josephoartigasia monesi*, the biggest species of rodent ever found in the fossil record. Actually a close relative of the guinea pig or porcupine, it lived about four million years ago in Uruguay and was a herbivore. It reached a length of eight feet and weighed as much as a ton and a half."

Marcus looked up from the picture. "You must be joking," he said.

"I am not saying this is what appeared from the tube at Parliament. I present this merely as evidence that extreme size is not unknown in the rodent world. Whatever killed and carried away three members of Parliament had to be much larger than any of our normal rats, and extremely strong. And it most definitely was *not* a herbivore."

"All right, all right," Forrester interrupted. "Marcus, since late last night these creatures have begun to emerge from the underground all over the city. By all accounts, they are big. They are ferocious. They are unbelievably strong. We have a report of one leaping straight from the ground to the top of a twenty-foot carport. They have been described as catlike, with powerful claws and teeth. To put it succinctly, London has been invaded. I have already mobilized every special police and military response unit in the city."

"You must bring me one," Jessmer said. "Alive preferably, dead if necessary, so we can examine it." He looked about the small group. "You do realize that if these creatures prove to be as prolific as normal rats . . . " his voice trailed off.

"I find that unthinkable," said Simonson. "If they were as prolific as normal rats, there would be millions of them. No way could they have remained hidden until now. We must be dealing with a finite number. Mutants, perhaps."

Rachel stared at Hopkinton. "I've been remembering, Marcus, what you told me about the secret research that went on beneath the city . . . "

The SIS director raised a hand. "That's top secret information, Madame Deputy Prime Minister. The men in this room do not have such clearance."

She looked at him as though he were an escapee from a mental institution. "For God's sake, we're way past worrying about security clearances. We're going to have mass panic on our hands. There are now two epidemics in this city, the Sweat and a plague of what apparently are the creations of your research scientists. When you told me that people had begun disappearing from the secret laboratories, frankly, I thought you were losing it. But now what I think is that your researchers not only tried to find a way to use the Sweat as a biological weapon, but they were also tinkering with developing a way to spread the disease using rodents. A very special kind of rodent, as we are now witnessing."

Hopkinton stood, visibly shaken. "They weren't *my* research scientists. I had nothing to do with setting the program up."

"Not when it was initiated during the war," said Rachel, "but I've done some research of my own. You were working for the SIS in the late sixties. It's a matter of record. You and your intelligence buddies kept it secret all these years and now it's exploded in your face."

"I . . . I order you to stop talking about this," he sputtered. "This is a matter of national security and the people in this room don't have clearance."

She gave a disgusted, dismissive wave of her hand.

The others were silent, aghast at the implications of what the deputy prime minister was saying and not quite sure whom to believe.

"What does the prime minister say?" asked Simonson.

Rachel shrugged. "No one knows where he is. I've asked the chief of his security detail to get a message to him, but so far, I've heard nothing."

Marcus suspected the PM had already heard about this new threat and had gone into hiding or even fled the country. His neck soon wouldn't be worth a farthing anywhere in England.

His secretary entered the room. "Sir, I have a message for the deputy prime minister."

He waved a hand for her to go ahead.

The woman appeared to be having trouble controlling herself. "Madame . . . the message is from the leader of the majority. Parliament has issued a vote of no confidence in Prime Minister Harris." She hesitated, trembling. "The government has fallen. In light of the national emergency currently taking place, they have requested, in the name of continuity, that the deputy prime minister take charge."

Hopkinton and Forrester both looked stricken. Rachel was the first to recover.

"I think we all realize this is unprecedented," she said, "and that the appointment will be temporary. Marcus, I want you to stay on for the time being to help mobilize our response."

He could only nod. For a moment, he had feared he would immediately be stripped of his powers. But of course, Forrester, in her inexperience, would need to rely on him. There might still be time to secure his treasure.

62

Prime Minister Forrester sat in the Cabinet Room at 10 Downing Street and surveyed the long faces. Incredibly, Nevil Harris had still not shown himself. The press was having a field day speculating on what had become of him. One tabloid even published a photograph of someone vaguely resembling the former PM wearing a thong on a beach and suggested he was engaged in a gay relationship with a Hawaiian surfer.

In his absence, Rachel could not move into Downing Street's private residence, but she had arranged to use the non-residential portions of the famous address as her base to fight the twin plagues that were now ravaging the country. Downing had superb communications facilities, which would be essential in dealing with their problems.

Health Minister Simonson, Drs. Jessmer and Westerling and SIS Director Hopkinton were there, as were Britain's senior military commanders from the Ministry of Defense. Heading up the military delegation was General Sir Richard Laurence, commander-in-chief, land command, British Army.

It was something of a miracle that Marcus had managed to attend at all, for while everyone else was focused on the Sweat and the giant rodents, he had been completely consumed by his search for the treasure. He had assembled a new crew of SIS men to replace those who, for all intents and purposes, had disappeared, along with Trimm, beneath London.

Of course, it was possible the men had simply decided to keep the treasure for themselves. But he had trouble believing anyone would defy him so directly. His reputation for ruthlessness was well known. He now suspected the large rats were responsible for the loss of his men.

While he had never known what was killing people in the secret laboratories beneath London in the 1960s, he had been responsible for security at the facility. It had been his first administrative position within the SIS, and he had taken it seriously.

When a cause could not be found for the mysterious disappearances, he was the one who took the order from up high to shut everything down and seal the facility. He was given full authority. No one had realized quite what that would come to mean.

Suspecting that many of the workers in the secret labs might be security risks or possibly even be infected with the Sweat, he had ordered the facility sealed with over a hundred people inside, condemning them to whatever fate had killed so many of their fellows. Their disappearance had never been revealed to anyone. Families simply learned that their loved ones had been mysteriously killed "in service to their country."

This time, he assured himself, there would be no mistakes, the biggest of which had been placing Trimm in charge. This time, he would lead the effort himself. There would be no further miscalculations. The force would consist of thirty well-armed men, all SIS agents. They would wear Special Forces Kevlar protective vests and helmets; carry explosives, flame-throwers, grenades and machine guns. No God damn rats were going to stop them.

The fact that he was taking men away from the all-important fight to restore order in the country was of no concern to him. His fellow citizens were under assault in the most sustained national emergency since the Blitz. No matter. His tenure at SIS was on borrowed time. He had to secure his future.

"Something on your mind, Marcus?" Forrester asked.

"Uh . . . sorry Madame Prime Minister. Too many things to think about and keep straight."

"Well let's try to keep the focus on the matter at hand. Dr. Westerling, you were saying that the Sweat is spreading rapidly?"

"Yes, sir . . . uh Madame . . . uh prime minister." Westerling looked momentarily nonplussed. Along with everyone else, he was having a difficult time getting used to the sudden change at the top. "Thousands of new cases are being reported daily. Many are dying, but we're getting a better rate of success in treatment since the word has gotten out. The public knows to get medical help now at the first signs of distress. Also, we've had one break."

"What's that?"

"We've managed to capture two of the rodents alive. After extensive testing, it does appear that they are carriers of the Sweat, along with our own common, brown rats. Our current theory is that the new, larger rodents infected the brown rats, which then fled the tunnels in their efforts to escape the vicious things that were killing them."

"I'd like to add," said Jessmer, "that we have determined that while there is a degree of genetic similarity between the rodents, the large rats are more complex and appear to have much higher intelligence. On the positive side, they have more primitive reproductive systems, almost as if they were designed to prevent the population from growing out of control. It would appear that at least someone working down in those labs had an iota of the possible ramifications of what they were doing."

"The rats have another interesting adaptation," said Simonson, "They have a vestigial eyelid which keeps out sunlight and allows them to move about in low-light situations. I believe they will be most active at night, but from the attacks we've seen, they can also operate in the early morning and late evening hours and perhaps even on heavily overcast days."

"Terrific," said one of the military commanders.

"They may have stayed below ground up to now," Simonson continued, "to avoid sunlight and the noise of the city. However, now that they are loose, they seem to be a most adaptable species. I hope humans will prove to be so adept."

One of the prime minister's aides entered and whispered something to her. Forrester stood up abruptly, a smile breaking out on her face. "Bring them in at once," she said.

The others turned in surprise as Sherwood, Carmen and Julia entered the room. Upon emerging from the underground in Russell Square, they had immediately alerted officials to the situation. But it had taken time—too much time for the details to work their way through channels. Mobilizing the bureaucracy, even in an emergency, was like trying to turn the Titanic. The delays had cost more than a few lives.

They were still operating on virtually no sleep. Carmen, in particular, appeared exhausted and almost on the edge of collapse. Sherwood stayed close by her side.

"Madame Prime Minister," he said. "Thank you for seeing us."

"I understand you were the ones to alert authorities to this awful situation," said Rachel. "Can you tell us anything further that might help us fight these plagues?"

"Some things, yes," said Sherwood. "We believe the Sweat was introduced via a WWII rocket fired by the Nazis and containing a biological payload."

You could have heard a pin drop in the room. Forrester swallowed hard and said, "How do you know this?"

"We . . . or I should say . . . Hans and Julia, discovered the rocket embedded in one of the tunnels. We also found an underground series of laboratories that date back to the war. Carmen read through enough of the files and reports to confirm that our British scientists tried to turn the Sweat that broke out in London at the time into a biological weapon of their own. They didn't know that it came from Germany. They only knew that it was deadly. And possibly useful.

"In their tinkering with it, they tried to develop rodents that would serve as carriers for the disease—as delivery mechanisms. They were playing God, altering the genetics of the rats. The war ended before they could develop the idea as a weapon, but the research continued for many years, under a series of SIS directors until, we believe, the laboratories were abandoned when the fierce rodents got loose and began to kill people."

He turned to face the current SIS director. "But you know all this, don't you, Director Hopkinton? It was your department that continued to hide this program's existence from the British people and from the government. Perhaps you may be interested to hear that Dr. Trimm and most of his men are dead, killed by those things out there. But then, you probably knew that too, or at least guessed it."

"I don't have any idea what you're talking about," Marcus said uneasily.

Carmen felt her anger rising. "Madame Prime Minister, Dr. Trimm and the men he had with him were working for the SIS, attempting to find the treasure that had consumed Trimm for years. And though we can't prove it, we suspect the SIS was behind getting us trapped below."

"That's the most absurd thing I've ever heard," said Marcus.

"It is a pretty serious charge," said Rachel. "Do you have anything to back it up?"

"One of the men who was helping Trimm remove the treasure mentioned Hopkinton by name," said Sherwood. "Those who survived with us have been arrested and are being interrogated. I suspect they will tell the truth in time."

"Remove the treasure . . . ?" Rachel looked stunned. "You're saying they *found* it?"

Carmen nodded. "It was right where I'd seen it when I floated the underground river. I think Trimm went to Hopkinton for help in getting it out."

Marcus stood up. "I'm not going to stay here and be libeled by this . . . this . . . museum functionary. I have better ways to serve my country."

He stalked out before anyone could overcome their surprise. He'd had a difficult time concealing his elation at hearing the existence of the treasure confirmed. Time was of the essence now. If Forrester decided to believe what Sherwood and Carmen were saying, he would be quickly stripped of his powers.

The prime minister stared at the door through which Marcus had just disappeared. She had too many things going on in her head. Perhaps the SIS director was a risk, but her own focus had to be on what was best for the country.

"Carmen, you're telling me that our own British researchers were trying to develop a biological weapon to send the Sweat to Germany . . . basically, that our scientists were every bit as cold blooded as the Nazis."

Carmen felt sick at the thought, but she knew it was true. "The Nazis didn't have a monopoly on immorality, Madame Prime Minister. I don't know, maybe the fact that we were forced to go to war to save ourselves gave our people a modicum of justification, but . . . " she shook her head.

"But I don't buy it," said Sherwood, finishing her thought. "The end doesn't justify the means. In any case, we can argue the morality later . . . if there is a later. Right now, I think your military heads here need to begin to plan how to deal with the rodents and your health people need to develop a vaccine for the Sweat."

Westerling nodded. "We have many people working on that. It's a difficult process. We can treat Sweat patients if we get to them quickly enough. But it will be some time before any viable vaccine appears. Our best hope is that the disease has a kind of natural life span. If that's so, we should begin to see signs of it dying down in just a few days."

"We can hope," said Rachel. "But I want all our health officials on high alert and fully informed as to what we are facing. I also want the public to know what to expect and where to go if they think they are sick. No more secrets. Is that clearly understood?"

There were nods around the table.

"All right. Lacking a working vaccine, that is all we can do about the Sweat for now. So let's focus on the rodents." She turned to her military officers. "Sir Richard, what is your plan?"

The commander-in-chief moved uneasily in his chair. "We've mobilized the army and police and special terror units," he began. "But I have to tell you, Madame Prime Minister, this is one of the most damnable situations I've faced in my thirty-six years in the military. We have no idea how many of these things there are. They act—as nearly as we can determine—like large, exceedingly strong, feral cats. Secretive, fierce, superb hunters, highly intelligent and adaptable, capable of hiding almost anywhere. As you know, we already have many reports of people being killed and hauled off to be eaten, including several members of Parliament. Just the terror of knowing that such a thing can happen is causing widespread panic.

"We can't use any sort of blanket bombing or poison in urban areas. About the best we've come up with so far is to warn people not to go outside in densely wooded areas, parks and so forth, especially at night or twilight times. We've stationed heavily armed units around the city for rapid response, but so far none of them have seen a thing. It's as if the animals know to avoid them. Frankly, our efforts so far have been ineffective at best."

Another officer cleared his throat. "Uh, there is one other piece of bad news, I'm afraid. We sent a heavily armed patrol into the gardens behind Buckingham Palace after the Queen said she'd seen some strange creatures on the lawn."

The PM looked aghast. "Did they find any?"

"Worse than that. They flushed a rat that refused to give ground. She was extraordinarily vicious and after she attacked she was shot. When they investigated the bushes where she'd been hiding, they found four babies. I don't know what you'd call them. 'Kittens' hardly seems appropriate. Two men were seriously injured by the juveniles before they managed to net them."

A chorus of horrified comments flooded the room.

"This is the worst possible news," said Jessmer. "If the creatures are entering into some sort of periodic breeding cycle, we could soon have many more to deal with."

"I don't know," Carmen said slowly, "I believe the scientists attempted to restrict the rats' breeding abilities. If they had not done so, I think we would already be facing millions of the things. But the fact that young have been found is worrisome. They may be changing and adapting to new conditions and a readier, more varied diet."

Forrester looked ashen. "I want you to fully mobilize the reserves. We have to find and destroy as many of these awful creatures as we can before any more of them begin to breed."

"It's not going to be easy, Madame Prime Minister," said Sir Richard. "A few years ago, Los Angeles decided they were going to eradicate coyotes that had begun to infiltrate the city. It was a major effort and it failed utterly. The coyotes were way too clever for the people trying to hunt them down. I fear these rodents will be even more adaptable and wary."

The PM waved a hand as if to say she didn't want to hear any more negative remarks. It was already clear they were going to need all the help they could get. She wondered where Marcus had gone. They needed his men on the front lines along with everyone else.

63

Sherwood drove Carmen home after the meeting with the prime minister. The streets were eerily quiet. Government pleas to avoid parks and lonely places in general had been taken to heart by the public.

"I never thought it would come to this," he said, as they drove down a deserted Whitehall. "We're prisoners in our own city."

Carmen had her head back against the seat. She was exhausted and still feeling the effects of the incredible stress they had been under. Yet she found herself wanting to find a bright side, hardly a normal characteristic of aspies.

"At least parking won't be a problem," she said.

He gave her a skeptical look.

"Seriously, Sherwood, I thought our biggest worry was going to be the Sweat, and it still may be. But if Dr. Westerling is correct that the sickness may have a natural life span and could begin to die down on its own, that's a very good thing. A disease like that could kill millions. As for the rats, as terrible as they are, I can't see them killing so many people. We may just have to learn how to avoid them and accept a certain number of casualties. Like the people of India accept the loss of life from Bengal tigers."

He glanced at her quickly before returning his eyes to the road. "I can't agree with you, Carmen. These creatures are much more vicious and attack oriented than tigers, which for the most part try to avoid people. Occasionally there might be a man killer, but these things seem to actually *prefer* a human diet. If they procreate into tens or even hundreds of thousands, humans will be relegated to living in blockaded compounds, bristling with weapons. That's a future I don't find the least bit attractive."

They entered Carmen's street and Sherwood pulled over to the curb in front of her apartment. She was right about one thing. There were plenty of parking spaces. He turned off the engine and looked at her.

She tried to give him a smile, but it felt awkward. Smiles weren't going to come easily for a while. She took his hand and held it tightly. They'd been through so much together the last few days.

"I know," he said. "I feel it too." He kissed her gently. "You were awesome down there. Very strong. I wouldn't have wanted to go through it with anyone else."

"Why don't I feel so strong right now?" she asked.

"There are bound to be some aftereffects. Hell, there's still probably residual adrenalin flowing in our veins. We'll both feel better after we get some rest." He stroked her cheek. "Even in a world of vicious rats and disease, I'd want to spend my time with you."

She smiled again and this time it felt real. "Thanks, Sherwood. Thanks for so many things. Saving my life, not least of all."

She started to get out.

"I don't think I should leave you alone," he said. "We don't know what Hopkinton and his SIS blokes will do next. They're dangerous and pretty much loose cannons right now. He's got to know his time is running out as a member of Rachel's government."

She batted her eyes at him. "That's a pretty good line, Inspector Peets."

She got out and he followed her up the steps. At the door, he put his arms around her and kissed her passionately. They felt their tiredness slip away to be replaced by a longing for peace and tenderness and love after all the horrors of the past few days.

But it was not to be. In an instant, everything changed. A black van squealed to a halt in front of the building. Sherwood barely had time to disengage from Carmen before half a dozen men in military-looking gear tore up the steps. One man dropped Sherwood to the ground with a vicious blow from his rifle butt that glanced off his head.

By the time he recovered his senses, Carmen was gone.

He sat on the cold steps rubbing his head, trying to think straight. Who would kidnap Carmen? There was only one possibility: Hopkinton. He needed her to lead them to London's underground riches. Without Trimm, the SIS director didn't have a clue where to look.

He felt his blood boil. What a fool he was not to realize that they would be watching her apartment. That Marcus would expose her to that sort of danger after all she'd been through made his skin crawl. Carmen was exhausted, her Asperger's acting up. This new trauma would be devastating.

There was no doubt in his mind what had just happened. The men who took her were highly trained and equipped. The clothes they wore did not reflect any military branch he knew of. They had to be SIS operatives. Hopkinton's new batch of professional treasure hunters.

There was no time to organize a police response team. The men had attempted to disable his car by shooting out the tires and spraying the interior with bullets as well. His radio had been destroyed, but the car still managed to turn on. His only plan was to go after them. The tires on his brand new cruiser shredded and kicked up sparks as he burned them into the pavement. His head thundered with pain from the blow. He shook himself, knowing he wasn't thinking straight. All he could concentrate on was somehow going after Carmen.

He decided to go to Russell Square where they had emerged from the underground. Maybe he could backtrack to the riverside rooms that held Marcus's loot.

Somewhere in his fogged thoughts, he understood the risk he was taking. To go back underground alone and unarmed would be foolhardy. It might not save Carmen and could very likely get him killed. Yet if he took time to raise support from Scotland Yard, she might be dead before they arrived. Hopkinton would have no reason to keep her around once he had his treasure. Every minute was important.

He made up his mind. His own apartment was on the way. When he got there, he raced inside, grabbed his spare pistol and went straight to his trash can. He had bundled up the clothes he'd worn underground and stuffed them in a garbage bag. They still reeked.

He nearly gagged as he put them on, but the residual smell of the dead creatures might still offer protection. He looked at his watch. He'd lost ten minutes. Still, a couple more minutes might pay off. He picked up the phone and dialed Harry's number.

The answering machine picked up. He cursed, explained as quickly as possible what had happened and what he intended to do. Then he fled the apartment.

As he ran down his front steps, two teenagers walked past, apparently oblivious to the public warnings.

"Blimey, mate," said one, turning away. "Take a bleedin' shower. You smell like a slaughterhouse."

Right you are, Sherwood thought. And that's exactly where I'm headed.

64

Carmen felt someone shake her roughly, so she opened her eyes. At once, a pounding started in the back of her head. A wave of nausea swept over her. She sat up, feeling the room spin. She felt drugged.

"All right," said a voice. "We've wasted enough time. Stand her up."

Two men lifted her to her feet and she found herself staring into Marcus's eyes.

"You?" she said in a disbelieving voice. "What are you doing?"

She tried to look around. They were underground in a large tunnel. It looked like all the other tunnels to her. She felt a cold fear rise in the pit of her stomach.

"Oh my God. You brought me back down here? Are you mad? We have to get out of here."

"I need your help. You're going to take us to the treasure."

"You must be out of your mind," she said. "Why would I help you?"

"Because if you don't, my men have orders to kill your boyfriend." He watched her reaction to his bluff. He'd been more than annoyed when his men reported that they'd left Sherwood behind. That was stupid. Good help was hard to find, especially when one had to rely on government workers.

"Oh, yes, I know all about you two. We've been following you for some time now."

Her fear was like a rising tide. She was back with the rats. There was no protection and she didn't even have Sherwood to lean on. She couldn't keep her eyes from darting one way and then another, searching for the creatures. "Even if I wanted to help you, I couldn't. We were lost most of the time we were down here. Just stumbling around. I have no idea how to get back to the treasure."

Marcus swore. He had feared as much. He took out a pistol and put it to her head. She flinched but held her ground. "Go ahead. You'll do me a favor by killing me." She looked at the men surrounding them. "Don't you know? You're all going to die down here."

Some of the men looked uneasy. They had no knowledge of the rodents. Hopkinton had been afraid to tell them for fear they wouldn't come. All they knew was that they would make a great deal of money and might have to fight—other men—for it. But there was no denying that this woman was terrified of something. Her fear was contagious.

Not having seen the rodents himself, Marcus had trouble imagining the degree of threat. Just rats after all. Big ones, no doubt, but his visions of treasure superseded all else. His men were well armed and capable of handling any conceivable threat.

He pointed his finger at Carmen. "Shut her up."

One of the men put a hand over her mouth. Another said, "Sir, I helped our men expand the tunnel Trimm planned to use to haul whatever they found out by tractor. I think I can find my way there. With luck, the tractor may still be useable."

"All right. You lead out," said Marcus.

"What about her?" asked the man holding Carmen.

Marcus was deeply tempted to kill her. But she might be useful later on. There was no hurry.

"Put a helmet and headlamp on her," he said. "Bring her along, and keep her God damned mouth shut."

True to his word, the man who had worked with Trimm took them to the correct tunnel, but here they were stopped when they reached the site of the cave-in. Marcus cursed a blue streak and ordered the men to begin digging it out.

It was slow work. Only a few of them had spades and no one had a pickax to pry out the larger stones and lumps of clay. Marcus fumed as they slowly dug and cleared away the debris, mostly by hand. Fortunately, it had not been a major collapse and after two hours, they had worked an opening big enough to get through.

The first thing they saw was the tractor, which sat where it had been left, still loaded with gold and jewels. They stared in disbelief. It was the first solid evidence that their entire endeavor wasn't a wild goose chase. Each man fingered the gems and marveled at the huge quantities of gold bullion and rare Spanish coins. Marcus ordered half the men to continue widening the entrance, so the tractor could get out. Moments later, the rest of the group reached the main treasure room, where they stood gaping before the greatest assemblage of wealth any of them had ever seen.

"It was all true," Marcus said, almost in a whisper. "Trimm was right. There's enough here to make every one of us rich beyond our wildest dreams."

The tractor roared to life back in the tunnel, and one of the men came out to report that they would have the way open in half an hour. That was when they heard the first of the sucking sounds.

"What's that?" asked Marcus.

Carmen's eyes darted around desperately. The man guarding her let go to lift his weapon. "That's your death warrant, Marcus," she said. "You and all the rest of us."

He stared at her for a moment, trying to determine if she was serious. In a loud voice, he ordered: "Set up a perimeter and prepare for a firefight."

The men looked uncertain. They didn't see anyone and heard nothing but that strange sound. Like an old man sucking on a tooth. Then, suddenly, a vicious blur raced out of the darkness and clamped its teeth onto the neck of one of the men. Without a sound, the creature hauled the body back into the darkness. The entire episode had taken no more than a few seconds, but it was long enough to burn the image into everyone's brain. This was the first time any of them other than Carmen had seen the horrific rodents with their muscular, three-foot bodies and needle-pointed teeth.

Now the men reacted to Marcus's orders. Several offered panicked cover fire into the darkness as they retreated to a corner to make a stand. As they fired, they heard the sound of a collapse. Their way in past the tractor had suffered another cave- in. A noxious cloud of dust floated out of the tunnel, leaving little doubt that the way out had been shut off. A handful of the men who had been left behind to dig emerged, filthy and soot covered, to join them. The others had been buried by the collapse.

The entire underground maze of tunnels, sewers, war rooms and tube stations was steadily weakening. London's depths were a Swiss cheese of porous, over-carved and undermined levels, riddled with hidden waterways eating away at the thick clay.

The men set up a skirmish line, backs against the wall, the river in front of them. They constructed a barrier of statues, gold ingots and baskets of gemstones. Everything was thrown into the mix. In short order, the riches had been reduced to little more worth than bags of sand. Marcus sent two men to explore the only other tunnel out, the one that went back to the roomful of King Henry's murdered workers. They quickly returned to report that they were completely trapped by another cave-in that looked fresh as well.

"No way out, Marcus," said Carmen. "Your greed has doomed us all to a horrible death from those things."

The SIS director felt a wave of panic seep through his body. The momentary glimpse of the creature that had taken one of his men had scared him more than he had ever been scared in his life. For the first time, he knew with certainty how those poor devils he had sealed into the laboratories so long ago had died. He and all of his men now shared Carmen's terror.

"Sir!" cried one. "They're coming."

Everyone peered into the gloom and dust, lit only by their headlamps.

The rats emerged in near heart-stopping numbers. It was difficult to say where they were coming from in the darkness. No doubt they had dug small openings everywhere down here, connecting the larger tunnels and further undermining the structures of London's vast underground.

Carmen noted that the creatures seemed to have lost whatever natural timidity they may have had to loud sounds, since the noise of the gunfire appeared to have little effect on them. She realized they were hungry. All of the normal rats had either fled or been eaten. The rodents were literally starving to death down here, and it was no doubt a major reason why many had begun to go above ground. The discovery of some thirty humans was driving them mad with hunger.

The men stared in utter, dumb terror as this scene out of a nightmare descended upon them. Hundreds of pale-skinned beasts, mouths open, mucus dripping from their horrific teeth, approached on all sides but one.

"Shoot them," Marcus cried. "Use your grenades."

The room turned into a holocaust of military explosions and gunfire. Carmen, back to the wall, watched as the rats darted in and out of the darkness. There seemed to be method to their attacks. Men were struck from behind or the side, whenever they had their backs turned even slightly and where the head-lamps were not directly focused. And each man who was targeted and then drawn into the darkness to meet his end meant one less lamp.

It was terrible to watch, but she couldn't turn away from the awful spectacle. Then, she saw an opening.

No one was paying any attention to her. The one direction the rats were not blocking was back down the tunnel to the tomb of King Henry's long dead workers. She realized that Marcus's men must have seen the obvious cave-in and returned immediately to report the bad news. But she knew that at least part of that landslide had to have been opened by Trimm and his men in order to get through. It was a slim hope but maybe, just maybe, they'd left enough of an opening that she could push her way into the next chamber.

In any case, it was a better option than staying here and being eaten alive. Slowly, she slipped back behind the men. No one cared what she was doing. Finally, when she was sure everyone was preoccupied, she made a dash into the tunnel. She feared some of the rats might follow her and her own terror was nearly overwhelming. She was completely on her own now in this nightmarish world.

It took only a moment to reach the site of the collapse, where she quickly pulled herself up to the crest of the thick, muddy clay and began to push and claw her way through. She tore at the clay until her nails broke. She was covered with mud. Every now and then she dared a look back. So far, none of the rats had seen her.

This had to be how Trimm had escaped. There was no other way. She pushed and crammed, turning in the tight confines, trying to use her feet to kick at the thick clumps. It was exhausting labor, but she was encouraged by a tiny hole that seemed to be opening, bit by bit.

She paused for breath and looked back again at the horrific firefight going on. Marcus's men were using everything they had. The caverns roared with the blasts of grenades, nonstop fire and the death screams of men. Scores of the creatures were being killed, but their hunger drove them on.

As she kicked out one stubbornly large clump, she heard a sound that stopped her cold. It was like the crack a frozen lake might make on a subzero night, reverberating, echoing through the chambers. The entire cavern seemed to shudder. In their terror, the men continued to blast and fire away, oblivious to the strange quaking.

Finally, the last piece of thick mud slid away and she felt a cool breeze come through the opening. She had her way out. Still, she hesitated. It was beyond logic, but she felt she should tell the men that there was a way to escape. She couldn't just leave them to such a certain, horrible death.

But even as she turned to cry out to them, that strange, low-quaking sound increased. She stared at the men, still firing blindly, enmeshed in a cloud of dust, soot, sulfur and pulverized rock.

And then it happened. The ledges that supported the enormous weight of the treasure reached the end of their endurance. With a sickening crack, they gave way, collapsing treasure, men and beasts into the river.

Carmen gaped in disbelief. One moment she had been witnessing the most awful battle. The next, everything was gone, submerged into the river and pulled under and away by the current. Weighted down with heavy protective armor and gear, the men sank like the golden ingots that surrounded them.

Marcus finally had his treasure, buried with him forever in the cold depths.

As the glow from the men's lamps disappeared, she was left only with her own, small light. She felt her heart race at the total calamity she had just witnessed. Then she turned away, slid through the hole she had created and tried not to wonder if still more rodents lay in wait ahead.

Sherwood had to admit it. He was lost. After descending into the subsidence at Russell Square, he'd quickly found his way to the research labs and quarantine cell where they'd been rescued by Julia. But from there, he began to wander aimlessly through the maze of rooms, tunnels and hallways.

They all looked alike in the dim glow thrown by his torch. At each branching of passageways, he shone his light and peered down as far as he could. There was a sameness to them all that had him biting his tongue in frustration.

Carmen might need his help this very minute and he was hopelessly lost. What a fool he was not to have gone for help first.

He entered a room that looked familiar and knew where he was when he saw the cages that held the bodies of long dead test animals. He stopped. There was a sound in the far corner. He wasn't sure what it was and turned his light on it.

One of the giant rats had gotten into a cage and was actually chewing the bones of a dead test subject. It must have been ravenous to try to make a meal out of that.

The creature looked up at him and added a snarl to the chorus of sucking and mewling sounds it was already making, before returning to its meal. Cautiously, Sherwood swung his light all around to see if there were more of the things. He didn't see any, and this one appeared to be completely absorbed in its repast.

Keeping his light from directly shining on the rat, he approached the cage, hesitated, then darted forward, shut the open door, and latched it all in one motion. The thing was trapped.

He stood beside the cage and stared at the genetically altered rodent. How, he wondered, could anyone have wanted to unleash such things on the world? The beast hardly paid any attention to him as it finished crunching the bones, offering forth that awful smacking of lips, its teeth dripping. He wondered if the stinging mucus that Hans had described might be some sort of stomach acid that enabled the beasts to digest bone so easily.

The beady eyes rolled over to contemplate Sherwood. Its immediate meal was finished but this unexpected new source must have looked considerably more delectable. Suddenly, the rat exploded in fury, banging again and again against the side of the cage.

He backed away. Clearly, the awful smell on his clothes had lost its potency. The thing didn't look like it could escape, but he wasn't inclined to stick around and find out. He was ten minutes away, still wandering through the maze of hallways before he heard the last echoes of the rat's fury.

Then he had his first bit of luck. He stumbled upon the lift shaft that had been their earlier avenue of escape. Quickly, he clambered down the metal sides and cautiously poked his torch through the hatch at the top of the lift.

He was stunned to find a familiar face looking up at him with a great smile.

"Carmen!"

"I knew you'd look for me if you knew what had happened," she beamed. "But I didn't think you would know for sure. God, this is an awful place to be alone in." She glanced away, then back with an anguished look on her face. "Sherwood, the rats have come through to the chamber."

"All right. Hold on. They couldn't get through the lift grates before remember?"

"Yes, but I couldn't get the gates closed all the way. They're stuck. Get me out of here, Sherwood. They're coming."

The panic in her voice galvanized him. He reached down with his long arms and lifted her up in one motion. Then he slammed the hatch shut, though he knew it would not serve as any kind of a deterrent. If the beasts came after them, they were in big trouble.

She grabbed him and held on fiercely.

"Are you hurt?"

Her body shook against his. She seemed different, somehow. Less certain of herself. More exhausted and terrified. Being thrown back into the darkness so unexpectedly must have been the last straw. Her AS had reached its limits of dealing with such unrelenting stress.

She couldn't speak, only shook her head.

He lifted her up so she could get hold of the metal sides of the shaft and together they climbed rapidly into the research lab. As they set foot in the first room, they heard the tormented sucking and mewling of the rats below.

They were already coming up the shaft.

Sherwood stripped off his shirt. "Put this on," he said. "It's got some of the rodent smell on it. Maybe it will fool them, though I don't think it's as powerful as it was."

Suddenly, he had an idea. "Come on," he shouted and raced down the hall.

Carmen was right behind him, still struggling to put on the rank t-shirt. "Where are we going?" she cried.

"Tell you when we get there."

Then they were back in the room filled with cages. Sherwood led the way to the cage with the captured rat in it. As soon as the thing saw them, it began to slam against the sides of the cage again.

"Stand back," he said. He took his pistol out and shot the thing twice. It fell dead, its strange, clawed toes still twitching.

They could hear the rats entering the lab. It sounded like there were plenty of them. Quickly, Sherwood opened the cage and stuck his bare hands into the animal's blood. He smeared the thick substance over both of them. "More," he said. "You spread it on me and I'll spread it on you."

They worked feverishly until they were coated with the noxious substance.

"That should be enough," he said finally. "Now we'll see if it works."

They slumped to the floor and waited. In just a matter of minutes, the rodents appeared. There were fewer than had been in the treasure rooms. Carmen suspected the collapse must have killed many of them.

About a dozen of the creatures entered the cage room, sniffing and mewling. But there was none of the sucking sound that always seemed to accompany their eating frenzy.

The two reeking humans sat, holding their breath, as the animals crept right up beside them. Carmen shook with terror. To have once escaped from such monstrosities, only to now have them literally crawling over her made her thoughts lurch—go someplace else, she willed her mind, not wanting to deal with what was happening.

But the beasts seemed unable to recognize the two humans as anything other than one of their own. They sat rigidly as the things climbed up and over them into the cage and began to eat the remainder of the dead rat.

"I don't understand," Carmen whispered. "The blood protects us but it seems to trigger their hunger at the same time."

"I don't know. Maybe they can detect when a thing is dead, not simply bleeding. Otherwise, they'd be eating each other every time they had a scratch. At least the dead rat should keep them busy for a little while. Come on. Let's get the hell out of here."

A few minutes later they were striding up the slope of the subsidence into Russell Square. A stream of police cars roared up. Men leaped out bristling with firearms and then Sherwood and Carmen saw Harry clamber out of one of the vehicles.

His face lit up when he saw them. "Boss. I thought you'd be dead for sure." He recoiled as he saw their blood covered bodies and smelled the stench of death on them. "What's the idea going back down there without me to protect you?"

Sherwood smiled. "It was my mistake, officer. I won't do it again."

Harry looked only partly mollified. "You do, I'll kill you myself," he said.

65

Mist rose from the Thames on a cold, December day. The streets were still largely empty. Most people only ventured forth in cars now, and they checked nervously in all directions while waiting at stop lights. There had been several instances of the big rats breaking through car windows and hauling people out to be eaten on the spot.

The cold seemed to have little effect on the beasts. Their thick, white fur grew heavier and gave them protection from the elements. Farmers reported finding more of the rats inside their barns. Most likely they took to the barns because they provided a ready food supply. Livestock losses had been substantial, though miraculously only a handful of farmers had been killed.

Prime Minister Forrester had moved permanently into 10 Downing Street after Nevil Harris finally surfaced in Australia, where he had been given asylum by his old friend, Prime Minister Martin. He was effectively out of reach to the assortment of legal actions being brought against him for keeping vital health and national security information from the people. For her part, Rachel was glad to be rid of the man. He would likely never show his face in England again.

She pored over her morning briefings. It was the usual litany of deaths, police actions and military movements. The horrific reports of killings by the rats were, sadly, becoming almost commonplace. But the economic effects were just beginning to be felt, as tourism had shut down completely. The rest of the world had no interest in becoming some creature's dinner while they attended the theater in Soho or went for nature hikes along the Dover coast or in Wales. Once spring came, there would be real hardship if the tourists refused to return.

Rachel had spoken only briefly to Sherwood on the phone following Carmen's ordeal. He informed her of Hopkinton's betrayal, of them, the prime minister, the British people whose safety he had been entrusted with and, ultimately, of himself. She hadn't really been surprised, and a new SIS director was already in place. His first order was to clean house and prepare a full report on the secret research conducted by his predecessors.

The PM checked her watch. She had a busy morning of meetings. But Sherwood and Carmen were first on the agenda.

For Carmen, it had been a long two months. Mentally, physically and emotionally, her nerves had been shattered by the awful experiences in London's underground. Sherwood struggled to help and to be understanding. He knew how hard the experience had been on Harry and himself, who were supposedly trained to deal with unusual, life-threatening situations. But Carmen's AS magnified everything. Every emotion Sherwood felt, he knew, Carmen experienced tenfold.

She spent a week in the hospital, recovering from simple exhaustion and had since been seeing a therapist who helped talk her through her experiences. Sherwood thought she was beginning to return to normal, but he still hovered over her to the extent that she sometimes snapped at him, then immediately apologized and hugged him, thanking him for all his help.

They'd drawn closer, as any such shared ordeal will do to people. It was as though they had served in combat together. Harry, too, shared a sense of comradeship with them.

Rachel smiled as she anticipated what their reaction would be upon hearing the latest developments. And she had a surprise for them as well.

Her secretary entered and announced the arrival of the guests. Rachel had invited them to join her for an early brunch.

"Thank you so much for coming," she said, greeting them warmly. "I had hoped we could get together before now, but I've been so incredibly busy. It takes a while to get used to the mad schedule prime ministers keep."

Carmen gave her a brief hug. "It's so good of you to invite us," she said. "I've been needing to get out of the house. Poor Sherwood's been going a little batty taking care of me, I'm afraid."

"Men, the poor dears, love to feel needed," said Rachel. "It's good for them."

Sherwood made a face and sank into a leather couch, while Carmen selected a wing chair in front of the fireplace.

"Well I for one," he said, "am impressed at what you've accomplished in such a short time, Madame Prime Minister. Just getting a handle on the Sweat was a great achievement. I'm still not clear exactly how you managed to develop a vaccine so quickly. I had thought that would be impossible."

Rachel smiled. "Part of why I wanted you to come in. The disease did begin to slow down as some had predicted it might, but the vaccine was what really shut it off quickly and prevented many more deaths. I'll explain how that came to pass in a few minutes when our other guest arrives."

Sherwood raised an eyebrow, but it was clear that the prime minister had no intention of telling them who the guest would be.

Carmen said, "What about the rodents still living beneath the city?"

"A real problem. Even though we believe only a small number remain underground, they have effectively shut down London's tube system. Obviously, no one wants to go down there, and who can blame them? No doubt you've personally experienced the havoc this has caused with the city's transportation. We need to get that system back on line."

Rachel leaned forward in her chair. "It's been a closely kept secret, but this coming week, everything will be in place. All entrances to the underground have been sealed. It took a great deal of effort and time to achieve this."

Sherwood looked puzzled. "I don't understand what good that will do. Most of the creatures have already come out. They're spreading across the country."

"On Thursday, precisely at noon, we will flood the underground with cyanide gas. Health authorities assure me that in tests done on captured creatures, they have shown unusual sensitivity to the toxic gas. They predict a low concentrate will deliver a near one hundred percent kill rate. We will still have to learn to live with the creatures who have surfaced and keep vigilant against any that want to return, but hopefully we can get our tube system back."

"I think it's unlikely they'll return to the underground," said Sherwood. "They appear to have adapted well to life in the real world, or at least in the world of shadows, of night and twilight. Thank God, they appear to have a very limited procreation rate. Perhaps we do have Dr. Carrel to thank for that. We may, as you say, learn to live with them, though it won't be pleasant."

Rachel looked at Carmen. "And now, perhaps you can tell *me* something. I understand the British Museum is looking into retrieving King Henry's Spanish treasure."

"It's being discussed, though we are only in the beginning stages. We still haven't been allowed to put anyone down there to see what can be found. Maybe, if your cyanide treatment works, we can move ahead. It seems possible that we ought to be able to bring up the heavier gold ingots, silver and coins which would have settled quickly to the bottom, even despite the current.

"There's been an interesting development, however, that you may have heard rumors of. Various priceless jewels and some smaller gold coins have been surfacing all over the city. People have found them in sewers, on the banks of the Thames and outflows. Fishermen and shellfish gatherers have brought in small fortunes for an afternoon's work."

"Rightfully, it should be the property of the government," said Rachel.

Carmen smiled ruefully. "Maybe so, but it seems downright penurious to go after those folks who've been lucky enough to find something. After all the troubles Londoners have had to go through in the past months, this has really perked them up. The chance that a fortune might back up into their loos has turned everyone into treasure hunters. People need a break. It's like a national lottery that you don't have to buy a ticket for."

"An unusual attitude for a museum official to take," said the prime minister.

"Maybe . . . but there was so *much* down there. If we manage to retrieve even a small portion, there will be more than the museum could ever display. I say let the people have their share. They've bloody well earned it."

Rachel's personal secretary entered once again. "Brunch will be served shortly, Madame Prime Minister. And your other guest has arrived."

"Wonderful," said Rachel. "How is she? Any trouble with the wheelchair?"

"None. She's just being brought into the outer room." Rachel rose at once. "I'll come greet her."

Sherwood and Carmen exchanged looks. Who was this mystery guest who came in a wheelchair and commanded the prime minister's personal attentions? They both stood as well and tried to see through the door.

Rachel bustled out. "Oh, my dear," she said. "It's so good to see you again. How have you been feeling?" She took the back of the chair herself and pushed her guest into the room, settling her close to the warmth of the fireplace.

The woman looked to be all of ninety at least, but except for the chair, she seemed quite bright eyed and cheerful, looking around the famous room and its furnishings as if they were old friends.

"I've been quite well," she said in a soft but not frail voice. "I so enjoy coming here to visit you."

"You are welcome any time," Rachel said. "I mean that." Then she turned to her other two, somewhat mystified guests. "I would like to introduce you to Inspector Sherwood Peets and Carmen Kingsley."

"Oh, a great pleasure," said the woman, holding out her hand. "I've followed news reports of your exploits beneath the city. You are both very brave. I have not seen such bravery in . . . many years."

They each shook her hand as Rachel completed the introductions.

"And this remarkable woman is Natasha Newman, former personal assistant to Prime Minister Churchill."

"A very great honor to meet you," said Sherwood, though he still had no idea why the woman was here.

"Why don't you take your seats again," said the prime minister, "and I will enlighten you of the questions you no doubt have." There was a twinkle in her eyes.

Once they were settled, she said, "Natasha is a survivor. Quite an extraordinary survivor. A participant in one of the great espionage efforts of the Second World War. She and a small group of commandos were sent by Churchill to determine if the Nazis intended to attack London with a biological weapon to be delivered by the new V-2 rockets."

Sherwood and Carmen's eyes went wide. "The V-2 that was discovered in the tunnels?" asked Sherwood.

Natasha nodded. "Only one rocket with such a payload was ever fired on London. Alas, our mission failed, and I feel I must apologize to you for being the cause of so much horror."

"Nonsense, my dear," said Rachel. "You were heroes to even try."

The old woman tilted her head slightly. "For many years, I thought we had done something good. When we found the journals Dr. Alexis Carrel kept on his research into the Sweat in the far north, we sent them back to England with our soldiers. Our hope was that if we failed to stop the missile, at least the documents might help British scientists understand and deal with the terrible disease. Instead, I have only recently learned, those journals were used by those very scientists— our own British scientists—to not only develop the Sweat as a biological weapon of their own but also to engineer what were called in my time, 'heroic rats,' as agents to deliver the sickness."

She paused, seemingly tired from the explanation. Rachel brought her a glass of water. Then she continued.

"Thank God, my Gunnar never learned the truth. It would have killed him, I think."

"I'm sorry," Sherwood said. "Who is Gunnar?"

"Another unknown hero," said Natasha. "There were so many from the war, you know. He saved me, even as he was giving his own life. I had succumbed to the terrible Norwegian cold during our attempt to destroy the rocket. Gunnar brought food and warm clothing to where I was hidden. I would not have survived without it. As it was, I lay there in the cold woods for three long days and nights until a local hunter found me."

"This is fascinating, I have to admit," said Carmen. "But I don't understand what it has to do with overcoming the Sweat today."

"When Gunnar brought me that warm coat, there were a handful of papers sewn into an inside pocket. I kept that coat as a remembrance of him, but I did not find the papers for many years. When I did, I realized at once who the owner of that coat must have been. Dr. Alexis Carrel. Dr. Carrel was not an entirely bad man, I think. He had hoped the Sweat program would not come to fruition before the war ended. In case he was wrong and unable to stop it, he secretly developed a vaccine for the disease.

"Perhaps he was thinking not so much of England as he was of his beloved Europe. He feared that if the Sweat got loose during transport to the homeland, all the deaths from the sickness that were supposed to take place in Britain might instead occur in France, Germany and possibly all the countries of the continent. So he brought the plans for how to devise a vaccine with him. Gunnar never knew that Dr. Carrel was on that train, yet incredibly, it was his coat that he stole for me and that contained Carrel's formula."

"And when she learned about our fight against the Sweat," Rachel continued for her, "Natasha brought us Dr. Carrel's instructions for the vaccine, which our scientists very quickly reproduced."

Natasha smiled. "I am a great believer in fate," she said. "Winston was right, you know. He believed absolutely that good would triumph over evil."

Rachel leaned over and patted her hand. "And so it has," she said. "You are living proof of that."

"So, you see," said Natasha, "my comrades and I were responsible not only for the terrible work done by British scientists on the disease and for the frightening creatures that now plague us but also for the answer to our prayers in the form of the vaccine. My Gunnar was not the failure he died thinking he was."

66

Carmen and Sherwood walked slowly along the Embankment. Small, white flakes of snow floated down from a slate-gray sky, magically disappearing into the coal-black waters of the Thames.

They now shared Carmen's apartment and were settling into life as a couple. The equanimity of that life had been a surprise after all they had endured. They discovered many wonderful things about each other and found that they could often finish each other's sentences, so connected had their experiences made them.

What *was* coming as a surprise was the degree to which their careers had begun to take off. Sherwood had been offered an important position at the SIS, but had turned it down for now. "Haven't really had a chance to be an honest-to-God inspector yet," he told Carmen. "I spent most of my life trying to achieve that. I want to see if I can do it for a while."

He'd had precious little time to himself. Seeking out and destroying the rats wherever they appeared had become a big part of the job. And there was a real sense that for each animal he managed to find, an untold number of lives were saved. There was no more rewarding feeling than that. Nevertheless, Deputy Commander Jarvis had made it clear that whenever Sherwood tired of the street, there would be a position for him in the hierarchy of New Scotland Yard.

And wonder of wonders, Harry had become an inspector too. He muttered a great deal about being promoted to "the other side," as he put it, but his wife wouldn't let him turn down the extra pay. Sherwood relied on his friend whenever there was something important to handle.

Dr. Jessmer retired. With his strong support and the added recommendation from the prime minister, Carmen was selected to succeed him as director of the British Museum. It was an unheard of elevation for such a young woman.

She agonized over whether to accept the job, fearing that her Asperger's would make it impossible. She spent days of pure misery, every element of her condition heightened to almost unbearable levels. But in the end, it was Julia who convinced her to take the leap.

"You love history," she said. "This is your destiny. Make of the job what you will. Be hands on, travel the world; visit every ancient site you always wanted to see. All expenses paid. You can hire minions to do the unpleasant stuff, the fund raising and administrative bullshit. No one will fault you, not with Jessmer and Rachel in your camp. Besides," she jabbed Carmen in the ribs, "I'll always be around to give you advice and bug you to fund my own projects."

And so, Carmen accepted the position. As suspected, she found her life turned upside down. An instant celebrity after her underground adventures were highlighted by an obnoxious, but competent journalist named Mitchell Harrison III, Carmen had found herself enmeshed in a whirlwind of fancy dinners, balls and hi-brow fundraisers. She met the Queen, J. K. Rowling and Princes William and Harry. And a funny thing happened. She discovered she liked all the excitement and her Asperger's began to decline in severity.

But lately, all the changes had strained her relationship with Sherwood. They were both so busy, they spent little time together and had begun to wonder if the relationship would survive.

Carmen poked her arm into Sherwood's and leaned her head against his shoulder. They stopped to stare at the London Eye as it majestically made its rounds in the snowflakes. They'd talked a lot about where their relationship was going.

"I miss you a great deal," Sherwood said. "When I don't see you for weeks on end. You travel too much."

"I miss you too, Sherwood. I worry constantly when you are out trapping rats. I'm a nervous wreck, even if I'm halfway around the world."

"Trouble is," said Sherwood, "I love you something awful."

"That doesn't sound like trouble to me." She squeezed his arm tightly.

There was nothing else to say. They stared down at the muddy flat below, where a large ruby glinted up at them.

They couldn't help but smile.